ZOFLOYA;

OR,

THE MOOR:

A ROMANCE OF THE FIFTEENTH CENTURY

ZOFLOYA;

OR,

THE MOOR:

A ROMANCE OF THE FIFTEENTH CENTURY

Charlotte Dacre

edited by Adriana Craciun

broadview literary texts

Canadian Cataloguing in Publication Data

Dacre, Charlotte, b. 1782
    Zofloya, or, The Moor: a romance of the fifteenth century

(Broadview literary texts)
Includes bibliographical references.
ISBN 1-55111-146-2

I. Craciun, Adriana, 1967-   . II. Title. III. Series.

PR4525.D119Z4 1997   823'.7   C97-930462-8

Broadview Press
Post Office Box 1243, Peterborough, Ontario, Canada K9J 7H5

in the United States of America:
3576 California Road, Orchard Park, NY 14127

in the United Kingdom:
B.R.A.D. Book Representation & Distribution Ltd., 244A, London Road, Hadleigh, Essex SS7 2DE

Broadview Press gratefully acknowledges the support of the Canada Council, the Ontario Arts Council, and the Ministry of Canadian Heritage.

Broadview Press is grateful to Professor Eugene Benson for advice on editorial matters for the Broadview Literary Texts series.

Typesetting and assembly: True to Type Inc., Mississauga, Canada.

PRINTED IN CANADA

For my mother, Magdelena Craciun

Charlotte Dacre as "Rosa Matilda," from *Hours of Solitude* (1805).
Reprinted from the copy in the Kohler Collection, with permission of the
Department of Special Collections, University of California Library,
Davis, California.

Contents

Acknowledgements   8

Introduction   9

A Note on the Text   33

Charlotte Dacre: A Brief Chronology   35

Zofloya   37

Appendix A: From *Nymphomania*   257

Appendix B: Select Contemporary Reviews of *Zofloya*   261

Appendix C: Poems from Dacre's *Hours of Solitude*   269

Appendix D: *The Dæmon of Venice*   279

Select Bibliography   299

Acknowledgements

My efforts to re-publish Dacre's novel began in 1993, and I am grateful to Don LePan of Broadview Press for making it happen, and to Barbara Conolly for her patient and thorough editorial help. Kari Lokke and John Logan have been enthusiastic fans of Dacre from the start, and have proved a tremendous source of support. Jerome McGann's enthusiasm for Dacre's work encouraged me to pursue the project. Randy Lewis came to the rescue on more than one occasion. Nan and Bruce Parker have always been a tremendous source of support, and Louise Millar and Andy Sievewright often provided me with a place to stay and with good company while I worked in the British Library. Thanks also to Rosanne Richardson for expert typing at short notice. I am grateful to Thomas Whitehead of Temple University Library for help in obtaining a copy of the chapbook, and to the Department of Special Collections, University of California Library, Davis, for permission to use the engraving.

Introduction

Charlotte Dacre and the "vivisection of virtue"

The protagonist of Charlotte Dacre's best-known novel, *Zofloya, or the Moor* (1806), is unique in women's Gothic and Romantic literature, and has more in common with the heroines of the Marquis de Sade or M.G. Lewis than with those of Ann Radcliffe, Charlotte Smith, or Jane Austen. No heroine of Radcliffe or Austen could exult, as Victoria does in *Zofloya*, that "there is certainly a pleasure ... in the infliction of prolonged torment." *Zofloya* is remembered today chiefly for its innovative revision of Lewis' *The Monk* (1796); the sexual desires and ambition of Dacre's protagonist, Victoria, drive her to seduce, torture and murder, and like Lewis' Ambrosio, Victoria is inspired to greater criminal and illicit sexual acts by a seductive Lucifer, disguised as a Moor, before she too is plunged headlong into an abyss by her demon lover. Dacre herself chose as her pen name "Rosa Matilda," a clear reference to the Satanic *femme fatale* of Lewis's *The Monk*. Dacre's conscious and public alliance with this demonic woman complicates any unproblematic reliance on the moralistic elements throughout her works, where she often urges female readers to follow sexually conservative and even misogynist moral prescriptives. Indeed, even Sade in his introduction to *The Crimes of Love* (1800) half-heartedly declared his purpose to be morally edifying: "I wish people to see crime laid bare, I want them to fear it and detest it, and I know no other way to achieve this end than to paint it in all its horror" (116).

Significantly, Swinburne admired the "remarkable romance of Zofloya" precisely for its Sadean overtones, and overtly linked Dacre's novel to Sade's *Justine* and *Juliette*:

> The action of the three volumes [of *Zofloya*] is concerned wholly with the Misfortunes of Virtue in the person of "the innocent Lilla" (who is generally undergoing incarceration and varieties of torment throughout the course of her blameless but comfortless career) and the Prosperities of Vice in the person of "the fiendish Victoria," who ultimately succeeds in accomplishing the vivisection of virtue by hewing her amiable victim into more or less minute though palpitating fragments.[1]

The "Misfortunes of Virtue" and the "Prosperities of Vice" are, of course, the subtitles of Sade's novels *Justine* and *Juliette*, respectively. Swinburne clearly saw in Dacre's "remarkable work" a fusion of Sade's two novels, wherein the libertine heroine Victoria, like Juliette, dismembered her "sister" Lilla in a Sadean "vivisection of virtue."

Contemporary reviewers of *Zofloya* were disturbed by precisely the pornographic elements of *Zofloya* that Swinburne delighted in, singling out the novel's sexual and criminal content as unfit for a woman writer and for women readers. *The Annual Review*, for example, lamented that the "principal personages in these wild pages are courtesans of the lewdest class, and murderers of the deepest dye," and concluded that

[t]here is a voluptuousness of language and allusion, pervading these volumes, which we should have hoped, that the delicacy of a female pen would have refused to trace; and there is an exhibition of wantonness of harlotry, which we would have hoped, that the delicacy of the female mind, would have been shocked to imagine.[2]

Not surprisingly, *Zofloya* sold well, not despite but probably because of its "voluptuousness of language" and "exhibition of wantonness," selling 754 of 1000 printed copies in six months, inspiring a pirated chapbook, *The Dæmon of Venice*, in 1810, as well as a French translation.[3] *Zofloya* also influenced Percy Bysshe Shelley's own Gothic romances, *Zastrozzi* and *St. Irvyne*, and Medwin relates that Dacre's novel had "quite enraptured" the young Shelley.[4]

Zofloya's relation to *The Monk* and to Shelley's Gothic novels may have maintained readers' and scholars' interest in Dacre's novel up to this point, but as we shall see, it is the text's unusual evocations of the female body and feminine subject that are most valuable in the context of the history of sexuality and of the body. After embarking on a series of violent crimes, Victoria's body actually begins to grow larger, stronger, and decidedly more masculine. Dacre's whole range of works illustrates the disturbing possibility that sexed bodies are not "natural," but are socially constructed and thus mutable, the most dramatic agents of transformation being the most "unnatural": women's violence, their desire for mastery, and their sexual assertiveness. It is not surprising, therefore, that a writer whose texts do not comfortably fit our current models of the female Gothic or of feminine Romanticism also has much to teach us about the subtlety of women's evocations of the body, and of their awareness that the female body, even on the most basic corporeal level, is anything but natural.

Dacre's female characters provide an important contrast to those of better-known Romantic women novelists, including Ann Radcliffe, Charlotte Smith and Helen Maria Williams. These writers, according to Anne Mellor's *Romanticism and Gender* (1993), are representative of women Romantics and distinct from male Romantics because they present a model of female subjectivity which favours rational and egalitarian intersubjective relations and rejects the use of power to master an Other, whether the Other is nature, knowledge, or another human subject. While "feminine Romanticism" does justice to and illuminates the writing of some women writers of this period, we need to begin to explore the works of women that do not neatly fit such gender-complementary models.[5]

In Gothic studies, similar gender-complementary models have shed light on the unique qualities and interests of women's Gothic writing. Dacre's revision of *The Monk* in *Zofloya* challenges gender-complementary models of the Gothic in such works as Kate Ellis's *The Contested Castle* (1990), and William Patrick Day's *In the Circles of Fear and Desire* (1985). Both of these critical works in effect identify a female Gothic that centres on an embattled heroine (typical of Radcliffe), and distinguish this from a male Gothic, which focuses on a rebellious hero (masculine because exiled from the domestic sphere, according to Ellis, and because he seeks to control rather than adapt to his world, according to Day). Dacre's heroine Victoria is exiled, seeks to master her world and those in it, and is decidedly sadistic, tormenting and murdering for the pleasure of exerting her will; she is thus neither within the female nor male Gothic traditions but somewhere in between. In one important respect, of course, *Zofloya* does fit the female Gothic tradition, for it reveals the marriage plot to be literally infernal. *Zofloya* shows that patriarchy and its central institution, marriage, are literally nightmares, and that these nightmares are real, and fatally so. Dacre's shattering critique of marriage as a compact with the devil (a "*bond* of destruction" in her poem "The Skeleton Priest")[6] marks a dramatic addition to the range of critiques of patriarchy found in the female Gothic.

But Victoria is not a female Gothic heroine, nor is *Zofloya*'s plot that of the female Gothic: Victoria's character and her quest are those of the male Gothic villain. Anne Williams terms the female Gothic a "revolutionary" genre because it counters the misogyny of the male Gothic such as Lewis's (in which the female and the maternal are vilified as dangerous Others), by imagining the male as a potentially dangerous Other who can be transformed by love; in Williams's words, "The Female Gothic plot is a version of 'Beauty and the Beast' "(145). As is *Zofloya*, of course, but in an entirely different way. Dacre's Beauty loves not the Prince she recognizes as the true self within the Beast, but instead the Beast himself, and the beast in herself. Williams argues, correctly I think, that "the line between the Male Gothic and pornography is not easy to draw" (106); Dacre's reviewers consistently pointed out that her novels crossed this line and were, in effect, pornographic. By focusing on a female subject of violence, with aggressive sexual desires, Dacre's Gothic is revolutionary in a different way than is female Gothic. While "negative" female characters such as Victoria do exist in women's Gothic literature of the period, they are typically secondary characters, dark doubles of the central heroine whose violence and destructiveness must be expelled from the text before the proper heroine can reach her desired goal (examples include Maria de Vallerno in Radcliffe's *A Sicilian Romance*, Laurentini in her *The Mysteries of Udolpho*, and most famously, Bertha in *Jane Eyre*). Because Dacre gives centre stage to such a villainess in *Zofloya*, as well as in her last novel *The Passions* (1811), her work marks an original and significant departure from the more familiar tradition of women's Gothic writing. The few details we have of Dacre's unusual life offer us some insights into her unusual female characters. Charlotte Dacre (b. Charlotte King, 1771-72?–1825) was the daughter of the famous Jewish self-made banker, writer, blackmailer and supporter of radical causes Jonathan King (b. Jacob Rey, 1753-1824), and his first wife, Deborah, whom he divorced in 1785 to marry a countess. Known as the "Jew King," John King was a visible figure in London society, "had direct dealings with Godwin, Byron and Shelley" according to Donald Reiman (vii), and "displayed a long record of political opposition" according to historian Iain McCalman (38). Dacre's novels and poems often take up the theme of women abandoned by unfaithful partners, as it appears her mother was, yet Dacre's own marriage in 1815 appears to have occurred after a lengthy extramarital affair. According to Ann Jones, Charlotte King, "spinster," married the Tory editor of *The Morning Post*, Nicholas Byrne, in 1815 (it thus appears that "Dacre" was itself a pseudonym), yet their children appear to have been born long before this date. Nicholas and Charlotte Byrne had three children, William, Charles, and Mary in 1806, 1807, and 1809, respectively, who were all baptized much later in 1811 (Jones 226).[7]

Placing Dacre on a political spectrum, given her texts and what little we currently know about her life, yields conflicting results. Her father's radical and scandalous politics, her own status as outsider because Jewish, and her long-term illicit relationship might suggest that she identified with outsider or opposition political causes, at least on the level of social policy. Yet poems such as "On the Death of the Right Honorable William Pitt" (1806), in which Pitt is elevated to "a Saint in Heaven," and "Mr. F[o]x" (1806),[8] in which the radical leader is lampooned, indicate that Dacre was politically conservative. We also know that her husband Nicholas Byrne, who was mysteriously murdered in his office in 1833, was "a zealous Pittite,"[9] and we can presume Dacre shared her husband's support of Pitt's politics, given that they named their son William Pitt Byrne. Moreover, passages in *The Passions* clearly and violently attack radical feminists such as Wollstonecraft, suggesting Dacre was anti-feminist; yet she also wrote a poem "To the Shade of Mary Robinson" celebrating the memory of that outspoken republican feminist and Della Cruscan poet (see Appendix C). We therefore must keep in mind the often sharp distinction between a writer's class and gender interests; Dacre's Pittite politics, and her questionable caricatures of feminism, need not (and do not) coincide with an acceptance of the ideology of domesticity and passionlessness.

Rather than lament our lack of access to Dacre's "true" intentions (e.g., in letters or memoirs), I suggest we use her relative anonymity as a test case for examining how gendered readings, especially according to gender-complementary models of "female Gothic" or "feminine Romanticism," to a large extent depend on an author's biography and their sex, and therefore in a sense re-produce a circular argument as to what constitutes a woman's text. How would we read *Zofloya*, for example, if we did not know the sex of the author, much less whether or not she identified herself as a feminist?

I believe that readers of Dacre's novel, past and present, would have assumed the author to be male if it had been published anonymously or with a male pseudonym, as readers had done with more famous examples such as *Frankenstein* and *Wuthering Heights*. The reviewer for *The Annual Review*, as we saw, was distressed by this dissonance between the sexual content of Dacre's novel and Dacre's sex, and the *New Annual Register* also confirmed that Dacre's writing came dangerously close to that of a male author censored and prosecuted for his novel's illicit and blasphemous content: "a stimulating novel after the manner of The Monk — the same lust — the same infernal agents — the same voluptuous language. What need we say more?"[10] We need say much more, of course, because this same lust, voluptuousness, and infernal temptation were those of a woman.

Ultimately it is not any subversive intention in Dacre's work that is most valuable, but the subversive effect in the pleasure she clearly takes, and her characters clearly take, in what Swinburne termed the "vivisection of virtue." Dacre, like Austen, Radcliffe and Wollstonecraft, clearly warns her readers against the dangers of excessive sensibility in women, a task that R.F. Brissenden argues Austen shares with Sade.[11] Yet unlike Austen and Wollstonecraft, Dacre does not attempt to persuade through reason or moral example, but rather to demonstrate a doctrine of destruction strikingly similar to Sade's. Gilles Deleuze explains the critical difference between persuasion and demonstration in *Masochism: Coldness and Cruelty* (1991), where he argues that if we understand Sade correctly, we expect no instruction from him, because

> the intention to convince [in Sade] is merely apparent, for nothing is in fact more alien to the sadist than the wish to convince, to persuade, in short to educate. He is interested in something quite different, namely to demonstrate that reasoning itself is a form of violence, and that he is on the side of violence, however calm and logical he may be. ... The point of the demonstration is to show that the demonstration is identical to violence. (18-19)

Dacre by no means demonstrates, in Adorno and Horkheimer's words, "the identity of domination and reason"(119) that Sade obsessively pursues. However, I think that she abandons persuasion for the morally questionable task of describing, in sexually charged terms, irrational, vicious and violent behaviour in women. Dacre in effect demonstrates the identity of passion and destruction, and the pleasures found in both.

Following Swinburne's example of more than a century ago, I suggest that, rather than rely on our knowledge of Dacre's gender (as reviewers had done) or her feminism — in other words, on our assumptions of what makes a "woman's" text or a "feminist" text — we recontextualize Dacre within the tradition she was writing in and against, namely that of Lewis and Sade, in order to trace a more complex relationship between women writers and "masculine" discourses. For although her anti-heroines may fail by traditional feminist standards (e.g., they are destroyed, and do not establish a stable, subversive subject position), they do succeed in Sadean, destructive terms, as Swinburne says of Victoria: she "ultimately succeeds in accomplishing the vivisection of virtue."

Dacre's association with Lewis's school of horror began with her first novel, *Confessions of the Nun of St. Omer* (1805), which she dedicated to Lewis, and her placement in the "male" Gothic tradition of horror, as opposed to Radcliffe's "female Gothic" school of terror, is significant. In that same year she also published *Hours of Solitude*, a two-volume collection of poems, many using the demon lover theme.[12] Dacre's demon lovers and revenants in these poems are remarkably diverse, however, ranging from the ghost of poet Mary Robinson that the speaker summons to haunt her, to sensual explorations of passionate love beyond the grave, to a female revenant who returns not to destroy but to warn the future female victim that her lover is a vampyre. In her third novel, *The Libertine* (1807), Dacre again explored women's sexuality in frank terms, leading one reviewer to protest that "readers who can be amused, with such prurient trash as the Libertines [sic], must have their mental appetites depraved, and their understandings warped in no common degree."[13]

The "self-conscious fleshliness" of Dacre's poetry, to use Jerome McGann's apt description, associated her with the earlier Della Cruscan poetic school of which Robinson and Hannah Cowley ("Anna Matilda") had been prominent members, and which had come under attack as excessively effeminate and self-indulgently sensual (as well as republican) in satires such as William Gifford's *Baviad* (1791) and *Maeviad* (1795).[14] Byron's infamous attack of Dacre's poetry as "prose in masquerade" and of herself as one of Della Crusca's last "stragglers" in *English Bards and Scotch Reviewers* is but one example of how Dacre's contemporaries associated her with this influential but now discredited group. The Della Cruscans lacked manliness, as the *Monthly Literary Recreations* remarked in an 1807 essay on the state of "poetical excellence":

> for ... an affected sensibility and glitter of imagery, they gave up energy of thought and diction, manly feelings, and even sense; such were the Laura Marias, the Robinsons, Jerninghams, Edwins of later years, and such the Rosa Matildas, the Hafiz, and other newspaper writers of the present day; though thanks to the keen satire of the above-mentioned author [Gifford], that sweetly-effeminately poetical junto are put to flight in a great measure, and an over affected simplicity has usurped its place, and crept into the works of some of our really otherwise excellent authors: such as Southey, Wordsworth, and others, who remind us very much, when they descend to

what they call their beautifully simple style, of the namby pamby songs of the nursery.[15]

Wordsworth is charged with affecting a "namby pamby" simplicity in response to the effeminacy and elaborateness of contemporary verse such as Dacre's, and as Jerome McGann and Roger Lonsdale have argued, Wordsworth's Preface to the *Lyrical Ballads* consciously rejects the language of women for the language of a "man speaking to men."[16] Thus Dacre's writing is excessively feminine when compared to the self-consciously manly new poetic standards put forward by Wordsworth, yet her writing, particularly her prose, is also dangerously unfeminine when compared to that of contemporary domestic women novelists such as Maria Edgeworth and Jane West. Not only as a novelist but as a poet, then, Dacre defies easy classification, falling either behind, or I would argue also ahead (and certainly outside) the trends, both of style and subject matter, of women contemporaries. Dacre's association with Lewis's school of horror thus marks a point where the "sweetly effeminately poetical" and the masculine pornographic meet, and where the gender of each discourse, poetic and pornographic, needs to be questioned.

Victoria's fearless appetite for sexual knowledge and pleasure was in fact the focus of much moral disapproval in reviews of *Zofloya*. As Ambrosio's sexual and moral liberation is inspired and perhaps directed by the infernal influence of Matilda in Lewis's *The Monk*, Victoria's sexual and moral liberation is influenced by Satan in the form of the seductive Moorish sorcerer Zofloya. But Dacre goes even farther than Lewis did in questioning the external origin of Ambrosio's lustful, violent desires, for unlike in *The Monk*, the infernal agent enters *Zofloya* midway through the novel, after Victoria has begun her seductions. The reviewer for *Monthly Literary Recreations* found Lucifer's superfluousness indicative of the novel's "disgusting depravity of morals," since Victoria is depraved before Satan arrives: "The supernatural agent is totally useless, as the mind of Victoria, whom Satan, under the form of Zofloya, comes to tempt, is sufficiently black and depraved naturally, to need no temptation to commit the horrid crimes she perpetrates." As many critics argue, in *The Monk* Matilda's influence is in effect a projection of the pious monk's own unspoken destructive desires; similarly, Zofloya's influence on Victoria, urging her on to increasingly violent crimes, is clearly a projection of her own destructive desires. Thus the submission of the protagonist to the infernal agent, through the selling of the soul, is in both novels, on one level, a liberation.

Yet Dacre also deliberately describes Victoria's eventual submission to Zofloya's will as a marriage, and his attempts to convince her to depend on him are expressed in the language of romantic courtship. Here Dacre highlights the subjecting (not liberatory) function of heterosexuality and its central institution, marriage, since as Foucault[17] has argued, the promise of "liberated" sexual desire is power's most attractive ruse. The story of Victoria's downfall is thus also the story of the loss of social identity, mobility and independence that a woman suffers in marrying her lover, who then becomes her legal master after having acted the part of her devoted and enthralled servant:

> "Now then, Victoria!" cried the Moor, but not in the gentle voice in which he had been wont to address her — "now then, thou art emancipated from falling ruins, from hostile guards, from fear of shame, and an ignominious death. ... I have watched thee, followed thee, and served thee until now: — If, then, I save thee for ever from all future accidents — all future worldly misery — all future disgrace; say — wilt thou, for that future, resign thyself entirely to me? ... wilt thou unequivocally give thyself to me, heart, and body, and soul?"

Thus, unlike Ambrosio, who is destroyed through liberating the excesses of his own desires, Victoria is destroyed through her submission to another, a husband, who ends her existence as mistress of her own will by gaining her wifely submission through the false promise of protection.

Dacre's contradictory accounts of Victoria's "evil" render any moralistic pretences the novel may profess dangerously unconvincing, as critics from the early reviewers to Robert Miles have observed:

> Four discourses offer competing explanations for the origin of Victoria's evil: a religious one of fallen nature and satanic temptation; a sentimental, libertarian one of nature/nurture; its Sadean variant ("Is not self predominant through animal nature?" (Dacre 1806, II; 171); and one of paternal and class responsibility. Typically, these explanations are left in contradictory and irresolute condition. (Miles 181)

Victoria's violence, and Dacre's intentions, cannot be neatly explained by any of these models of evil, and though the bad example set by her mother is repeatedly cited by the narrator as the cause of Victoria's "love of evil," the narrator contradicts herself repeatedly by also offering competing explanations, which leads Gary Kelly to conclude that the novel is "hopelessly self-contradictory on the causes of the evil" (106). Yet as the *General Review* pointed out, "Zofloya has no pretension to rank as a moral work."[18] *Zofloya*'s resistance to rank as a moral work is formidable, and goes against the grain of most women's writing of the period, which, I suggest, again invites us to read Dacre as we would Lewis or Sade.

Zofloya celebrates Victoria's capacity for sexual desire and pleasure; her desire for Zofloya the Moor is itself transgressive, not because it is blasphemous as is Ambrosio's desire for Matilda (who modeled for the portrait of the Madonna) in *The Monk*, but in part because it grows as the novel progresses and Zofloya grows more demonic. Unlike the conventional woman in a demon lover ballad who is horrified to see her lover revealed as infernal, Victoria, like several of Dacre's poetic narrators, finds his supernatural and infernal origins arousing:[19]

> Never, till this moment, had she been so near the person of the Moor — such powerful fascination dwelt around him, that she felt incapable of withdrawing from his arms; yet ashamed, (for Victoria was still proud) and blushing at her feelings, when she remembered that Zofloya, however he appeared, was but a menial slave, and as such alone had originally become known to her — she sought, but sought vainly, to repress them; for no sooner (enveloped in the lightning's flash as he seemed, when it gleamed around him without touching his person), — did she behold his beautiful and majestic visage, that towering and graceful form, than all thought of his inferiority vanished, and the ravished sense, spurning at the calumnious idea, confessed him a being of a superior order. (3: 130-31)

Victoria's desire, because it is for a Moorish servant who was once a slave, also "crosses class and racial taboos" (Miles 188), but her desire grows as does Zofloya's class status (and stature, literally) in her eyes, undercutting the subversive charge and highlighting the novel's significant racist and orientalist dimensions. Dacre in fact may have read an earlier novel, *Zoflora, or The Generous Negro Girl* (1804), and may have transformed the persecuted slave Zoflora into the persecuting former slave Zofloya, thus offering an unsympathetic and unsentimental (though thoroughly exoticized) portrayal of a black slave in the year preceding the passage of the anti-slave trade bill.[20]

Reviewers picked up on *Zofloya*'s racism (casting the devil as a black man, and vice versa): the *General Review* thus parodied the novel's faint attempt at moralising: "if the devil should appear to them [young ladies] in the shape of a very handsome black man, they must not listen to him."[21] The *Literary Journal* made the connection between Zofloya's race and his evil origins even clearer: "Satan ... had the decorum to lodge himself in a black body, so as to be something in character."[22] But the irresistible beauty of Zofloya's black body, of his eyes and voice, is emphasized throughout the novel, so that while Victoria's desire for him cannot be separated from the racism and orientalism inherent in conflating a black man and the devil, neither can her desire be reduced to these racist dimensions.

It is in this unusual and conflicted heroine that *Zofloya*'s greatest value lies. The novel traces the progress of Victoria and her brother Leonardo, who are exiled from an "idyllic" patriarchal family because of their mother's adultery and her abandonment of them. It is Victoria who is the novel's protagonist, who actively pursues her desires for wealth and power, never submitting and seldom wavering in moments of personal danger. Possessing an "unflinching relentless soul" filled only with the "ambitious, the selfish, the wild, and the turbulent" sensations, Victoria's ability to "inflict pain without remorse" and revenge her own injuries likens her more to a Satanic hero than to any heroine of the period (with the exception of Sade's). Her brother is overshadowed in the narrative by his lover, Megalena Strozzi, who like Victoria derives her pleasure from mastering others. The women in *Zofloya* strategically use their sexuality to enchant or command men, and it is this process of mastery itself that is the source of their pleasure.

The "vivisection of virtue" that Dacre undertakes in *Zofloya* is, as Swinburne's vivid metaphor suggests, conducted to an important extent on a corporeal level. Victoria violates the natural difference between the sexes to such an extent that her body itself is transformed into a larger and decidedly masculine form. Victoria's increasingly physical masculinization reveals the anxiety (and hope) of Dacre's age that perhaps the two sexes themselves (and not merely the gender identities they supposedly establish) are not fixed or natural.

According to Foucault, the eighteenth century's fascination with hermaphrodites and the question of their "true" sex is indicative of modern Western society's pursuit of the truth of sex.[23] The truth of Victoria's sex becomes increasingly unclear as she proceeds to seduce, dominate, torture and murder. Her body, no longer a "natural" entity, is redesignated as unnatural (specifically, "unnaturally" large and masculine) according to her actions, in an illustration of Judith Butler's (and Foucault's) problematization of the supposedly stable distinction between "natural" sex and "cultural" gender: "Gender is not to culture as sex is to nature; gender is also the discursive/cultural means by which 'sexed nature' or a 'natural sex' is produced and established as 'prediscursive'" (Butler *Gender Trouble*, 7). Dacre illustrates exactly how sex is a product of gender, and not the other way around.

Victoria's corporeal transformation makes sense given the period's increasing suspicion that the natural, and especially the naturally sexed body, was not fixed but mutable. In addition to growing larger and more masculine, Victoria's body also grows darker, so that one can read her corporeal degeneration also as a sign of miscegenation. Her darkness is increasingly emphasized, as is Zofloya's, particularly in contrast with the milk-white Lilla, as in the scene where Henriquez awakes after having slept with Victoria while drugged, and is horrified at her appearance: "those black fringed eyelids, reposing upon a cheek of dark and animated hue — those raven tresses hanging unconfined — oh, sad! oh, damning proofs! — Where was the fair enamelled cheek — the flaxen ringlets of the delicate Lilla?" (3:89). Victoria and Zofloya's increasingly large bodies also owe something to the racist discourse of miscegenation, for as H.L. Malchow has recently argued, "[b]y the early nineteenth century, popular racial discourse managed to conflate ... descriptions of particular ethnic characteristics into a general image of the Negro body in which repulsive features, brutelike strength and size of limbs featured prominently" (18). Yet darkness and "more than mortal" size and strength also belong to other competing discourses of the period, among them medical and supernatural.

The mutability of body shape and size with which modern readers are most familiar — weight control — also emerged as a socially desirable possibility in the early nineteenth century, particularly in the novel according to Pat Rogers, and it is the novel that "responds to, and creates, a growing uncertainty about the reliability of body shape ... it starts to seem malleable rather than eternally given"(183). Victorian scholarship has already begun to explore the period's interest in politics of the body, especially regarding women. Jill Matus, for example, has recently explored how in the Victorian era, "although being sexed was understood as a natural, pre-given biological condition, it was at the same time conceived as unstable, even precarious" (10). Of course the Romantic and Gothic traditions can claim one of the most spectacular novels of corporeal mutability, Shelley's *Frankenstein*, and it is significant to note that the primary reason Frankenstein destroys the female creature prematurely is his fear that her great size will allow her to rape men and choose her own destiny (like Victoria).

Yet for the most part, women's own perspectives on the body in the Romantic period have only begun to be examined, and it has typically been assumed that the burden of bourgeois propriety was simply too powerful for (middle-class) women to seriously resist. As Mary Poovey argues, "by the last decades of the eighteenth century, [for women] even to refer to the body was considered 'unladylike'" (14). Yet Thomas Laqueur has argued that this ideology of passionlessness and incommensurable sexual difference was one of several competing sexual ideologies: "Whatever the issue, the body became decisive. ... It may well be the case that almost as many people believed that women by nature were equal in passion to men as believed the opposite" (152). Laqueur argues that in the eighteenth century, while the two sex model based[24] on natural difference between men and women gained credibility, this epistemological shift did not eliminate the previous one sex model in which the sexes existed along a continuum, and women's sexual passion was a given.

Despite the growing emphasis on a "biology of incommensurability" (Laqueur 152) and women's passionlessness, women writers such as Dacre, Radcliffe and Wollstonecraft clearly rejected the ideology of women's passionlessness, and perhaps even questioned the immutability of the binary two-sex-model. Though it is in many ways productive to generalize, as Mary Poovey does, that "[b]y the end of the eighteenth centur ... 'female' and 'feminine' were understood by virtually all men and women to be synonymous" (6), I find Laqueur's emphasis on the unresolved struggle over both the meaning of the sex "woman," and whether or not such a distinct sex even exists, more compelling. By emphasizing the struggle over the categories of sex and gender, rather than the struggle's outcome (the conflation of sex and gender), we can give women's perspectives greater visibility.

Dacre rejected the doctrine of incommensurability in which women's passionlessness was grounded, not only by writing of women's passions, as had Radcliffe and Wollstonecraft, but by also showing how the two incommensurable, distinct sexes were capable of mutating. Early in *Zofloya*, when she seduced her lover, Victoria had been described as possessing a countenance "not of angelic mould; yet though there was a fierceness in it, it was not certainly a repelling, but a beautiful fierceness," and a figure that was "graceful and elegant." After committing two murders (one of her husband) and attempting to seduce her affianced brother-in-law Henriquez, Victoria is described as possessing a "masculine spirit," whereas she had been consistently described as bold, independent and inflexible, without reference to gender. After this degeneration of her feminine "spirit," it is her body that is suddenly masculine when compared to that of her rival, Lilla, Henriquez' fiancée, whom Victoria has kidnapped and will soon murder. No longer a stunning seductress, in comparison to Lilla Victoria is suddenly less feminine and perhaps no longer female, as if a "hidden deformity" similar to Appollonia's had emerged:

> "He would have loved you [said Zofloya] had you chanced to have *resembled* Lilla."
> "Ah! would," cried the degenerate Victoria, "would that this unwieldy form could be compressed into the fairy delicacy of hers, these bold masculine features assume the likeness of her baby face!"

It is the fluidity of corporeal identity that is significant, for Victoria will indeed transform her body into that of the absent and ideally feminine Lilla. Henriquez, drugged and spellbound, will believe Victoria to be his Lilla and will make love to her under this spell, thereby temporarily granting the masculine Victoria the "fairy form" of the properly feminine and unquestionably female Lilla. Victoria's "materialization" as Lilla is much more than a Gothic trapping: materialization, to use Judith Butler's rather Gothic term, is inseparable from issues of power and how one (or in what form of "woman" one) can exercise more of it. As Butler succinctly puts it, "what constitutes the fixity of the body, its contours ... will be fully material, but materiality will be rethought as the effect of power, as power's most productive effect" (*Bodies That Matter*, 2).

That a degenerate and "unwieldy" woman such as Victoria can resemble and become the fragile Lilla suggests the primacy of performance over fixed essence. Butler's concept of performative gender, and of sexual difference as one of its ongoing productions, can thus be effectively applied to Romantic female subjectivity and corporeality in Dacre: "*woman* itself is a term in process, a becoming, a constructing that cannot rightfully be said to originate or to end. As an ongoing discursive practice, it is open to intervention and resignification" (*Gender Trouble* 33). Dacre reveals how her women characters enact such an ongoing process of self-creation and self-destruction as they take whatever actions and roles are necessary for survival, which in their eyes is synonymous with increased power over self and others. In constantly drawing attention to the desire to master shared by Victoria and Megalena (and Appollonia in Dacre's *The Passions*), Dacre offers a version of female subjectivity that is not complementary to male subjectivity, but which dissolves the boundaries that her contemporaries and ours would like to fix between the genders and between bodies. If a fixed feminine subjectivity embodied in a "natural" female body was and is crucial to a larger ideological process of naturalizing a rational and benevolent bourgeois identity, then Dacre effectively deprives her readers of the consolations of femininity and benevolence.

Dacre insists that female and male subjects are driven by a will to power and possess an infinite sadistic capacity, which in her age translates into a "love of evil." The metaphor she typically uses to characterize the subject is that of struggle, as in this quotation from *The Passions*, spoken by the novel's sole survivor: "mine is a fearful struggle. I oppose myself to myself. ... My heart is as a land which is the seat of war, the rival powers combat, but vanquish which may, the wretched land is savaged and destroyed" (4: 18). The outcome of the internal struggle, like that of the external one, is always destruction and fragmentation (or vivisection), so that her characters' inter-subjective and intra-subjective struggles collapse into one another, and problematize the boundaries between external reality and internal experience, a feature characteristic of the Gothic's psychological complexity.

In the last line of *Zofloya*, Dacre poses the novel's central question regarding this "love of evil" in such as way as to suggest that the widely-held and supposedly "reasonable" faith in human benevolence is in fact as reasonable as believing in "infernal influence" as the cause of crimes "dreadful and repugnant to nature":

> Either we must suppose that the love of evil is born with us (which would be an insult to the Deity), or we must attribute [such crimes] (as appears more consonant with reason) to the suggestions of infernal influence.

The world Dacre's characters inhabit never operates according to reason; on the contrary, the unreasonable "love of evil" is shown by Dacre to be neither "repugnant to nature" in general, nor to women in particular, but rather to constitute a will to power which is both constructive and destructive.

Bienville's *Nymphomania, or, A Dissertation Concerning the Furor Uterinus* (1775)[25], the first medical treatise devoted to this disorder, provides an excellent medical context against which to read Dacre's novel, for Victoria on one level illustrates the dangerous degeneration a sexually active woman is capable of undergoing, and there are indications that Dacre had read Bienville. Reviews of Dacre's novels consistently expressed disgust with the excessively sexual language of her prose (complaints about her "bombastic" language are typically linked to her language's shocking voluptuousness), and one review noted the singular inappropriateness of a woman novelist knowing, much less using, medical terminology for female sexuality:

> Here the language in general is bombastical; new words are introduced, such for example, as *enhorred* and *furor*, the latter of which is certainly used in the language of medicine, but in a sense which delicacy will not permit us to explain.[26]

The *furor* the reviewer (and *Zofloya*) refers to is the *furor uterinus*, or nymphomania, medical language fit for a misogynist medical treatise such as Bienville's , intended to demonstrate women's "imbecility" (Bienville vii), but absolutely "odious and indecent" in a woman writer's Gothic romance.

Bienville's text embodies the contradictory claims regarding sexual difference and women's propensity for sexual desire and pleasure that Laqueur described; Bienville argues that women's sexuality is natural and that its suppression is "capable of ... causing a revolution, and disorder in the physical system of their nature" (160), while simultaneously emphasizing "the fragility of [women's] nature" (vii) and their greater vulnerability to their distinctly sexualized bodies, which therefore demand regulation. Bienville describes nymphomania in lurid detail as an "incredible ... metamorphosis" (136) that "can debase, afflict, and as it were unhumanize" (186) women, and, like Foucault (who discussed Bienville's work), argues that the ultimate danger in nymphomania is social disorder through corporeal disorder: "it is from this general overthrow of all their relations to each other, that a delirium arises to destroy the order of ideas, and impels the person afflicted to affirm what she had denied, and to deny what she hath affirmed" (70).[27]

Dacre's heroines in both *Zofloya* and in her last novel, *The Passions*, follow a similar process of nymphomaniacal degeneration, but because Dacre gives us complex characterizations of the women and their motives, her novels critique, and do not merely internalize, such medical representations of women's sexuality and subjectivity. In fact, *The Passions* unites a critique of Rousseau's *La Nouvelle Héloïse* with a rendering of one of Bienville's case studies from *Nymphomania*, and like *Zofloya* focuses on the mental and physical degeneration of women under the influence of violent passions. In Bienville's narrative, a young innocent woman, Julia, is "initiated into the secrets of Venus" by a "voluptuous procuress of lascivious pleasure," her young friend and waiting-woman, Berton (165). In *The Passions*, Dacre focuses her attention on this minor character Berton, giving her the ambitious, intellectual aspirations of Lucifer, and setting her against the domestic, Eve-like ideal of Rousseau's Julie. Dacre's Appollonia not only destroys the emotional and sexual tranquillity of

Julie's domestic isolation, but she destroys the lives of all but one of the characters in the novel, and is herself a victim of the violent passions she inspired. Rather than simply embodying the misogynist stereotypes of women as either virtuous virgins or degenerate whores, Dacre's two types are both shown to be dangerously unstable.

Both in *Zofloya* and *The Passions*, Dacre uses a similar (and popular) narrative device of two complementary female characters, much like Sade's Justine and Juliette; most significant for the purpose of this discussion, however, is the degree to which these two types are embodied differently, and most interestingly, how one type of body, that of the proper woman, can degenerate into an unsexed, unfemale, and unnatural body through physical and emotional violence.[28] The virtuous and the vicious body, Dacre repeatedly demonstrates, are dangerously mutable, and the catalyst for their degeneration is most often female sexual desire.

Dacre's vivisections of virtue, like Sade's, do not merely invert the terms of the debate by focusing on "masculine" behaviour (e.g., cruelty, violence) in women; these portraits of destructive women leave neither vice nor virtue intact, but show how both categories, not just the "unnatural" one, are socially constructed, and similarly destroyed. Because Dacre deals so often with complementary doubles, her *femmes fatales* could be dismissed as nothing more than misogynist stereotypes of improper women, of women who take on masculine qualities without challenging the underlying assumptions about gender. Dacre's *femmes fatales* subvert the persistent category of the proper woman, however, not only by embodying its antithesis, but by demonstrating the instability of these categories themselves. Her *femmes fatales* are thus subversive in the same way that masquerade is according to Terry Castle: through their ambiguity, not their simple role reversal. Though the atomizing ideology of bourgeois individualism was persistent and the ambiguity of the masquerade temporary, we should not underestimate the force of such ambiguity, Castle argues in *Masquerade and Civilization*. Similarly, though the proper "natural" woman was established as a distinct, pervasive norm by the end of the eighteenth century, we find in literature of the period examples that she existed alongside temporary anomalies, monsters and phantoms. Though at the conclusions of Dacre's narratives transgressors are punished, the temporary exploits of such transgressive women momentarily reveal (to a largely female audience) the violent disorder of female subjectivity, and its violent repression by demonic masculinity, a significant accomplishment. And the bourgeois moral order is not re-established at her novels' conclusions, because generally most of her characters do not survive — the innocent and the guilty are alike destroyed, as the chapbook version of *Zofloya*, *The Dæmon of Venice*, emphasized in its closing sentence: "Thus the precipice was the grave of two, the innocent Agnes [Lilla] and the wicked Arabella [Victoria]."[29]

The contagious potential of Dacre's critique lies in the process of reading itself, in its controversial function in the production (and destruction) of subjects and even bodies. The danger of reading sentimental fiction is a ubiquitous theme in this period, and it is central to all of Dacre's novels, as well as to Bienville's *Nymphomania*. *The Literary Journal* had warned in mock medical terms that Dacre's imagination (like the nymphomaniac's) is both diseased and infectious:

> this malady of maggots in the brain is rendered still more dreadful by its being infectious. The ravings of persons under its influence, whenever they are heard or read, have a sensible effect upon brains of a weak construction, which themselves either putrefy or breed maggots, or suffer a derangement of some kind. (Appendix B, 5)

The medical context this reviewer provides, albeit satirically, highlights Dacre's own exploration of the dangerous properties of imagination, and of nymphomania, in *Zofloya*. Dacre's "extravagant language," her "overwhelming all meaning in a multitude of words" (*Literary Journal*, 635), marks a fascinating intersection of medical and poetic discourses of passion and imagination, of how they are experienced physiologically, psychologically, socially, and even supernaturally, and why they are each both pleasurable and dangerous.

Significantly, Dacre gives her readers access to the immoral pleasure felt by her vicious heroines as they set out to seduce and destroy (and the epistolary format of *The Passions* allows us, like Rousseau's original text, to read the first-hand accounts of adulterous passion, and more importantly, of Appollonia's passion to destroy). In focusing on the productive power of literature (whether it is withheld or provided) on young women, Dacre foregrounds the extent to which the proper woman and her improper complement are alike effects of power. Dacre's texts instruct women readers not only that women's sexual desires are capable of destroying both self and others, a conservative and often misogynist concept, but that the naturally asexual and domestic woman held up as the alternative ideal is as unnatural as her "degenerate" double.

Though the anti-heroines in both Dacre's *Zofloya* and *The Passions* are punished and denounced by the narrator as improper models for female behaviour, both novels (like Bienville's treatise) simultaneously and ambiguously instruct readers how to reach such depths of depravity. Thus, not only are such disturbing examples of female behaviour allowed to flourish temporarily, but Dacre's novels celebrate the powers of the poisonous texts they claim to warn against. The prohibitions against novel reading, especially of Rousseau, in Dacre's own novels make transparent, or demystify, how normative sexuality and the normal female body are constructed through the exclusion of negative examples. Dacre's dire warnings against Rousseau, that "sentimental luxurious libertine," are ultimately as prescriptive as they are prohibitive,[30] for Dacre rewrites Rousseau's text in even more lascivious terms, focusing in minute detail on Appollonia's decidedly lascivious pleasure in destroying the virtuous

Julia, as well as on Julia's and her lover's adulterous desires. For example, the anti-heroine Appollonia celebrates her sexual corruption of the virtuous Julia through the "sovereign poison" of books in such a way that Dacre's implicit warning against such novels, occurring in precisely such a voluptuous novel, amounts to an endorsement. The warning ensures that readers will, if they haven't already done so, immediately seek out a copy of Rousseau's novel:

> I know that there is not in the world a more subtle poison than that which is extracted from and administered by books ... there is not in my estimation a more dangerous work extant, or one better calculated for the purposes of seduction [than *La Nouvelle Héloïse*]: for I defy the female, however pure in her heart, however chaste in her ideas she may be, before reading this book, to remain wholly unaffected, and unimpressed by its perusal. I aver that it is utterly impossible so many highly-coloured and voluptuous images as are there depicted, can be permitted to take their passage through the mind, and leave no stain behind. (*The Passions*, 1: 207, 209-210)

One might argue that in deploying this familiar argument against women reading sentimental novels, Dacre perpetuates a misogynist concept of women's sexuality as dangerous, much as Bienville had done when he repeatedly warned against the "venomous" power of novels to unleash nymphomania in women: "The perusal of a novel, a voluptuous picture ... soon excite those emotions, of which but the moment before, she seemed herself the mistress" (76).[31] Yet because Dacre, unlike Bienville, is precisely the sort of novelist she warns us against, her narratives of sexually transgressive women who destroy properly asexual women, and are themselves punished, are in fact sophisticated accounts of the discursive construction of both natural and unnatural women and their sexuality. In Dacre's novels the asexual feminine ideal is produced only by isolating the young woman from corrupting social influences such as novels and fashionable society, yet Dacre, like Wollstonecraft and Radcliffe before her, insists that such an "ideal" woman is artificial, vulnerable, and destined for destruction precisely because of her isolation in the domestic sphere.

Dacre's model of subjectivity as struggle parallels (without resolving) the larger cultural struggle over the term "woman," and raises to a more disturbing, even pornographic, level the parody Barker-Benfield (like Brissenden) locates in Austen's *Sense and Sensibility*:

> The alternatives offered to women in the 1790s — the approved vision of mindless sensibility or the outlawing bogey of the strong-minded Amazon — can be seen as a parody of the conflict represented by Marianne and Elinor Dashwood. As Wollstonecraft recognized, the conflict existed both within women, and between women and the surrounding male and female authorities, telling them what it was to be female. (Barker-Benfield, 382)

The unique value of Dacre's doubles lies in their process of degeneration, in the way they experience increasingly perverse gradations of pleasure and pain as they reach the parodic extreme. This process of degeneration they undergo is not indicative of an unstable, fluid female subject, characteristic of "feminine Romanticism" and its use of feminist psychoanalytical models that emphasize women's "permeable ego boundaries." Dacre's emphasis on emotional and physical violence is significantly different, because it does not allow for the peaceful harmony between woman and woman, or woman and nature, which such models of subjectivity privilege.

In *The Passions* Dacre isolates two contemporary models of female subjectivity at their most extreme and shows how easily (and violently) one "natural" type can degenerate into the other, thereby undermining the possibility for fixed identity. The narrative of *The Passions* is set in motion by the Countess Appollonia Zulmer's desire for vengeance against the man who rejected her, Count Weimar, and this vengeance is directed at the object of his love, his new bride Julia. Weimar presents Appollonia as the *ancien régime* model of femininity that is actively sexual, aggressive, and intelligent:

> The Countess Zulmer ... does not endeavour gently to steal into the heart, but attacks it by storm, as able generals strive to carry all by a *coup de main*. Sensible of her power in conversation, whatever the topic, she takes a part, and enters freely; she obtains admiration, astonishment — but not love ... fearless, regardless of prejudice, an ardent spirit and daring intellect, she discusses opinions, combats errors, exposes systems, detects folly; in each and all she appears great; in every act of her character, full of power. Her fierce and penetrating eyes seem to look into the heart, with a glance so quick, so piercing, that other eyes are unable to meet them, and are cast down, as with a feeling of conscious guilt. Soaring, and eccentric in her flights, she leaves her wondering sex far behind. ... (1: 27-28)

Embodying both Wollstonecraftian feminism and *ancien régime* flamboyance, Appollonia is a fascinating contradiction, possessing a bold and articulate intellect, and exercising this intellect, along with considerable seductive powers, in the public sphere. Like Milton's Satan (and unlike Shelley's Prometheus), she is trapped in a cycle of destruction which leaves the question of free will (or of feminist subversion as autonomy) out of reach: "I [will] now ... sell myself to destruction to destroy him. ... Toppled from my high eminence, I will not singly fall, others shall be dragged down, and struggle with me in the depths of my despair" (1: 282-3).

Appollonia, like Victoria, is a Satanic heroine, one who consciously identifies herself with Lucifer's rebellion and accursedness, a criminal artist figure who repeatedly refers to her machinations as an art of enchantment and destruction. Appollonia destroys the domestic tranquillity of Weimar and Julia by awakening Julia's sexuality in the same terms Milton's Lucifer seduced Eve:

> I will initiate you! I will shew [sic] you the extent of your dominion, and how infinitely you are sovereign over the fate of him you obey. ... The secret of your slavery must be unfolded to you. You must taste of the tree of knowledge. (1: 173)

It is thus Appollonia's own sadistic pleasure in causing the suffering and death of all those close to Weimar that generates the narrative of *The Passions*; as Appollonia rightly claims, it was "*I*, who seduced her heart from [Weimar]!... *I* bade her give the reins to loose illicit love and pleasure!" (4: 85, original emphasis).

The political Satanic subtext of *The Passions* can be read as either an endorsement of the masculine Romantic model of autonomous heroic subjectivity, or as a literal demonization of Wollstonecraftian feminism, since Wollstonecraft was popularly associated with sexual corruption of young women;[32] yet I think the most productive reading rejects both pure subversion (Appollonia as autonomous hero) and pure normalization (Appollonia as demonized and defeated feminist). Instead, like Milton's Satan and *Zofloya*'s Victoria, Appollonia embodies the conflicted status of a subject who is necessarily, by definition, subjected.

The suggestions of Appollonia's lesbianism, since she does indeed "seduce" Julia, are clearly lesbophobic, as they were in attacks on Wollstonecraft's influence on young women. Like *Zofloya*, *The Passions* illustrates that the female homosocial continuum, to use Eve Kosofsky Sedgwick's formulation, was neither stable nor unproblematic in the early nineteenth century, as Emma Donoghue has demonstrated in *Passions Between Women: British Lesbian Culture 1668-1801* (1993). It is Appollonia's sexual effect on other women that particularly disturbs the men in Dacre's novel:

> such a woman as Appollonia Zulmer is calculated to do more mischief to her sex than the most abandoned libertine of ours, the most avowed profligate of her own. She is an enchantress — a Circe; and her arts enable her to conceal her deformity under the mask of the most seducing beauty. (1: 149-50)

Appollonia's monstrousness, like Victoria's, is increasingly emphasized as the novel progresses, her vaguely phallic "deformity" (which also suggests lesbianism and nymphomania, which Bienville claimed were accompanied by a large clitoris), and her masculine associations (Apollo, Apollyon, Lucifer, Prometheus) all contribute to the indistinctness of her sexual identity, to the indistinctness of the truth of her sex. Both Victoria and Appollonia are outside their proper sex, they both betray a hidden "deformity" suggestive of lesbianism, particularly in Victoria's rape-like, sadistic murder of Lilla, which reveals the author's and the age's awareness that women's sexual desires and activities went well beyond the prescriptions of the "natural" they were urged to embrace.

The value of Dacre's Victoria and Appollonia is ultimately not as subversive models of female subjectivity, however, for they are as much products of normative discourses on femininity as their tamer complements. The value of her *femmes fatales* lies in the dialectical relationship they have with their "innocent" victims, Julia and Lilla, for Dacre ultimately makes these asexual martyrs as repugnant and inhuman as their destroyers. Angela Carter's insights into Sade's *Justine* and *Juliette* apply just as well to Dacre's novels: "Justine is the thesis, Juliette is the antithesis; both are without hope and neither pays any heed to a future in which might lie the synthesis of their modes of being" (79).[33] The true subversive potential of Dacre's female characters lies thus in their mutual annihilation, and in the pleasure Appollonia and Victoria find in this destruction. Destruction, and its accompanying violent sublime which Dacre's heroines revel in, have historically been neglected by scholars of women's literature in favour of creation, nurture, and the "female" sublime, yet as Patricia Yaeger has argued, the "female sublime of violence ... needs, again and again, to be rewritten" (211).

Dacre's *femmes fatales* belong in a Sadean world but remain in and are limited by the English Gothic and sentimental traditions; yet even in their self-destructive, melodramatic outbursts we see a radical critique of the subject which is remarkably similar to Sade's:

> Oh! for ten thousand scourges, applied at once — for the stings of knotted scorpions — for any species of corporeal suffering, that for a single instant might divert to it the superior and unspeakable agony of my soul — that for a single instant one might be swallowed up in the other. — But, no, it may not be; I am sadly free from physical pain — all, all is soul, the nerve of mind. (*The Passions*, 1: 41-2)

In this remarkable passage Appollonia comes close to articulating Sade's (and Foucault's) desire that the self be swallowed up in the body, and that the body no longer be subjected to the self. Appollonia here echoes Olivia's speech in Radcliffe's *The Italian* (1797),[34] but Dacre transforms the "generous purpose" of Olivia's desire for self-denying martyrdom into a highly questionable desire for a literal annihilation of the self (not suicide) and the annihilation of others. Like the nymphomaniac and Victoria, Appollonia "sinks into a state of perfect reconciliation with the powers of her body" (Bienville 70). When the self is swallowed up by, or is "reconciled" with, the body, its destruction is both violent and suggestive of violence to others. Such female characters belong in a virtually unexplored tradition of women's *femmes fatales*, and demand that we go beyond the familiar reduction of *femmes fatales* to a "symptom of male fears about feminism," to use Mary Ann Doane's formulation (2-3). Dacre's works, like Sade's, are potential examples of "pornography in the

service of women" (Carter 37). Her *femme fatale* heroines are unacknowledged precursors to those of Victorian sensation novelists such as Mary
Braddon and decadent writers such as Vernon Lee (and Swinburne), and
we could begin to reconstruct from these *femme fatale* heroines a neglected counter-tradition in nineteenth-century British women's writing, a tradition which for too long has been dominated by the realist novel and its
heroines. Simultaneously, however, we need to consider how Dacre's
strong Sadean affinities and decidedly pornographic subject and style
challenge this notion of a "woman's tradition," and of gender-complementary readings of the Gothic and Romanticism in particular.

Notes

1   Algernon Charles Swinburne, letter to H. B. Forman, November 22, 1886.
    174-75.
2   Rev. of *Zofloya*, *The Annual Review* 5 (1806) 542. (See Appendix B.)
3   In addition, *The Morning Post* of June 28, 1806, announced that a dramatic
    piece from *Zofloya* was expected in the following season (see D. Varma's intro-
    duction to the Arno edition of *Zofloya*, p. xxvi). *Zofloya* was translated into
    French in 1812 by Mme. de Viterne (Paris, Barba).
4   Dacre's influence on P.B. Shelley has attracted some critical attention, exam-
    ples of which are Stephen Behrendt's Introduction to Shelley's *Zastrozzi and
    Irvyne* (1986), and A.M.D. Hughes' early essay, "Shelley's *Zastrozzi* and *St.
    Irvyne.*" Walter Edwin Peck, in vol. 2 of his *Shelley: His Life and Work*, includes
    an Appendix (A) which outlines Shelley's *Zastrozzi*'s debts to Dacre's *Zofloya*.
5   The best examples of gender-complementary models of Romanticism remain
    Marlon Ross' *The Contours of Masculine Desire* (1989) and Anne Mellor's *Roman-
    ticism and Gender* (1993). Both scholars, despite their differences, clearly distin-
    guish between canonical male Romanticism and women's writing of the peri-
    od, either arguing that women were not and could not be Romantic (Ross), or
    that women had a complementary "feminine Romanticism" (Mellor).
6   Charlotte Dacre (original emphasis), "The Skeleton Priest; or, The Marriage
    of Death," *Hours of Solitude* (1805) 71. (See Appendix C).
7   Charlotte Byrne died in 1825 at the age of fifty three, thus placing her birth in
    1771 or 1772, ten years earlier than her own prefatory remarks indicated in the
    1805 *Hours of Solitude* when she gave her age as twenty three. Most of the bio-
    graphical information on Dacre in the modern introductions to her works (e.g.,
    by Summers, Reiman, Varma, Knight-Roth) contain significant inaccuracies;
    the information presented here is based largely on Ann Jones' account in *Ideas
    and Innovations: Best Sellers in Jane Austen's Age* (1986), which corrects previous
    mistakes, acknowledges lingering mysteries, and to which I would only add
    the confirmation that Charlotte Dacre was indeed the sister of Sophia King.
    Along with her sister Sophia King (later Fortnum), also a novelist and poet,
    Charlotte (King) first published *Trifles of Helicon* (1798), which the two sisters
    dedicated to their father by name. Although her identity as the daughter of
    John King has been disputed in the past (by Reiman and Summers), this ver-
    sion of Dacre's biography is substantiated by the reappearance of Charlotte
    King's poems in Charlotte Dacre's *Hours of Solitude* (1805). Dacre's obituary in

The Times stated that she died in London on 7 November 1825, "after a long and painful illness." Garland's *Encyclopedia of British Women Writers* (2nd. ed., eds. Paul and Jane Schlueter) and *The Feminist Companion to Literature in English* (eds. Blain et al.) also contain helpful brief accounts of Dacre's life and works, as do other such reference volumes.

8   Dacre's poem on Pitt appeared in *The Morning Post*, Jan 27, 1806 (Pitt had died earlier that month). "Mr. F[o]x" is part of a series of poems Dacre published in *The Morning Post* in 1806 satirizing prominent contemporaries, called "The Dream; or, Living Portraits." (Knight-Roth's dissertation reprints the series in part, from which these quotations are taken. (See her Appendix I.)

9   Harold Herd tells the story of Nicholas Byrne without any reference to Charlotte Dacre in his "The Strange Case of the Murdered Editor," *Seven Editors* (London: Allen and Unwin, 1955). Herd suggests that Byrne's murder, closely following the passage of the 1832 Reform Bill, may have been politically motivated (because he opposed reform), and for that reason remained unreported, hence a "strange case."

10   (See Appendix B.) Rev. of *Zofloya. New Annual Register* 27 (1806) 372-3. The *Oxford Review*'s review of Dacre's *The Libertine* confirmed that all of Dacre's productions, her "worse than wild nonsense," were suited for a male author (and presumably a male readership): "we might have hoped, for the honour of that sex whose brightest ornament is modesty, that the author of such flights as the Nun of St, Omer's, Zofloya, and the present florid rhapsody could not be a female" (*Oxford Review, or Literary Censor* 2, August 1807) 190.

11   In his excellent *Virtue in Distress: Studies in the Novel of Sentiment from Richardson to Sade*, Brissenden demonstrates a strong continuity between the critiques of sensibility found in Richardson, Sade and Austen (see esp. Part I, chaps. 1 & 5). Sade was a great admirer of Richardson, and his *La Nouvelle Justine* ruthlessly attacks Rousseau's *La Nouvelle Héloïse*, as does Dacre's *The Passions*. Brissenden notes many similarities between the doubled female figures in *Sense and Sensibility* and *Justine* and *Juliette*; Dacre's doubled female characters in *Zofloya* and *The Passions* demonstrate a similar critique of Rousseauesque sensibility, in particular his construction of the virtuous, submissive woman.

12   Dacre (as Charlotte King) had published an earlier volume of poetry with her sister Sophia King (later Fortnum) titled *Trifles of Helicon* (1798), dedicated to their father John King. All of Charlotte's poems from that volume reappeared in *Hours of Solitude*, and some were also reprinted in periodicals.

13   Rev. of *The Libertine*, by Charlotte Dacre. *Monthly Magazine* suppl. v. 23 (30 July 1807) 645. *The Libertine* was translated into French in 1816: *Angelo, comte d'Albini, ou les Dangers du vice, par Charlotte Dacre Byrne connue sous le nom de Rosa Matilda, traduit de l'anglais par Mme. Élisabeth de B****. Paris: A. Bertrand, 1816. 3 vols.

14   For an excellent discussion of Byron's debt to Dacre, and of the relationship of Della Cruscan poetry to canonical Romanticism, see Jerome McGann's "'My Brain is Feminine': Byron and the Poetry of Deception."

15   "An Essay, whether the present age can, or cannot be reckoned among the ages of poetical excellence," *Monthly Literary Recreations*, no. xv (September 1807) 172.

16   See Lonsdale's Introduction to *Eighteenth Century Women Poets*, ed. Roger Lonsdale, and Jerome McGann, "Mary Robinson and the Myth of Sappho," *MLQ* 56 (1995).

17 See in particular Foucault's *History of Sexuality, Volume One: An Introduction* and his Introduction to *Herculine Barbin*.

18 See Appendix B.

19 Max Milner makes this important point regarding the novel's original use of the demon lover motif in *Le Diable dans la littérature française* (290); Milner praises the novel in positive terms rarely seen since Swinburne: "Comment ce roman plein d'originalité et de sombre poésie ne rencontra-t-il qu'indifférance en ce temps où les plus médiocres productions du genre noir étaient assurées du succès?" (288).

20 Picquenard's *Zoflora* is set before and during Haiti's rebellion following the French Revolution of 1789, and features a noble and selfless Creole slave, Zoflora, the epitome of virtue in distress, who is persecuted and nearly raped by sadistic (white and black) fathers and would-be lovers. Zoflora eventually falls in love with a "good white man" (as she refers to him), the novel's hero, for whose love she twice offers to sacrifice her life. In some respects, Zoflora's imprisonment in a gruesome cave and her persecution by a Sadean father loosely parallels Lilla's torture and captivity by Victoria, but both these conventions are also present in *The Monk*.

21 (See Appendix B.) *General Review of British and Foreign Literature* v. 1 (London: D. Shury, 1806) 590-3.

22 (See Appendix B.) *The Literary Journal* ns. v. 1 (June 1806) 632.

23 Michel Foucault, ed. Introduction to *Herculine Barbin: Being the Recently Discovered Memoirs of a Nineteenth-Century French Hermaphrodite*. Trans. Richard McDougall (Brighton: The Harvester Press, 1980).

24 Until the eighteenth century, female bodies were essentially inferior and "cooler" versions of male bodies, with complementary though internalized genitals, and human bodies in general were related to other natural bodies and phenomena through correspondences and homologous features.

25 First printed (in French) in Amsterdam, 1771. For a feminist account of *Nymphomania*'s role in the construction of female sexuality, see Carol Groneman's "Nymphomania — The Historical Construction of Female Sexuality."

26 (See Appendix A.) Rev. of *Zofloya*, *Monthly Literary Recreations* 1 (1806) 80.

27 In the third, "desperate" stage of nymphomania, which is accompanied by sexual aggression and violence toward men, the nymphomaniac "sinks into a state of perfect reconciliation with the powers of her body" (70) and the body itself undergoes a physiological degeneration/transformation. Foucault discussed Bienville's *Nymphomania* in *Madness and Civilization*, pp. 97-8.

28 For a fuller discussion of the complex meanings of "violence," which went beyond physical assault, see Raymond Williams' discussion of "Violence" in his *Keywords*.

29 The authorship of this chapbook remains unknown; the first page gives the author as "A Lady." Thomas Tegg, the publisher, was an innovative chapbook publisher from Cheapside, who sold "one-shilling coloured" prints as well as chapbooks, often illustrated by Thomas Rowlandson. The illustrator for *The Dæmon of Venice* is unknown and is probably not Rowlandson, though Rowlandson had illustrated another chapbook published by Tegg, *The School for Friends*, whose author was "Miss Dacre." Because Dacre's name was associated with this other chapbook by Tegg (though her authorship is not confirmed), it is possible, though I think unlikely, that she was the author of the *Dæmon of Venice* as well. On Rowlandson's work for Tegg, see Edward Wolf's *Rowlandson and His Illustrations of Eighteenth Century Literature* (1945).

30 Lewis had similarly manipulated the terms of this debate over the dangers of novel reading by naming the Bible as the most sexually suggestive and dangerous text, a gesture deemed blasphemous and censored after the first edition of *The Monk*.

31 Bienville also considers the possibility that a young woman may come across his own volume, but assures us that after reading *Nymphomania*, a woman "would feel the fragility of her nature; she would respect, and even cherish the principles which could certainly preserve her from that impending wreck to which the sex are, by reason of their imbecility, exposed" (vii). Though Dacre also focuses on the "impending wreck" facing sexually transgressive women, her dramatization of this wreck is a critique of the impossible double bind sexually active women are placed in, not a meditation on women's "imbecility."

32 After the publication of Godwin's memoir of Wollstonecraft's life in 1798, her feminist politics were intimately and unfortunately connected with the sexual "scandals" in her own life, as critics such as Richard Polwhele made clear (see Polwhele's poem *The Unsex'd Female*, London, 1798). One unfortunate incident of which Godwin reminded readers involved the Kingsborough family for which Wollstonecraft was governess, the daughter of which eloped with her married uncle, who was himself murdered by her family. After the shocking trial, "the *European Magazine* explained it as a result of Wollstonecraft's 'system of education'" (Barker-Benfield 369). Bienville's Berton in *Nymphomania* has a similar function of initiating young middle class women into sexual immorality with hints of lesbianism, though Bienville is unable to give his readers any insight as to why she would want to do this, whereas Dacre gives us many good reasons (e.g., power, pleasure, revenge) which we aren't necessarily intended to reject as unattractive.

33 Angela Carter's illuminating *The Sadeian Woman and the Ideology of Pornography* (1978) is an early and important work that explores "pornography in the service of women," and specifically the feminist uses of Sade. Some of the most dynamic Sade scholarship in the last twenty years has been produced by feminists. See for example Alice Laborde's "The Problem of Sexual Equality in Sadean Prose" in *French Women and the Age of Enlightenment.*, ed. Samia Spencer and Lynn Hunt's Introduction to *The Invention of Pornography*.

34 "I think I could endure any punishment with more fortitude than the sickening anguish of beholding such suffering as I have witnessed. What are bodily pains in comparison with the subtle, the exquisite tortures of the mind! Heaven knows I can support my own afflictions, but not the view of those of others when they are excessive. The instruments of torture I believe I could endure, if my spirit was invigorated with the consciousness of a generous purpose; but pity touches upon a nerve that vibrates instantly to the heart, and subdues resistance" (Ann Radcliffe, *The Italian*, 127).

A Note on the Text

This text is based on the first edition of 1806, published in three separately paginated volumes; 754 of the 1000 copies had sold by February 1807. According to Montague Summers' Introduction to the 1928 Fortune Press edition of *Zofloya*, in 1806 the *Morning Post* announced that a "dramatic piece" based on Dacre's novel would be performed in the next season. Summers also noted that the *Morning Post* announced that *Zofloya* had been translated into German in 1806, though this is not confirmed.

Because Dacre's style has been assailed by both her contemporaries and our own (Ann Jones concluded that "In all she wrote her style was a weakness," 241), I have maintained her original punctuation and spelling so that modern readers can examine her stylistic excesses in context. I have regularized the spelling of Megalena's name, which fluctuated between "Megalina" and "Megallena" in Dacre's text.

Charlotte Dacre: A Brief Chronology

The few biographical details we know about Dacre's life are drawn largely from the information provided in Ann Jones' chapter on Dacre in her *Ideas and Innovations*. Although she was born Charlotte King and later became Charlotte Byrne, she remains best known as Charlotte Dacre. There is no information to suggest that Dacre was the name of another husband, and it seems likely that it was a pseudonym.

1771?–72? Charlotte Dacre born, daughter of Jacob Rey (known as "John King") and Deborah Lara.

1798 John King, Dacre's father, arrested for bankruptcy. Charlotte King and her sister Sophia King (later Fortnum) publish *Trifles from Helicon* (London) and dedicate it to their father.

1804 Dacre publishes poems in *The Poetical Register* under the name of "Rosa."

1805 March: *Confessions of the Nun of St. Omer* published, dedicated to Matthew Lewis.

1805 Dacre publishes *Hours of Solitude*, a two-volume collection of poems, many of which had been published in *Trifles of Helicon*.

1806 May: Dacre publishes *Zofloya; or, The Moor*, and is known as "Mrs. Byrne" in the Longman archives.

1806 July: Charlotte Dacre (as Rosa Matilda) publishes in *The Morning Post* a series of poems on contemporary political figures, known collectively as "The Dream; or, Living Portraits."

1806 September: Charlotte Dacre and Nicholas Byrne's first child, William Pitt Byrne, born.

1807 *The Libertine* published, and reaches three editions by the end of the year.

1807 November: Charlotte Dacre and Nicholas Byrne's second child, Charles, born.

1809 July: Charlotte Dacre and Nicholas Byrne's third child, Maria, born.

1810 *Zofloya* pirated in a chapbook, *The Dæmon of Venice*, by Thomas Tegg's press.

1811 *The Passions* published.

1811   June: The three children of Nicholas Byrne and Charlotte baptized.

1812   *Zofloya* translated into French by Mme. de Viterne as *Zofloya, ou le Maure.*

1815   July: Charlotte King, spinster, marries Nicholas Byrne, widower, the editor of *The Morning Post.*

1816   *The Libertine* translated into French as *Angelo, comte d'Albine, où les Dangers du vice.*

1822   *George the Fourth* published.

1825   November 7: Charlotte Dacre dies in Lancaster Place, London, "after a long and painful illness," according to the obituary in *The Times.*

ZOFLOYA;

OR,

THE MOOR:

A ROMANCE

OF THE FIFTEENTH CENTURY.

IN THREE VOLUMES.

BY

CHARLOTTE DACRE,

BETTER KNOWN AS

ROSA MATILDA,

AUTHOR OF THE NUN OF ST. OMERS, HOURS OF SOLITUDE, &c.

VOL. I:

These shall the fury passions tear ——

COLLINS.

——Let me not let pass
Occasion which now smiles, beho'd alone
The woman, .opportune to all attempts——.

MILTON.

LONDON:

PRINTED FOR LONGMAN, HURST, REES, AND ORME,
PATERNOSTER-ROW.

1806.

ZOFLOYA;

OR,

THE MOOR.

CHAPTER I.

The historian who would wish his lessons to sink deep into the heart, thereby essaying to render mankind virtuous and more happy, must not content himself with simply detailing a series of events — he must ascertain causes, and follow progressively their effects; he must draw deductions from incidents as they arise, and ever revert to the actuating principle.

About the latter end of the fifteenth century, on the birth-night of the young Victoria de Loredani, most of the youthful nobility of any rank in Venice were assembled at the pallazzo of her parents to do honour to the festival — the hearts of all appeared in unison with the hilarity of the scene; even the lovely and haughty Victoria smiled with an unchecked vivacity; for no fair Venetian had presumed to vie with her, either in beauty of person, or splendour of decoration. Another circumstance contributed to elevate her spirits, and render her triumph complete. Leonardo,[1] her brother, ever haughty and turbulent in his manners, had acknowledged that she outshone every female present.

At this time the Marchese di Loredani had been married seventeen years to Laurina di Cornari, a female of unexampled beauty, and of rare and singular endowments. If she possessed a foible, it arose from vanity, from too great a thirst of admiration, and confidence in herself. At the period of her marriage with the Marchese she was scarcely fifteen, and he himself not more than twenty — it was a marriage contracted without the concurrence, without even the knowledge of respective friends, resolved on in the delirium of passion, concluded in the madness of youth! Yet, unlike the too frequent result, disgust and repentance did not follow this impetuous union; for chance and circumstances happily combined to render it propitious. Time had not yet perfected the character of Laurina: she saw beside her an husband whose ardent love appeared to suffer no diminution; no temptations crossed her path — it required, then, no effort to be virtuous; and as, in revolving years, reason approved the choice of a passion at the time undiscriminating, she gradually adored as an husband him she had thoughtlessly selected as a lover.

Two children, within two years after their marriage, had been its only fruits: from this circumstance, lavish and imprudent was the fondness

---

1 Leonardo: Leonardo Loredani was the Doge of Venice from 1501–1521, and the subject of a famous painting by Giovanni Bellini.

bestowed by the parents upon their idolized offspring — boundless and weak was the indulgence for ever shewn to them. The youthful parents little comprehended the extent of the mischief they were doing: to see their wayward children happy, their infantine and lovely faces undisfigured by tears or vexation, was a pleasure too great to be resigned, from the distant reflection of future evil possible to accrue from the indulgence. The consequence was, that Victoria, though at the age of fifteen, beautiful and accomplished as an angel, was proud, haughty, and self-sufficient — of a wild, ardent, and irrepressible spirit, indifferent to reproof, careless of censure — of an implacable, revengeful, and cruel nature, and bent upon gaining the ascendancy in whatever she engaged.

The young Leonardo, who was a year older than his sister, having been as much the victim of an injurious fondness as herself, possessed, with all the bolder shades of her character, a warm impassioned soul, yielding easily to the seductions of the wild and beautiful, accessible of temptation, and unable to resist, in any shape, the first impulses of his heart. This disposition, though it perhaps might never lead him into vice, would prevent him from repelling its inroads with the iron shield of energy: he was violent and revengeful, yet capable of sacrificing himself to a sentiment of gratitude; he had a quick impatient sense of honour — feelings noble, though impetuous, and a pride (encouraged infinitely by the Marchese) of birth and family dignity, which, sooner than by an act of meanness have disgraced, he would have perished. Thus it could not be denied, that in his ill-regulated character were some bright tints.

Such were the children whom early education had tended equally to corrupt; and such were the children, whom to preserve from future depravity, required the most vigilant care, aided by such brilliant examples of virtue and decorum as should induce the desire of emulation. Thus would have been counteracted the evils engendered by the want of steady attention to the propensities of childhood.

Yet, with all these causes for reflection and deep regret — causes which did not strike the broad beam of conviction upon the eyes of the infatuated parents; yet they were happy; the whole city of Venice contained no pair so happy. Laurina di Loredani, still in the meridian of beauty, and still adored by an husband, though not with the fantastic delirium of a boy, yet with an enthusiastic and approved affection; the most beneficent, the noblest, and the best of human beings, was the Marchese, admired by all, yet living alone for her whom his boyish heart had worshipped: his unsuspicious and generous nature gloried in the attractions of his wife — to see her followed and admired yielded to *his* heart a pleasure exquisite and refined — to *hers* a sentiment less noble, because it centered in self-gratification, and considerations of self ever debase the heart.

At this juncture it may not be amiss for a few moments to digress, in stating, that at the period which commences this history, the Venetians were a proud, strict, and fastidious people — in no country was the pride of nobility carried to a greater extent; their manners, also, received a deep and gloomy tincture from the nature of their government, which in its character was jealous and suspicious, dooming sometimes to a public, sometimes to a private death, on mere surmise or apprehension of design against the state, and always by secret trial, its most distinguished members. This power was exercised by Il Consiglio di Dieci, or council of ten,[1] by ordering nobles to be hung by the feet between the pillars of St. Marc, or else dispatching them more privately, that the order might not suffer in the opinion of the people, by plunging their bodies in the Orfano, or otherwise. The Venetians were fond of their mistresses, and jealous of their wives to a degree, uniting the Spanish and Italian character in its most sublimated state of passion. To avenge an injury sustained, or supposed to be so, to atchieve a favourite point, or gratify a desire otherwise unobtainable, poison or the dagger were constantly resorted to. Sanguinary and violent by nature, climate, habit, and education, the hatred of the Venetians once excited became implacable, and endured through life.

Having thus briefly reverted to the character of a nation where the principal scenes of the following history are laid, we proceed with matter more immediately connected with it.

It was in the midst of the gay revelling in the Palazzo di Loredani that a stranger arriving at the gates, requested admittance to the Marchese. On being told that one acquainted with his name desired to see him, the Marchese ordered immediately that the person should be admitted; when, the doors of the saloon being thrown open, a graceful figure entered, respectfully bowing, and presented to Loredani a letter from the Baron Wurmsburg, a German nobleman, and most intimate friend of his; wherein he requested of the Marchese, that he would exercise his hospitality in favour of Count Ardolph, the bearer, a German likewise, of high rank, fortune, and unblemished character. No sooner had the Marchese di Loredani perused the letter, than, with conciliating politeness, he extended his hand to the count, and led him immediately to the upper end of the saloon, where Laurina, her daughter, and the rest of the company, had assembled, that the stranger, on his entrance, might not be disconcerted or pained by fancied observation. He introduced him first to the Marchesa, and then to the company in general. There was that in the air and striking appearance of the count, which created at once a sensation of awe and admiration; his figure was noble and commanding, and in his features shone a dignity and fascination, which, while it irresistibly attracted the regards of all, flattered and delighted, if his could be attracted in return; yet, once attracted, those powerful regards overpowered by their beauty

---

1 council of ten: The Council of Ten was first established as a temporary committee of public safety to punish the Tiepoline conspiracy of 1310, and was made permanent in 1335. The Council of Ten moved against all conspiracies secretly and rapidly.

and their brilliancy those on whom they turned. Such in his personal semblance was Count Ardolph; and, as such, drew speedily around him a bright circle, of which he became the focus: every one forgetting, in the ease and gracefulness of his manners, the recentness of his introduction, while his presence diffused around a spirit, a vivacity, and an interest, of which before the assembly had seemed unconscious.

Victoria, as the young divinity of the festival, was presented to him by her beautiful and scarce less blooming mother: the eyes of the count dwelt momentarily upon her charms; he complimented her with politeness, but not with warmth, and turned immediately to the Marchesa with an air so expressive of admiration, that an insignificant observer might have remarked the difference of his regards.

At a late hour the company separated, and Count Ardolph was conducted to a splendid apartment in the Pallazzo of the Marchese.

CHAPTER II

Before we proceed, some account must be given of Count Ardolph, as to the bent of his principles and character; as to his introduction amid the ill-fated family of Loredani, may be ascribed the origin of those misfortunes which subsequently overwhelmed them.

By birth he was German: being left early in life, from the death of an only surviving parent, to his own disposal, he quitted his native country, and visited France and England; in both places, instigated at once by inclinations naturally vicious, and the contamination of bad example, he plunged into such a stream of depravity as rendered him in a few years callous to every sentiment of honour and delicacy; but the species of crime, the dreadful and diabolical triumph which gratified his worthless heart, was to destroy, not the fair fame of an innocent, unsullied female — not to deceive and abandon a trusting, yielding maid — no, he loved to take higher and more destructive aim — *his* was the savage delight to intercept the happiness of wedded love — to wean from an adoring husband the regards of a pure and faithful wife — to blast with his baleful breath the happiness of a young and rising family — to seduce the best, the noblest affections of the heart, and to glory and to exult in the wide-spreading havoc he had caused. Endowed with a form cast in nature's finest mould, blest, or rather cursed, with abilities to astonish and enslave, possessed of every grace and every charm that could render a man the most dangerous, or the most perfect of his sex, he employed these rare and fascinating qualities, as a demon would put on the semblance of an angel, to mislead and to betray. Yet, even of perpetual conquest the heart of man will grow weary. Ardolph, as the fury of passion or excitement of vanity became gratified and assuaged, sunk into inanity; and, despising all he had acquired, disdaining those females whose blandishments, while they had momentarily enchanted his senses, had been incapable of touching his heart, he quitted Paris, the hot-bed of his vices and profligacy, in disgust, and hoped by change of scene to give a zest to those feelings which excessive and unlimited gratification had blunted and almost destroyed. Yet, in change of scene, he had as yet failed of finding what he sought with an anxious and impatient curiosity — a woman who should be capable of inspiring his *heart* with continued sensation; for the proud Ardolph denied, in his mind, the possibility of the existence of such a woman. He analysed and investigated, with too contemptuous and prejudiced an eye, not to find in the sex an infinity of folly, weakness, and inconsistency. Thus it was, that having triumphed over them, he disdained his conquest, and disdained himself to have been attracted by them.

Such was the sceptical, the cruel, the dangerous Ardolph, at the period of his arrival in Venice; for which place the Baron Wurmsburg, a friend and distant relative of his family, seeing him only such as he appeared to be (for Ardolph had deigned to revisit for a short period his native land), gave him to the Marchese di Loredani an introductory letter: little suspecting the depravity of his heart, he recommended him in strong terms to the kindness and hospitality of that nobleman, building that recommendation upon the strength of an honourable friendship formerly subsisting between them.

To Venice, Ardolph had only come in search of novelty and amusement, to find, if possible, fresh scope for the gratification of his seductive and destroying talents; little expecting, however, that he should meet with aught to attract or to retain him there. — We now hasten to the more circumstantial part of our history.

He had not been long an envious and ungrateful guest in the house of Loredani, ere he beheld with evil eye the happiness which reigned among them; his soul burned to disfigure the beautiful fabric of a family's happiness, and to scatter around him misery and devastation. But, to achieve this, on whom did the malignant fiend fix his regards? Not on the young, the ardent, and self-confident Victoria, but on her lovely and attractive mother! — on the wife of his hospitable unsuspecting host! — of the man who daily and hourly showered down civilities and attentions on him. It was *his* honour and *his* happiness that he sought to blight — it was *his* offspring whom he sought to destroy and to disgrace — it was *his* Wife whom he sought to seduce! Such was the gratitude of man to man! and such still it continues to be!

But it so happened, that, susceptible as was Laurina to admiration, and more particularly so from a man of the high accomplishments and endowments of Count Ardolph, she still loved her husband with an undiminished love, and considered him as the god of his sex. The attention and the admiration she excited, were certainly a source of gratification to her; but then she excused herself with the belief, that it was as much on his account as on her own, and hence was a most powerful barrier opposed to the machinations of the wily Ardolph. But, unfortunately, opposition and difficulty were what he had long and ardently sought; it strung his dangerous energies anew; and while he gazed on the glowing charms of the devoted wife, and beheld with darkened eye their faithful vassalage to her husband, he vowed, even in the centre of his guilty heart, that he would conquer, or perish in the attempt.

He had now been nearly three months under the roof of the Marchese, when a profound melancholy (partly occasioned by a view of happiness he had not yet destroyed, and partly by the gradual increase of sensations to which he had till now been a stranger) appeared to take entire possession of him. Whether it was the beautiful and unobtrusive virtues of Laurina, or whether it was that her high and protected situation, by enhancing the danger and boldness of his attempt, added fuel to his passion, cannot be ascertained: certain it was, women, more *beautiful* than the Marchesa, had been tempted, obtained, and forsaken by him; it could not, therefore, all-

seducing as she was, be her person only that enslaved him; and for the beauties of *mind*, further than they added glory to the destruction he caused, he had little devotion. How then happened it, that on frequent occasions rushing from her presence, in a delirium of rage and passion, he discovered, and avowed to his proud heart, the ascendancy she had gained over its hitherto frigid insensibility. Sometimes, in imagination, he would reduce her in an instant to the level of those unfortunates he had betrayed and abandoned: but even so, she was *still* Laurina, and he felt that over *her* he could gain no triumph. Thus, in the maddening passion which hourly consumed him, did he experience some slight retribution for the misery he had so often caused to others.

Mean time Laurina, on remarking his increasing melancholy, had experienced sensations in her bosom which she wished not to investigate: she could not help perceiving (for so the insidious Ardolph had desired) that it was a melancholy not independent of herself. His stolen, yet purposely betrayed, ardent glances, directed towards her — his deep sighs, the tumultuousness of his frame, if by accident he touched her hand, or even any part of her dress — all, all failed not to be observed by the Marchesa, and to make its unfortunate impression; yet, had she never, even in thought, strayed from her husband — for so gradual, so unsuspected, are the first approaches of a guilty passion to the heart, that she would have started on being told she felt more for Ardolph than the interest of friendship.

It was one evening, that, straying pensively down an avenue in the garden, she suddenly encountered him; not, however, accidentally on his side, who was forming, unconsciously to herself, a portion of her thoughts: he appeared before her, pale, haggard, and with an expression of wretchedness on his countenance deeper than any he had yet worn. Involuntarily she stopped; and, looking with kindness in his face, asked, in a soothing voice, if he were ill. An enquiry into the cause of his complaint was all he had anxiously desired, but had not yet ventured to expect: thrown for once, however, off his guard, no longer master of his violent emotions, he threw himself at her feet, and acknowledged, in hurried accents, the passion with which she had filled up his heart. Confounded, bewildered, and overcome, the trembling Laurina knew not how to fly; yet to remain an instant after an avowal so base, would, she felt, be infamous, and participating in its guilt. She made an agitated attempt to disengage herself from the Count, who on his knees grasped wildly between his hands one of her's. But in admitting to her *thoughts, even for an instant, any other man than her husband* — in listening for an instant to an acknowledgment of the passion with which she had inspired him, the unhappy Laurina had advanced *one step* in the path of vice, and to recede required an energy and resolution almost incompatible with the weakness of which she had been already guilty! — At length, inspired with sudden resolution, touched, as it were, by a keen sense of the impropriety of her situation, she snatched her hand from the deluding Ardolph, and, flying from his presence, sought, in the solitude of her chamber, vent to her emotions.

There, sunk in shame, and absorbed in retrospection, she dared not analyse the feelings excited in her bosom: a thousand times did she wish that Count Ardolph had never entered the Pallazzo Loredani; but the reigning, the only foible of her nature, whispered to her the brilliant triumph of captivating such an heart as his, whose every smile, whose every look, seemed a condescension from the superiority of his nature.

Oh! self-love! — dangerous and resistless flatterer! — thou immolatest at thy shrine more victims than all the artifices of man!

Earnestly did Laurina desire to be virtuous, earnestly did she pray for fortitude to preserve her from the power of temptation; but she had not strength to fly from it, and in that alone her safety would have consisted. Her mind became torn with conflicting sentiments; her reason, her gratitude, the secret and powerful ties of early habit, taught her to adore her husband; but the insidious Ardolph daily led her senses wandering, and corrupted the purity of her heart. In his company she became thoughtful and embarrassed; in his absence, restless and unhappy. The cruel Ardolph perceived his advantage, and pursued it: like a keen blood-hound he hunted the wretched victim of his pursuit, even to the brink of destruction — no friendly hand extended to save her, no guardian angel hovered nigh; and, ere she knew the extent of her danger, she was far beyond the reach of preservation.

CHAPTER III

That it is but too often an ungenerous principle in human nature, first most ardently to desire the possession of a certain object, and despise it when obtained, cannot be disowned. In the present instance, however, there was an exception to this principle. A real passion had absorbed, for the first time, the heart of the seducer Ardolph. To have estranged from an husband the honour of his wife, to have gained over her sacred virtue a dreadful ascendancy, did not satisfy him; he resolved to possess her wholly — to blast the doting husband with conviction of his dishonour — to plunge his offspring in eternal ruin and disgrace, and to despoil them of the protection and tender services of a mother.

For the atchievement of this purpose, he found it necessary to degrade completely in her own eyes the miserable and deluded Laurina; then, profiting by her agony and despair, he represented to her, that it was in fact adding to her guilt, in a most flagrant and abominable degree, to remain under the roof of him she conceived herself to have so deeply injured — was it not adding treachery to dishonour? and was it not, in reality, the crime of deceiving, under such circumstances, far beyond that of acknowledging her guilt by an immediate and honourable flight: — "If the treasure is gone," pursued the sophisticated Ardolph, "the casket can but little avail; and could you then, Laurina, live a life of deception, deluding your husband in the idea of fondly possessing a treasure that is no longer his?"

"Oh! — no, no!" cried the wretched wife, "leave me, oh, cruel Ardolph! — fly for ever from me! — Here will I remain, and die; and may the tortures I now endure expiate, in the sight of a merciful God, the most infamous of crimes!"

But Ardolph, the eloquent *friend*, whose seductive blandishments had so *far* destroyed the delicate fabric of connubial happiness, was not to be diverted from the most material part of his task; for slight is the perseverance required to atchieve that which is already more than half accomplished. He vowed, and he even believed at the moment that his vow was sincere, that, while life endured, he would adore her who, for his sake, had forfeited so much.

"My children! — oh, my children!" deeply sighed the frantic Laurina.

"May those children," exclaimed Ardolph, calling upon outraged heaven to attest the prayer, "may those children *witness* — nay, *perpetrate* my destruction, should ever my heart become cold towards thee!"

Let us forbear to dwell on this scene of weakness on the one hand, and depravity on the other. Complete as he could wish was the triumph of the seducer; he bore his victim from the scenes of her past honour and her happiness! — he bore her from her home! — from the arms of her husband! — from the embraces of her children! — and far from Venice, the place of her nativity!

To paint the horror of Loredani when he discovered the perfidy of those whom his noble heart had cherished and relied on — the wife he had fondly adored, the guest he had received and trusted — would, if expression could do justice to it, be superfluous: he beheld himself, at once, the wretched, the desolate, and the *only* guardian of his forsaken children, forsaken by *her* who had given them birth! — From the wildness of despair he emerged and strung himself to virtuous resolution, determined, while his heart would hold from breaking, to live for his children, and to supply to them, as far as the love and protection of a father could, the fallen but once virtuous mother they had lost. Thus did the Marchese court to his aid those divine energies of which good minds are ever susceptible. But another trial awaited him still: scarcely had he acquired fortitude to leave the gloomy solitude of his chamber, ere fresh wounds were inflicted upon his lacerated heart, by the horrid tidings that Leonardo his son, the pride and heir of his house, had, soon as the flight of his mother became known, rushed from his home, and never since returned! — Well did the proud, though agonised father, trace in this action of his boy, his noble, tenacious, and impetuous spirit — well did he trace, exult, and participate in the glorious feelings, whose ebullition could not be restrained; and while he deplored the rashness of such conduct, he adored the sentiment that had impelled it. Yet fondly he hoped, that the young enthusiast, when the indignant fervor of the moment should have subsided, would return to be pressed in the arms of his widowed parent, and to mingle his tears with his. He entertained the idea, that, under the first painful impression of shame and grief, he had perhaps secreted himself at the house of a friend; but when every friend had been questioned, and day after day had elapsed, and still he came not, the expectant, heart-sick, and disappointed father, with bitter reluctance, resigned all hope; and, pressing his solitary daughter in his arms, saw concentered in her all that must attach him to existence, and preserve him from despair.

Victoria, thus the idol, the hope, and only solace of the heart-broken Marchese, was become the deity to which the house looked up: her word was law throughout; and to dispute the smallest of her wishes, would have been deemed amounting to sacrilege. Ever of a bold and towering spirit, haughty, fond of sway, it was with difficulty that her partial mother could occasionally administer a slight reproof; but now, with an unlimited scope for the growth of these dangerous propensities, they bade fair soon to overtop the power of restriction. Vainly did the Marchese hope that time, by maturing her reason, and improving her ideas, would correct the wrong bias of her character; for strict education alone can correct the faults in our nature; they will not correct themselves. If improper tendencies are engendered by early neglect, education may still work a reform; for we are in a great measure the creatures of education, rather than of organisation: the former can almost always surmount the defects of the latter. Thus, though Victoria in childhood gave proofs of what is termed, somewhat injudiciously, a corrupt nature, yet a firm and decided course of education would so far have changed her bent, that those propensities, which by neglect became vices, might have ameliorated into virtues. For example, haughtiness might have been softened into noble pride, cruelty into courage, implacability into firmness; but by being suffered to grow entirely wild, they overrun the fair garden of the mind, and prevented proper principles from taking root. What then must be thought of the unfortunate and guilty mother, who, making light of the sacred charge devolving on her, the welfare of her children, as depending on the just formation of their minds, not only neglects that sacred charge, but seals the fiat of their future destruction, by setting them in her own conduct an example of moral depravity — depriving them of the world's respect, and rendering them thereby indifferent to their own?

With saddened eye the Marchese traced occasionally the progress of his daughter's character; but he endeavoured to disguise from himself the suspicion that her heart was evil. To add to his unhappiness, the society of Victoria was generally shunned, not in reality on account of the disgrace brought upon her by her mother's conduct, but on account of her own violent and overbearing disposition, which rendered her obnoxious to the young nobility of Venice. The haughty girl, however, attributed the neglect she experienced to the former cause; and as such, conceiving herself deprived of the world's consideration, became daily more indifferent regarding it. Thus do vicious minds lay hold of every excuse for the pursuance of evil.

One evening, about a year having elapsed since the departure of Laurina, as she sat in sullen silence by her sorrowing parent, he turned affectionately towards her, and said —

"Wherefore, Victoria, dost thou debar thyself of the amusements befitting thine age and situation, to sit in chearless solitude with me? Why dost thou not invite to thee thy friends and acquaintances, and visit them in return?"

Victoria haughtily returned — "Because they would neither come to me, nor suffer me to go to them."

"And why so?" eagerly enquired the Marchese.

"Because my *mother* has disgraced us," gloomily replied the unfeeling Victoria.

Never had the name of his unfortunate wife been uttered by the Marchese since her ignominious flight — never had he reverted to, or even breathed a reproach upon the baseness of her conduct. The cruel Victoria had roughly touched a string that reverberated to agony! — the wretched father struck his forehead; and, springing from his seat, cast a look of anguish on his daughter, and rushed from the apartment.

But the recollections she had awakened, the feelings of bitterness she had renewed, rent his bosom with renovated torture. Never, never had the memory of the misguided Laurina's ingratitude left his torn mind: in secret he had brooded over his misery; in secret, where no eye could reproach him for his weakness, he had deplored and fondly loved; but never, in the presence of a human being, had he appeared to remember that he had once possessed a wife. Pride preserved him from public regret; but his lacerated heart paid for it when alone.

Unable to bear longer in solitude the keenness of those sensations excited by his daughter, he left, as the cool breezes of night came on, his secluded chamber; he sought by motion to disturb the chain of thought that formed heavy in his mind, and to fly, if possible, from himself. He had wandered about some time, when, in an unfrequented part of the city, he beheld a man walking swiftly before him: he was enveloped in a cloak; but the outlines of his figure were such as to send through the frame of the Marchese sensations of tingling horror, followed by a rage so frantic as almost to deprive him of sense. He thought that in the stranger he beheld Ardolph, the machinating villain who had blasted his every hope and happiness.

Unknowing what he did, unaware of the violence and rapidity of his own emotions, he darted after the person, and tearing aside his cloak, discovered indeed the wretch he had imagined!

"Draw, monster, devil, and incendiary!" exclaimed the frantic husband, at the same time snatching his stilletto from his bosom.

"I have no sword," cooly returned the count; "but I have, like yourself, a stilletto, that shall be at your service."

The Marchese heard no more: he struck and struck again with desperate fury at the body of his antagonist; but his aim was rendered unsure by his thirst for vengance, by the raging and uncontrouled passions of his soul. The count, calm, and self-collected, parried with hellish dexterity his indiscriminate attempts; but receiving, at length, the point of his adversary's stilletto in his shoulder, he suffered an impulse of rage to nerve his hand; and, retreating for an instant, then furiously advanced, and plunged his dagger to the hilt in the breast of the unfortunate Loredani.

Thus did he become the *murderer* of the *husband*, as he had been already the *seducer* of his *wife*; and his guilt, at the bar of Heaven, assumed a dye seven times deeper than before.

The instant that the Marchese fell, Ardolph hurried from the spot, first taking care to conceal his stilletto, and to wrap his cloak closely around him. To seek assistance for the being he had inhumanly sacrificed, entered not his ignoble mind. There, then, weltering in his blood, might the Marchese have remained, but for the arrival of some passengers, who, soon ascertaining his rank and residence, conveyed him to the Pallazzo Loredani. Thither a surgeon being immediately summoned, dressed his wound; and to the feeble yet earnest enquiries of the Marchese, felt compelled to pronounce it mortal.

"Tell me the utmost," in a firm though low voice, said he, "that it is possible for me to exist?"

"Not longer than to morrow, I fear," the surgeon slowly replied.

" 'Tis enough," said the Marchese; "let my daughter be sent to me."

"My lord, you must not talk," observed the professional attendant.

Loredani looked upon him with an anguished smile. "If I have so few hours to *live*," he said, "what have I to guard against? — Let me see my daughter."

"My lord, your death will be hastened."

The Marchese feebly waved his hand — Victoria was called: she entered the room with slow and trembling steps — she gazed upon the death-marked features of her father with horror and regret — horror at the situation in which she saw him, and regret at the thought of having given him, a few hours before, a pang so deep. Of this emotion was Victoria susceptible; therefore, at this moment, her heart was not *utterly* depraved.

She approached the bed-side of her father — her naturally stubborn heart now deeply and profoundly affected. The dying Marchese stretched forth his parched and trembling hand: she took it; and, pressing it to her bosom, sunk upon her knees beside him.

"Oh, my child! — my Victoria!" he faintly began — "I am snatched from thee at a time and season when least thou canst afford to lose me; — yet, ere I die, let me — oh, my love! — perform my duty to Heaven and to thee. Let me implore thee to suffer my dying counsels to sink deep into thy heart. — My Victoria, correct, if thou canst, the errors of thy disposition — think upon what we are — think on life, how unsure, how unstable is its possession! — think that, in the midst of buoyant health, elate in youthful pride, surrounded by riches, and every gratification they can procure, that still, even for a moment, we cannot ensure it; some dreadful unforeseen event, some accident arises, and cuts us off; let not, therefore, the riches thou wilt in all probability be mistress of, render thee proud or self-confident; let them not cause thee to forget we are but the creatures of a day, existing we know not how, and reserved for — we know not what! — let not the independence of thy fortune render thee unfeeling or inaccessible; nor think that the accidental circumstances of birth and riches render it unnecessary for thee to abide by the strictest rules of virtue. Remember, that in proportion to the elevation of thy rank, thy inferiors will look up to *thee*; and, therefore, it becomes a moral obligation on thee, to keep a guard over thy conduct, so that no possible evil may be derived from thy example; for thou wilt be hereafter responsible for whatever vices are imitated from thee, and for whatever contamination thou

---

* Cicero [Dacre's note]. Perhaps a combination of two Cicero quotations: "Glory follows virtue as if it were its shadow" (Gloria virtutem tanquam umbra sequitur, *Tusculanarum Disputationum* Bk.1, ch.45, sec.110), and "That which stands first, and is most to be desired by all happy, honest, and healthy-minded men, is ease with dignity" (Id quod est praestantissimum, max imeque optabile omnibus sanis et bonis et beatis, cum dignitate otium, *Pro Sestio* XLV., 98).

mayest cause in the society of thou art a member. Be not deluded with the ignoble idea, that it is less incumbent on *thee* to be virtuous than those below thee; for, in proportion as thou hast power and scope for the commission of evil, and the gratification of self, so in proportion is thy merit in forbearance, and a steady rectitude of conduct. 'How glorious is it to live with dignity and decorum!*' to reign in the fiery wildness of the passions, to place happiness in the highest perfection of which our nature is capable, and to remember that we live to become worthy of a higher state than that which we at present move in!"

Overcome with pain and weakness, the Marchese suddenly ceased; nor had his counsel been delivered but in a faltering voice, broken every now and then from excess of anguish. The exertion which, from a principle of duty, he forced himself to make, struck forcibly to the heart of Victoria. The time was past midnight — a pale lamp emitted its faint rays over the spacious chamber, and shewed the pallid features of her father — of that father whose love for her, even in death, taught him to despise his own agony. The pause he had made was solemn and affecting. The scene impressed her imagination, and his words her mind; while the silence, the gloomy silence, that reigned around, was only interrupted by her sobs.

The wan hand of the Marchese hung over the bed — Victoria held it to her heart: his dim eyes were fixed upon her with an expression of love and bitter regret — "Oh my Victoria! thou wilt be unprotected," he faintly said, and a deep sigh rose from his heavy heart, as dreadful recollections passed through his brain. Suddenly a noise was heard, the door of the apartment flew open, and in rushed — no, it was no delusion — the figure of Laurina!

"Heaven! do I behold aright!" feebly cried Loredani, endeavouring to raise himself in his bed — "or is death so near, that already dim shadows, the semblance of former friends, hover before my eyes?"

"Oh, my God! — oh, Loredani, my injured husband! — bless me, I implore — oh, you cannot! — yet forgive — oh, forgive me, ere you die! — Curse me not with your last breath!"

So saying, the frantic Laurina threw herself prostrate on the ground by the side of the bed where lay her dying husband, cut off, by her guilt and misconduct, in the flower of his life.

Loredani succeeded for an instant in raising his head upon his hand: a heavenly and celestial expression irradiated his features; he gazed upon the prostrate wretch beside him with the look of a pitying angel; then, motioning to Victoria, he said — "Retire, my child, for a moment." When she was withdrawn —

"Laurina!" said he, in a low solemn voice, "arise."

She raised herself upon her knees, but covered her face with her hands.

"Laurina!" said he again, in the voice of a man who, conscious he has not long to live, desires to say nothing idly — "Laurina, look upon me."

There was that in his manner which impelled obedience, and the eyes of his guilty wife met his.

"Laurina! — it is yet in thy power to repair, in some measure, the evil thou hast done. — When I am laid in the grave, seek out, if possible, thy son — that son who fled his home, on his discovery of thy perfidy — seek him; and, if it should please Heaven that thou shouldst prove successful, retire with him, and thy daughter Victoria, far from Venice; for Venice, methinks, is no longer a place for thee. Endeavour to expiate, by a life of penitence, the great crimes thou hast been guilty of; for, dreadfully as thou hast marred the happiness and the honour of thy children, perhaps it is not destroyed. Retire, then, to where thou art unknown; and hereafter in the world they may claim consideration and respect — But, oh, Laurina! tremble, if thou returnest to guilt and infamy! — eternal destruction *then* betides both thee and them! — There is no redemption! — Never will the impression of this night fade from the mind of Victoria, if thou wilt *yet* have courage and resolution to abandon thy guilty career, and to instil into her mind, by thy *future example*, principles of virtue and honour. — Laurina, unfortunate and once-loved wife! thou wilt make thyself answerable, by thy conduct, not only for the life and future actions of thy daughter, but for the *fiat* which will go forth respecting her, when she renders up her great account! — Ponder, then, well upon the mighty charge, that, by appearing before me at this awful moment, thou bringest upon thyself — yes, on *thy example* — Oh! thou who couldst desert thine innocent and lovely offspring — on *thy example* will the life and conduct of thy daughter *now* be formed!"

"Oh, spare me! — spare me!" cried the wretched Laurina, in accents of despair. "I swear — "

"Let my Victoria enter," said the Marchese, gasping for breath: "I have — I have not a moment to live!"

Laurina rose, and bade Victoria enter. As she approached — "Quick, my child!" cried Loredani, "and embrace thy mother. — Laurina! — *now* swear to protect and cherish thy daughter, to preserve her from evil, and from the *contamination of bad example*!"

"I swear, I swear!" articulated Laurina, in a voice drowned by sobs, and pressed convulsively her daughter to her bosom.

"Victoria — *swear*!" murmured the Marchese, "that thou wilt forget the errors, and imitate the *future virtues* and *example* of thy mother!"

"*I swear*, father!" in a solemn voice, answered Victoria.

"Oh, God! — I thank — thee — thank thee!" gasped the dying Loredani. — "Kiss me, my — Victo — ria — my — Thy hand, Laurina — I *forgive* — *thee* — Oh, God! — my God! — I die content!"

Thus perished, in the flower of his days, the noble Loredani, the victim of a FRIEND's ingratitude, and of a WIFE's depravity!

CHAPTER IV

After the fatal rencontre of the ill-starred Marchese with Ardolph, the latter hurried, as has been already observed, from the spot. Having had sufficient time to escape from the scene of action, and being of course completely unsuspected, he reached, by bye and circuitous ways, his own
house, which, having had occasion to return to Venice, he had hired for a
short time only, at some distance from the populous city, under a feigned
name; hoping, for the little while he had to remain, completely to elude
discovery from the injured Loredani. — To return, however. When he
entered the room where the apostate wife Laurina was sitting, she was
struck with an appearance of sternness in his countenance, and an unusual seriousness of manner.

Approaching him, and tenderly taking his hand — for deep was the
sway the traitor had acquired over her he had betrayed — she asked if
aught had occurred to which she might attribute his altered looks.

Pressing the hand which held his, and looking steadily in her face, he
said — "Laurina, I have this night committed that which my heart condemns, but which the necessity of the case enforced. Say only, before I
tell thee all, that thou wilt not hate me for what involuntarily I have
done."

"Hate thee!" passionately exclaimed the deluded wife — "I could not
hate thee, Ardolph, if thou hadst committed murder!"

"Murder!" gloomily returned Ardolph — "I hope not, Laurina; but I
have wounded, I fear mortally, thy — husband!"

A piercing shriek was the only answer of the horror-struck Laurina: her
avenging crimes flew in her face — they flashed like lightning through
her brain. She rushed from the presence of Ardolph, and flew, as the
resistless impulse of her frantic remorse dictated, to the well-known mansion of her martyred husband. Ardolph, who merely imagined that she
had flown from him, impelled by the overflowing anguish of the moment,
suspected not, till some hours had elapsed, whither she had gone. When
at length, however, he surmised and ascertained the truth, his rage and
apprehensions knew no bounds; for the passion with which the wretched
Laurina had first inspired him, that fatal passion, which in its *consequences*
and progress was the cause of such immediate and such wide-spreading
evils, had not as yet subsided: opposition, too, or difficulty, could only
tend, in the breast of such a character as Ardolph, to give it strength and
violence. Sooner, at this period, would he have endured death than her
loss; and he determined, therefore, whatever the chance of being suspected, whatever the risk of being discovered, to respect no sanctuary
which could detain her from him, nor permit her even to exist independently of himself.

For this purpose he completely disguised his person; and wandering near the Pallazzo Loredani, now the mausoleum only of its once happy master, resolved that from that spot he would never depart, but with her whom he knew to be enclosed within its walls.

It was on the eve of the second day after the death of Loredani — and Laurina, in the bitterness of remorseful anguish, was weeping the consequences of her unhappy conduct — that a letter was put into her hands. Upon opening it, she found it to run as follows —

"Your present residence is no place for you, having forfeited, by a preference most gratefully recognised, all title to act as the wife of the deceased Loredani. I would recommend it to you, to depart from the place where you now are, with all possible expedition. The haughty relatives of the Marchese will soon fill the house: you will be considered as the boldest and most infamous of women, and treated with all the ignominy that revenge and illiberality can dictate.

"ARDOLPH."

Laurina, whose mind was still acutely smarting under the wounds inflicted by the last words of her husband, and whose heart was deeply and sensibly impressed with a conviction of her unworthiness, wrote, without hesitation, the following answer —

"Ardolph, dare my guilty heart admit the horrible acknowledgment that I love you still? — you whom my bewildered reason shews me at once a *seducer* and a *murderer*! — Oh, wretch! that can cherish such sentiments! — for what am I reserved? — But mark my determination — it is to see you *no more*! — With Victoria, the innocent sufferer for her mother's crimes, it is my intention to quit immediately the roof under which I am: I shall retire for a time into a remote province — then, when the remembrance of my infamy has ceased, I shall again endeavour to mix with society — not for my own sake, but for the sake of that daughter I have so cruelly wronged; ask not, therefore, to see me, for the request will be vain. — I dare not load with such a weight of guilt my blackened soul!
"For ever farewel."

Having dispatched these few lines by the messenger, who still waited, the wretched, half-repentant Laurina expected, with an agitation and horror of mind she vainly attempted to quell, some further notice from the unworthy Ardolph. Scarcely dared she acknowledge to herself the base, the lurking hope, that he would not so easily resign her. With trembling frame, then, and mind of anarchy, did she compel herself to prepare for speedy necessary departure from the roof of her husband, where she felt, with impunity she must not long remain.

An hour, however, had not elapsed since the departure of her letter, before the same messenger returned with an answer — an answer which, to the eternal shame of Laurina be it said, conveyed to her breast a sensation of smothered unacknowledged delight, equal, at least, to the irrepressible feelings of shame with which it was accompanied. It ran thus —

"You would retire from Venice with your daughter — Mark me, Laurina — with me there is no trifling — leave at midnight your present abode, and bring with you Victoria. On the canal, opposite your window, I shall await you. — You must go with me to Monte Bello, the villa which I hired on my arrival here, as a retreat during my necessary stay: the situation is retired and distant from the city: there we may remain free from suspicion; for it is the opinion of everyone that the Marchese met his death by the hands of bravoes. I have only this to add — When there, if you *still continue to desire it*, I will myself accompany you to any seclusion you may point out, and leave you there for ever unmolested. — Let this however be fully understood between us — I swear, by every thing that is sacred and holy, whether you accede or not to my present proposition, you depart not unaccompanied by me from the city of Venice — through the world will I pursue you, Laurina, for ever cross your path, haunt you eternally, if for a moment you dare hesitate or think to escape,   "ARDOLPH"

From her variously agitated heart Laurina heaved a deep and tremulous sigh. Essaying to believe herself irrecoverably fixed in the resoluteness of virtue, and without daring farther to investigate the real workings of her mind, she wrote as follows —

"Confident, most cruel and invincible of mankind! — confident, that I shall live and die in the performance of my promise to — I dare not write the name, for my conscious beating heart unnerves my fingers. I accede to your proposition; and trust — since I must — to your *honour* for the performance of your promise."

Thus far being arranged, the weak and misguided Laurina again commenced her preparations — but, ah! with renewed alacrity; for, though undefined perhaps by herself, her sensations were those produced by a conviction of still being loved, and still being seen once more by him, whom, of all men, she should have shunned and abhorred. Such, such is the picture, too often, of a guilty human heart.

At midnight, Laurina, accompanied by Victoria, left the Pallazzo Loredani. The determined Ardolph was punctual to his appointment: he received them with a proud seriousness; and, conducting them to a gondola which he had in waiting, they speedily arrived at Monte Bello.

It is not necessary to enlarge upon this incidental part of our history: suffice it, that arrived at his villa, the seductive Ardolph called to his aid all those dangerous and seductive blandishments which already had been the cause of so much guilt and mischief; and successfully, too successfully he called them. The wretched Laurina yielded at first to the delay of a few hours under the roof of the unprincipled betrayer, and well he knew how to improve this short delay; for what man, having once corrupted the *heart* and *principles* of the woman he deludes, has ever found it difficult to maintain his victory, if he thought it worth his while? Most literally, indeed, did Ardolph keep his conditional promise, that Laurina should have free liberty to depart if still she continued to *wish* it. Unhappy wretch! she wished it *not*; for, blinded by the fascinations of her lover, she found it impossible to live but in his presence.

Gradually and imperceptibly their intercourse, now doubly criminal, became dearer and more strongly cemented than ever: yet was the wretched farce of journeying in various directions, and even to considerable distances, (under the pretext of discovering some suitable situation for the young Victoria and her deluded mother) steadily persevered in; for, did not Ardolph know, that change of scene was conducive to the plans he had in view, of restraining from compunctious reflection the mind of Laurina? and by so ordering, that in his society she should experience no moment of melancholy, make her view with horror the idea of abandoning him, and secure her entirely to himself.

The plans of Ardolph, ever well arranged, rarely failed of success. Infatuated by his seductions, Laurina sought, eagerly sought, to evade refection; and as a wretch writhing with pain flies to the relief of opium, so did Laurina, from the pangs of conscience, to the soothing and intoxicating presence of him who destroyed her; for she could ever endure the *secret* horrible conviction of her guilt — that she had rushed from the *death-bed* of her husband — from where his sainted spirit still lingered, to the very arms of his *murderer*! — that she had forfeited her *solemn vow*, which his soul had tarried to hear sworn? — Could she, even with all the aid of sophistry, attempt to seek in her own mind a palliation of this? — She had no resource, then, but in Ardolph; in his eyes she idolatrously beheld an excuse for her crimes, and in his fascinating voice was recorded a temptation she imagined no heart could have resisted.

Gradual and terrible are the approaches of vice! The only absolute original imperfection of Laurina was vanity and love of admiration. This error, trifling when in a dormant state, but dangerous when improperly called forth, of what a catalogue of dreadful evils did it not become the cause! — what awful mischiefs had not already ensued! Should not this lesson, then, be conveyed to the mind — that the propensity of our natures to evil should be vigilantly checked, and that the guard which should be constantly kept over the wanderings of the heart, should never be suffered to slumber on its post?

CHAPTER V

A year had now elapsed since the death of Loredani. The melancholy events which had characterized that period, had become fainter and fainter in the mind of Laurina: the journies of enquiry had long since ceased; and on the subject of her departure from the society of Ardolph the perjured wife no more expatiated.

They did not reside in the city of Venice, but still at Monte Bello, some few miles distant; for the circumstances, still unforgotten, with which their names were connected, would have caused them to be viewed with disdain and indignation by the higher classes of society: they remained, therefore, at their villa, and thither contrived to attract most of the dissolute and many of the thoughtless inhabitants of Venice; for the aggregate of the world will run even into the very dens of profligacy for amusement, as in a few individuals alone is it vested to be the censors of vice. Monte Bello resounded to the voice of mirth and folly; reflection appeared to be banished; and those events which should have been engraved in characters of blood upon the hearts of its inmates, appeared rapidly sinking into oblivion, or to be remembered only with indifference.

It happened, that among the gay Venetians who frequented their society, was one called Il Conte Berenza: he was a man of peculiar sentiments, and extraordinary character; he came not to Monte Bello in search of amusement, nor merely from indolence: he came from an investigating spirit, to analyse its inhabitants, and to discover, if possible, from the result of his own observation, whether the mischief they had caused, and the conduct they pursued, arose from a selfish depravity of heart, or was induced by the force of inevitable circumstances: he came to investigate character, and to increase his knowledge of the human heart.

He found, however, or fancied that he found, but little to interest the consideration of the liberal philosopher in the relative situations of Ardolph and Laurina: he concluded in his mind that they had voluntarily rushed into evil, and had possessed the power to have withdrawn themselves in time from the dangerous vortex — he therefore viewed them with contempt and dislike, unmixed with the slightest portion of pity — he beheld wretches who had studied alone their own gratification, wholly unmindful of the mischiefs they might cause in its atchievement. Under this impression, he regarded, with eyes of no common interest, the young Victoria: pride alone forbade his soliciting her hand; for never yet had Berenza beheld a female whose character he had imagined so formed to constitute his happiness: nay, so ardent in his admiration was the misguided philosopher — misguided in this instance — that, had no dishonour in his idea been attached to the unfortunate girl, he would have made her his wife upon speculation, and relied upon the power he believed himself to possess over the human mind for modelling her afterwards, so as perfectly to assimilate to his wishes. Her wild and imperious character he would have essayed to render noble, firm, and dignified; her *fierté*[1] he would have softened, and her boldness checked. Berenza knew not, so unconscious is the heart of man of the springs of its own movements, that it was the graceful elegant form, and animated countenance of Victoria, that led him to form of her strongly-marked character the best and most flattering estimate. She was at this period about seventeen: the age of Berenza was five and thirty; his person was majestic, and his countenance, though serious, possessed a sweetness of expression, that riveted and delighted the eye: it it was not this so much that engaged the attentions and allured the fancy of the young Victoria — no, it was the flattering remark that herself exclusively attracted his regards — regards, which the natural haughtiness, and apparent coldness of his character, rendered peculiarly gratifying to her vain mind. It was for this she sought his society, and courted his notice, till Berenza, wound almost to a pitch of enthusiasm, scarcely lived but in the hope of calling her his. Attachments his philosophic mind had none, excepting to a brother some years younger than himself, who was at this time absent from Italy, to divert the melancholy of an almost hopeless passion: his thoughts and wishes, therefore, centered in Victoria with undivided ardour.

It may naturally be supposed that the character of Victoria, by nature more prone to evil than to good, and requiring at once the strong curb of wisdom and example to regulate it, had not, since the death of her father, obtained much opportunity of improvement. She saw exemplified, in the conduct of her mother, the flagrant violation of a most sacred oath — she saw every principle of delicacy and of virtue apparently contemned — and, although the improper bias of her mind led her infinitely to prefer the gay though horrible state of degradation in which she lived, to the retirement and seclusion so strongly insisted on by the dying Marchese, yet had she reflection and discrimination enough, fully to perceive and condemn the flagitious disregard those dying commands had received. But Victoria was a girl of no common feelings — her ideas wildly wandered, and to every circumstance and situation she gave rather the vivid colouring of her own heated imagination, than that of truth.

Berenza had awakened in her breast feelings and passions which had till now remained dormant, mighty and strong, like the slumbering lion, even in their inactivity. Slight, indeed, was the spur which they required to rouse them. She had ever contemplated the seductive, and, in appearance, delightful union of her mother with Ardolph, with such sentiments as were at the time inexplicable to herself; but when Berenza singled her out, when he addressed her in the language of love, she then discovered that her sentiments were those of envy, and of an ardent consuming

---

[1]*fierté:*   Literally "pride" in French, with overtones of haughtiness and boldness.

desire to be situated *like* that unhappy mother — like her, to receive the attentions, listen to the tenderness, and sink beneath the ardent glances of a lover. Such, such were the baleful effects of parental vice upon the mind of a daughter — a mind that required the strongest power of precept and virtuous conduct to correct it.

"At length, then," with secret exultation, she exclaimed — "at length, I too have found a lover — I shall now be as happy as my mother, at least, if Berenza should love *me* as Count Ardolph loves *her*."

But it happened that the heart of Berenza had acquired a *real* passion, while that of Victoria was susceptible only of novel and seducing sensations — of anticipations of future pleasure. Berenza *loved* — Victoria was only roused and *flattered*. Upon consideration, but not certainly impartial consideration, the enamoured philosopher concluded that it would not be an act of baseness or guilt to withdraw Victoria from her present dangerous and ineligible situation — to acknowledge his passion to her, and induce her, if possible, to abandon the contaminated roof under which she resided. The pride of the Venetian, however, must have been stronger than his love, for it rejected the idea of making her his wife; while he determined to leave no means untried to cause her to become his mistress.

Pursuant to this idea he sought the earliest opportunity of obtaining a private interview with Victoria. An opportunity early presented itself; and having declared to his delighted auditress the ardent love with which she had inspired him, he delicately but frankly proposed to her the plan upon which he had for some time past suffered himself to dwell enraptured.

The boldly organised mind, the wild and unrestrained sentiments of Victoria, prevented her from being offended at the proposition of Berenza: had she for an instant conceived, that his strict ideas deemed her incapable of being legally his, she must, with all her desire for a lover, have spurned him indignantly from her; but pride here acted as the preservative of pride, and her vanity easily led her to believe that Berenza thought marriage a degrading and unnecessary tie to love like his.

Under this impression she gave him her hand: Berenza seized it with ardour, as the earnest of consent; and, seating himself at the feet of his mistress, who smiled with high and unusual joy, he entered more fully into his arrangements, and the means by which he proposed she should quit Monte Bello unsuspected. Victoria listened with lively emotions; pleasure flushed triumphant her animated cheek, and shone in her wild eyes with an almost painful brilliancy: her heart glowed with the love of enterprize; she felt capable of deeds which, though in their *conception* they dilated and seduced her soul, she could neither *comprehend* nor *identify*; but she felt inspired for action, and the enthusiasm which burnt in her bosom, lighted up every feature with lambent and etherial fire. Suddenly, in the very midst of her felicitations, while Berenza, still at her feet, was pouring in her intoxicated ears his various plans for their future happiness, in rushed, rage and horror depicted in her countenance, the half frantic Laurina!

"Wretch!" she exclaimed, seizing violently the arm of Victoria — "wretch! is it thus you recompence my indulgence towards you — the fond, the foolish confidence, which your mother has ever placed in you? — And *you*, Signore Berenza, monster of depravity! is it thus *you* recompence the hospitality of Count Ardolph, in seeking to seduce our only happiness, the innocent Victoria?"

"Signora," replied Berenza, with a distainful smile, "*you* are indeed well qualified to arraign those who *trample on the rights of hospitality!*"

The eyes of the conscience-struck Laurina sought for an instant the ground — her countenance became suffused with a guilty blush — her heart beat with violence, and scarcely could she support her trembling frame! Berenza, with dignified calmness, took the hand of Victoria — "I do not," he continued, in a firm deliberate voice, "I do not plead guilty to the charge of attempting to *seduce* your daughter. — I wish," he added, in a severe accent, "to *save* her from seduction. Pardon me, if I say, that under *this* roof, I conceive it inevitably awaits her."

"Victoria," cried Laurina, recovering from her agitation, but awed by the manner of Berenza from replying to *him* — "Victoria, I command you to leave the room — yes, for the first time in my life, I *command* you never more to hold converse with Il Conte Berenza!"

Berenza fixed his proud and enquiring eyes upon the countenance of Victoria. Whether she caught a spark of the fire which emanated from them, or thus for the first time asserted the bold and independent sentiments of her bosom, is immaterial; but, withdrawing proudly her hand from Berenza, as though she needed not his aid, and advancing a few steps towards her mother, she thus replied —

"That you never, Signora, *commanded* me till now, is true; that you command me now, when it is too late, is equally so. I *determine* to quit this roof, which is no protection to me, for that of Il Conte Berenza, which I trust will be."

"Oh, Victoria! — Victoria! — art thou *mad!*" exclaimed Laurina, clasping her hands, and now beginning to feel the terrible commencement of those retributive pangs so justly ordained as the punishment of those parents who corrupt their children — "Art thou mad, my child? or wouldst thou voluntarily plunge me in eternal disgrace?"

"Plunge *you* in disgrace!" contemptuously returned Victoria.

"Oh, my child! my child!" cried the distracted mother, sinking under the overpowering excess of remorseful anguish, "wouldst thou indeed *abandon* me?"

"*You* abandoned *me* — my *brother* — and my *father!*" sternly replied the torturing Victoria.

"Oh, daughter! — oh, Victoria!" groaned Laurina — "this from thee!"

"Mother — *eternally* hast *thou* disgraced us!" she replied. "For me, no one has ever thought me worthy of love but Il Conte Berenza. Let me, then, *accept* his love, and be happy. Why, I ask you, should considerations of *your* happiness sway me in opposition to my *own?* When *you* loved Count Ardolph, you know, mother, that you fled with him, regardless of the misery you gave my father. — Do you not remember too —"

"Cease, scorpion! — cease, for *God's* sake!" shrieked Laurina, in agony.

"Let me, then depart with Il Conte Berenza. Remember, it is your fault," pursued the pitiless girl, "that ever I saw him. Had *you* but kept the oath — the *oath*, mother, that — that you swore at the death-bed of my father —"

The images conjured up by the forked tongue of a reproaching child, were too much even for the guilty Laurina to endure; and, in a convulsion of irrepressible anguish, she sunk upon the floor.

Berenza, who had at first listened with delight and surprize to the independence of spirit, as he considered it, evinced by the undaunted Victoria, now became visibly shocked at her persevering and remorseless cruelty to a mother, whose personal tenderness for her had at least merited some little gratitude. Scarcely willing to analyse if his love for her had not already somewhat diminished by the display of a trait so offensive to a delicate and feeling mind as filial ingratitude and unkindness, he approached, and raised Laurina from the floor. When she became in a degree recovered, he assisted her, with respectful forbearance, to her chamber; and whispering to Victoria, in rather a serious voice, to be tender towards her mother, retired, and left them together.

But the slight shade of reserve which marked the countenance of Berenza, as he waved his hand to Victoria in parting, had not failed to make even more than its due impression on her: her vivid imagination easily led her to trace the occasion of his altered air. She saw that her cruel recriminations on her mother had excited his disgust: alarmed at the remotest idea of becoming indifferent to him, she instantly determined on regaining his esteem. Approaching her weeping mother, therefore, with a conciliating air, she endeavoured to soothe her into composure; but having awakened the remorse of the conscious Laurina, she no longer beheld in the artful Victoria a disposition to softness, than she resolved to take immediate advantage of it to withdraw her, if possible, from the vortex of guilt and libertinism into which she saw her plunging. A keener pang assailed the heart of the mother, as she acknowledged, in dreadful conviction, the fatal effects of her own example: to alleviate, therefore, the tortures of her mind, to save her loaded conscience from such an addition of guilt, she sought with energy to preserve her daughter. To every persuasion, however, even to every supplication to give up her distracting resolution without reserve, the wild impassioned Victoria was wholly deaf. The utmost that Laurina could obtain, was a reluctant promise to see Il Conte Berenza no more for that day. Even this would not have been granted, had not the deeply-meaning Victoria imagined, that, by debarring her lover from seeing her for a few hours, he would begin so far to feel the loss of her society, as wholly to forget, in his uneasiness, the cause he had had for displeasure against her.

Laurina, after some hours of more poignant wretchedness than she had almost ever experienced, separated at length, for the night, from her daughter. She flew instantly to Ardolph, and imparted to him this new and unexpected cause, to her, of unhappiness. So keen, indeed, were her compunctious feelings, that, with bitter tears, she vowed she would quit him on the morrow, and retire at once, with Victoria, to some seclusion, where, experience now convinced her she ought long since to have been.

Ardolph listened without interruption. When Laurina paused, he looked at her with tender seriousness, and said —

"That a union like ours, Laurina, cemented by ties and by circumstances, which, however they may be considered by the prejudiced and misjudging, nothing should have the power of annulling; that such an union should either be innovated or destroyed by the impudent caprice of a forward girl, admits not of a thought. Listen to what I have to propose, and let Victoria, as she ought, reap the fruits of her audacity. It would be easy for me to forbid Il Conte Berenza to remain here another hour — it would be easy to imprison Victoria in her chamber, and prevent them seeing each other; but we shall have recourse to no compulsory measures; on the contrary, to such only as shall be at once simple, cool, and effective. It is most probable that Il Conte Berenza has never had occasion to correspond with your daughter; he is, therefore, ignorant of her hand-writing. Do you then draw up a few lines, suppose to the following effect —

'Dear Berenza, owing to the unhappiness manifested by my mother, I have agreed to deny myself, for a little time, the pleasure of seeing you. I therefore entreat of you to return to Venice; and when the effect produced by present circumstances shall in some degree have worn off, I will gladly write to you to return.'

"Let these, or a few similar lines, be conveyed at once to Berenza, and you will find the effect produced will be an immediate and voluntary absence from hence. The instant he departs for Venice, Victoria shall quit this abode."

"Without me, do you mean, Ardolph?"

"We will both escort her *hence*, Laurina, and she shall be too securely lodged, ever more to interrupt our happiness; — and, now that an idea strikes me," he hastily added, perceiving that Laurina was on the point of speaking, and determined to drown her objections, "I have an admirable seclusion for her. In our excursions last year, Laurina, we made at one time a short stay, as you doubtless call to mind, with your cousin the Signora de Modena: she resides, I think, near Treviso. Nothing can be more retired, more fitted for Victoria, than her abode. The Signora de Modena was singularly polite and courteous towards *me*," smiling as he spoke. "Come, come, my Laurina, no objections: but on this matter we will talk further — mean time, should even Berenza, finding that he is not recalled by his mistress, venture hither we can receive him with marked coolness. When he no longer perceives the lode-star of his attraction, he will naturally conceive that we have purposely withdrawn her; and having certainly no *claim* to an explanation, he will speedily and in chagrin desert us."

"Thus," he added, in a gayer tone, "shall we be rid of every source of trouble and uneasiness; and thus, my beloved, you perceive, there is no immediate necessity for separating the soul from the body. To tear yourself from me, to whom you are more even than soul — no, we must not bend to circumstances, we must make them subservient to us. No human being, nor any consideration on earth," he added, in an emphatic voice, "must now, Laurina, separate thee and me. But, come," resuming the gaiety of his manner, "to business."

Laurina mechanically took up a pen, and, as Ardolph dictated, traced something similar to what has been already given. The letter finished, it was conveyed to Berenza by a female servant of Laurina's, who was ordered not to wait for any answer.

The feelings of Berenza, as he read characters, which he never for a moment doubted had been traced by the hand of Victoria, were such, as to the line of conduct they instigated him to adopt, highly favourable to the views of Count Ardolph. But Berenza was not displeased by the perusal; nay, it is uncertain, if he had not even a contrary sentiment; for he believed that Victoria's declining to see him for a short time, was merely an atonement offered by her for her recent misconduct to an insulted and wounded mother. As such, therefore, he felt, with genuine goodness, disposed to concede to her idea; and, believing that his departure might assist to establish that harmony which his presence had interrupted, and which it was absolutely requisite to the ultimate achievement of his own wishes should be restored, he determined to lose no time, but to quit Monte Bello at once, for the purpose of being enabled to return to it hereafter with better prospects of success. He experienced, too, something like a sensation of pleasure, that Victoria should evince remorse for the pain she had inflicted upon a doting parent: and perceiving, in addition, that a prompt departure would avoid some unpleasant, and perhaps very serious explanation with Count Ardolph, he called instantly, under the impression of these ideas, for his servant, and ordered him to get ready for returning to Venice. He had indeed a slight inclination to leave a line for Victoria; but, upon reflection, thinking it might only tend to irritate Laurina against him, he determined to dispense even with this; and all being very soon prepared for his short journey, with a bright Italian sky sparkling over his head, and the moon to light him on his way, Il Conte Berenza bade adieu to Monte Bello.

CHAPTER VI

On the following morning, Laurina entered the bedchamber of her daughter, and after some slight conversation, informed her, in a tone of affected surprize, of the departure of Berenza.

The intelligence, for an instant, gave to the haughty bosom of Victoria a pang of acute mortification, but this emotion was speedily succeeded by one of violent and uncontrolled rage. Looking fiercely at her mother, she said —

"Il Conte Berenza went not willingly from hence. At whose instigation was he driven to depart?"

"Not at the instigation of any one, Victoria," mildly but faulteringly replied Laurina.

Victoria withdrew her keen eyes from the countenance of her mother, and in a musing but stern voice said —

"If Il Conte Berenza departed voluntarily, he will rest passive, and take no measures to see me; but if he was impelled hence, then he will write to me, and inform me of the truth. Thus, even at all events, will the mystery be cleared up."

"And in the mean time, cruel girl," said Laurina, who had been accurately tutored by Ardolph, "and in the mean time, we, to amuse ourselves, will plan an excursion somewhere."

From the air of innocence so well assumed by Laurina, the unbending Victoria almost believed it real: she relaxed into a smile, and half soothed, half angry, she suffered her mother to take her hand.

"When are we to depart, and whither are we to go?" she haughtily enquired.

"We shall depart, if you do not object, my love, almost immediately," mildly returned Laurina, "and it is the wish of Count Ardolph, that we should pay first a visit to the Signora di Modena, at her delightful retreat, Il Bosco, near Treviso."

"What! to that forbidding, formal old creature?" sullenly muttered Victoria.

"Come, my love, she is a relation, you know. There, however, we need only remain a few days, and afterwards our little tour shall be prescribed by Victoria."

Victoria deigned a haughty smile. Her mother tenderly pressed the hand she still held, and rising, said —

"Adieu for the present, my love; prepare, as I am going to do, for our departure."

Not unpleasing was this request to Victoria, for her wounded pride now again usurping the place of regret and love, "Surely," thought she, "had Berenza really loved me, he would not so coolly, so suddenly have departed, without leaving even a line. No, perhaps, he began to imagine, that by persevering in the plan he had intended, he might become involved in some embarrassment or inconvenience; therefore, if even his departure was not voluntary, no doubt he readily embraced the slightest hint to disentangle himself from his engagement with me; can he then be worthy of regret? And yet I may wrong him, perhaps — Some combined artifice, some circumstances, of which I am not aware! But I will not reflect; let time, for time only can convince me."

With an unsettled mind, and an heart ill at ease, Victoria began to arrange a few things for her departure. She was not suffered by the Count or Laurina to remain long in solitude, the nurse, too often, of dangerous reflection. They entered her chamber together, and in a gay, unembarrassed tone, Ardolph enquired if she was ready. "I am," was the laconic answer of Victoria.

"Then so are we," said he, and took her hand to lead her from the room.

With coolness, but without anger, the proud girl withdrew her hand, and followed them in silence from the apartment.

Ardolph, who resolved that no danger should arise from delay, had caused every thing to be prepared: they embarked, therefore, immediately for Treviso, on the Terra Firma, and Victoria, though she little dreamt it at the time, bade a long adieu to Venice.

Every attempt at conversation was for some time baffled by the sullen taciturnity of Victoria; but by degrees (perhaps from a feeling of shame at the idea of being thought to regret a man, who, after all, might have voluntarily abandoned her) her sullenness relaxed, and she determined to assume a chearfulness that she was far from feeling. This change delighted Laurina; so powerfully indeed did it affect her misguided heart, that she even began to repent the precipitancy of her conduct, and to feel some pangs at the idea of immuring in a disgusting solitude a young creature, who, but for the mischievous tendency of her own example, might have been rendered to society a value and an ornament.

Ardolph read in her eyes the increasing softness of her heart, and that her purpose wavered. She even ventured to cast towards him a look expressive of her feelings; but he, whose aim it was to remove every barrier to his continued possession of Laurina, instantly by a stern look of the most unshaken resolution, convinced her every attempt would be vain to alter his purpose. Laurina sighed; for the eyes of Ardolph had told her there was nothing to hope; she sunk into painful thought, and it now became the task of Victoria to rally her mother, and to shew, vain girl, how far she could conquer her feelings, and become mistress of herself; her every endeavour, however, but added to the compunction of mind experienced by the unhappy Laurina.

As they had departed from Venice at a late hour, it was dusk when they reached Treviso, and arrived at Il Bosco, which was so named from its situation in the midst of a wood: its gloomy appearance, however, did not depress Victoria, who was by this time absolutely in spirits. The mother's heart was rived: she knew it was the intention of Ardolph, after her relation should be instructed as to the conduct it was his wish she should pursue towards Victoria, laying infinite stress upon the levity and freedom of her principles, to abandon her solely to the guardianship of this person, with whom even Laurina herself had never been much in the habit of associating; she therefore ardently longed to alter the severe resolution of the unyielding Ardolph; but the effort she knew would be vain. With him she could atchieve nothing, when not under the immediate apprehension of losing her. Divested of that, he became stern, unrelenting, and inaccessible, which was indeed his natural character. To have obtained from him a remission of the sentence, she should have begun earlier, before even her departure from Monte Bello. Now, having gone so far, to suppose he would retract, was supposing impossibilities. In vain she anxiously examined his countenance; she saw there nothing but a complacent, cool expression, the result of a settled purpose in the mind.

The Signora di Modena welcomed Count Ardolph with all the warmth she could command. Laurina anxiously examined her countenance, to see if she could augur aught of kindness or gentleness to reconcile her to her guardianship of her daughter; but in the frigid features of this forbidding female nothing was discernible but the austere pride of ungracious virtue, with an aukward attempt at condescending kindness, which shewed how much it cost her to assume.

Acquainted with the unhappy misconduct of Laurina, and likewise that it had lost her her place in society, she, with the arrogated superiority of little minds, ever triumphing in the fall of others, contented herself with a solemn curtsey towards her, while on Victoria she scarcely deigned to glance.

The Signora di Modena, as has been already observed, was distantly related to Laurina. She was not more repulsive in person than in character; a long yellow visage, small grey eyes, and a stiff unbending meagre figure, constituted the former. She was proud, fastidious, and possessed of a mercenary soul. From her youth, alarmed at the idea of conventual seclusion, yet being portionless, as the daughters of the Italian nobility frequently are, she preferred residing an occasional dependant in such noble families as would permit her lengthened visits, where she would act alternately the overseer, the companion, the governess, or the servant. By these, and other winding paths, by flattery, peculation, and hypocrisy, she had actually amassed, as the friendless period of age approached, sufficient to make it pass with comfort, though not with affluence; and, to recompense herself for the contempt she had in her early life experienced, becoming, as far as she could, the torment and scourge of all who were miserable enough to be subject to her controul. No man, even in the best of her days, had ever glanced toward her with the eye of admiration, much less attempted to solicit her in marriage; and for this reason, her bitterness against all females who could attract, or dare to yield to the regards of the other sex, knew no bounds, and they could hope from her no mercy. Such was the Signora di Modena, whose self interest would not permit her to quarrel with Laurina, because, though she had never much associated with her, she had often proved herself a generous friend towards her. Still her wretched affectation and rancorous envy would not suffer her to display much warmth. No such reason, however, operated in her conduct to Ardolph; of him she was desirous to *make* a friend; and hence her mercenary homage was directed towards him, and she paid him chiefest court. He had not therefore entirely jested when he had remarked to Laurina the courtesy of the Signora toward him on a former visit. Nothing, however, could excite in him a desire to prolong his stay beyond what was necessary under her roof; he, therefore, presuming upon her uncommon deference towards him, requested an early supper, that Victoria might then retire, and he might be enabled to enter at once upon the grand object of their visit.

Supper was at length announced, and the unsuspecting Victoria detesting the very looks of the old Signora, which had already succeeded in damping her spirits, requested to be shewn to her chamber, as soon as it was concluded. Beneath her stern and scrutinizing regard, her haughty mind felt a sentiment of impatient disgust, and an oppression never known before to the buoyant carelessness of her disposition. On bidding her mother good night, she felt impelled, from the very uneasiness she experienced, to throw her arms around her neck, with unusual affection, and whispered to her, that she hoped they should not long remain under so gloomy and uncongenial a roof. Scarcely could the anguished mother reply; her heart smote her, for her deception and conscience whispered to her truths that brought the blood into her cheeks. She however pressed the hand of Victoria, and faultered out 'good night;' while the reflection that it might be perhaps for the *last time*, filled her bosom with acute pain, and her eyes with tears.

Victoria left the room almost reproaching herself for having ever pained a heart of such fond sensibility as her mother's. She was scarcely gone, ere the impatient Ardolph, turning towards the Signora di Modena, entered abruptly upon the business he was most desirous of accomplishing.

"Will you, Signora," he began, "allow me to say a few words to you?"

The Signora stiffly bowed, endeavouring to smile graciously, but succeeding only in a ghastly distortion of feature.

The well bred Ardolph, however, took it for a smile of acquiescence, and thus proceeded: —

"Your courtesy and politeness to me, Signora, and above all, the high opinion I entertain of your character, induce me to place in you a confidence I could not certainly repose in any other female. — I am to inform you, then, that the young girl, who has just left the apartment, I am desirous to commit for a certain period to your care. Naturally evil disposed, of a haughty and audacious temper, she has been nearly by flattery and indulgence destroyed. Her ideas are entirely corrupted, and, child as you may think her, for she is scarcely eighteen, there have not been wanting those of the other sex who have sought to undermine her principles." — Here the Signora heaved a loud tremulous sigh, and, turning up her eyes to heaven, made the holy sign of the cross. The Count with external gravity and secet contempt proceeded: — "What I would therefore presume to request of you is, that you will condescend to keep over this proud and forward girl so strict a watch, as scarcely to suffer her ever from your sight."

"But do not, do not treat her severely, dear cousin," interrupted Laurina with a faultering voice.

The immaculate Signora replied only by a cool half-scornful look, and scarcely seemed proud of the appellation which Laurina had given her, though once it was the chief boast of her little mind. She now thought *herself* superior to the fallen wife of Loredani.

"I would have you, Signora," continued Ardolph, endeavouring to call back her attention to himself, "I would have you confine her, if it be necessary, to the solitude of her chamber, for a short time."

"Oh, Ardolph," cried Laurina, unable to command her feelings, "you are too cruel, there can be no occasion for such harshness."

Another look from the unbending Signora chilled her into silence, who then turned again with the utmost deference towards the Count.

"Laurina, you are no judge," coldly observed Ardolph, "the Signora will only act as circumstances may require; to her conduct and discretion you may safely commit your daughter, when by a due course," he pursued, looking towards the Signora, "of restraint, and privation of every incitement to evil, a change for the better shall be perceptible in her disposition, we will withdraw her hence, and you, Laurina, may again receive her. Mean time, Signora di Modena, it is my intention to depart early tomorrow morning from this place, leaving Victoria still asleep. When she arises, astonished at not seeing us, she will enquire of you respecting us. You will then gently disclose to her the truth, and her own destination for the present. By degrees you will, I doubt not, reconcile her to what she will perceive to be inevitable. Deign to act in this affair, Signora, with that zeal and punctuality, which your piety will teach you to exert for the salvation of a soul, and with that prudence, which has hitherto appeared so eminently to distinguish your own conduct in life: in which case, allow me to add, you shall not find me ungrateful." Again a smile, which appeared hideous, because it seemed unnatural to the hard features it dilated, was the return for this last significant remark of the Count's. He had skilfully touched the spring, the only spring upon which any feeling, or any principle of the Signora, hung — Interest. She found, as she had all along imagined, that it was her *interest* to court and to oblige the Count; she therefore determined to yield to whatever he should require, fondly promising herself in return, some splendid remuneration.

"Be assured, my Lord Count," she said, in a grating, discordant voice, intended to be gentle and conciliating, "I will observe your wishes to the uttermost; and as for you, Signora Laurina," looking towards her with a pitying air, "for all I intend to observe my Lord Count's wishes, you shall not have any reason to complain of the treatment your daughter will receive."

At these words, the grateful Laurina flew towards her, and, seizing her hand, which she fervently pressed, she said, "Oh, you have no child, my dear Signora, yet pity the feelings of a mother, and be kind to mine. She has never, no never been opposed, nor treated with harshness." Hastily, and with a look almost amounting to horror, the pure and dignified Signora withdrew her hand, as from the touch of pollution; then rising, and retreating three steps, stretching out her arm at full length, to prevent the nearer approach of so sinful and impure a being, she said —

"I will do the duty of a good catholic towards your child. I shall study the preservation of her soul, and more her spiritual interest than her temporal vanities."

The conscious and abashed Laurina turned aside, with shame, even from the *shew* of virtue in its most ungraceful form, pride and affectation.

"There appears no occasion for further discourse," observed Ardolph coldly, "we shall rely upon the proper tenor of your conduct towards Victoria. When we think that time and reflection shall have shewn her her faults, and taught her to amend them, we will visit you again; if we find her sufficiently improved in her character, we shall receive her once more. Mean time, cousin di Modena, good night, have the goodness to direct that we may be awakened early for the purpose of commencing our journey homewards, before sun-rise. And that you may bear us in mind till our return, deign to accept this ring, as a small token of the respect we cherish towards you." So saying, Ardolph took from his finger a magnificent ring, which he placed on one of the Signora's, whose half-closed eyes had more than once been rivetted upon it. Then gallantly bowing on her withered hand, he withdrew, leaving her in admiration at his singular politeness, and her own dexterity, as she thought, in having turned him already to such good account.

Pursuant to his determination, long ere the sun had risen, Ardolph, with his weeping and remorseful companion, were far from the villa Il Bosco. Perceiving, however, that Laurina was not yet reconciled to the prompt and severe measures he had so obstinately pursued, he forbore for the present to touch upon the subject, though his heart exulted to think, that what he willed he executed, and that nothing now could intervene to deprive him of a woman, whom his pride, equally at least with his love, made him so desirous of retaining. Had no obstacles ever existed to his possession of her, and even to his retaining her afterwards, the depraved and cruel Ardolph had either never sought, or long since have disdained her. But his passion and his pride, kept in continual alarms, gave a renewed vividness to feelings, which, but for such excitements, would have sunk into apathy or disgust. Such was the vitiated mind of Ardolph, that he could taste no delight that possessed not the poignant zest of having caused misery or destruction to others. Innocent and easily acquired pleasures suited not his profligate soul. Beauty to him was but a slight attraction, if not surrounded with difficulty, and shielded either by the doting fondness of a husband, or cherished as the glory of an admiring family. Such had been the situation, when he first beheld her, of the the unfortunate and now degraded Laurina; of her, whom he beheld himself, as he proudly thought, in the future undisturbed possession of, even till she should outlive, if such could be, his present love and admiration of her — if such could be, oh, then Laurina, in bitterness of heart, mightest thou curse the hours when first thou wert seen by the cruel and insensible Adolph.

Those feelings so base, yet not unparalleled in the nature of man, which actuated the mind of Ardolph, gave an elation to his spirits, which dispensed itself in a brilliant animation over his fine features and ever fascinating manners. Without alluding to the cause of Laurina's grief, he contrived, by the most gentle and tender blandishments, gradually to dispel it. Such a seducing influence did he still possess over her ruined mind, that there were moments when she literally forgot there was a being in the world but himself. When she listened to his attractive converse, and gazed on the dignified beauty of his form, she felt rising in her breast a sentiment of that vanity, which had already proved her destruction. She even conceived towards him (such was her infatuation) an increase of love and gratitude, when she reflected that it was the unbounded ardour of his attachment to her which had induced him to act with severity towards any one who had sought to embitter it. Thus, even the sacrifice of her child, sacrificed at the shrine of *her* errors and her crimes, by him who had been the cause of all, she began to contemplate with emotions of less poignant regret. Scarcely could she grieve in earnest at anything which bound closer to her the object of her idolatrous love. It seemed as if every occurrence which should have made her view him with sentiments of horror, but increased the delusion of her soul; each moment that carried her further from the child she had abandoned, effaced more and more her image from her mind: her ideas became more strongly rivetted upon him, whose artifices had rendered her an infamous wife and a cruel mother; while himself was the exclusive charm of her unhappy existence. Let us leave then for a time this guilty pair to enjoy the society of each other, and return to the deserted Victoria.

When she awakened, and looked round the large and desolate chamber, which the ill light afforded by a lamp on the preceding night had prevented her from viewing, the first feeling of her mind was renewed disgust against the owner of the mansion, and an impatient hope that the Count and her mother would not prolong their stay under a roof so hateful. Finding, however, that no one attended to call her, and imagining that she must have slept many hours, the morning appeared to be far advanced; she arose, and, dressing herself hastily, descended from her chamber, and entered the garden. Here she had not been long, before she beheld advancing towards her a short muscular looking girl, habited in the costume of a peasant. She approached Victoria, and informed her, that the Signora di Modena desired her company at breakfast. With a haughty and supercilious air, and a smile of derision on her features, Victoria glanced over the figure of the humble girl, and, without deigning a reply, preceded her into the house.

Entering the apartment where breakfast was laid, she saw there seated alone, at the table, the old Signora, in unbending state. Without even offering to her the customary salutations of the morning, the haughty Victoria enquired impatiently if Count Ardolph and her mother still slept.

"I think it improbable," coolly returned the Signora.

"Why are they not here, then?" pursued the offended girl in a quick tone.

"Because," answered the Signora, with malicious and ill-disguised exultation, "they must by this time, I imagine, be some way on their journey from hence."

"Gone!" almost shrieked Victoria; "did you say gone?"

"I said so," with unaltered countenance carelessly returned the Signora — "Is there anything so dreadful, young lady, in being compelled to remain with me for a while? Come, be charitable," she tauntingly proceeded — "I have been long very solitary, and you will be noble company for me, I think."

The rage of Victoria knew no bounds; she gazed wildly round the apartment; the whole truth rushed through her mind at once — the base, the unpardonable artifice that had been used — she struck her head violently with her clenched hand, and passionately exclaiming — "I am deceived and entrapped!" rushed from the room before the Signora was aware of her intention; and, reaching the apartment where she had slept, she secured the door.

There, casting herself upon the floor, her passion vented itself in a violent paroxysm of tears; but becoming suddenly ashamed of yielding, as she thought it, to a weakness so ignoble, and angry with herself that the ill treatment of any one should have power to excite in her either grief or lamentation, she checked a rising gush, while rage and the most deadly hatred against those who had thus dared to dupe and to betray her, took possession of her swelling heart. An ardent desire of revenge followed; and thus from the conduct, misjudging and inexcusable, that had been pursued towards her, did every violent and evil propensity of her nature become increased and aggravated.

No sooner had Victoria called to her aid the loftier and more dangerous passions, than she became to appearance calm; and though now and then, when reflecting upon the deception of her mother, and cold deliberate artifice of Ardolph, her eyes shot fire, and the pulsation of her heart increased; yet, in her general aspect, there were no longer traces of grief, but, on the contrary, a superior and dignified expression, which would have done honour to a nobler motive: her head no longer drooped; and rising hastily from the floor, on which, after her first paroxysm, she had remained sitting, with firm and measured step she traversed the apartment to and fro. In the course of her cooler reflection, it occurred to her that Il Conte Berenza must have been impelled by artifice, and not his own desire, to quit Monte Bello. This idea soothed the sovereign pride of her bosom: she felt that her charms had not been slighted; and, at some future period, she did not yet despair of convincing him that the separation was neither on her side voluntary. But then she recurred to her present situation — was it intended she should remain for ever a prisoner in this gloomy abode? Again she yielded for a moment to the influence of circumstance, and her heart became chilled at the idea. Yet she determined to observe minutely — to make no enquiries — to betray no vexation, but to act precisely as events might shew necessary.

Soothed and calmed by these mental arrangements, and by the victory which reason, as she conceived, had obtained over her weaker feelings, she resolved, as evening drew on, to quit the solitude of her chamber, and breathe for a short space the air of the garden. For the whole of the day she had not tasted food; and though she heeded not the calls of hunger, she became sensible of the privation. The cold and unfeeling Signora, happy to have a human being, and, above all, an ardent and high-spirited creature, to tyrannise over, resolved that no refreshment should be offered her till she herself came, and, with proper apologies for her conduct, requested it: but of this Victoria formed not the remotest intention; and it is probable that, rather than have done so, she would have fallen a victim to the pangs of hunger. Fortunately for her, however, though infinitely to the regret of the tantalising Signora, she was not put to this trial. Having walked for a while in the garden, and refreshed her weary faculties with the dewy fragrance of the atmosphere, she entered the house, and proceeded, though unintentionally, to the very apartment where supper was prepared; there quietly seating herself opposite to the old Signora, she partook, without ceremony, of what was before her: she even made some attempt at conversation; but, foiled in her proposed plan of ungenerous mortification, the Signora di Modena was too vexed to make any reply. She had hoped to have found her inmate stubborn, refractory, and violent, giving fine scope thereby to her favourite art of tormenting. How grieved and disappointed then was she to find the fury of the morning sunk into calm, and, as it appeared, patient submission.

Victoria, perceiving the Signora determined upon sullen silence, requested permission to withdraw for the night, in a tone of the utmost politeness. The only answer she obtained was a stiff inclination of the head. More determined than ever at this, that she should not have the gratification of provoking her, she coolly rose, and wishing her, with a profound curtsey, good night, left the room.

When she was gone, this worthy and pious catholic began to reflect, that, by means like these, Victoria would escape from all the arrangements she had been making to punish and mortify her. "This will never do," she cried, while ruminating how best she might vex and harass the mind of her unfortunate guest: "she has become *reconciled* to her situation without any attempt on my side to render her so; but she shall not escape thus — I will break that proud spirit, and make her submit afterwards."

Such were the reflections of the charitable devotee; and, with these thoughts at work in her brain for the comfort and happiness of others, she said a long prayer, during which she frequently struck her breast, and retired to repose.

Victoria, after sitting for an hour at the window, with a mind still persevering in the resolution to be firm, sought likewise her bed, and soon forgot the vexations of the day in slumber.

On the following morning, she awakened at an early hour; and, after having drest herself, she prepared to pass from her chamber into the garden. Trying her door, she found it was fastened on the outside; and discovering soon that every attempt on her part to shake it must be ineffectual, she opened the window, and stationed herself beside it.

In about half an hour the door was unlocked, and the young muscular girl already mentioned entered the room, with a bowl of milk and and a slice of coarse bread. These she laid upon the table, and was retiring —

"Come back!" imperiously cried Victoria. The girl sullenly turned half round.

"I chuse to walk in the garden," she pursued.

"The Signora will not permit," gruffly returned the girl.

"Will not permit!" repeated Victoria.

"No," laconically answered the girl, again laying her hand upon the lock of the door.

"Why do you leave these things behind you?" cried Victoria, smothering the rage she felt rising in her breast.

"It is your breakfast," replied the girl, quitting the room, and locking the door after her.

"So, then, I am made a prisoner!" muttered Victoria, and her cheeks assumed a crimson dye, as she endeavoured faintly to smile at the impotent malice of the Signora. "How have I incurred this? Not, surely, by my conduct of yesterday!" But the malevolent disposition of the tyrant devotee became evident to the haughty girl, and she deemed her a being too insignificant to excite a moment's pain. "This cannot last for ever," thought she; "and when the wretch is weary of confining me, she will, for variety, set me at liberty; mean time, I must amuse myself the best I can."

She then searched her trunk, which, on the night of her arrival, had been brought into this chamber. Here she found some drawing materials. The surrounding scenery, beautifully romantic, furnished ample employment for her pencil; and, with mixed sensations contending in her bosom, she seated herself by an open window, and endeavoured by occupation to banish reflection.

This unworthy procedure and system of torment, on the part of the

Signora, continued in full force for some days, till want of exercise, and inferior food, began, though the proud Victoria disdained complaint, to have a visible effect upon her health. At this the Signora, who was informed of the circumstance by the young girl who attended her, began to be slightly alarmed, and to apprehend likewise that she might overstep, by such measures, the limits that had been prescribed her, and render herself amenable for any ill consequences that might arise; such, for example, as the sickness of Victoria, which, by distressing and aggrieving Laurina, might bring her into disfavour with the Count; perhaps, as he appeared so tenderly to love Laurina, even excite his anger against her, for such unauthorised severity. For though Adolph had said, she might, if *necessary*, confine Victoria to her chamber, he had not bid her do so without cause, much less deprive her of her accustomed food, and give her only a scanty portion even of the worst. Under these considerations, therefore, she determined to relax a little; and Victoria, from being confined the whole of the day, and visited only twice in the course of it by Catau, her attendant, with a small quantity of bad bread and milk, was suffered, accompanied, however, by Catau, to walk an hour in the garden, morning and evening. To attempt to describe the indignant feelings of Victoria at this treatment, or the struggle it cost her, amounting almost to phrensy, to subdue the expression of the violent rage that fermented in her bosom, would be indeed vain; yet she bore all, and was determined sooner to die than betray the smallest symptom of vexation or impatience.

But desire of revenge, deep and implacable, was nurtured in her heart's core, and gave to her character an additional shade of harshness and ferocity: thus she became like the untameable hyaena,[1] that confinement renders only more fierce.

A few days after this comparative liberty had been allowed her, the Signora, by Catau, requested her presence in the drawing-room. In strict pursuance of the conduct she had prescribed herself, she instantly obeyed, and regretted only that her pallid cheek and sunken eyes were evidences of suffering beyond her power to conceal, and would gratify, as she feared, the malignity of her tyrant. She entered the apartment, however, with an air neither of sullen reserve nor acknowledged resentment, but placid, cool, and unembarrassed. Thus, too, did she learn the most refined artifice, which, by practice, became imbued into the mass of her other evil qualities.

The Signora, somewhat discomfited by the unexpected demeanour of Victoria, having previously arranged her hard features for the intended expression of severe reprimand, knew not for the moment how to receive her: at length, she said — "Be seated, child."

With secret scorn and hate, Victoria obeyed.

---

1 became like the untameable hyaena: The hyaena was commonly believed to be hermaphroditic.

"It is not my intention," solemnly, and in a laboured accent, began the Signora, "to revert, at present, to your violent and improper conduct, when first you became an inmate under this roof; nor, upon account of what is past, to punish you further. I merely wished to evince to you that softness, humility, and obedience, are indispensable requisites here, and that nothing can be tolerated that shews an overbearing, haughty, or ferocious spirit. You are by this time, I trust, properly convinced of your error."

The heart of Victoria rose in her bosom — it swelled with indignation to reply — but again she conquered her emotions, and the only evidence of them was a momentary rush of the blood into her cheeks. The Signora proceeded —

"Under this impression, I deem it no longer necessary to confine you. You will not, however, be suffered to go beyond the walls of this mansion: the garden, at all events, must be the extent of your wanderings, and your only society Catau, and, at meal-times, myself."

How the pride of Victoria battled for vent! — "Society for Catau!" but still she spoke not.

"I shall likewise expect that you peruse such religious book as I shall put into your hands, and which, I humbly hope, will tend to amend the stubbornness of your proud heart. Moreover, that you abjure the vanities of dress, and meekly comply with every requisition, that, as a good and pious catholic, anxious for the salvation of your soul, I shall think it my duty to make of you."

The Signora now paused for breath — Victoria still remained silent, as not seeming to suppose an answer was required.

The Signora then resumed — "How much ought you to thank Heaven, proud child, that has caused you to be placed under my care — that has rescued you from the abode of vice and abomination, and placed you beneath the roof of purity and virtue. Count Ardolph even tells me, unhappy girl! that young as you are, you have already suffered your corrupt imagination to wander after man! — Oh! Santa Maria! that ever I should live to speak the word," continued the devotee, turning up her eyes, and making the sign of the cross — "teach me to bear with patience, admitting to my presence one of passions and propensities so vile, and whose mother has already trespassed before her, beyond redemption, in the paths of sin! — You may retire, child," she said, changing her tone of raphsody into one of haughty severity; "retire, and seek Catau: she is a meet companion for the contaminated offspring of one who is immersed many fathoms deep in guilt and shame."

This last bitter, illiberal, and uncalled for reproach, tingled with burning heat through every vein of the insulted Victoria. "Oh, mother! — cruel mother!" she faintly murmured, and hastened from the room.

CHAPTER VII

It would be endless to dwell on the varied and unworthy artifices which the pious Signora di Modena had recourse to, for the torment and annoyance of her unhappy charge. Suffice it to say, that in time their effect became blunted and despised, and the whole thoughts of Victoria turned to the possibility of escaping from such vulgar tyranny: for long she revolved in her mind even the remotest probability, but in vain; she could never penetrate farther than the allotted garden, and knew not even the precise path or door that might lead beyond it — even were that difficulty obviated, she was ignorant of the means of getting to Venice, whither, could she but once escape, she was determined to hasten.

Under these circumstances, the image of Catau presented itself to her mind. Confined as she was almost wholly to the society of this untaught girl, she had leisure to remark in her, certain traits of docility and goodnature, ill concealed beneath the sullen sternness she had evidently been commanded to assume.

Catau was a peasant of Switzerland, short and thick in her person, hard favoured, of rude and vacant features, ignorant and inured to labour: she had been selected by the Signora to attend and watch Victoria, first to mortify her by the careless clumsiness of her manner, and the inferiority of her station; and, secondly, from an idea that Victoria would despise her too much to endeavour to corrupt or make a friend of her. Should she even make the attempt, the Signora presumed the extreme stupidity of Catau would render it abortive. But here, for once, the infallible Signora, as she believed herself, was mistaken in her fancied penetration. Catau was not only not so stupid as she was supposed, but was possessed of a certain shrewdness, and power of combining ideas, which, hid beneath an habitual silence and placidity of disposition, had drawn upon her the mistaken imputation of heaviness and insensibility. Catau could think; and, what was more, she could *feel* — yes, infinitely beyond those who so proudly sat in judgment upon her character.

To return, however, to Victoria. No sooner had the remotest glimmerings of a possible attempt beamed upon her mind, than instantly she determined, by every means in her power, to attach Catau to her interests. Time and experience had already made her so far acquainted with the malevolent and tormenting spirit of the Signora di Modena, that she well knew one great step towards the scheme in embryo, was not, by any means, to appear reconciled to the society of Catau, but, on the contrary, to seem to shun and despise her; for it was sufficient for this worthy catholic to be aware of the particular circumstance, that could yield a moment's satisfaction to any one, instantly to reverse it, and continue with unwearied perseverance in that line of conduct which appeared to give most pain and uneasiness: therefore, when she seemed to dislike being accompanied by Catau in the garden, which she often did purposely, the Signora, with a distorted smile of fancied triumph, would tell Catau to take her arm, and lead her thither, thinking by that to inflict on the proud heart of her charge the deepest mortification. But here again the Signora was fallible; for no sooner was Victoria out of her sight, than she smiled on Catau with an air that said — "There is no other way of preserving your attendance." This smile would penetrate the heart of her humble companion; and she would feel so gratified and affected, that, perhaps, at those moments, Victoria might have made an attempt not destitute of success. Such, however, was not her plan; she had not yet sufficiently arranged it, and she resolved to do nothing from crude undigested ideas. She was but now in the infancy of her attempt, sounding the disposition of Catau; and her mailed heart was not to be thrown off its guard by any effusions of softness of feeling, attributable to the effect of the moment alone.

It so happened, that one evening they perambulated to a part of the garden which was yet unknown to Victoria: it was a beautiful close avenue, the sides and roof of which were interwoven branches of vine and honeysuckle; the entrance was almost concealed by a thick shrubbery, which it required no slight ingenuity to penetrate; and, from the serpentine direction of the path, it appeared wholly impossible to ascertain its extent. Still having made their way through, they proceeded, Victoria with a vague and indefinable feeling of hope and fear, and Catau merely with that vacant curiosity incident to vulgar minds.

At length, after walking for near half an hour, they only reached the extent of the garden, bounded by the high circular wall, which had so often, since the comparative liberty she had enjoyed, filled the mind of Victoria, in contemplating it, with a despondency almost hopeless. The winding path they had traversed, had alone deceived her as to the imagined distance; and, as she gloomily surveyed the strong and lofty enclosure, she almost doubted if any outlet whatever existed. "Surely," thought she, "there is only an entrance to this garden from the house, and no outlet from the garden itself." While thus she ruminated, walking slowly along by the side of the wall, she became convinced, as she proceeded, that the precise part of the garden in which she now found herself, she had never seen before. At length, a small wooden door, formed in the wall, and secured by two rusty bolts, and a heavy iron lock, presented itself to her eager view. She instantly called to Catau to approach: and, pointing to the door, enquired of her if she knew whither it led. Catau readily applied an eye to the key-hole —

"It leads into the wood, Signora, which surrounds this house; but, unless we were outside, I cannot tell the exact spot."

The first part of her reply fixed the breathless attention of Victoria. "Into the wood!" repeated she mentally, and applied her eye likewise to the key-hole. "And is there no way, Catau," said she, "of opening this door?"

"None that I know of, Signora," replied Catau; "and even if there was, you know, Signora," she added, in a hesitating voice, "you know that — "

"I understand you, Catau," answered Victoria; "but you know there could be nothing wrong in rambling now and then about the wood, and, supposing the Signora has forbid it, how could it ever become known?"

"Why, that is true," replied Catau, thoughtfully. "I must own, it is a hard thing to be so confined; but, holy Jesu, Signora, we could never open this door!"

"Oh, Catau!" said Victoria, in a gentle voice, "nothing is impossible to those who are willing. You could easily procure the key, under some pretence or another; and think, then, how delightful it would be for us to be quite out of the reach of the horrible Signora!"

"Ho, ho," cried Catau, with quickness, as if suddenly awaking from a reverie, "I have a *thought* — To make any enquiries about the key belonging to this door, Signora, would only make us suspected. I now remember, that when, before you came, the Signora used to send me to Ambrosio, (the gardener) that I have seen hanging up under the little shed where he keeps his tools, a large bunch of rusty keys. I think, Signora, I could lay my hand blindfold upon the very spot where they hang."

"Well!" cried Victoria, her natural impatience breaking forth through her assumed gentleness and forbearance.

"Well, hasten then, fetch them, and let us try them all immediately."

"No, Signora," answered Catau, with genuine mildness, "that will not do: the evening is drawing in — the Signora has already begun to miss us — by this hour Ambrosio, too, has most likely returned home, and may be in the very place I speak of. To-morrow, when he shall be in a distant part of the garden, I will watch the moment when no one is near, and slip through his little cottage to the spot; for I must pass through Ambrosio's residence, Signora, to get at it — I shall then whip down the keys as quick as lightning; and if you will *promise*, Signora — if you will promise not to betray me, nor to stay out too long, I will do all I can to oblige you. — I do not think," she continued, "this door has been opened for a long time — perhaps the very key that belongs to it may be in this bunch."

Victoria was fearful to appear too eager; and, ardently as she longed to penetrate beyond the unvaried precincts prescribed by the Signora, she acquiesced with apparent readiness to the arrangements of Catau, and reluctantly agreed to bend her steps homeward.

The whole of the night was past in giving way alternately to trembling hope and the deepest despair. The perpetual ferment of her brain, and, above all, the violent restraint she imposed upon her feelings and natural disposition, scarcely ever suffering herself to be provoked, for an instant, from the cool and systematic conduct she prescribed herself, had began long since to have a visible effect upon her personal appearance: she had become thin and pallid; but still her eyes burnt with an ardent though melancholy lustre, that bespoke the *trammelled unsubdued* ferocity of her soul.

About noon the following day, Catau, who had been absent since she had risen, (for she occupied the same apartment as Victoria) rushed suddenly into the room, and, first carefully securing the door, drew from her pocket a huge bunch of rusty keys. At this sight Victoria's eyes sparkled, and the orient tint revisited momentarily her pallid cheek: she devoured them with eager look, and in fancy applied them in turn to the lock of the door. It was, however, as yet, too early to venture forth; for they might be tempted to remain longer absent than would be prudent, and suspicion might be excited; they therefore agreed to defer till evening their destined trial.

Now, in all this active conduct of the simple Catau, there was absolutely not the smallest intention of aiding or abetting Victoria to escape; she would, on the contrary, have shuddered at the idea: but though, in obedience to the orders of the Signora, she had, in the commencement, treated her with sullen coldness, yet in a little time, as is natural for a young uncorrupted mind, she had become weary of this assumed character, and returned to the kind, gentle, and respectful conduct, more consonant to her feelings. Besides which, the involuntary awe with which superior rank inspired her, was not to be done away; for superior rank, if accompanied with any dignity, makes resistless impression on the vulgar mind.

Victoria, who beheld with pleasure this gradual change of conduct, divested herself as much as possible of her natural *hauteur*; and, having a point to carry, she behaved towards Catau with the utmost condescension, now and then bestowing on her such trifles as were still within her power (for of the greatest part of her little possessions, clothes, &c. the Signora had deprived her, under the pretence of curing her of a sinful vanity detrimental to the good of her soul). But what Victoria could, she did; and the trifles which, with grace, she pressed upon Catau, were acceptable, and had their desired effect; for vulgar minds are *almost always* mercenary: therefore, as far as *she* could, in return, she enlarged the slender sphere of Victoria's comforts, and her solitary unvaried amusements. Thus, in procuring for her the keys, she had it merely in contemplation to obtain for her, if possible, a few moments of satisfaction.

Early in the evening they descended to the garden, and hastened to the avenue already described. Strong anxiety winged the feet of Victoria, and soon she reached the door which had already excited in her mind ideas so various and confused. Snatching the keys from Catau, who had toiled after her, she applied them in turn, with trembling impatience to the lock: one at length appeared to suit the best; she essayed to turn it, but in vain — it was reserved for the sinewy hand of Catau to triumph over the united strength of rust and iron. She wrenched the key with violence; it turned in the lock: she applied her force to the bolts alternately with her hand and a stone, which she had picked up: the door at length yielded to her perseverance, and flew open.

Happy and joyous sight for the imprisoned Victoria! — she darted, like a wild bird newly escaped from its wiry tenement, into the beautiful and romantic wood that presented itself to her ravished view. The cautious and less ardent Catau closed the door after them, and followed. Victoria looked wistfully around: she beheld no boundaries, nothing to retard her, should she effect her escape. For a moment she ruminated; then calling Catau towards her, she said, in a careless tone — "Catau, canst thou tell now in which direction lies the city of Venice?"

"Venice, Signora!" answered Catau, pausing and gazing around, "Venice lies there," pointing with her finger.

"Then," said Victoria, clapping her hands, while her cheeks crimsoned with rage, "Monte Bello," pointing contemptuously towards the left, "must be on that side." Reflections too bitter and too strong to be endured, rushed through her mind: she turned abruptly away, and with a look that seemed to say — "Accursed be the quarter where I was deceived and duped, and accursed every breeze that is wafted thence!"

But far, far different sensations actuated her, when she cast her eyes forwards. "There," thought she, "is Venice itself, and there dwells *Berenza!*" Distance, which, like death, always magnifies to the imagination the charms of those who were beloved, together with the deception that had been used to separate her from him, induced her to think of him with a tenderness, that, but for those circumstances, perhaps, she had never felt in so powerful a degree. — "Ah, dear Berenza!" she mentally continued, "might I but hope to see *thee* once more —"

She turned towards Catau, anxious to rally her thoughts; and, taking her arm, she walked on with her in silence. A thousand unconnected ideas still floated in her mind: time passed unheeded, till Catau, respectfully reminding her that it would be expedient to return, roused her from her visions of the future, and she readily acquiesced in the propriety of the movement.

CHAPTER VIII

It may be naturally presumed, that the mind of Victoria remained bent upon escape; not a day past, that she did not induce Catau to extend their walks farther and farther from the outlet, an outlet the Signora little thought they would ever discover, much less dream of attempting. Every day, too, did she contrive to make silent, though accurate observations, as to the direct course it would be most proper for her to pursue.

At length, unable to bear continued procrastination, she determined to put in execution the plan that had been so long arranging in her brain. Accordingly, on the following evening, when the unsuspicious Catau had been lured, by her kind and condescending manner, to accompany her far, infinitely farther than they had ever yet ventured, she suddenly stopt short, and thus addressed the astonished girl —

"Catau, I will never more return to Il Bosco — my term of slavery is now over — I shall bend my course whither I please — to the East, the West, the North, or the South. Listen, therefore, to what I have to propose: exchange instantly your apparel for mine, and by your prompt acquiescence merit this diamond ring, which has been concealed from the old Signora, and which I will in that case immediately bestow upon you. You can easily, as we have hitherto done, return into the house unperceived, and array yourself in some of your usual attire. Should you be questioned as to my escape, swear, what will be true, that you was not privy to it. Should you be questioned as to whither I am gone, swear, what is true, that you cannot tell. If, even after this, the Signora should think fit to discharge you, I do not see that you will have anything to regret; and with regard to any advantage you might think you lost, this ring, which is extremely valuable, will more than indemnify you. Now these are the *pacific* terms which I propose to you: if you refuse them, I am equally determined to fly; and, if nothing but violence will avail to oppose *my* strength to yours, my strength, it is true, may not *equal* yours; but you may find, to your cost, Catau," she added, with meaning in her eyes, "that victory may not always depend upon that alone."

Catau trembled like a leaf in the gale: the firmness and decision with which she had been addressed, left her not the power of reply. Victoria, marking her consternation, began calmly to take off her robe; and, in that gentle tone she knew so well how to assume, thus went on — "I see, Catau, that you have the good sense to feel the propriety of my resolution, and the kindness to wish to assist me in it. — Come, my good girl, prepare to undress."

"Oh, Signora!" faltered out Catau. At length, involuntarily taking at the same time the first step to divest herself of her attire — "oh, Signora, what are you about to do?"

"To leave a tyrant!" answered Victoria, with quickness, her eyes darting fire; "and I wish you, Catau, speedily the same good fortune. — Come, hasten your movements," she proceeded, handing her the robe she had now taken off.

Poor Catau mechanically proceeded to do as she was ordered. Hurried in hger naturally slow conceptions, yet in the native goodness and simplicity of her heart, seeing something in the conduct of Victoria which she could not blame, (for who, more than the poor drudge Catau, had reason to hate the tyrannical and never-satisfied Signora?) she went on, but not so quickly as Victoria desired, to exchange with her gradually every necessary external part of her dress, to render the disguise complete.

Though the imperious, unaltered Victoria had acquired, by assumed gentleness, the love of the humble Catau, yet had she still the power of inspiring her with awe. Conscious of that, and knowing that her weak mind must, in the present case, be taken by surprise, and subdued by the force of language, she had preferred this mode to that of attempting sudden flight. Such an act would have roused her drowsy faculties; and, once impelled, it was possible she might have excelled her in swiftness of foot, which would have delayed, perhaps destroyed, her entire project. Besides, it was infinitely more politic to make Catau a friend, than, by apparent ingratitude and want of confidence, render her perhaps an enemy.

The transformation was at length completed; when Victoria, presenting Catau with the promised ring, slightly pressed her hand, and said — "My good, my honest Catau, if you possibly can, return to the house unseen, and enter the chamber we have usually occupied — secure the door. Should the Signora see nothing of us for the night, she will conclude, that, supperless, we have retired to bed, and will not have the foolish goodnature to disturb us, perfectly satisfied to have saved a meal. We are never in the habits of seeing her late in the day. I shall then be safe from the reach of tyranny, at least, I hope so; and, should we ever meet again, you will have no cause to repent the part you have acted. — Adieu, my kind girl, for time flies — adieu; return homewards, and do not attempt to follow me."

"Oh, Signora! Signora!" sobbed Catau, while the tears streamed copiously over cheeks resembling the full-blown damask rose.

"If you *really* love me, Catau," said the calm Victoria, who felt not a shadow of regret at leaving her faithful companion, "if you really love me, detain me no longer, but turn at once, and let me behold you on your return."

Catau, with a violent burst of tears and sobs, seized the hand of Victoria, and impressed on it a kiss forcible in proportion to the affection it was meant to convey. She then turned hastily away; and, without power to speak a word, proceeded towards the house with a speed almost sufficient to satisfy the impatience of Victoria.

She remained, however, upon the spot, thinking every moment an age till the poor girl was out of sight, who, unconsciously however, turned frequently round to obtain a last look of her she so much regretted to leave. At these periods, Victoria, though with a feeling of vexation and anger, would hastily wave her hand, as if to say — "I see thee, but pr'ythee go on." At length, some trees intervening, excluded entirely from her view the object she desired to lose sight of: then, hastily turning from the spot, she bent her steps forward, fondly congratulating herself, that every step she took brought her nearer and nearer to Venice.

The sun had set about an hour. Victoria, who had walked, or rather ran, with the utmost celerity, from the moment that she beheld Catau no longer, had hoped in a short time to have penetrated the wood; she, however, found herself mistaken, for the wood was of extensive dimensions; and, ignorant of its windings, she had not taken the shortest way to emerge from it. Though she continued her speed with unabated eagerness, night, to her confusion, began to draw in, and still she was wandering in its mazes. As it grew darker, the necessity of abstaining from her journey became evident. "And whither can I seek for shelter to night?" she mentally ejaculated, casting her eyes around. A small white shed, embosomed at a distance among some trees, caught her view: she felt an emotion of gladness, and was hastening towards it; but, suddenly recollecting, that when her flight should be discovered, it was not improbable but the very road she had taken might be searched, and that, in such case, this shed being liable to the observations of others as well as herself, might undergo some scrutiny, she determined instantly to avoid, as much as possible, the habitations of man, and to pursue the path that appeared the most unfrequented. Sooner than incur the smallest risk of being traced, the firm-minded Victoria decided on passing the night in common with the race of animal nature, beneath no other canopy than the star-sprinkled heavens.

In pursuance of this resolve, she turned from the path that led, as she now perceived, to various scattered seclusions of humble life; and, beneath the umbrageous shade of a self-formed bower, composed of jessamine and the luxurious vine, o'erhanging and intertwining from a wild hedge on one side of the forest, she cast herself for repose.

"Here," thought she, "why may I not enjoy a few hours of more refreshing rest than hitherto I have obtained on more luxuriant beds? I am safe too in doing so; for the Signora will not even hear of my escape till noon to-morrow."

Thus reflecting, sleep stole gradually over her senses. Fatigued by the unusual exertions of the day, for some hours she enjoyed undisturbed repose; nor, till the sun-beams playing through the tender branches upon her closed eyelids, and the carol of the birds, exhilirated by the divine rays of the morning, burst melodiously forth, did she awaken.

She no sooner opened her eyes, than, starting upon her feet, she again commenced her journey with the utmost speed. A few Naples biscuits, which she had the day before thought of securing, served her for breakfast, and she ate them as she proceeded. Her chief desire was now to leave behind her the wood; for this she increased her speed, and, after two hours walking, she found herself in a kind of path that she hoped would give her some unerring clue to proceed by. Eager with this idea, she swiftly measured its winding way: it terminated, at length, in a lonely canal, bordered on each side by poplars and acacias; and Victoria beholding this, cast herself almost hopeless close to its edge.

"Oh!" she cried, "how deeply must I have wandered! — on this melancholy canal no gondola, most likely, ever passes! To retrace my steps would be certain destruction to my hopes — here, then, may I as well remain and die!"

She had thrown herself upon her face, and despondently leaned her forehead upon her clasped hands. The soft gale sighed among the trees — no human being seemed nigh to interrupt the solitude. The melody of the birds among the lofty poplars and the spreading acacias, alone broke the heavenly silence of the scene; and Victoria, indifferent to these wild beauties, so hostile to her wishes, remained prostrate and in despair.

At length, a low distant sound struck upon her ear: she started — "Did it not resemble the remote noise of oars, dipping, at measured intervals, in the canal? — No, no! it was but the breeze agitating the leaves of the trees." And again she reclined her head.

Presently the sound returned, but with increased effect: it was accompanied — most joyous conviction! — by a rough voice, singing a song common among the gondolieri. In an instant, Victoria was upon her feet: she bent eagerly over the canal, and descried a gondola most leisurely approaching, and containing only a single rower, who was coasting coolly along the edge of the lake.

"Oh!" thought Victoria, "on that careless being depends *my* fate! — How slowly he approaches, while I burn with impatience!"

Without increasing an *iota* in speed, by degrees the gondola came near. Victoria eagerly hailed it —

"Whither go you, friend?" she asked.

"To Venice."

Victoria's heart leaped —

"Wilt thou permit me," she asked, "to enter thy gondola?"

"Canst thou pay, my pretty one?" asked the gondolier in turn.

Victoria was silent: all she had possessed, her ring, she had given to Catau. The gondolier was silent likewise, and her hopes began again to fade.

At length, she cast her eyes upon the countenance of the gondolier: though coarse and brawny, she perceived that he was a young man. "Alas!" she said, "I *have* no money, friend; but I have a lover in Venice, and if thou wilt convey me thither, the blessed Virgin will ever send thee luck."

The gondolier in turn, cast his eyes upon Victoria: he beheld, beneath her peasant's hat, that she was beautiful. He conceived her, from her garb, to be a peasant in reality, and readily believed that she had no money. The gondolier himself had a mistress that he loved; but, on account of his poverty, her parents refused the match, and he saw her by stealth alone. He conceived a fellow-feeling then for Victoria; and, towing his gondola close to the edge of the lake, he stretched forth his hand to her, which she joyfully seized, and vaulted into the gondola.

Who can describe the sensations of Victoria? She could not speak — a thousand gay anticipations revelled in her mind, and their enjoyment was too sweet to be unnecessarily interrupted. The gondolier, however, thinking he had at least a right to her conversation for his kindness, did not long permit her to indulge —

"But how, my pretty one, "he began, could you ever think of meeting a gondola where I found you perched? It is not once in a century that any of us pass thereabouts, except indeed at an odd time or so. Why, if it had not been a cavalier that I took up this blessed morning, before the heats began, to carry him to a pretty villa that he has close almost to the borders of the canal — and, between you and I, I carried a pretty Signora along with him — his reason, no doubt, for setting off at such an hour, so private you know — Well, if it had not been for that, I say, which is no business either of mine or yours, (I was well enough paid) — the devil a gondola you might have caught that way these six days. So you see, my pretty rogue, how lucky you are — and to get such luck for nothing too!"

Victoria, who had long ceased to attend to the long-winded dissertation of the gondolier, catching only his last words, most cordially assented to them, at the same time expressing her gratitude for his goodnature.

To this the gondolier made no other reply than a broad significant grin, winking at the same time one eye, alluding, as Victoria supposed, to the lover she had told him of; and then began again with the song he had been singing before she hailed him.

Soon, to her infinite joy, Victoria beheld the towers and domes of stately Venice rising proudly from the Adriatic, encircled round by its green arms. It was the time of the Carnival: multitudes of gay and splendid gondolas appeared upon the lake, as they drew near; they were now upon the point of landing at St. Mark's. Victoria turned to thank the gondolier for his kindness — he nodded and smiled, and helped her out of the gondola, whispering in her ear, that he should never at any time object to do so pretty a girl a service.

Once more at liberty, and at her own disposal, secure too in her disguise, Victoria, without trepidation, mixed with the gay crowd of St. Mark's Place, in the faint hope, perhaps, of discovering among them one to whom her heart involuntarily pointed. Fatigued, at length, by exertion and want of food, for she had tasted nothing but a few biscuits since the preceding evening, and evening again was now far advanced, she quitted St. Mark's Place, to seek a spot less thronged and confused. As she proceeded, a sudden faintness, the consequence of exhaustion, overcame her so far, that, to prevent falling in the street, she hastened beneath a lofty portico, and seated herself upon one of its steps. Leaning her swimming head upon her hand, she remained for some moments unable to move; her heart palpitated, and she began to fear that mind might not *always* prove omnipotent over matter. By degrees, however, the faintness went off: she raised her head. The gay appearance of the streets and the canals, every window illuminated, and the splendid apparel of the masks, ill and overpowered as she felt, yielded her a sensation of the highest delight: she could remember only that she had escaped from a dreary solitude and the most abominable tyranny, and every feeling of sickness vanished at the idea.

As still she continued sitting, (her symmetrical figure habited in her homely garb, and those strong-marked features shaded by a large and simple hat) amid the gay and hurrying crowd, that still continued to pass, a group of masqueraders caught her attention. Among them was one of a tall and noble figure, far surmounting the rest: he wore a domino of blue silk wrapped carelessly round him, so that his left shoulder with part of his vest was displayed, which sparkled with jewels; on his head he wore a Spanish hat of black velvet, surmounted by a lofty plume of snow-white feathers, confined in it by a diamond loop.

Upon this attractive figure her eyes fixed as he past with a sort of confused recollection of having before seen it. The hasty glympse she had caught, however, was insufficient to ascertain where, and involuntarily she started up to have a better view of his person: as she did so, he turned round. True, he was masked; but conviction flashed upon her senses; — sudden and irresistible was the impulse — she flew towards him, and laying her hand upon his arm, exclaimed — "Berenza!"

"Yes! — oh, yes!" in a low but eager voice answered the mask, pressing her hand upon his arm; "mark me, but retire."

Victoria drew back — the mask rejoined the group he had a moment separated from, and was soon lost in the crowd.

Bitter was the vexation and disappointment of Victoria; — by happy accident was thus discovered, and in the same moment lost, him on whom her chief hopes depended! But still the splendid illusion of the scene remained — the mind of Victoria was supremely elastic, and she consoled herself with the reflection that she was still in Venice, and at liberty. She continued mechanically moving along, till at length she found herself in a more retired part of the city, where resided some of the inferior inhabitants. From this place she hastened; but every where the brilliancy of the scene began now to fade; the night was considerably advanced; the gay crowd, visibly diminishing, had entered their houses to carouse; and the splendid light decreasing, assumed the appearance of a twilight gilded by the last rays of the setting sun.

The adventurous Victoria now began to perceive the possibility there existed of passing another night without shelter: the reflection was unwelcome to her feelings; but she preferred it to the remotest risk of discovery, by seeking out any of her former acquaintances, or dependants. Again, therefore, seating herself beneath a portico, she leaned her head upon her hand, and gave way to reflections of a gloomy tendency. She was hungry and fatigued; and these circumstances added to the depression of her spirits. Suddenly a voice sounded in her ear — "Follow me." She raised her head, but perceived no one; again therefore she covered her eyes with her hand, and endeavoured to resume her train of thought.

"Rise," said the same voice again. She started, and instinctively arose. The portico at which she had seated herself was the first in the street. A tall figure darted as it were from behind her: it appeared enveloped in a dark cloak; and retreating swiftly to such a distance as to render its actual presence dubious, beckoned in an inclining attitude to Victoria. Glad even of so mysterious, perhaps dangerous, a mandate, she hastened to obey as fast as her enfeebled limbs would allow. The stranger perceiving that she did so, again retreated; but still continuing to invite, Victoria still pursued: at length, in a deserted part, he stopped. Victoria approached: he encircled her waist; and, drawing aside his cloak, she discovered the spangled habit, and the figure of Berenza!

"Hush!" he hastily exclaimed, perceiving she was about to express her joy; then again withdrawing himself, he proceeded towards a small door in the street, at which he gave three distinct knocks. It opened cautiously: he put forth his hand, and beckoned Victoria; she drew near; he seized her arm, and conducting her into the house, the door closed. They had not walked many paces through a dark narrow entry, before Berenza stopped; and, taking a handkerchief from his pocket, bound it lightly over the eyes of Victoria, saying to her, in a low voice — "Fear not; this shall not be for long." Victoria only smiled, and did not answer.

At length they ascended some stairs, and appeared to enter an apartment. The Conte pressed the hand of Victoria, and bade her take the bandage from her eyes: she did so, and instantly uttered an exclamation of pleasure and surprise; for a sumptuous and brilliantly illuminated chamber struck upon her dazzled sight: the walls were covered with large resplendent mirrors, that variously reflected her simply attired but graceful figure.

Berenza appeared for a moment to enjoy her surprise; then, fervently pressing her in his arms, he said —

"Here my lovely and beloved Victoria will be sole mistress; she will no more fly from the man who more than life adores her."

"Fly!" repeated Victoria — "I never fled from thee, Berenza!"

"Didst thou not, my love? Much then requires explanation, but not at this juncture. You look pallid and fatigued; rest here awhile, till some slight refreshment is procured."

So saying, he gently seated Victoria upon a superb sopha, and for a few moments left her to herself.

The most pleasing ideas now took possession of her mind, as in a recumbent posture she awaited the return of Berenza. Her fatigues, her difficulties, even her imprisonment, all was forgotten in her present prospect of long desired happiness.

"Now, then, cruel and ungenerous mother," she exclaimed, "thou canst no longer deprive me of a happiness similar to that which thou so selfishly enjoyest! — a happiness which, but for *thee*, my awakened fancy had never conceived, nor my soul coveted. Ah! mother, mother! thou didst deceive and betray me; but I shall still live to thank thee for teaching me the path to love and joy."

As she concluded this wild expression of her misguided sentiments, Berenza entered: he had heard what she had uttered; and, pleased as he undoubtedly was that chance had thrown in his way the girl he had admired and loved, yet his delicate and refined mind experienced a sensation of regret at the avowed freedom of her principles. Yet still more severe were his reflections against the *authors* of this mischief, the *parent*, whose example and conduct had corrupted the sentiments of her *daughter*, and the *wretch*, whose seductions had corrupted the *parent*. But mentally he promised himself to restrain and correct the improper bias of Victoria's character; for Berenza, though a refined voluptuary, possessed a noble, virtuous, and philosophic soul.

He seated himself by the side of Victoria, and gently took her hand. It was dry and feverish. "You have undergone considerable exertion this day," he said, gazing on her countenance, "have you not, my sweet Victoria?"

Victoria smiled, and great was the dismay of Berenza, when he learned that for upwards of twenty-four hours she had not tasted food. He instantly forbade her to utter another word till nature was recruited, and the moment a collation he had ordered made its appearance, he tenderly pressed her to eat; nor till he thought her sufficiently refreshed, would he reply to the most pressing of her eager interrogatories respecting the real cause of his precipitate departure from Monte Bello.

At length, when he explained to her this circumstance, and his conviction at the time of having acted expressly consonant to her own wishes, nothing could exceed the rage she evinced at the deception which had been practiced; and unwilling as was Berenza to countenance or encourage the undue violence of her disposition, he could scarcely avoid participating in the expression of her sentiments. "The gross unworthiness of the parental duplicity had surprised and disgusted him; and if for a moment before be had been disposed to lament the effect of her daughter's flight upon the mind of Laurina, he *now* felt that compassionating sentiment give way to one of pleasure that Victoria had escaped, and escaped to him. It appeared too, in the course of his explanation to Victoria, that surprised at not receiving from her the smallest intelligence for a length of time, though according to the intimation in the note, he was taught to expect he might shortly hear from her, he had, impatient at the delay, presented himself uncalled at Monte Bello; there had he learned, that by her own desire his fair mistress had taken her departure from thence, and had expressly required that he should be kept in ignorance of her retreat; for that reflection having convinced her of the impropriety of encouraging his attentions, she had determined to endeavour at least to overcome it, and therefore conceived that absence was the most likely, nay the only mode of forwarding so desirable a point. "I confess," pursued Conte Berenza, "from the knowledge I possessed of your character, I thought such sudden variation of sentiment almost incompatible with it; but having no alternative, for I felt I had no right to request an explanation from your mother or the Count, (you, according to the law of things appertaining rather to them than me,) and urged by the cool looks I received, I took my departure, secretly hoping that time would bring me some satisfactory elucidation of a circumstance that I could not help considering as somewhat mysterious."

Ere their mutual explanations had ceased, the night was far advanced. The history of Victoria's sufferings at the Signora de Modena's; the mode of her escape; her difficulties, her precautions to avoid being traced — all, all must be detailed and expatiated on ere she would think of retiring. Berenza at length ventured to recur to the necessity there was for her taking some rest. Unwillingly, at his delicate solicitation, she agreed to do so, when summoning some female attendants, he ordered them to shew her to the chamber which had been hastily prepared for her.

No sooner had Victoria reached her apartment than she requested her attendants to withdraw, for she was desirous of indulging alone the influx of her ideas; delight and pleasure had such complete possession of her, that scarce could her trembling hands perform the office of disrobing herself. Long too after she had entered her elegant bed (which rose in the form of a dome, bordered with deep gold fringe) did her buoyant spirits drive sleep from her pillow. At length, however, her ardent imagination became overpowered; she fell asleep, and brilliant fantasies gamboled before her in the dreams of the night.

Berenza too retired to repose, but his reasoning mind, though in such recent attainment of a desired good, was placid and unruffled; the images which occupied it were devoid of the romantic trappings of fancy; he beheld Victoria such as she really was, unembellished, unornamented; his keen eye that perceived her beauties, discerned likewise her defects. He appreciated her character; he beheld at once her pride, her stubbornness, her violence, her *fierté*. "Can I," asked himself, "be *rationally* happy, with a being imperfect as she now is? No; unless I can modify the strong features of her character into the *nobler* virtues, I feel that all her other attractions will be insufficient to fill up my craving heart." — Pursuing these reflections, Berenza fell asleep. Victoria beneath his roof, *voluntarily* in his power, he had leisure to *repose* and *amplify* on those errors, which, while she seemed *unattainable*, struck him in a point of view infinitely less momentous. *Such* is the nature of man!

CHAPTER IX

The sun had risen far above the horizon when Victoria awakened: she hastily arose, and perceived that the peasant's garb had been exchanged for habiliments more resembling those she had till now been accustomed to wear. This she with justice attributed to the delicate attention of Berenza. Dressing herself, she summoned attendance, and was informed, that Il Conte Berenza had been long waiting breakfast for her, and desired them to conduct her to the apartment where he was. She found him sitting upon a sopha, with breakfast things before him. On her entrance he rose, and conducted her to sit beside him. His demeanor towards her was rather that of a sincere and a tender friend, than of an ardent lover; for the mind of Berenza, ever aiming at perfection, felt, that ere he could avow himself the latter, he must himself new model the object.

During breakfast he conversed upon indifferent subjects; but more sedulously and more anxious than ever did he scrutinise her, as though in her air and in her eyes he would read every movement of her soul. Yet true it was that Berenza was a voluptuary, but a philosophical, delicate, and refined voluptuary; — it was not the perfection of *body* only that he required, but the perfection also of *mind*.

Victoria perceived that embarrassment clouded the manners of the Conte. She sought by every means to draw him from his apparent abstraction, and gaily taking his hand, she said —

"Berenza, why are you not chearful? You were wont to tell me, that I should constitute your happiness, if once I became yours — now then, that fortune has united us, you appear *less* happy than when you despaired of gaining me; nay, indeed, dear Berenza, almost indifferent to her you so professed to love."

Berenza rose during the speech of Victoria. A new idea had taken possession of his mind — it was the tormenting, the useless reflection, that perhaps he was not particularly distinguished by the confidence of Victoria; that perhaps she had flown to him merely as a refuge from discomfort and oppression, and that had *another* addressed her, she would equally have flown to him. This suggestion struck a pang to the heart of the refining philosopher; suppressing his emotion, however, and taking the hand of Victoria, he only said —

"You have often, my love, known me abstracted and thoughtful, without any particular reason occurring at the moment — heed me not, and I shall speedily be myself again."

"Then I will withdraw to my chamber, my Lord," said Victoria, secretly piqued and disgusted that her presence should not be a talisman against *every* species of uneasiness.

"Do so, my love. Consider yourself here as mistress, and all I have at your disposal. Make such arrangements as you may think fit, without hesitation. Employ yourself a few hours apart from me — we will meet at dinner, and in the evening repair to the Laguna, where my Victoria will be the fairest.

Victoria withdrew, but her air was indignant; and Berenza observing it, sighed as he gazed after her, mentally exclaiming, "Victoria, how imperfect thou art — fool that I was," he continued, I never possessed either the heart or the mind of this girl — *circumstances* only have impelled her towards me — Oh! could I but penetrate her thoughts; could I but discover her actual *feelings*, my mind would be at rest; were I only convinced of her love, I could easily new model her character, because the precepts and the wishes of those we love sink deep into the heart. But no matter; I will be the friend, the brother, the protector of the girl who has thrown herself into my arms. I will love her too, but never, no never will I meanly take advantage of a fortuitous circumstance. I will be *convinced* of her affection, — her absolute, her exclusive affection; and till I am thoroughly convinced, I will be her *friend*, and not her lover.

Such was the determination of the reasoning philosopher, whose delicate and fastidious mind made its own food, and took for ever a pleasure in repining upon itself.

At dinner they again met, and when the heat of the day was succeeded by the cooling breezes of evening, Berenza led his fair charge to St. Mark's Place, along which multitudes of gay Venetians were flocking to get into their gondolas. The Conte assisted Victoria into his, which was splendid and gaily accoutred. Happy was the vain Victoria to find herself thus in the midst of the gay world. The Laguna was covered with an innumerable quantity of gondolas, soft music sounded from every side, and sweet female voices sometimes accompanied the strains. The scene elevated her spirits: she blest the moment when she had escaped from the tyranny of a discontented bigot. She cast her eyes around, and she perceived that she had excited that attention and admiration she so much loved to obtain. She even fancied that the Venetian belles viewed her with an air of envy — the idea was doubly pleasing, and her animation increased. But she did not for a moment suppose that this envy was excited on account of the companion who sat beside her. Berenza was indeed accounted the most accomplished cavalier in Venice — the very phoenix of grace and elegance. His opinions, his taste, his approbation formed the standard of fashion; — for, though no one knew or appreciated the dignity and delicacy of his mind, yet was he considered the most graceful and fascinating of men. His society was universally courted, even by the women, though they well knew his refined and superior judgment. His was not the heart of a sensualist, if indeed a sensualist hath a heart; he could not gaze enraptured on the accurate formation of a limb, waste his hours in contemplating incessantly a beautiful form, or resign his independence, while admiring some harmonious combination of feature or complexion. Even his most irrational hours were never spent at the feet of a simpering coquet. No, it was necessary that Berenza's beauties should be polished, that they should possess the talisman of mind. Well was this general trait in his character understood, yet his society and his notice were eagerly courted by females; — since to attach him would indeed have been triumph, who then could forbear the attempt?

Victoria excited therefore universal envy in one sex, and she likewise excited universal admiration in the other. The notice she attracted filled her vain ambitious heart with exultation, and it was with infinite regret she left the gay covered lake, to return to the Pallazzo of her lover.

Flattered by the attention she had excited, the philosophic Berenza viewed her involuntarily with a feeling of encreased approbation; for true it is man is too apt to be guided in his estimate of things by the degree of estimation they may obtain from others, and to be influenced in his opinion by the standard (often depraved) of the public taste.

Supper being prepared for them, the Conte began wholly to relax from the restraint he had imposed upon his manner; he seated himself with a smiling air by the delighted Victoria, who instantly availed herself of the gaiety and unreserve of his manner to ask an explanation of what had more than once obtruded itself upon her mind. Looking somewhat archly in his countenance, she said —

"Tell me, Berenza, if the question be not improper, why with so much caution and mystery you first acknowledged your recognition of me, and conducted me hither, yet now carelessly exhibit yourself with me in public?"

"Oh woman, curious woman!" said the Conte, laughing; — "but I will tell thee, Victoria."

"Frederic Alvarez, a friend of mine, and a Spanish nobleman of high rank, had a mistress called Megalena Strozzi; by birth a Florentine. Of this mistress he was passionately fond, and often pressed me to be introduced to her, but having many other engagements, I always declined.

"At length one day he succeeded in securing me, and I was reluctantly dragged into the presence of his syren. Mark the untoward result. On the honour of a Venetian, I solemnly assure you, I paid her no extraordinary attention, nor any whatever of a nature that could be considered dishonourable towards my friend; yet she exerted her utmost artifice, she used every blandishment to allure me. Megalena was beautiful; she was beside elegant and accomplished. I am not, as I think, either a philosopher, or a stoic, but a man refining on my own sensations. I yielded, I own, to the witcheries of Megalena, and I felt no compunctious visitings from a consciousness of treacherous conduct toward my friend — I had not attempted to seduce his mistress; it was she, on the contrary, who had so powerfully addressed my feelings and *my* senses, that was in the fullest acceptation of the term the seductress. At length, however, the jealous Alvarez discovered the infidelity of her to whom he was devoted heart and soul; he sought me out, foaming with rage and outraged love, and gave me my choice to meet him in honourable combat, or be passively run through the body. Breathing death and vengeance, it was vain to reason with him. I therefore preferred the former offer, and we met. Fury rendered his hand unsteady, and when I succeeded in drawing a little blood from his arm, some of our mutual friends who were privy to the affair, endeavoured to explain to Alvarez the folly of fighting for an abandoned wanton. He heard them with a gloomy air, but appeared convinced by their arguments. I offered him my hand, but he refused it with rage, and soon after left Venice. Since that period I have occasionally visited Megalena, but never could I prevail upon myself to consider her as a mistress, from the very obvious and unerring reflection, that a female who could abandon a sincere and doting lover for *me*, would as readily abandon *me* for any other who might attract her wandering eye. Still, however, the jealous, the alternate fits of love and resentment which she thought proper to exhibit whenever I presented myself before her, have long been a source of extreme unpleasantness to me. She has frequently sworn, with a frantic air, that though she bears with my insulting indifference towards her, that should she ever have reason to attribute my coldness to regard for another, my death alone would satiate her vengeance. Thus, though I know the irregularity of her life, and that her undisciplined passions hurry her into the most abject excesses, I do not wish, insolent and unjustifiable as such conduct would be, to induce her phrensied attacks against my life, or peace. I therefore, in my research after you, used all possible precaution; nor did I, though you saw me not, even for once lose sight of you. My reason for placing a fillet[1] over your eyes was merely to enjoy your astonishment when it should be removed, for I introduced you by a private way into my house. "I believe, fair Victoria," pursued the Conte, smiling, and taking her hand, "I have now explained all that may have appeared mysterious to you."

"You have, my Lord," answered Victoria; "but you *still* — still visit Megalena then?" she pursued, while her jealous eyes wandered.

"I have, as I said," replied the Conte, smiling, "been accustomed to visit her."

"And — and you *still* intend, my lord Berenza — "

"My *future* intentions," replied Berenza, seriously, "will be considerably influenced by *you*."

"But, my lord," said the artful Victoria, with an air of innocence, unwilling to proceed too far, "you love me too well, I hope, to think of another while *I* am with you?"

"Sweet Victoria," exclaimed Berenza, "that is spoken like yourself. The Signora Megalena must now be tranquil — she *must*, for she will see us together, and it will be beyond her power to separate us. Yesterday I had visited at her house; she knew the colour of my habit for the Carnival; her eyes, no doubt, followed me every where; and had she perceived my attention attracted to you, she would either have had you entrapped,

---

1. fillet: a ribbon or band

and conveyed out of my reach, of have followed me even into my apartment like a vengeful fury; therefore it was I conveyed you into the Pallazo by a secret way, wholly unknown even to her. But let us dismiss this unworthy subject. Once for all, Victoria, be assured it is not in the power of a Megalena to attract me from thee. I have known her, 'tis true: she has been the companion of my looser hours; but she was never the mistress, the beloved acknowledged *friend* of Berenza. No, it is not enough for me that *my* mistress should be *admired* by men; they must *envy* me in their hearts the possession of her. She whom Berenza can love must tower above her sex; she must have nothing of the tittering coquet, the fastidious prude, or the affected idiot: she must abound in the graces of *mind* as well as of *body*; for I prize not the woman who can yield only to my arms a lovely insipid *form*, which the veriest boor in nature can enjoy in as much perfection as myself. *My* mistress, too, must be *mine* exclusively, heart and soul: others may gaze and sigh for her, but must not dare approach. It is she too, who, while her beauty *attracts*, must have dignity sufficient to repel them. If she forfeit for a moment her *self-possession*, I cast her for ever from my bosom. But if," he added, with increasing energy, "it be within the verge of possibility that she forfeit her honour, then — oh! then, her blood alone can wash out her offence! — Victoria!" grasping her hand, "dost thou mark me? — hast *thou* courage, hast thou firmness, to become the friend, the mistress of Berenza?"

Victoria smiled with ineffable dignity: she laid her hand upon the arm of Berenza, and said —

"Yes, I have courage to become every thing to you. Why these doubts, these stipulations, Berenza?" she pursued with a serious air.

"But thou must *love* me, Victoria, *me* alone," said Berenza, fixing his eyes upon her countenance.

"And do I not, my lord, love *you* alone?" she said.

"Not certainly — not *enough*," he replied. "Thou art a stranger to the turnings and windings of thine *own* heart," mentally added he; then rising hastily, he took the hand of Victoria — "Retire," he said, in a gentle voice, "retire to repose, and to-morrow we shall meet again."

He led her to the door, and saluted her hand. How few in character resemble Berenza! — yet in such perfection are some minds regulated, ultimately enhancing by their forbearance the pleasures they obtain.

CHAPTER X

Some time passed on thus, and still Berenza, languishing for positive *conviction* of Victoria's love for him, continued to treat her as a beloved and innocent sister, rather than as a destined mistress; for though his taste in female beauty led him to view that of Victoria with the eye of an enraptured amateur, still was he too scrupulously refined to accept the privilege fortune had thrown in his way, or anticipate, by premature encroachment, the smallest of the pleasures he promised himself for the future, when she should *prove* to him (delightful idea!) that her heart was intrinsically his. Charmed as he was with the boldness of her natural character, charmed as he was with the graces of her face and figure; yet was Berenza a man of too *proud* a mind to be swayed to a conduct that his peculiar delicacy contemned. In vain would he sometimes seek for a trait of innocent tenderness in the countenance of Victoria; something that should *convince* him he was beloved. No, her's was not the countenance of a Madona — it was not of angelic mould; yet, though there was a fierceness in it, it was not certainly a repelling, but a beautiful fierceness — dark, noble, strongly expressive, every lineament bespoke the mind which animated it. True, no mild, no gentle, no endearing virtues, were depicted there; but while you gazed upon her, you observed not the want of any charm. Her smile was fascination itself; and in her large dark eyes, which sparkled with incomparable radiance, you read the traces of a strong and resolute mind, capable of attempting any thing undismayed by consequences; and well and truly did they speak. Her figure, though above the middle height, was symmetry itself; she was as the tall and graceful antelope; her air was dignified and commanding, yet free from stiffness; she moved along with head erect, and with step firm and majestic; nor was her carriage ever degraded by levity or affectation. Living under his roof, almost perpetually in his company, she became daily a more dangerous object to the peace and to the forbearance of Berenza; yet even in those times, when his ideas and actions were least subject to the controul of his reason, it was but for an instant to admit the tormenting reflection, that perhaps she felt not for him a genuine and ardent affection, for a sudden gloom to take possession of him, and overspread his countenance.

The singularity of his conduct surprised Victoria: she endeavoured to investigate the cause, and to trace, if possible, the workings of his mind. To this end she watched, with scrutinizing eye, every movement, every look; she listened to and weighed every word he spoke; then, combining the whole, discovered ere long the secret which pressed upon his feelings.

"What, then," would she exclaim, confiding her reflections to her pillow, "Berenza fears that I love him not? This idea, then, is the grand source of his constrained mysterious conduct towards me." Then reverting to herself, she examined the state of her heart respecting him.

"And do I *not* then love Berenza?" she said: — "I know not; nor what may be the precise nature of love; but this I know, that I prefer him to all men; that I think him elegant and accomplished; and that, if death snatched him from me, I should grieve. True, my sensations towards him have nothing ardent in them, nor do I feel that oppression of soul, that doubt, that uneasiness, respecting his attachment for *me*, that he seems to entertain of mine. Yes, I feel it is requisite to my future prospects, to those plans and views, yet vague and indefinite, which are floating in my brain, that he should not entertain any, not the smallest doubts of my regard for him. I must endeavour, then, to suit my conduct to the fastidious delicacy of his ideas."

So reasoned, from combined inferences, the subtle Victoria. True indeed it was, she did not *love* the scrupulous, the refined Berenza: she was incapable of loving such a man; nay, she was by nature unfitted to admit so soft, so pure a sentiment as *real* love. Victoria's heart was a stranger to every gentle, noble, or superior feeling. The ambitious, the selfish, the wild, and the turbulent were her's. Her's were the *stormy* passions of the soul, goading on to ruin and despair — Berenza's were mild, philosophic, though proudly tenacious. His were as the even stream, calm, yet deep — her's as the foaming cataract, rushing headlong from the rocky steep, and raging in the abyss below! She was not susceptible of a single sentiment, vibrating from a tender movement of the heart: she could not feel gratitude; she could not, therefore, feel affection. She could inflict pain without remorse, and she could bitterly revenge the slightest attempt to inflict it on herself. The wildest passions predominated in her bosom; to gratify them she possessed an unshrinking relentless soul, that would not startle at the darkest crime. Unhappy girl! whom Nature organised when offended with mankind, and whom education, that *might* have corrected, tended only to confirm in depravity.

Berenza, as before has been remarked, was the only man who had ever paid her particular attention, consequently it was natural that what feeling of preference she was capable of entertaining should be given to him. She voluntarily sought his protection, because she knew not whom else to solicit. She remained under his roof, for she knew not of another; and though any heart but her's would have been deeply and enthusiastically affected by the nobleness and delicacy of conduct he had, under all these circumstances, observed towards her, yet did she remain wholly unimpressed; nor was a single idea awakened by it that did not revert to self. She saw only that it would be necessary and politic to answer his sincere and honourable love at least with an *appearance* equally ardent and sincere. The peculiar cast of Berenza's disposition was in reality melancholy; sombre, and reflective, though in society seeming gay and careless; she then must become melancholy, retired, and abstracted. Berenza would hence be induced to scrutinize the cause. Artifice on her side, and natural self-love on his, would easily make him attribute it to the effects of a violent and concealed love: thus would an explanation be the result; and the reserve, the doubts, the hesitations of Berenza at an end.

Her plan arranged, she entered on it gradually: her eyes, no longer full of a wild and beautiful animation, were taught to languish, or to fix for hours with musing air upon the ground; her gait, no longer firm and elevated, became hesitating and despondent. She no longer engrossed the conversation; she became silent, apparently absent, and plunged in thought. It was now Berenza, who had to call *her* from a melancholy abstraction, to enquire if any hidden uneasiness preyed upon her mind. Victoria saw, exultingly saw, the gradual operation of her plan. New and rapturous ideas, scarcely admitted even to himself, began to occupy the soul of Berenza; but as yet he spoke not, he hoped not; — he was slow, because he was fearful to believe.

It was one night, after a day of well-acted gloom and oppression of spirits, that Victoria, having left the apartment occupied by the Conte, retired into the saloon, and throwing herself upon a sopha near one of the windows, enjoyed the delicious fresco of the evening. She had not been long in this situation, before Berenza, unable to bear her absence, determined to seek her in the saloon, and perceiving her reclined upon a sopha, imagined she slept. Closing gently the door, therefore, he softly approached her. In an instant, an idea had glanced across the mind of Victoria: she determined to avail herself of this circumstance, and of Berenza's mistake. Shutting her eyes, she affected in reality to be asleep: the Conte drew near, and gazing upon her for a few moments, he seated himself beside her.[1]

""Oh, Victoria!" in a low voice, he tenderly said, "why, why, my love, art thou unhappy? Oh, that I — that I might only hope I were the envied cause! — Ah, were it indeed so, Berenza would be too happy!"

He paused. Victoria, as if disturbed in her sleep, heaved a broken sigh, faintly giving utterance to the name of "Berenza."

Berenza scarcely ventured to breathe.

"Why wilt thou not love me Berenza?" she murmured.

Berenza's heart beat high; he drew his breath quick.

Victoria was sensible of his emotion — "One word more," thought she.

"Indeed — indeed, Berenza — I love *thee*!" she articulated, starting up, and stretching out her arms, as if under the impression of her dream, attempting to embrace him; when opening her eyes, and affecting surprise and shame at the sight of Berenza, she covered her face with her hands and turned aside.

The violent emotion of Berenza was such, that for some moments he

---

1 Victoria's calculated revelation of feigned desire for Berenza echoes Melliora's genuinely unintentional revelation of her desire for D'elmont during a dream in Eliza Haywood's scandalous novel, *Love in Excess* (1719-20).

was deprived of the power of speech. The blood rushed from his heart to his head; his senses became confused, when, seizing wildly in his arms the artful Victoria, he exclaimed, in hurried accents — "Thou art mine! — Yes, I now *know* that thou art mine."

Proud of her achievement, it was Victoria's care that her lover should not recover from his delusion: well did she support the character she had assumed; and the tender refined Berenza became *convinced*, that he possessed the first pure and genuine affections of an innocent and lovely girl!

CHAPTER XI

Berenza became daily more attached to Victoria: his scrupulous doubts, his reserves, wholly vanished, and fondly he flattered himself, that he was as much the possessor of her dearest affections, as she was the mistress over his. Still, though his love for her was carried in some respects to a romantic height, his pride forbade him to marry her. There was a certain stigma in his idea attached to her, through the misconduct of her mother, which it was impossible for his delicate mind to overlook. Of this sentiment, however, the haughty Victoria was unconscious, and she simply imagined that her present union with the Conte was chosen by him expressly for the purpose of convincing her, that his devotion towards her needed not the aid of artificial ties to rivet it. Under this impression, her vain spirit was flattered; and little did she ever suppose, that while the proud Venetian deemed her *worthy* of becoming his *mistress*, he conceived her unfit for the high distinction of becoming his *wife*.

It was one beautiful evening, that, accompanied by the admired Victoria, Berenza, in his splendid gondola, mixed with the gay concourse upon the Laguna. Every one appeared exhilarated; and, Victoria, gazing around, felt in the moment that she excited the admiration so dear to her soul, that she required nothing more in the power of man to bestow.

While her eyes still wandered, exacting attention from all, a gondola passed close by that of Berenza's: it contained only one female besides the gondolieri, who, in the moment of rapidly passing, fixed her eyes upon Victoria with a rage and malignity so exquisitely bitter, that it was impossible, momentary as was the glance, that its expression could be mistaken. For an instant Victoria was awakened from her dream of vanity: she looked at Berenza; but perceiving, from the unaltered expression of his countenance, that he had not observed the circumstance, she thought it too insignificant to advert to, and other objects soon made her forget it altogether.

At length they returned home, and the evening was concluded with a convivial party and a dance, to which many were invited that had not been present during the early part of the evening.

At a late hour the company separated, and Victoria and the Conte retired to repose. Victoria, however, felt no inclination to sleep: the festive scenes of the evening passed in mirthful review before her, the music still sounded in her ears, and the dancers still figured in her sight. She skimmed over in her mind the adulation, the elegant and well-turned compliments she had received, and in idea again she enjoyed and smiled at them. Then she reverted to her evening's amusement on the Laguna; and, on reverting to that, she suddenly remembered the look she had received from the female who had passed so swifly by. She was on the point of mentioning to the Conte this circumstance; but perceiving, that, overcome by wine and the fatigue of the evening, he slept, she would not awaken him, and pursued the diversified current of her ideas. Still, however, she could not lose the remembrance of this malignant glance, and was embarrassing herself in vain conjectures as to the cause which should induce any one to view her with particular rancour, when a gentle rustling at the further end of the chamber caught her attention: this interrupted her thoughts, and called them to external objects. The bed on which she lay was surmounted by a superb canopy, the curtains were drawn on each side, but remained opened at the foot. The rustling increased; she fixed her eyes on the opposite side of the room, where a large window jutted out and opened into a balcony on the outside: the window itself was concealed by a thick curtain; by degrees this curtain was moved a little on one side; half the figure of a man became visible, and presently the whole. The chamber was faintly enlightened by a lamp; and she observed, as softly, though with long strides, the figure approached, that his face was concealed by a mask: at length he reached the side of the bed at which the Conte slept, and gently divided the curtains.

Victoria now firmly believed some evil was intended, yet feared to awaken Berenza, lest his surprise and alarm, by depriving him of requisite presence of mind, should hasten any attempt against him, which she hoped herself, by being awake and remaining tranquil, to circumvent.

The intruder now stood at the side of the bed, and paused; then stooping down, he examined earnestly the face of the Conte: the countenance of Victoria he could not see, for her arm was thrown over her head in such a manner that her hand concealed her eyes, though she could observe all that passed, and the lower part of her face was shaded by the covering. The stranger, however, appeared to imagine that she slept; for, drawing a dagger from his bosom, he waved it to and fro near the closed eyes of the unconscious Berenza; then gently uncovering his bosom, approached the point of the dagger towards it. His hand appeared to tremble; he stifled a sigh, and retreated a few steps; then again he drew near: with his left hand he held back the curtain, and raising his right, as if with sudden resolution, he prepared to strike! Just as the dagger was descending, the undaunted and watchful Victoria caught his wrist: the force of the intended blow being thus broken, the assassin, who was in an inclining attitude, lost his equilibrium, and falling across the bed, the point of the dagger entered the shoulder of Victoria. At this instant the Conte awakened: his first impulse was to seize the man, but he struggled violently, and Berenza being unable to obtain a firm hold, shackled as he was by the weight of his body, which lay across him, he contrived swiftly to disengage himself. As he did so, he could not, however, prevent his mask from falling off: he sought to recover it, and rush from the spot; but, ere he could atchieve his purpose, the eyes of the wounded and fainting Victoria were rivetted upon a countenance that memory immediately identified for her brother! — that brother who, on the desertion of his mother from her home, had fled the paternal roof, and now was recognised as an intended murderer.

"Monstrous assassin!" she feebly exclaimed; while Leonardo, with horror depicted in his countenance, fled across the apartment, and, gaining the window, appeared to precipitate himself from it.

Berenza, now released, started from the bed; but, as he was flying after the assassin, a faint groan from Victoria arrested him: he turned, and beheld the bed-clothes dyed in blood. The sight distracted him — "You are wounded, my life!" he franticly exclaimed.

"Only slightly, my lord," murmured Victoria; "but I do — I do not regret it!"

Berenza, in agony, vociferated for assistance: he dispatched the servants fifty different ways for medical aid; then taking Victoria in his arms, he examined the wound, while the big tears of love and anguish fell upon her bosom.

"Ah, do not weep, Berenza!" faintly ejaculated Victoria. "I would suffer ten thousand times more to prove my *love* to thee — nay, I rejoice to prove it!" And, in fact, Victoria *did* rejoice; for she felt that the wound obtained in defence of her lover's life (and of which her firm mind entertained no apprehensions) would bind him inseparably to her; — the triumph she experienced, then, when she beheld his violent anguish, more than repaid her for the pain she felt. She essayed to take his hand, and press it to her bosom; but all her firmness, all her contempt of pain, could not conquer the weakness of nature, and she fainted from loss of blood.

The Conte was half mad. The medical men arrived; they dressed the wound; they announced that it was not dangerous, and that repose and quiet would, in all probability, avert the appearance of fever. By degrees she was recovered from her temporary insensibility. The Conte seated himself by her bedside, and gazed in agony upon her. She turned her eyes upon him, the brilliancy of which had given place to a seducing languor, that penetrated Berenza's inmost soul, and in his mind he vowed that his whole life henceforth should be dedicated to her happiness. He now felt that she was dearer, far dearer to him, than he had ever imagined. On the noble and enthusiastic soul of Berenza the conduct of Victoria had wrought the most powerful effect — such cool intrepidity, such contempt of her own life in the defence of his — the patience, nay the pleasure with which she bore the unhappy consequences of her courage: — "What woman in existence," thought he, "would have done thus much for me?" These reflections swelled his heart with a love almost idolatrous, and his violent feeling sought relief in an irrepressible gush of tears.

Victoria determined carefully to conceal from her lover her conviction that the intended assassin was her brother. A certain indefinable feeling prevented her from confessing her knowledge, and she was fain to rejoice in his escape; but of his motives for an attempt so heinous she could form not the smallest idea. As for Berenza, he merely concluded that he was some daring and determined robber, who might easily have obtained an entrance into the house during the careless festivity that had generally prevailed during the evening; but respecting a circumstance that he now deemed immaterial, he gave himself but little concern." His whole thoughts were concentered in Victoria, and he looked forward with impatient anxiety to the much desired period of her recovery. Scarcely could he be prevailed on to quit her bedside, even to obtain necessary repose, and what little food he could be induced to take, was taken without stirring from her chamber.

In a few days, however, to reward such unwearied anxiety, Victoria was enabled to leave her bed, and by marks of attachment, apparently more strong than ever, repaid the care and tenderness of her lover. Raised by her seducing manners to a pitch of enthusiasm, Berenza sometimes wavered in his pride, and almost determined that he would make her his wife, the moment that her re-established health should permit him to do so.

One day, while sitting with her in her apartment, (a fortnight having nearly elapsed since the accident which had confined her there) a letter was delivered by a servant into his hands — opening it he read as follows: —

"Wretch! by the time you receive this, I shall be far from pursuit, if such your meanness or your revenge should lead you to attempt. Know that it was *I* who directed to your faithless and unworthy breast that hand which failed in executing its office! — it was *I* who intended, and who hoped, that the accursed stilletto, which erred in its duty, should have found a bloody sheath in the recesses of your heart! Yes, miscreant, it was *Megalena Strozzi*, who beheld you on the Laguna, accompanied by the minion, whose temerity robbed her of your love — oh! and if a look could *kill*, mine should have blasted *her* to the earth! What, durst you openly exhibit your novelty, and believe that your audacity would remain unpunished? Did you not know me? You should have carefully guarded your late found gem; you should not have suffered her to sparkle in the light of day, in the eyes of Strozzi! But she, and even you, for the present have eluded my vengeance — yet ha! my heart beats, it revives in the faint hope, that she perhaps may *not* have escaped! — if it be not so, nothing shall bind me to life, but the dearly cherished hope that the time will *yet* arrive, when no barrier shall intercept the blow I would aim at your life — no, not even the hated form of your *newly* acquired love. Couldest thou indeed hope, fond fool, that with impunity thou mightest despise the passion and insult the feelings of

MEGALENA STROZZI."

"Vile and abandoned wanton!" exclaimed Berenza, "is it then even so? and is it to thee, and to thy absurd and insolent jealousy, that I am to attribute my present misfortune? But it is well," he continued, "the worthless fury will molest us no more; she has left Venice." As he concluded, he gave the letter to Victoria, who, after hastily perusing it, exclaimed —

"That look! that look then, which so strongly impressed my mind, is now accounted for — it was Megalena Strozzi, who would have blasted me to the earth." Then turning towards Berenza, she explained to him the circumstances to which she alluded, and which, at the moment of its occurrence, so forcibly called her attention — nay, had even employed her thoughts just before the projected attempt upon his life took place. While she spoke, Berenza did indeed recognize the vindictive Florentine; but anxiously, though silently, did Victoria ransack her brain, to discover what connection could possibly subsist between this female and her brother; a connection evidently of no slight nature, that could already so deeply have influenced his character and conduct as to drive him to the intended commission of murder! to the very brink of destruction, for her sake. Recurring frequently to vain surmises upon this subject, and rapidly recovering from the effects of her wound, for the present let us leave her, to explain certain events which will carry us back to an earlier period of this history.

CHAPTER XII

It may be remembered, that when detailing the misfortunes which befel the family of Loredani, in consequence of the desertion of Laurina from her husband and children, to the arms of an adulterer, we related at that epoch the sudden flight of the young Leonardo from his paternal roof, to which he had never more returned. It is *his* progress from that time, and the events which led him ultimately to determine on the commission of the most horrible of crimes, that we are now going briefly to revert to.

The high and susceptible feelings which actuated the bosom of this youth, when little more than sixteen years of age, caused him (under their uncontroulable influence) to rush from the house of his father as soon as he learned the unfortunate dereliction from the path of honour of his other parent. Scarcely to the youth himself were his sensations definable; but his naturally soaring spirit, unbroken by restraint, strengthened too by the high notions of family honour, which the Marchese had delighted to inculcate in the heir of his house and fortunes, gave him a feeling confused and agonized, that to remain longer on the spot where his mother had heaped disgrace upon her ruined family, would be vile and unworthy. Impressed with this idea, he took his rash determination; it was to fly from Venice, never, perhaps, to behold it more! In the shortest possible time he endeavoured to accelerate his distance from a city now grown hateful to him, and to lose by motion, and change of scene, the uneasy reflections that oppressed his proud but noble heart. Even to fly from Venice was not enough; to remain near it was death to his soul. Nor did he for an hour intermit the rapidity of his movements, until almost without knowing, certainly without designing it, he found himself in the delightful country of Tuscany. Awakened to cooler recollection, "Here then," he energetically exclaimed, "here then, I may *breathe* without an oppression of the heart!" — (and here too, necessity compelled him to rest; for the enthusiastic youth, careless of the future, when he left his luxurious home, was but scantily supplied with money, and all he had possessed was by this time expended.) "And what then," he cried, as sober reason suggested this reflection to his mind; "better to die an exile in the furthest corner of the globe — better to die in poverty and want, than live in a luxury which the soul despises!"

It was evening, and the young Leonardo reclined pensively on the bank of the majestic Arno — the sun had sunk in the west, and misty shadows were collecting upon the mountains. For the first time he began to reflect upon his situation, whither he must now continue to bend his steps, and how he should support life, having thus cast himself upon a friendless world. His thoughts became painful and embarrassing — he sought again to lose them in activity, and sprang hastily from his recumbent posture. He had not proceeded far ere he beheld a large and elegant mansion, which, from the extreme beauty of its architecture, standing too wholly by itself, rivetted his attention: he continued to approach, and when he drew near stopped involuntarily to contemplate it. While he was thus employed, a gentleman of a noble and superior appearance came from the house, and being attracted by the animated countenance and figure of Leonardo, he was induced to approach him, and enquire by what chance he had wandered to this beautiful solitude. Leonardo replied firmly, and without hesitation, that he was a youth whom misfortunes, not to be explained, had driven from his home, and that he was straying, he neither knew, nor was solicitous whither.

Struck by the singularity of this reply, in which there was something to interest an expanded mind, the stranger, who was called Signor Zappi, felt impelled to increase if possible his acquaintance with the youth, whom chance had thus introduced to his attention.

"Well, my young friend," he said, "if you will enter my mansion, which seems to have attracted your notice, we may have some conversation that perhaps may not prove unsatisfactory to either of us. Your appearance and manner please me, and I should feel happy to know more of you."

To this frank invitation the warm hearted youth readily assented, and accepting with an ingenuous air the proffered hand of Signor Zappi, they entered the house together.

Leonardo was conducted into an elegant apartment, where desiring him to be seated, Signor Zappi enquired of him if he stood in need of refreshment. Leonardo replied in the negative. Some indifferent conversation then ensued; when (though with the utmost delicacy) his liberal host expressed a desire to be informed of his name.

The youth blushed. — "My name," he replied, "is Leonardo — that which is subjoined to it, I must be excused from revealing. Circumstances have impelled me to leave my home; and I feel it impossible, Signor, utterly impossible," he added, rising hastily from his chair, "to gratify a curiosity so proper, and so natural, for you to feel respecting one you have admitted beneath your roof, I will, with your permission, take my leave, and no longer intrude upon your hospitality."

"That must not be indeed, my young friend," answered Signor Zappi — "There is that in your appearance and manner, as I have said, which interests me considerably — keep then your secret, if you wish it; and since you are avowedly at present a child of fortune, indifferent and undecided whither you bend your course, remain for a short time where chance has directed you, and forbear (young and enthusiastic as you appear) to cast yourself upon the careless world."

Leonardo's heart was penetrated with gratitude at the kind words of the benevolent stranger. His dreadful, and as he conceived it disgraceful, family secret, his pride shrunk from acknowledging; but feeling in an instant the good fortune he experienced in having met, in the forlornness of his situation, one who appeared inclined to befriend him, he cast himself at the feet of Zappi, unable to restrain his tears. This excellent being, whose philanthropic heart led him to seek every opportunity, not only of befriending his species, but if possible of preserving them from ill, v as deeply affected. That the nature of the youth was noble, he easily conceived — that some sentiment of a high and honourable (though, perhaps, misguided) tendency had induced him to fly his home, he likewise believed; therefore, gently raising him in his arms, he said —

"Come then, Leonardo — I desire to know you by no *other* name — Come, let us quit this room; and, as the son of a friend, I will introduce you to my wife and daughter."

The wife of Zappi, however, chanced to be in every respect the reverse of her husband; for she possessed an intriguing spirit, and a profligate heart. But it is not intended to dwell minutely upon every progressive incident that befel the young Leonardo; to skim lightly, on the contrary, over all, excepting that which led to his connection with Megalena Strozzi, is the present purpose.

The Signor Zappi then daily grew more attached to the youth of his adoption; — when absent, his conversation to his wife teemed with his praises; when present, he continually sought modes of drawing forth his character, and every trait he discovered added to the warm impression that his pristine ingenuousness had made upon his benevolent mind.

It so happened, unfortunately, that Zappi was not singular in his admiration of the youth, for he had not been very long an inmate in his house, before the Signora Zappi became a warmer eulogist in his favour than even her husband: she paid him beside the most pointed attentions. Yet it was not his ardent character, his talents, or his virtues which attracted *her* distinguished regard; — no, it was the charms of his person, the beauty of his form and face, which had drawn towards him her attention; and true it is, they displayed a manliness and grace far above his years. Yet not similarly disposed in her favour was the object of her growing passion; his admiration, his thoughts, and all he knew of love, was bestowed upon Amamia, her lovely and more approximating daughter. This, to her dismay, the wife of Zappi soon discovered; but, bent upon carrying her point, she resorted to all the fascination of dress, to all the allurements of softness, and the most tender attentions; — that all this too might the more forcibly impress his mind, she, as much as possible, upon various pretexts, removed the fair Amamia from his view. Still all was unavailing. The youth felt gratitude for the kindnesses shewn him by the wife of his friend, but he felt no more.

About a year had now elapsed since his first introduction to the house of Zappi, yet still the secret of his alienation from home was locked in the recesses of his heart, guarded by an impenetrable aegis of punctilious pride and delicacy. The good Zappi, indeed, had long ceased to hint at any desire for information upon the subject; he felt happy in the society of the youth, and he required no painful acknowledgments on his side for the friendship he had delighted to shew him. He had never yet, from any act, or any conduct of Leonardo, had occasion to regret his intimacy in his family: no trait of vice, of meanness, or ingratitude had ever yet exhibited themselves in his character. Zappi was a plain and pure professor of morality, as well as a benevolent being, and if he had had reason to suspect aught amiss in the *heart* of his young friend, painful as would have been the task, he would have felt it his duty to drive him from beneath his roof, lest, by appearing to protect and cherish vice, he should inculcate lessons of dangerous tendency into the mind of his daughter, and by an inevitable progression, *injure* rather than *benefit* society.

The passion of Zappi's wife had by this time grown to such a height, that she felt it utterly impossible longer to conceal it from the object that had inspired it; — She determined, therefore, whatever the consequence, to make it known to him. For this purpose, she seized an opportunity, when her husband and the fair Amamia were absent, to follow him into the garden, whither he had retired, to think, without interruption, and with all the enthusiasm of an innocent *first* love, upon his mistress. As he reclined upon a seat, he beheld coming towards him the mother of her he loved, and respectfully he would have arisen; but as she drew near him, gently laying her hand upon his shoulder, she prevented him from doing so, and seated herself beside him.

"You were absorbed in thought, Leonardo," said she.

"I was indeed," answered the youth, blushing.

"You were thinking of her you love, I would wager," pursued the wanton wife of Zappi, and heaved a sigh, fixing upon him her eyes at the same time, in which were depicted the troubled emotions of her agitated soul. Leonardo, who was thinking of Amamia, re-echoed her sigh. The sigh was electric fluid through her breast, and fanned the fires which were raging in her heart. She took his hand, and fervently pressing it, said —

"You are beloved in return — yes, Leonardo, most charming of youths, you are indeed beloved."

"Are you certain," replied the transported boy, springing from his recumbent attitude.

"Oh, I am but too certain," franticly replied the degraded female, falling at his feet, and thrown completely off her guard — "you are beloved — oh, how madly, by *me*.

"By you, Signora?" cried the astonished youth, "you jest surely — Rise, rise, I beseech you, from your unbecoming posture — unbecoming towards me," he sternly added.

"Oh, Leonardo, I love, I adore you!" cried the abandoned wife. "Spurn me not then, I conjure you, for I cannot, cannot conquer the fatal passion with which you have inspired me."

"Signora Zappi, you strike me with horror!" exclaimed the youth — "It is your *daughter*, it is your blooming daughter, that I love.

"What — and will you never love me, boy?" in an accent of rage and grief, she cried.

"*No*, never while I have breath — *never*!" emphatically replied Leonardo, disengaging himself from her wild embrace. "Allow me, if possible, to *respect* you."

"Curses then seize thee, miscreant!" shrieked the wife of Zappi, in an agony of rage and disappointment, and casting him from her with vehemence: "I will live to blast thee for this!"

"Most infamous of women!" returned Leonardo passionately, "let me fly from thy loathed presence — let me again in the wide world seek a refuge from infamy and shame; for infamy it is to be the object of thy love!"

So saying, with impetuosity he rushed from the spot, and would have fled from the house altogether, but that a thought of Amamia darting across his mind, he felt an irresistible desire to see her once more, ere he quitted for ever a roof that had sheltered him so long: he therefore hastened to his chamber, where he determined to abide till the arrival of Zappi and his daughter.

Mean time, his disappointed enamorata, rendered half frantic by the contempt and indignation with which her abandoned overtures had been received, resolved, in the tumultuous vengeance of her soul, to destroy and blacken the youth whose virtue she had failed to corrupt; or, it was not virtue that actuated him, but merely that the temptation offered him was not sufficient to seduce it; still the reflection was, in either case, maddening and humiliating, and how she might most bitterly cause him to repent his conduct was now her sole consideration. At length the demon of hate and revenge suggested to her a plan sufficiently diabolical.

With eager and triumphant malice she instantly began tearing her apparel to tatters; then taking some gravel between her hands, careless of pain, in pursuance of revenge, she rubbed it with violence over her face and hands till the blood flowed; and in this state determined to await the return of her husband. Presently she heard him arrive: she flew round the garden; and, as he entered the house, met him at the door, and cast herself, as if in agony of shame and horror, before him.

Zappi, who tenderly loved his wife, was shocked and dismayed; he caused her to be carried into the house, and laid upon a bed, and then tremblingly entreated to be informed what terrible event had befallen her.

The false and unworthy wife then motioned for every one to withdraw; and pressing, with seeming love and agitation, his hand to her lips, she replied thus to his anxious enquiries —

"Oh, my beloved husband! that scorpion we have nourished so long, behold, what has been our reward! It is to that audacious, that hypocritical stripling, you must attribute what you now behold. Finding me alone in the garden, he first presumed to insult me with professions of a dishonourable love — I rebuked the saucy boy, and attempted to rise, when suddenly seizing me in his arms, I soon found my strength unequal to his. I shrieked aloud: he became, I suppose, apprehensive of discovery, and fled from the garden, leaving his infamous purpose unaccomplished!"

The wife of Zappi ceased; and, bursting into tears as if oppressed with a sense of shame, covered her face with her hands.

"Depraved, ungrateful viper!" exclaimed the deluded Zappi, "could I ever have imagined of thee this? But instantly shall he — no, first he shall appear before us, and be forced to reply whether sudden madness, or deliberate villainy, impelled to this criminal attempt."

So saying, Zappi, summoning a servant, bade him tell the young Leonardo that his presence was immediately desired.

At this mandate the infamous wife of Zappi felt somewhat alarmed; but, resolving to persevere in her plot, she offered no objection. In the course of a few moments the youth entered the room: he started on beholding the maimed figure of his accuser; but his step was firm and unhesitating; his eye was open, and on his blooming cheek guilt had set no mark.

"Wretch!" began Signor Zappi, unmindful of these appearances tallying so little with imputed crime, "wretch! dare you to appear before me with that audacious front? See there your work, young but most infamous monster! So green in years, so old in the basest profligacy, what — might not the wife of your benefactor have been held sacred by you? Durst you endeavour to break through the nearest and the dearest connections that are respected between man and man? Could you trample thus on every principle of honour, and of gratitude? attempt the subversion of moral order, and trespass upon sacred social affinities? Worthless profligate, and unfeeling boy! quit instantly a roof which has sheltered you too long, and never let me more behold your face."

During this bitter language, which was addressed to him, Leonardo made no attempt to speak: he folded his arms upon his bosom, and as the deluded Zappi proceeded, he saw the depth of the plot which had been imagined against him by his depraved wife. The instinctive pride, however, of his nature, spurned at the unmerited imputations which had been cast upon him, and the poignant invective with which they were accompanied: he scorned, proudly scorned, to attempt a vindication; and, perhaps, a magnanimous sentiment of gratitude made him desire to spare his friend and benefactor too accurate information of his wife's depravity, if such his indignation would have allowed him to listen to; therefore, when he perceived that he had concluded, in a gentle but firm voice, he thus replied —

"I am ready, Signor Zappi, to depart your house. I thank you for all the favours you have conferred on me, and wish you may never experience from others greater ingratitude than you have met from me."

So saying, be bowed respectfully, and moved towards the door; yet, ere he quitted the room, turning his eyes full upon the wife of Zappi, he looked at her for a moment with such dignity and scorn blended, that her soul trembled within her, and involuntarily she passed her hand over her eyes. With firm and majestic step he then retired.

His first impulse led him to the chamber he had been taught to call his:

there, with swelling heart, but tearless eye, he placed, with indignant eagerness, upon a table, every trinket he had about him, which his benefactor, in the plenitude of fond affection, had bestowed upon him. Of money he retained not a marevedi. Then unlocking a drawer, where, on first becoming an inmate in the house of Signor Zappi, he had deposited (from a certain feeling at the moment indefinable) the clothes which he had worn on entering it, and the only ones he possessed: he cast off hastily those in which he was now clad, and substituted for them such of his own as his increased height and bulk would allow him to make use of. Bitterly did it corrode the heart of the youth, that he could not in like manner return every benefit he had received; yet, since that was impossible, he could only determine to retain nothing that might be resigned. Then surveying himself from head to foot, with a mingled feeling he exclaimed — "These are my own; *all*, too, that I can well call *mine*. — Oh, mother, mother! — for *this* may I thank thee!"

Becoming now more violently agitated from succeeding reflections, he rushed from the chamber, and fled hastily through the house. Once he stopped, with the fond wish to take a last leave of the fair Amamia; but on the recollection that he must either expose to her the infamy of her mother, or himself appear culpable in her eyes, he conquered the impulse, and pursued his way hastily across the garden.

Anxious to lose sight of the house, he halted not till he found himself at a considerable distance from it, and had walked at a rapid pace for several hours. Actual weariness at length compelled him for a moment to rest. The energy of his mind had till now supported him: he became conscious that he had walked many miles; nature felt overpowered, and reluctantly he seated himself at the foot of a tree. Uneasy reflections began to enter his mind: with his head reclining on his hand, involuntarily he suffered a deep gloom to take possession of him. It was past noon when he quitted the abode of Zappi: he now strained his tearful eyes, and beheld the east beginning to be obscured by the shades of evening. His oppression increased, but his strength of mind shewed him the necessity of combating it. He started on his feet, and turned his face to the west: there he beheld the glorious sun, declining indeed, but declining in a blaze of radiance; the sky around represented a thousand brilliant figures; the tops of the mountains, catching the last rays, reflected many different degrees of light and shade. The youth felt no longer overcome by melancholy; his heart cheared; painful ideas gave place to indefinite hopes; and he determined that he would no more indulge in the weakness of useless regret.

Pursuing a path that chance alone directed, he soon found himself winding among those beautiful mountains, whose fruitful bosoms are covered with olive and the luxurious vine. Wherever a beautiful villa met his eye, instinctively he turned aside. The shades of evening began to thicken, and the young exile from home was still unsheltered for the night. At length, wandering onwards, he beheld, situated in a kind of glen, a small and low roofed cottage: to perceive it fully, it was even necessary to ascend a considerable way the mountain at the foot of which it humbly rose. It was embosomed by trees, and surrounded by a garden, seeming the abode of industrious poverty, rather than the seclusion of romantic whim. At all events, Leonardo shunned it not, but resolved to investigate it nearer, and ascertain by whom it was inhabited. As he continued to approach, the voice of moaning and distress sounded on his ear. This hastened his steps, and he speedily gained the little narrow path which led to the cottage. There, seated on the outside of the door, he beheld an aged female, weeping and wringing her hands. Sorrow was in unison with the heart of the youth, and in a gentle voice he asked, if her grief might admit of consolation and assistance.

"Alas, no!" she answered, redoubling her tears: "death admits no remedy; it has deprived me of my only hope and comfort in this world — of my poor Hugo, my darling son. — Oh, Signor, that he should go before me! Who now will support my tottering limbs? — who provide for the short remnant of my days? — who work for, who befriend, the poor forsaken Nina?"

"But weep not so bitterly, good mother," said Leonardo. "Admit me into your cottage; and if you will be kind enough to give me a draught of milk, we will talk further upon the subject of your sorrow. Perhaps things may not prove so bad as you at this moment apprehend."

The voice of consolation is always sweet, but doubly sweet when coming from buoyant youth to age. The poor Nina rose with the utmost alacrity she possessed from her seat, and hobbling into her cottage, she set in silence before him (while her tears continued, though more slowly, to flow) the best that her cottage afforded.

When Leonardo had a little satisfied his hunger (for the almost unremitting fatigue he had undergone, for the last seven or eight hours, had completely exhausted him,) he took the hand of his aged hostess, who involuntarily had seated herself beside him, and said —

"Tell me, my good mother, how old was your son Hugo?"

"He was twenty, Signor, on the blessed day of Saint Gualbert."

"And tell me, Nina — "

But Nina would not allow him to proceed —

"Oh, Santo Pedro! was he not every thing to poor Nina? — Signor, I have a little garden, and Hugo it was who turned it to account. I have a vineyard too, and Hugo looked to it. But he would seldom leave his aged mother, Signor: for — 'Mother,' would he say 'it is better to give this, or that, or a little, upon what we dispose of to Pietro, or Varro, and let them manage for us, than for me to leave you, mother, who can't well help yourself.' — Signor, I have lately got a little the better of a terrible pain in my poor limbs; and now — oh, misericordo! — to lose my staff, my dear boy! — Oh, Signor! I vex my heart, and think he worked beyond his strength; for he was always weak and sickly from a dear child.

Here poor Nina was interrupted by her tears, at the recollection of what her son had been to her.

An idea had entered the mind of Leonardo while she spoke, which every moment acquired fresh force from a view of its eligibility — a garden to cultivate — a vineyard to attend to — no occasion for public exposition in the market, or even the town — her son in a declining state too, and yet capable of doing all that was necessary to be done — "Surely I — "

He turned towards Nina, who was still bitterly lamenting —

"Come, worthy Nina, dry up your tears — what if I could supply to you the place of your son, would you allow me to remain under your roof, and accept of my best endeavours?"

"Oh! Cielo be praised, be adored for this!" joyfully exclaimed the aged Nina, dropping on her knees, and fervently kissing the ground. "Oh! as I live, my heart began to feel lighter the instant I set my eyes upon you; and though I did continue to weep, Signor," weeping again, "for my dear lost son Hugo, yet I vow and protest, by the blessed Maria, I felt as if a ray of light shot through my breast."

"Well, rise now, my good Nina, and let us talk further."

Nina, trembling, arose.

"You must give me some instructions, my good Nina; for though I understand sufficient of gardening, there are many things I shall require you to explain to me."

This Nina, her heart almost bursting with conflicting joy and regret (joy that she had found a protector, and regret that she had lost one,) readily promised. Some necessary conversation then ensued; and Leonardo, feeling within himself no doubt of success in his new situation, consented at an early hour to retire to repose, sensible of intense fatigue from the exertion of the day.

The aged Nina conducted him to the little chamber which had appertained to her deceased son; and, with a heart infinitely lightened, Leonardo took possession of the homely bed which it contained.

As he reclined his head upon the pillow — "This is the second time," he exclaimed, "that the heir of Loredani has been indebted to the benevolence of strangers for shelter, that the humanity of strangers has compassionated his forlornness, and that the bounty of strangers has cherished and protected him. Oh, mother — mother unkind! to thee, and thee alone, do I owe all this!"

With this bitter though just reflection burning at his heart, he fell asleep; and had the son of Laurina *expired* in that sleep, he would have appeared at the bar of Heaven with an accusation against his mother registered in his heart. — Let other mothers tremble at this reflection, and pause on meditated guilt.

END OF THE FIRST VOLUME.

VOLUME TWO

ZOFLOYA;

OR,

THE MOOR.

CHAPTER XIII

At an early hour the following morning, Leonardo awakened, and immediately repaired to the garden, to enter upon his self-allotted task. While
in the mansion of Zappi, he had obtained considerable knowledge with
respect to gardening, from having, at leisure hours, resorted to it as an
amusement; Signor Zappi likewise felt pleasure in giving him instructions, because he himself passed much of his time in botanising, in plant-
ing, and trying various experiments upon the fecund earth. The young
Leonardo had additional motives to strengthen his perseverance; for he
felt, though he should in reality reap the benefit of his own exertions, that
he laid himself under no obligations to be again (bitter reflection!)
reproached with them; he repaid, by the service he rendered, the benefit
he received; his proud heart was therefore at rest, and his spirit became
even buoyant with pleasing anticipations that banished for a time the recollection of his real woes — woes no less real, because his peculiar sentiments (whether romantic, or otherwise) induced him to prefer their pressure to the ease and splendor which he would have deemed disgrace and
infamy.

Nothing assuredly calms the mind like a settled purpose. Leonardo
had determined to persevere (while circumstances should render it expedient) in a course of labor and activity. Each successive day brought with
it lighter, because more habitual toil, with an increase of pleasure to his
heart, in the conviction of being no idle member of society. In his knowledge, superior to that of Hugo, the poor Nina soon discerned a multiplied
advantage; every thing flourished beneath his fostering hand and excellent arrangement: his mind, warm and enthusiastic, slackened not in the
pursuit of his object; he became gradually enamoured of his peaceful,
innocent, and industrious life — his humble retirement, and total seclusion from the world. He felt no want, he received no favor; he beheld the
little store of the aged Nina daily increasing, and, while he experienced
the sweet reward of constant employ, his heart bounded, for the first time,
with the exulting consciousness of being useful to a fellow-creature.

He anticipated the future, however, with a feeling of melancholy. His
uncertain destination occasionally employed his thoughts — "Can I
always remain thus?" he would exclaim. "Alas! No. Yet, surely, these are
halcyon days; but still I have an unquenched sentiment in my soul, that
tells me, this for ever (though in itself laudable) would be but an inglori-
ous life for the heir of Loredani!" — "What," said I, "the *heir* of Loredani
is disgraced! He may be happy, he may be honoured in the *shade*, but

despised, contemned, if he offers to emerge in the betraying light of day! — No, no, Loredani; the world is no place for *thee*, in thine own character; never mayest thou appear among men!"

These reflections sometimes overwhelmed his mind with gloom. He had then no refuge but in redoubled activity, resolving to allow himself no leisure for useless anticipation of future fate.

It happened, however, one morning, that the aged Nina complained of an unwonted sensation; towards noon it amounted to indisposition, and Leonardo, whom she had ever called her son, assisted her to her bed, from which she was doomed never more to arise. Of this, in a few hours, the worthy creature became conscious; she felt undeniable symptoms of approaching dissolution, and knew them for what they were. "Alas!" said she feebly to the youth Leonardo, "I feel, my beloved, my second son, that I have not long to survive my dear Hugo; let me behold thy sweet face in the moment of death, and let me bless thee with my last breath."

Leonardo was deeply affected; he beheld, on the point of departing for ever, her who had admitted him unhesitatingly, beneath her humble roof, to a share of her little comforts, to the disposition of her trifling all. True, the event had *rewarded* her kindness, but that was not the consideration of the moment, of her genuine hospitality — could he then forsake her lonely pillow? No longer than to procure every assistance, every necessary that might contribute to her ease, or tend, perhaps, to revive the feeble embers, yet lingering, of life. But vain were his attentions, vain his endeavours; ere long the extinct became every hope. After some hours of painful watching by her bed-side, during which she had not spoken, and her breath had been heard to fluctuate, she, in a low and almost inarticulate voice, desired Leonardo to raise her in his arms. He obeyed with tender anxiety. "All I have is thine," she murmured, making an effort to open her eyes, and fix upon him her last look. No sooner had she beheld that ingenuous countenance, then her wishes seemed fulfilled; her head sunk heavy on his bosom, and she expired in his arms with the serenity of a child.

Great was the grief of Leonardo: he summoned her few friends and neighbours, who occupied here and there a cottage on the mountain, to perform the last sad offices for his humble but affectionate friend; and, feeling now the inutility of remaining on the spot, he resolved to defer his departure only till he had seen her decently consigned to the earth.

In a few days, therefore, Leonardo dividing her slight possessions among those who had obeyed his call at her decease, and reserving to himself only a trifling sum of money, the produce of his own labor since he had resided beneath her roof, he left the simple cottage where he had passed some happy hours, and, furnished with a small stock of provisions, once more renewed his wanderings. Of shelter for the night he was no longer solicitous, for his late toil, and regular healthful habits, had so far increased his hardihood and vigor, that he no longer shrunk at reposing in the open air; nor would he, he resolved, while possessed of sufficient for half a meal, attempt to enter the habitation of man.

Night at length overtook him; he threw himself carelessly upon the earth and began to reflect. The vagueness of his own intentions, the desultoriness of his mode of life, forcibly struck him. — "It is now two years and three months," thought he, "since I left my native city of Venice — since I left the disgraced abode of my father — that dear, that tender father, who so much loved me. Since that, I have been once accused of the most dreadful crimes, and driven with ignominy from the shelter to which I had no claim; then I have been inured to poverty and toil, and earned my bread, like the meanest peasant, by the sweat of my brow; now am I again an outcast on the wide expanse of creation, no friend, no home, nor a prospect of obtaining bread for to-morrow's sub-sistence: Oh, mother! and all this for *thee*," he exclaimed, clasping his hands fervently together; "through thee have I endured all this." Now the probable fate of that mother, how his father had supported her loss, and the situation of his sister, with a thousand dear and tender recollections, pressed upon his mind; the fond wish of revisiting his home flashed across his mind, but scarcely at first would he admit the idea. Irresistibly, how-ever, it hung around his heart. "And why not, then," said he, at length, in an eager voice, "why not?" as he contemplated the alteration of his appearance: "who, in the present hardy Leonardo, (robust by toil, embrowned by the fierce rays of the mid-day sun, and habited too in the coarse costume of the humble peasant,) shall trace the once luxurious heir of Loredani? Yes, I am determined," he pursued, starting on his feet; "I may with safety, without danger of being known, once more revisit my home; I can satisfy my mind respecting my unfortunate family, and then take of it an eternal adieu."

He walked rapidly a few steps, forgetting, in the enthusiasm of the moment, that it was night: at length he grew calm. "Early in the morning, then," said he, mentally; "meantime here is my bed." Once more he cast himself upon the earth, and sleep stealing over him, soon calmed the agi-tation of his mind.

Prompt was the decision, and prompt ever the execution of Leonardo: leaving, at early dawn, the mountains of Tuscany behind him, he pursued his journey with the most eager rapidity that his humble means would allow, ever cautious that no one should suspect him for other than he appeared. Who can describe his sensations when he found himself even near the city of Venice! yet he resolved not to enter it during the day; and when he arrived at Padua, determined to proceed as far as he could on foot, thinking by this means that it would be impossible for him to reach Venice before nightfall.

Curbing his impatience, therefore, after taking some slight refresh-ment, he deliberately set out on his allotted task; but, notwithstanding that he walked, as he conceived, at a moderate pace, by the time he reached the extremity of the Terra Firma, he perceived the sun still far above the western hemisphere: he continued therefore slowly to wander along the borders of the lake, idly stopping to remark whatever villa or splendid domain attracted his eye, of which the Venetian nobility have many on the Terra Firma. At length, however, feeling somewhat weary, he threw himself upon the bed of the earth, to him no longer unfamiliar as such, and fell as usual into a train of thought. Tears involuntarily filled his eyes, and coursed each other down his cheeks: he closed those eyes, filled as they were with tears, and ruminated over the sorrows of his youth. Ah! tears, painful as you were, as yet rising from an unpolluted heart; from a heart, though bursting with grief, yet unstained by guilt. Why, why must it so soon become changed, destroyed, and plunged into an abyss of shame and infamy? Why art thou doomed, Leonardo, to add another blot to the page which registers Laurina's crimes?

Nature will often become exhausted by the intenseness of its own sensations. Leonardo sunk by degrees from keen feeling into a temporary insensibility; a soft sleep stole over his faculties, and he forgot for a time the unhappiness of his situation. While unconsciously he thus reposed, a female chanced to wander near the spot. She had quitted her house for the purpose of enjoying more fully the *fresco* of the evening, and to stroll along the banks of the lake; the young Leonardo, however, arrested her attention, and she softly approached to contemplate him — his hands were clasped over his head, and on his cheek, where the hand of health had planted her brown-red rose, the pearly gems of his tears still hung — his auburn hair sported in graceful curls about his forehead and temples, agitated by the passing breeze — his vermeil lips were half open, and disclosed his polished teeth — his bosom, which he had uncovered to admit the refreshing air, remained disclosed, and contrasted by its snowy whiteness the animated hue of his complexion.

Beautiful and fascinating, though in the simple garb of a peasant, did the wondering female consider the youth before her. Struck with lively admiration, she knew not how to quit the spot, when an insect suddenly alighting on his cheek, he started and awakened — somewhat confused, he hastily arose, for the female that met his eyes appeared to him supremely beautiful; approaching him gently, and with a smile, she laid her hand upon his arm, and in a gentle voice said:

"You appear a stranger here; and though your dress bespeaks inferiority of situation, pardon me if I distrust what it seems meant to convey. Without therefore deeming me impertinently curious, allow me to inquire whither you intend to bend your course, as the evening is already far advanced, and I know not of any house near this that could yield you accommodation for the night."

This was the first beautiful and attractive female (save the innocent Amamia, whose attraction too was of a nature wholly different to that of hers before him) who had ever addressed herself to the warm imagination of Leonardo. His cheeks became suffused with deepening blushes, and his eyes, with which he longed to gaze upon her, were yet cast bashfully towards the earth. In a faultering voice he replied, while every consideration but of the object before him vanished from his mind:

"I have — no, I have not any particular destination for this night, Signora — but I have — I have it in contemplation where to bend my course soon; at least I am solicitous — " He stopped, unable to proceed from a confusion of idea.

"Well, but then," in a voice of tender anxiety, answered Megalena Strozzi (for her it was who addressed the youth), "if you are not absolutely decided — if you are not particularly desirous of proceeding further to-night, perhaps you will for the present deign to enter my villa, and allow me the happiness of offering you a dwelling for the night."

Leonardo raised his eyes, and was about to reply. "Come, I perceive you will not deny me," gaily resumed the fair Florentine, taking him lightly by the arm, and leading him onwards; "my house is but a small distance from hence: look, you may behold it as you stand," (she added) pointing with her finger to a small and beautiful edifice built in the form of a pavilion. — "Impossible, lovely Signora, to refuse *you* any thing," said the youth, enthusiastic at her charms, and the gracefulness of her manner: "impossible to refuse *you* any thing."

The fair Florentine only smiled, and proceeded with alacrity, as though apprehensive that the youth should retract. They soon reached the villa, and a smothered sigh, as he entered it, was the last tribute paid to the memory of his neglected home.

The character of Megalena Strozzi has already been so far revealed, that to amplify upon it here, or the excesses into which it perpetually hurried her, would be vain. Suffice it to say, that, enraptured with the novel graces of the young Leonardo, she spared no artifice or allurement to induce him to protract his stay beneath her roof. She devoted herself to fascinate and seduce him, and day after day contrived fresh causes to prevent his departure. By degrees these artifices, as Megalena had hoped they would, became unnecessary: it was now him who forbore to press the subject, who sought excuses to remain, and who constantly trembled, lest the necessity of departing should be pointed out to him. It was not with the beautiful Megalena, as with the profligate wife of Zappi; for, though equally depraved herself, she knew better how to disguise, beneath an artificial delicacy and refinement, the tumultuous wishes of her heart. It was not vainly, then, that she sought to seduce the imagination, and lure the senses of the youth. No; he had in his own high-wrought feelings, in his susceptible soul, powerful and treacherous advocates in her cause. He beheld her with a mixed sentiment of admiration and passion, far different to the sentiments with which he had regarded the young Amamia. Those he had entertained for her were innocent, peaceful, and refined; for Megalena, turbulent, painful, wild: *her* charms kindled his soul; Amamia's had filled it with a halcyon tenderness: his sensations for the one were like the burning heat of a fierce meridian sun; for the other, like the gentle calmness of a summer eve.

Megalena, who had only retired to the villa which she at present occupied, with the intent to remain there a few days, (and that merely on account of a slight quarrel that she had had with Conte Berenza, wherein she had bitterly reproached him for the infrequency of his visits to her,) now forgetting the cause of chagrin that had induced her to leave Venice, found herself, from the delightful chance that had introduced Leonardo to her, inclined to protract her stay far beyond what she had originally intended.

It so happened, that about this time Berenza had recovered his beloved Victoria; the absence, therefore, of the fair Megalena remained not only unnoticed, but unknown; while she secretly congratulated herself upon the revenge she believed herself to be taking upon the indifference of Berenza towards her; yet, indifferent as he was, the Florentine could not forget that she had loved him once with a passion almost equal to that which she now felt for Leonardo: and whether or not he still continued to repay her diminished regards with all the ardent gratitude she had the vanity to conceive her due for having *once* preferred him to all other men, she vowed in her heart that the hour in which she should discover in *him* a preference to another should be the last of his existence.

Yet for her own conduct she had no standard but her wishes. Inconstancy and duplicity towards him, from whom she presumed to require such implicit devotion, were esteemed as nothing: *her* excesses, her irregularities, if she had ingenuity enough to conceal them from his knowledge, she considered perfectly allowable, and far from affording to Berenza a sufficient excuse for attaching himself elsewhere.

With these sentiments she gave unbounded latitude to her passion for Leonardo, and to such an excess did it speedily arrive, that she almost felt as if for him she could resign every other man.

CHAPTER XIV

Three months had now elapsed since Leonardo, fatally for himself, had become known to the syren Megalena. He was not yet nineteen; Megalena was his senior by several years; yet so far had her full-blown but unfaded charms, her playful yet elegant manners, her various seductive blandishments, obtained the ascendancy over his imagination, that the bare idea of separating from her became to him at length distraction: she had bewitched and enslaved his heart, she had awakened his soul to new existence; the image of the delicate Amamia faded from his mind, and a more wild, a more unbounded passion took possession of it, in the form of Megalena.

With a novel delight, superior to aught she had ever felt at any former conquest, did the artful Florentine behold her triumph: she had sown (as she believed) the first gems of love and passion in a pure and youthful breast; she had seen those germs shoot forth and expand beneath the fervid rays of her influence, and she enjoyed the fruits with a voluptuous pleasure.

At length however the vanity of her sex became predominant: assured of the perfect regard of Leonardo, enamoured of his beauty, and proud of her conquest, she had yet another feeling to gratify; she longed to exhibit him at Venice, to the females of her acquaintance, to excite their envy and their admiration, for of their attractions she entertained no fear; no dread of rivalry with herself had the haughty Florentine. But how to conceal from Berenza her new and highly prized lover — she resolved then to let her return to Venice remain a secret to him, and, in order to maintain it such, go but little from home; this point determined on, she expressed to Leonardo her desire to revisit Venice.

At the mention of Venice he became visibly agitated; the colour forsook his cheeks, and returned to them again with deepened dye. That very event which he had a little time before so eagerly desired, he now contemplated with mingled sensations of terror and reluctance. But could he refuse aught to his seducing mistress? Impossible! for her he forgot the firmest purpose of his soul; to her he laid open the painful secret, which till now, with scrupulous care, a high mindedness that shrunk from the idea of divulgement, he had undeviatingly guarded — the secret of his name and family.

Throwing himself into the arms of Megalena, he acknowledged himself for what he was, and hesitatingly expressed his unwillingness openly to revisit Venice, at least in his proper character.

"Are you then," exclaimed Megalena, (the fire of increased exultation sparkling in her eyes), "are you then the son of Loredani?"

"I am, beautiful Strozzi," answered he; "but," dropping on his knees, and fervently clasping his hands together, "guard, guard, I beseech you, the secret which your charms have extracted from me; respect my honor, my happiness, and my life; and never, by any chance, oh, never let it transpire from your lips, that I am the disgraced, the wandering offspring of that unhappy house; or that, to the name of Leonardo I add," — his voice faltered — "I add that of *Loredani*!"

"Never, never," solemnly answered the Florentine.

"Swear it! lovely woman — swear it, ere I rise," passionately added Leonardo.

"I *swear*, solemnly swear," answered Megalena, laying one hand upon his shoulder and raising the other to heaven, "I swear never to divulge thy secret to mortal being, and in the moment I forget my oath, may the lightning of heaven blast me!"

"Megalena, I thank thee," cried Leonardo fervently, rising from his knees, and embracing her with a tender solemnity, while tears trembled in his eyes, "I earnestly thank thee; for the discovery of my secret I would never survive!"

"But you will go to Venice then, Leonardo."

"Oh, Megalena, does not my father dwell there? — how, going with thee, might I remain concealed from his knowledge?"

"Know you not then, dear youth, that the Marchese is no more! That event, and those which followed, are sufficiently known in Venice, and none of your family at present reside there."

Leonardo heard only the words, "The Marchese is no more!" His hands were raised in mute anguish to heaven, the eloquent tears rolled slowly down his cheeks, and emphatically he exclaimed, "Merciful God, I *thank* thee!" Then turning towards Megalena, he said, in a voice of assumed calmness, "Inform me of what you know; I can bear to listen."

The Florentine, appearing deeply affected at the visible emotion of Leonardo, stated (and certainly with all possible regard to those high and susceptible feelings which she perceived in him,) whatever had come to her knowledge respecting the occurrences in the family of Loredani. She concluded her detail, (which she had rendered as concise and as little painful as possible,) by again observing (as she believed justly) that no part of that family resided now in the city of Venice.

"Oh, lost — oh, miserable mother!" silently ejaculated the youth; "thou hast completed, then, the measure of thy crimes: adieu, for ever, to the honor, to the happiness of thy children; thou hast now blasted them irretrievably!"

To Megalena, however, his smarting pride, his anguished feelings, suffered him to make no remark; his heart was too full, it was too towering, even in its humility, to ask a sharer in such griefs.

"And wilt thou not, then, accompany me to the city?" interrogated Megalena again, taking his hand, and looking fondly in his face.

"Yes, yes, fair Megalena," he replied, passing his hand hastily across his forehead, as if to chase away every uneasy thought; "yes, I can *now* do any thing — but, remember, I am only Leonardo."

Delighted to have gained her point, the Florentine promised obedience to his smallest desire; anticipated, and entered warmly into his every wish, arranging with eager facility a plan for his remaining concealed, and unknown. Leonardo, yielding to all she proposed, hastened from her presence to wander awhile in gloomy retrospection; for his mind, incapable of recovering immediately from the shock it had sustained, required, in solitude, to wear off its effect, and conquer the gloom that oppressed it.

Megalena, however, determined that her lover should not retract, resumed, as soon as she again beheld him, the subject nearest her heart, and fixed the following day for their departure from the villa Aqua Dolce, to whose friendly seclusion she considered herself indebted for pleasure, beyond any she had ever enjoyed.

Accordingly, in the cool of the evening, on the following day, they embarked for Venice. It began to get dusk as they arrived; they soon reached her luxurious residence, but nothing could remove the oppression which momentarily had been growing upon Leonardo, increasing at every step that brought him nearer to the place of his nativity. Megalena perceiving this, exerted herself, by every tender assiduity and insinuating art, to lighten and disperse. She welcomed the youthful lover to her home, and caused a splendid supper to be prepared. At length her powerful influence began to prevail; the melancholy of Leonardo gave way before it; potent goblets of wine assisted her efforts; the uselessness of regret becoming manifest to his mind, it was displaced by a vivacity, resulting rather from the animation imparted to the spirits, by wine and luxurious viands, than the sober reasoning of philosophy. The bland[1] seductress Megalena possessed over him an unlimited power; she had caused a new world to open on his view; even yet he was not awakened from the dream of pleasure with which she had bewitched his soul: feelings and ideas, unknown before, swelled in his bosom, and his heart was rapidly becoming immersed in an infatuating sea of voluptuousness.

Megalena, to his heated enthusiastic fancy, appeared an angel, at once beneficent and beautiful. Jealous of every idea that was not directed to herself, she sedulously endeavoured to banish from his mind all painful recurrence to the past; to this end, she thought it expedient to seek for him amusement and recreation, but of a nature that should not involve publicity; for, in his determination of concealment, Leonardo continued firm, and tremblingly alive to the remotest idea of discovery.

Accordingly, at her own house Megalena assembled most of her female friends, and such of her male acquaintance who, while from vacancy they affected to admire her, professed not to be lovers: to all these she presented her cherished lover as a young Florentine, and distant relation of her

---

1 bland: soothing

own; for even Megalena, bold and unprincipled as she was, did not desire to have known the real circumstances of her acquaintance with Leonardo.

Among the visitors that frequented this abode of levity and ignoble pleasure, it was not probable that any should be found who had formerly visited at the Marchese Loredani's; yet, had such an accident occurred, nearly three years of absence from Venice, joined to the life which he had led amid the mountains of Tuscany, had so far changed his originally delicate appearance, that it would have been almost impossible for any but a near relative to recognise the pampered boy, Leonardo, in the hardy and robust-looking Florentine, increased to the most elegant stature of the full-grown man. But yet, although unknown and undiscovered, Megalena vainly flattered herself in believing that the tale of his relationship to herself was credited. Enamoured as she appeared of the eminent beauty of his person, and evidently incapable of remaining at ease if for a moment he quitted her presence, it required no singular degree of penetration to discern, that ties more tender and more animated than those resulting from consanguinity attracted her towards him.

It so happened, that among the females, to which the vanity of the Florentine incited her to introduce her lover, was one, by name Theresa. This girl was of exquisite beauty, but deeply immersed in a stream of vice and dissipation. To the further disgrace of Megalena, it must be acknowledged, that she was in a high degree accessary to her fall from virtue: the unfortunate girl (though she appeared to court her society, and to entertain towards her, friendship and affection,) was in her heart deeply sensible of this, and, when reflection transiently pervaded her wretched mind, in the bitterness of an abhorrent half-repentant spirit, she silently cursed the enemy that had betrayed her.

Soon her penetrating and observant eye remarked the fond expression of regard with which Megalena Strozzi so frequently regarded her lover; the concealed exultation with which she viewed him, was discovered by the watchful Theresa; she felt convinced in her mind, that he bore no relationship to her, excepting that of love, (if love it might be termed,) and rejoiced at a prospect of obtaining revenge for the misery that an envying and fallen female had induced her to partake of. Inspired, too, by something of passion for the attractive Leonardo, she resolved, if possible, to detach him wholly from her hated associate, by courting him to herself. Eager in the prosecution of this plan, she left untried no artifices that could facilitate it; she invited Megalena frequently to her house, and, in spite of her watchfulness and care, contrived to have her attention engaged, that she might steal Leonardo from her side, and hold private conferences with him; she appealed, as the Florentine had done, to his imagination and his senses; and by younger, therefore more blooming charms, sought to reduce his heart from its allegiance to her. But while Theresa angled, as she thought, thus securely and unsuspected, the demon of jealousy had taken possession of the Florentine's soul! Enraged to madness at what she saw, yet wily and apparently cool, with vengeance burning in her breast, she resolved still to appear unconscious, and see how far the daring treachery of Theresa would carry her. To this end, she forbore to circumvent her various plans to inveigle her lover; and, while Theresa believed herself wholly unobserved, she only fell the readier into the snare which was laid for her.

At length her incessant and evident assiduities began to attract, in return, the attentions of Leonardo. Now no longer diffident, no longer retiring, he sought not to repress the sensations she excited — sensations not so ardent indeed, because no longer new, as those he had experienced for Megalena, but yet gradually acquiring strength, and, from the novelty of the object, at least increasing in allurement. His eyes and his language began to assure Theresa that she had in some measure atchieved her anxiously-desired object. Desirous, if possible, to rivet him at once her own, she, with eager and ill-concealed delight, appointed an evening when, by a plan of her own suggestion, he might, unsuspected, steal to her house. The sentiments of Leonardo, though high, and tremblingly alive to whatever regarded his pride or dignity of birth, were not yet so punctilious as to shrink from the idea of infringing on the fidelity of love. Unused, even from childhood, to curb the slightest of his wishes, and his self-love flattered by the early acquired regard of so young and lovely a female, he hesitated not in accepting her invitation, though his native delicacy taught him to consider it as somewhat premature. But what then? Megalena herself had first inspired him with a taste for ignoble pleasures, and it could scarcely be dishonourable to pursue with another the path her fascinations had pointed out.

The evening then was mutually agreed on, and even the very hour fixed: to this length did the secure and artful Strozzi permit every thing to advance. Leonardo was suffered to make his escape, to enter the house, and even the apartment where his impatient fair one awaited to receive him; but then so well, so accurately had the Florentine arranged her plan, she burst upon them like a thunder cloud. For a few moments she even surveyed them, but with that kind of horrible tranquillity that betokens an approaching storm.

Theresa had greeted Leonardo with a fervent embrace, and such was still their attitude. With a look, wherein was depicted the blackest rage, the deepest vengeance, and the bitterest scorn, without advancing a step, she continued to contemplate them; then, firmly and deliberately approaching Leonardo, she seized him by the arm. So unimpaired was her power over his soul, such was the awe, almost the terror, which he involuntarily felt, while sinking abashed beneath the powerful glance of her eye, that he had no power to resist the decisiveness of her action. There was a something at this juncture, in their relative situations, that made her, even in his own eyes, appear the injured person, and himself the worthless aggressor. Without a single rebellious struggle, therefore, on his side, the Florentine retained his arm, which she grasped with the violence of smothered rage; then, casting on the trembling and foiled Theresa a look, which spoke volumes to her trembling soul, she led, with step haughty and indignant, her recovered captive from the room.

Returning homewards, Megalena preserved a gloomy silence; Leonardo essayed twice or thrice to speak, but his tongue refused its office, and accents, half formed, quivered on his lips. Shocked and repentant, his mind suggested nothing that could allay the resentment he knew was boiling in the breast of his mistress. At length they reached home, and entered an apartment: the Florentine still preserving an uninterrupted silence, threw herself upon a sopha, and, covering her face with her hands, remained apparently absorbed in thought.

Leonardo could bear no longer this terrible demeanor; he became agonised: the remembrance of the happiness he had till now enjoyed with his still adored Megalena, rushed impetuously over his ardent soul. Of Theresa he knew little or nothing; he felt an emotion, bordering on rage and disgust, rising in his bosom against her, for having, even momentarily, alienated his thoughts from her to whom fondly he conceived that he owed so much. No longer master of himself, he rushed towards her; he threw himself with violence at her feet, kissed them, and bedewed them with his tears. This was only what the artful Florentine had expected; knowing well the haughtiness of his nature, yet knowing likewise well the susceptibility of his feelings, she had forborne to irritate, by reproach, him who was to be conquered by an appeal to the heart.

"Oh! lovely, oh! adored Megalena," cried the repentant lover, "forgive, forgive me. I feel, yes, I feel that 'tis you alone I love; pardon then, in this conviction, your unhappy, guilty slave!"

The Florentine answered not.

"What! not a word, not a word. Oh! Megalena," resumed he, almost distracted, and snatching his stiletto forth, "I have lived too long then, and thus let me force existence from my worthless, though agonised heart." As he spoke, he tore open his vest, and franticly made an attempt to plunge it in his bosom.

Megalena, starting up, wrenched it from his furious grasp, and threw it far. Still the devoted youth remained at her feet. She cast her eyes downwards upon his graceful form, and tenfold love assailed her softened soul. She stretched forth her hand and bade him rise. Her voice re-animated him, and, springing up, he folded her with ardor to his breast.

The artful Strozzi returned his embrace, but suddenly pushing him from her, she exclaimed:

"Go, bring me that stiletto?" He felt surprise, but obeyed her imperious command.

She took it hastily from his hand, then said in a solemn serious voice:

"Leonardo, do you *love* me?"

"*Love* you!" he eagerly repeated.

"Then, mark me," she resumed, "by this stiletto, and by *your* hand, Theresa dies!"

The youth shuddered, and recoiled a few steps; for human nature shrinks instinctively at murder.

"Ah! false wretch! do you hesitate?" fiercely exclaimed the Florentine; "go then! go to your Theresa, and quit my sight for ever!"

"And will nothing less then appease thee, oh Megalena!" faltered out the enslaved Leonardo.

" 'Tis plain he *loves* her," gloomily muttered the vindictive Strozzi.

"Oh! no, by Heaven I do not!" eagerly replied Leonardo.

"*Prove* it then, by plunging this stiletto in her heart! nought else can, or shall, convince me that you do not."

"Oh! Megalena, my first, my only mistress! you will not, you cannot surely require proof so dreadful!" — and imploringly he looked in her countenance.

That fierce countenance still retained its unchanging expression — in it he read, "*Consent*, or *leave* me!" — This dreadful fiat made her appear, from the apprehension it excited of losing her, more beautiful than ever in his eyes. Her symmetrical form shone forth with redoubled loveliness to his heated fancy, and, while he gazed, his struggles died away, or were displaced by sensations which overpowered them. — He stretched forth his burning hand; it trembled with the consciousness of intended murder; and, in a faint faltering voice, he said —

"Give me the dagger!"

"You *consent* then, said the seductress Megalena, "to let it shed the blood of the insolent Venetian."

"I do — I do —"

"And to bring it me again, stained and dripping with her gore!"

"All — all — you require!" groaned the miserable Leonardo. "I love you — cruel Megalena — oh! how much — when, to prove it, I would murder —"

The Florentine cast the stiletto with violence away, and opened her fair arms wide. The bewildered Leonardo rushed into their embrace, and sunk overpowered on her bosom!

"I forgive thee," she cried; "I *now* forgive thee, Leonardo! I wanted, after thy cruel dereliction from me, some proof that I was still loved — that proof I have obtained, and thou art mine again!"

"Oh! I was thine ever," replied the infatuated youth, tears gushing from his eyes.

"I now believe that thou wert," answered the Florentine, gazing exultingly upon her victim, and then gently seating him beside her with a smile.

Such was the *fatal* empire that a worthless wanton had acquired over a young and susceptible heart, left to its wild energies, ere reason could preponderate; and thus darkly coloured became the future character of one, yielding progressively to the most horrible crimes, which, if differently directed in early youth, might have become an honor and an ornament to human nature.

CHAPTER XV

Megalena Strozzi, from this instance of the envy and treachery of female acquaintance, became disgusted with Venice, and resolved to retire again to her villa near the banks of the lake, that she might retain her captive in solitary safety. Having but rarely quitted her house during her stay at Venice, and even then avoiding the most public resorts, she had, as she desired, escaped the observation of Count Berenza, who indeed, had he chanced to have espied her, would have been more anxious to shun, than recognise her. Venice, however, she with Leonardo hastily quitted, and repaired to Aqua Dolce, secretly happy that she had borne away her lover from all further temptation, and exclusively appropriated him to herself.

For a time she remained tranquil and satisfied: she found means to diversify the scene, and amuse the youthful taste of Leonardo, by rambling about the beautiful walks that environed her dwelling, or sometimes, in her gondola, taking the fresco upon the lake. Yet, spite of all this, spite of being unceasingly in the society of him she preferred, her restless spirit could not be restrained, and again she panted for the gay pleasures of the city: *ennui* began to take posession of her ill-organized and resourceless mind; for it is the pure, *intellectual* soul alone, that can receive delight from solitude.

Venice, with all its dangers, became preferable in her eye to the gloomy sameness, though security of the country; and, after a residence of a few weeks there, she again resolved to brave the allurements of the city. Leonardo was equally desirous as herself to emerge from seclusion, but, having now acquired artifice, he affected indifference to the proposed change. Megalena, pleased at this appearance, and flattering herself that he was now too firmly riveted to allow himself to be again seduced by the charms or incitements of others, with as great eagerness as she had flown to it, now hastened from her weary solitude.

Arrived once more in Venice, she boldly resolved that she would no more, as formerly, debar herself from going, as she had been wont to do, to the most public resort of the gay Venetians; and she even decided in her mind, that should Berenza, as she fully expected he would, question her with respect to the nature of her intimacy with the youth Leonardo, to impose upon him, if possible, the same story that she had attempted to pass upon others.

In consequence of these arrangements it was that she no longer held herself from figuring in St. Mark's Place, and on the Laguna. Leonardo, however, constantly declined accompanying her in these public exhibitions; and the artful Florentine procured him such amusements at home, as should inform her on her return how he had employed his time.

Thus it was that, on a certain evening, during one of her excursions on the lake, she encountered Berenza, whom so long she had feared to meet; but encountered him under circumstances that she had little expected. Bitter and offensive to her jealous soul was the situation in which she beheld him, with a young and lovely rival seated by his side, in gay and amorous converse; with a basilisk's eye she gazed upon her, breathing destruction and revenge.

"And is it for this, then," she exclaimed, "that I have till now so anxiously concealed myself? Well might the wretch be incurious respecting me: well he might leave me unmolested by his visits. But why? Ah, little could I guess, and dearly shall he pay, for the short-lived raptures his inconstancy has procured him."

Thus, bursting with rage, swore the vengeful Megalena; and, rushing immediately, as she entered her abode, to the apartment where she had left Leonardo employed in finishing a drawing, she threw herself upon a chair beside him, and exclaimed —

"Throw, throw aside your pencil, Leonardo, and seize your dagger; for, by Heaven, this night he dies!"

"What said'st thou, Megalena?" inquired the youth with evident surprise, fixing his eyes upon her countenance: "*who* is it dies to night? and what dost thou mean?"

By the rage which flamed on her cheek, and sparkled in her eye, Leonardo easily discerned that somewhat unusual had occurred. Taking her hand, and tenderly kissing it, he pursued: "Tell me, Megalena, what has befallen thee?"

"Yes, he *shall* — by all my hopes of salvation he shall *die!*" frantically cried the vindictive Florentine; "and *thou*, Leonardo, yes, thou shalt execute my vengeance on him!"

Murder again! — the theme was still horrible to Leonardo, and again he shuddered and recoiled.

"Wilt thou not consent, Leonardo?" she said, in a hollow voice, fixing upon him her large and fiercely gleaming eyes.

"But say, *who* must die?" cried the youth, "and what is the offence against thee?"

"The treacherous, the ungrateful betrayer! But you know him not, Leonardo — yet, mark me; my resolution is taken, and it devolves on you to execute it! The time is at a length come, wherein you must prove the strength, the devotedness of your attachment to me. Now then hear me: — Il Conte Berenza is a noble Venetian; he was the betrayer, the deceiver of my youth; to him do I owe — yes, to *him*," added the artful Florentine, "that first my soul wandered from the paths of virtue! that I am now unworthy," hiding her countenance upon the bosom of her agitated lover, "to become ever more than the mistress of my Leonardo." The heart of Leonardo became infinitely affected. Megalena proceeded: "This day I encountered him on the Laguna, accompanied by a female: he passed me by; he uttered words the most gross, the most insulting; I regarded him with horror and surprise painted in my looks;

when, fearful I suppose that the mere sight of me should contaminate the purity of his present love, he rudely waved his hand, with an air of scorn and indignation, as if to say, "Impure wretch, how darest thou appear to recognise me in the presence of a superior female? — Leonardo!" she pursued, furiously starting from her chair, strung with new rage by the relation of the falsehoods she had invented — "Leonardo! shall I tamely submit to this? Canst *thou* submit to it? This to *thy* mistress — it is for that he dies! — thy love has *ennobled* me, and I will not now suffer degradation tamely!"

The high susceptible feelings of Leonardo, thus artfully played upon, became enkindled: he participated in her well-feigned outraged delicacy, so flattering to his own self-love; but still the revenge was dreadful to his mind, proportioned, too, far beyond the offence.

Perceiving that, though his cheek glowed with indignation, and his eyes with ardent love, that still he spoke not, determined, then, to work him to the pitch she required, she resumed:

"Oh, Leonardo! if, in love for thee, I have outstepped the bounds of delicacy and decorum, oh! let me not, therefore," with faltering voice, she pursued, "let me not be with impunity outraged or trampled on by others!"

"No, no, no!" cried the overpowered Leonardo, raising her in his arms; "no, never, sweet mistress of my soul, while I have life! He who offends thee, dies!"

"Thou art, then, thou art my own," cried the delighted Florentine; "that assurance reanimates my sinking soul. Secure now of my cherished revenge, I will discuss with thee further the steps to be pursued: come, my beloved Leonardo, let us go to the supper room.

Obedient to her will, Leonardo accompanied her. Seated now at supper with the machinating Florentine, she, fearful that his enthusiastic ardour might relax, pledged him repeatedly in goblets of the most potent wine; taking sufficient care, however, to elude swallowing more herself than would permit her to preserve her empire over him. As it fatally happened for Leonardo, Megalena never appeared more beautiful to him than at those times when she was urging him to the commission of some horrible evil; so that deeds, however repugnant tp his nature, and the loss of her love, bore in his deluded eyes no comparison. Megalena well aware of this, by appearing in her conduct and by her language as though she considered herself to have received his promise of avenging her, took from him in fact the power of refusing to do so. How to acknowledge to her, that his soul, shuddering, recoiled from the idea of murder, he knew not. From his knowledge of her disposition, he shrunk at encountering her direful rage, her bitter reproaches, and resentful looks; but more he shrunk even in thought from the possibility of her abandoning him, and, with a violent but expiring struggle, he decided in his mind to acquiesce, and give up every attempt to alter the current of events. As the fumes of the wine mounted to his brain, the reasoning of principle subsided, and the delusions of fancy increased. The Florentine became every moment more beautiful in his sight, and he began to think, that, in *her* cause, crime itself must become a virtue. She who, as she had persuaded him, seduced by her wild unconquerable love towards him, to forego and cast aside every principle of delicacy; she who had braved for him the scorn and contumely of the world; who had even this day, through him, as he conceived, endured gross insult; — no, it was no longer the representations of his lovely mistress which aroused him, but honor, justice, and gratitude. So wild and erring, in the increasing heat of intoxication, reasoned and believed the deluded Leonardo. It was now him who led to, and followed up the subject, while the exulting Megalena, by a refinement of artifice, added fuel to the fire she had excited, without appearing to do so.

At length, unable to contain the burning rage she inspired him with, he started suddenly up, and drinking down an overflowing goblet of Lacrymæ Christi, he prepared to rush from the house, without even taking the necessary precaution of a cloak and a mask, as enforced by Megalena. For a moment she succeeded in calming him, but only to direct his furor to unerring and surer destruction. Covering his face with a mask, she armed him with a stiletto, which she took from her girdle, and covered his figure with a cloak; then, straining him in her arms, she cried, "Success attend thee!"

Strung anew by her seductive embrace, stiletto in hand, he flew from the house, to plunge the deadly weapon in the heart of a man who had never injured him — whom even he did not know. Such is the influence to be obtained by female profligacy over the warm feelings of unaided youth.

Directed by the subtle enchantress, Leonardo easily gained the pallazzo of Berenza. As it had been a night of festivity, he found an easy access to the house, and, unobserved, into the chamber, where he concealed himself behind a wide curtain that covered a window, which, as has been said, opened into a balcony. On hearing Berenza and Victoria enter, he had stepped into it for greater security, and perceived, with no indifferent feeling, that it would, in case of necessity, afford him an opportunity of escape. There, in a state of mind bewildered, yet dreading to be reasonable, he remained till occasion seemed favorable for the execution of his purpose: the success it met with has been already related. To a hand rendered unsteady by a confused consciousness of the meditated crime, was added the intense and overpowering horror of at once recognising a sister, and burying in the same moment (as he believed) his dagger in her heart. Wild and dismayed, precipitately he had fled, a murderer in thought, at least, if not in deed, and sought, in a state of mind inexpressible, the vile Strozzi, who, like Sin, sat expecting to hear tidings of death.

"Well," exclaimed she, starting from the restless couch where she had thrown herself, as, pale and disordered, the unhappy Leonardo rushed into the room, his mask in his hand, and his vest torn open to admit the air to his burning bosom: "Well, is it done?"

"Yes, yes, vengeance is executed upon *one* of your enemies," he cried, in hurried accents.

"Upon the false, the infamous Berenza, I hope," eagerly returned Megalena, approaching and gazing in his pallid face.

"No, no, upon *my sister*!" gloomily answered Leonardo.

"Your sister! You rave, young coward," cried Megalena, shaking him by the arm.

"I do not — I have mortally wounded Victoria de Loredani, my sister! wounded her mortally in the arms of him, for whom my dagger was intended!"

"Thy sister, *thy* sister!" in a voice of fiend-like exultation, cried the infamous Strozzi; — yet secretly enraged that Berenza had not perished, and thrown by the furor of disappointment off her guard. — "Then Megalena Strozzi is not the *only* fallen female upon earth; no longer need she bow her head with shame to the ground — for Laurina, *mother* to the heir of Loredani! and Victoria, his *sister*! both *high* and *noble* ladies, raise her to *their* level by sinking to *hers*! — Oh, this is a balm to my soul," she continued, clapping her hands with a wild laugh; "Berenza, proud and accomplished seducer! the woman who loves *thee* may sacrifice to thee her innocence and her fame; but thou wilt never sacrifice to *her* thy liberty, or grant her thy *honorable* love!" — Thus continued the unfeeling Florentine, wreaking upon the wretched Leonardo the avenging scorpions of her tongue, for having failed in the precise purport of his dreadful mission. This was the first time, since their ill-advised union, that she had ventured to breathe aught concerning, much less taunt him with the agonising secrets of his family misfortunes! His high soul sickened and shrunk within him at allusions so barbarous: for an instant he regarded with horror the infamous Strozzi; he essayed to speak, but could not, and, overpowered with violent and conflicting emotions, he fell prostrate on the floor.

It was then Megalena began to think, and even admitted the conviction, that she had proceeded too far; she almost feared that, by the inhuman stab she had given to the high feelings of the youth, she had destroyed for ever in his heart every particle of love for herself. This reflection served in an instant to change the tenor of her conduct: from the malice of rage and disappointment, she softened to the suggestions of her interest, which whispered to her, that in losing now the regards and future devotement of Leonardo, upon which she calculated much, she should lose her all.

Throwing herself beside him, therefore, she passionately implored his forgiveness, and sought, by the repetition of every well-tried artifice, to soothe and alleviate the agonising tumult she had excited. By degrees her blandishments began to prevail over the infatuated youth; and even the horrible recollections she had awakened in his mind, of his being in reality a disgraced and wandering outcast, drew him but more closely to *her*, who, knowing him for what he was, still loved, and took an interest in his fate. He adored her, though she had wounded him to the soul, and, when to her caresses and ardent professions of eternal attachment she solicited some reply, he raised her in his arms, as kneeling she bent over him, and, pressing her with violent emotion to his bosom, passionately cried:

"Megalena, I am thine *still* — yes, I feel that I am, and shall be so *for ever*! — Oh, lovely and seducing woman, eternal must thy empire be over me; and, if I forsake thee, may the curse of Heaven light upon my head!"

"Then," cried the Florentine, delighted at the strength and solemnity of this assurance, "let us from this moment be eternally devoted to each other! let us *swear*, that nor time, accident, nor circumstance, shall *ever* disunite us!"

"I swear," answered Leonardo ardently, "I swear it again;" and kissed with rapture the extended hand of Megalena.

"Receive too *my* oath of perpetual allegiance to *thee*, loved youth," with ardour, exclaimed the Florentine, "for I solemnly swear to be ever true, and devoted to thee. Now then," she added more calmly, "let all past differences be buried in oblivion, and the more material circumstances of the moment obtain our consideration."

Seating herself beside Leonardo, she then desired a minuter detail of the occurrences of the night; when suddenly, in the midst of his relation, she missed the dagger which she had given to him! Her high-flushed cheek became immediately blanched by terror, and eagerly she interrupted him to ask him concerning it. In an instant the recollection flashed upon his mind, that, in endeavouring to recover his mask, he had never thought of retrieving his dagger likewise, which he did not even remember to have drawn from the bosom of Victoria, where fully he believed himself to have plunged it. Such had been the horror and agitation of his mind, he could retrace nothing distinctly; yet the dagger was unquestionably left behind, and this was enough to distract the Florentine.

Gasping for breath, "We are undone!" she cried, "we are betrayed; for on the hilt of *that* dagger is engraved, at full length, the name of "Megalena Strozzi!"

Leonardo was silent, for he dreaded the reproaches which he almost felt he merited.

Suddenly recovering, however, her presence of mind, she exclaimed: "We must fly, we must fly instantly; the night is not yet spent; before daybreak we may be far from this detested city. To some future period I must defer the completion of my just revenge! — You tremble, young man; but let us hope," she added with a horrible smile, "that you will not *always* be thus dismayed at the thought of blood; — why, Leonardo, thou art not half a Venetian!"

"Am I not, Megalena? When occasion calls, I can prove myself one; but I feel that, were I even abject by blood, and in my heart, that *thou* couldst render me equal to any thing." Still, as he spoke, his eyes refused to meet the unshrinking gaze of the Florentine.

"We shall fly then together, beloved Leonardo," said she, "and I shall not so much regret our enforced departure from this gay city; for, now to be frank with thee, my love, my resources diminish daily: this place affords me no longer the exhaustless mine I once imagined it would; the Venetians have become wary, or can it be, that *I* am changed from beauty to deformity?[1] Be it as it may, we will quit it unreluctantly, and let us hope that elsewhere better fortune may be ours."

Though some parts of Megalena's speech had surprised Leonardo, he forbore (unwilling to diminish her fascinations in his own eyes,) to require more ample explanation; he took her hand hastily, and said —

"I will follow thee, fair Megalena, wheresoever thou wilt, even unto the end of my life, as we have mutually sworn."

Smiles of pleasure chased from the brow of the Florentine the gloomy traces of rage, and unsatisfied revenge; she looked upon her lover with eyes of gratitude, and ardent affection: he was indeed become her all, her sole dependance in the plans of her future life; for, vicious, profligate, and unsteady, though still not past the zenith of her charms, they were deemed so far from counterbalancing the violent passions which deformed her mind, that she had but few admirers among the jealous and suspicious Venetians.

She now hastened from the room to make every preparation for an immediate flight: in less than two hours, she had gathered together all the valuables she possessed, and which were capable of being taken with them — every requisite was arranged, and the grey eye of the morning beheld them far from Venice.

Unhappy Laurina! whose criminal desertion of thine offspring entailed upon them such misery and degradation. In this early career of their lives, behold the guilt and unworthiness for which thou art amenable. Yet, darker still, and disfigured by greater crimes, will be the days which are to come. Faultless example would have shamed into efforts of virtue, the proud and violent nature of thy daughter; yet behold her now, without even a remorseful struggle, abandoning its precepts. Thy son, the dark hue of his character decided, the slave of an artful worthless wanton, who presumes, and justly presumes, to call herself *thy equal*! while, through a terrible and unforeseen combination of events, he has been on the eve of becoming the murderer of his sister! — Tremble, unfortunate and guilty mother, for longer and more gloomy becomes the register of thy crimes!

---

1 from beauty to deformity: Megalena had been compared to Sin awaiting Death earlier in this chapter, and here she echoes Sin's speech to Satan after he fails to recognize her in her new form as "snaky sorceress." "Hast thou forgot me then, and do I seem / Now in thine eye so foul, once deemed so fair / In heav'n" (*Paradise Lost* II 747-49).

CHAPTER XVI

The letter, which was written by Megalena Strozzi, and which, from an obscure spot in the island of Capri, she had caused to be conveyed to Berenza, has been already given at full in a preceding part of this history; and was received, as stated, about a fortnight after the mutual flight of Leonardo and herself, well knowing that pursuit must then be vain, and (from the precautions they had taken) to trace their route impossible. Still undetermined where eventually to fix, but resolving to be guided by circumstances respecting their future plans, we must now, for a considerable length of time, leave them, and return to the thread of our narrative.

Youth, and that strength of mind which precluded hypochondriac malady, did not permit Victoria to languish long under the effects of her wound; she grew rapidly convalescent, but, during her inevitable confinement, external objects not intervening much to distract her regards by flattering her vanity, she had full leisure to concentrate her great and varied powers into one point — that of rendering herself an object of such moment to her lover, that he should consider, with horror, the bare possibility of losing her, and be anxious to bind her more completely his, by ties esteemed indissoluble.

But such had already been the effect produced upon Berenza, by conduct which he could not help considering proof of the most heroic love, as well as courage, that he no longer viewed her with tender passion only, but with the strongest sentiments of gratitude and enthusiastic admiration.

What could woman more, than voluntarily, nay eagerly, oppose her own life in defence of his? Who but Victoria could possess, at once, such tender and such exalted sentiments towards a lover? Longer to doubt the truth, the romantic ardour of her attachment, would, he esteemed, be sacrilege; his ideas underwent a wonderful, but natural revolution — no more the haughty Berenza, proud of his noble, his unsullied blood, fearing to dash it with a tincture of disgrace! — no more looking *down*, with protecting air, a high and superior being, upon a mistress beloved indeed, but not considered as an *equal*, because, though innocent in reality, in his eyes she was a scion of infamy and shame; — no, his heart now throbbed with excessive tenderness, and now ached with compunctious pangs, that he could ever have deemed unworthy of his honorable love the creature before him, shining superior in a glory emanating from *herself*! — the creature to whom he now thought himself inferior! So complete and powerful a dominion had the act of Victoria obtained over his mind, that his *proud* and dignified attachment, softened into a doating and idolatrous love. He was no longer the refined, the calculating philosopher, but the yielding devoted lover! devoted to the excess of his passion. In short, he felt that *now*, to be happy, to conciliate his conscience, and to atone to Victoria for his past injustice, he must make her his wife.

No sooner had he formed this resolution, than he believed himself to have discovered a balm for every thing, and to experience a pure sensation of delight till now unknown. Unable long to contend against the strong impulse of his heart, he waited only for the re-establishment of Victoria's health, to pour out his feelings at her feet, and to offer to her the unworthy gift of himself.

When, therefore, he thought her sufficiently recovered to permit him to touch upon a subject, that must, as he supposed, occasion some emotion, he no longer withheld himself from giving utterance to what had of late so often risen from an overflowing heart to his lips. Victoria heard him with a look of complacency, and all that softness she knew so well how to assume; but pride having always kept her from surmising the struggles of Berenza upon her subject, and that he had not till this period offered to become her *husband*, because till this period he had deemed her unworthy to become his *wife*; having never surmised this, she betrayed no immediate emotion, or unspeakable delight; no overpowering transport, or surprise; but listened to him in silence, with an acquiescent smile. This being considered by Berenza as a coolness of demeanour uncongenial to the subject, he mentally attributed it to wounded pride in Victoria that he had not *sooner* made her an offer of his hand. His own noble delicacy caught the alarm, and his liberal soul acknowledged the justice of her feeling; anxious then to remove from her mind every uneasy impression, the ardour of his manner increased, and he prayed of Victoria to pardon the unworthiness of his past scruples.

Here Berenza erred; had he stopped at the simple intention of offering his hand to Victoria, he had done right; but his last insinuation, though broken and obscure, darted like lightning through her brain, and struck to her proud heart as a three-edged dagger! That proud heart had now indeed taken an alarm far beyond any that Berenza's imagination could have conceived. Her brow lowered, she turned of an ashy paleness, as sudden hatred and desire of revenge took possession of her vindictive soul. The conviction flashed upon her, that she had till this moment been deemed by Berenza unworthy of becoming his wife.

"The secret then is betrayed," thought she; "the sort of union into which he entered with me , and which vainly I preferred as a proof of his love for me, was desired by him only as being least offensive to his dignity and pride — 'tis well —"

Rapidly these ideas passed through the mind of Victoria; and, while secretly vowing the offence should never be forgotten, she again harmonised her features, and clothed them with smiles: since such had been the sentiments of Berenza, it now became unquestionably a desirable point to become at once his wife. To have triumphed by any means over his stern and detested pride was something, but it could not obliterate the crime of having ever dared to view her in an inferior light. Unhappy, Berenza! all thy delicacy, thy forbearance, and nobleness of mind, will not save thee from the consequences of having proceeded thus far.

The changes of Victoria's countenance were only attributed by her lover to an unconquerable emotion, which she struggled to conceal, at this undeniable proof of the strength of his attachment to her; delicately solicitous to raise her in her own eyes, he, with pressing earnestness, entreated of her a prompt compliance to their union. Victoria fixed upon him her eyes, pregnant with an unusual expression, for busy were her evil thoughts against him.

"Why is that look, my love?" inquired Berenza.

"I look upon thee as I love thee!" answered Victoria.

"And thou wilt be mine — honorably and solemnly mine, then?" said Berenza, with eagerness.

"I will; answered Victoria — I most ardently *desire* to become thy wife."

Berenza, who understood nothing by these expressions but simply what met the ear, viewed her with an increase of tenderness and admiration; for it is a principle in human nature to exalt in our *minds* those objects we are determined to favor and elevate.

A very short period from this beheld Victoria di Loredani the wife of Il Conte Berenza; and becoming so, her faults in the eyes of an admiring husband were wholly obliterated, and her better qualities appeared to shine forth with redoubled effect.

With what a different and far more refined feeling did he *now* walk with her in St. Mark's Place, or exhibit her on the Laguna, amid thousands of gay Venetians, in their gondolas. With what pleasure, with what delight, with an air how unembarrassed, did he *now* introduce, as his *wife*, to an elegant and respectable society, her whom he could have felt but a vain and inconsiderable triumph in introducing as his *mistress* to the gay and dissolute! In having made his Victoria an honorable wife, he experienced a noble and benevolent satisfaction, which had for its basis the reflection of having raised to a level with the higher class of society, her whom he might have been instrumental in sinking to that of the lowest.

But though the conduct of the refined Berenza was such as to claim and to deserve the highest gratitude and love, the vindictive spirit of Victoria could not forget that he had *once* deemed her unworthy of ranking on an equality with himself; for this, in her moments of solitude, her heart swelled with unforgiving hate: she despised and undervalued the advantages she possessed, and fed the discontented repinings of her mind, by recalling to memory the moment when he unfortunately betrayed the state of his sentiments respecting her. Sometimes she even regretted that, under circumstances so humiliating, she had consented to become his wife, and almost determined to shew her contempt of his fancied condescension, by abandoning him. If at these times her unconscious husband by chance obtruded, he was received with a gloomy and discontented air, which, when he pressed her to explain, she attributed either to indisposition, or an involuntary depression of spirits.

When the mind is dissatisfied, whether upon grounds just or unjust, it ever views objects through an exaggerated medium; trifles which, when in a sane state, would have passed unnoticed, are twisted from their proper insignificance, to aid the conceptions of a disturbed imagination. Thus was it with Victoria: she knew, and felt, that Berenza was her superior, and she imagined that he must feel it likewise; every word, every look, every action, she thought reproached with her former degradation, and the abjectness from which it had pleased him to raise her. Her fits of gloom and abstraction increased; she forbore to cultivate any society, from a sentiment of most unpardonable pride — pride which, like a worm in the heart, the more it was cherished the more corroded; and the luckless Berenza was sometimes, in the momentary sting of disappointed hope, compelled to acknowledge, that though the situation of a wife might have rendered more *respectable* the object of his love, it had for ever destroyed the charms and fascinations of the mistress: yet still he loved her with the tenderest, the truest affection.

Five years had now rolled on since a union but little productive of real happiness to either party, when, one evening, a violent ringing at the gate of the pallazzo bespoke the approach of an impatient visitor. Soon a stranger was announced, and almost in the same moment entered the saloon. Berenza rose from his chair, but scarcely did he cast a glance towards him ere he flew into the arms that opened to receive him, exclaiming, "Welcome to Venice! welcome home, my beloved Henriquez!" Then, turning towards Victoria, as surprise and delight permitted him to recover himself, "Behold a beloved brother, my Victoria," he said; "and you, my brother, behold an adored wife: now, now, indeed, may I expect to be truly happy."

Henriquez pressed the hand of his brother, and paid some graceful compliments to Victoria, who, gazing upon him with admiration, in an instant drew ungrateful comparisons between their persons, to the disadvantage of him in whom her soul should have discerned *no fault*. But that benevolent and unsuspicious being seated himself between them, and felt, as he deserved to be, truly happy.

Hitherto it has not been thought requisite to enlarge materially upon the cause that induced the departure and stay of Berenza's brother from Venice. It has been hinted, however, that it was to divert, if possible, by activity and change of scene, the ardour and impetuosity of a passion that he had conceived for a young lady, whose father had, on the plea of their mutual youth, opposed their union, but who in reality was desirous only of obtaining a higher match for the blooming Lilla, his daughter, at that period little more than thirteen years of age; for although he could not bestow upon her the smallest dowry, he conceived that the nobility of her birth entitled her to the first Duca in Venice. The circumstance of his having lately become deceased, which event Lilla, in corresponding with, had imparted to her lover, was the means of bringing him thus in anxious eagerness to Venice, fondly hoping that now every obstacle to their union was removed, which still remained the first fond wish of his bosom, undiminished by time or an absence of years; for where, as with impassioned earnestness he demanded of himself, could he ever hope to find in another that purity and innocence which his heart told him still dwelt incorruptible in the bosom of his young and lovely mistress?

Berenza, to whom, during supper, he related the delightful cause of his sudden return, and dwelt with all the ardour of a lover upon the fond hope he entertained of being soon enabled to call Lilla his, fondly took pleasure in flattering him that nothing indeed was now likely to disappoint the desires of his heart. Victoria listened in silence to the conversation, and an indefinite sentiment, resembling regret, glanced through her bosom, when she thereby discovered that the affections of the young Henriquez were so deeply engaged.

At length they separated for the night: the lover to dream of the fair creature that in the morning he hoped to embrace; and the disturbed Victoria to arrange, if possible, the confusion of idea that floated in her mind.

Scarcely had the first beams of morning enlightened the east, ere Henriquez awakened, ardent and impatient to visit the object of his love. Soon as propriety might in the least admit, he flew to her residence: the fair Lilla received him indeed with all the warmth, with all the affection he could have wished, but his buoyant hopes were quelled by what she said in reply to his eager solicitations to become immediately his.

Her father was indeed dead, but still impediments existed; she was under the protection of an ancient female relative, who with herself had remained with him in his last moments. It was the dying request, nay command of that father, (cruel and relentless even in death,) that she should not marry till the expiration of a whole year from the time that he should be consigned to the earth. To this she had solemnly and implicitly promised obedience, and to this requisition, hard as it was, she professed to Henriquez her fixed resolution to adhere.

Educated in sentiments of the severest piety, it was in her idea a sacred and religious obligation in her to fulfil a promise to the dying; nay, she would have deemed it horrible sacrilege even to hesitate or waver respecting its performance; and all the entreaties of her lover to make her forego adherence to what he considered an arbitrary and most unjust command, were not only vain, but tended almost to shake him in his long and deep-rooted sentiments of esteem, by giving her doubts of his moral character. Little more than one month had as yet elapsed, since the interment of the tyrannical parent; nearly a whole year even now must roll over their heads, ere they could become united; yet even against this grievous representation on the side of Henriquez the pious Lilla was proof, and, with a heart nearly as agonised as if he had been compelled to resign for ever his hopes, the unhappy lover returned to his brother's pallazzo.

His first impulse was to seek him in private, and relate to him the disappointment of his wishes with Lilla. The kind Berenza listened with attentive sympathy, and it occurred to him that, since Lilla would not immediately become the wife of Henriquez, the pains of delay might be infinitely alleviated by prevailing on her to become a constant visitor at the pallazzo, which, as Berenza was now married, and she herself under the protection of a female relative who would always accompany her, could not certainly be in the least an objectionable alternative. This was indeed pouring balm into the wounds of Henriquez; scarcely would the eager and impassioned youth permit his brother to conclude, ere he rushed from his presence, and appeared again before his beloved Lilla, to impart to her the proposition of Berenza, and to implore her to accede to it. This the scrupulous and innocent girl offered no objection to, and the heart of her lover was once more rendered comparatively light.

On the evening of the same day she consented, accompanied by her relation, to visit Victoria; for it was under that shape alone that Henriquez had ventured to propose her seeing him at the pallazzo of his brother: he then once more departed, and related to Berenza his second attempt, with the success it had met upon the conscientiousness and delicacy of his mistress.

In the evening, according to promise, the fair girl made her appearance, and was by Henriquez introduced to the Conte and to Victoria, as his destined wife: but never, ah, surely never, was unconscious guest received with feelings and with thoughts so hostile as was the innocent Lilla by Victoria! Yet still the smile played upon the disciplined features of the accomplished hypocrite, and the hand was extended to bid her welcome.

Throughout the evening her conduct was such as to excite a timid gratitude and respect in the breast of her lovely visitor, and to make her appear admirable in the eyes of the delighted Henriquez. Why were unreal, appearances that shed around such pure, expansive satisfaction? Dark and dreadful are the intricacies of the human heart, when debased as was Victoria's. Almost unknowing to herself, she conceived immediate hatred for the orphan Lilla, because she was dear, because she was beloved by Henriquez, and Henriquez had appeared charming in her eyes. It was the early influence of this new-born sentiment that had generated one so base, and Victoria's was not a noble and an honorable mind, that would combat in itself feelings that were improper to be indulged, rather would she have sought their gratification, unmindful of the misery that might be produced to others.

CHAPTER XVII

As though the curse of Laurina were entailed upon her daughter, (that of becoming absorbed by a guilty and devouring flame, with the single exception that, in the case of the former, the heart and mind had been *involuntarily* seduced by a designing betrayer, while the other cherished and encouraged an increasing passion for one who attempted her not, and which common honor should have taught her to repel), Victoria dwelt with unrestrained delight upon the attractions of the object, that had presented itself to her fickle and ill-regulated mind.[1] From her infancy untaught, therefore unaccustomed to subdue herself, she had no conception of that *refined* species of virtue which consists in self-denial; the proud triumph of mind over the weakness of the heart, she had ever been unconscious of; education had never corrected the evil propensities that were by nature hers: hence pride, stubbornness, the gratification of self, contempt and ignorance of the nobler properties of the mind, with a strong tincture of the darker passions, revenge, hate, and cruelty, made up the sum of her early character. Example, a *mother's* example, had more than corroborated every tendency to evil, and the unhappy Victoria was destitute of a single actuating principle, that might, in consideration of its guilt, deter her from the pursuit of a favorite object. Her mind, alas, was an eternal night, which the broad beam of virtue never illumined.

Henriquez was the subject of her thoughts by day; he employed her fancy by night; his form presented itself if she awoke; he figured in her dreams if she slumbered; daily, nay momentarily, her unchecked passion acquired strength: already she viewed with disgust, heightened by unfading remembrance of the sentiments he had once entertained respecting her, the being who had claims so strong upon her gratitude and affection.

For the young Lilla she cherished the most unprovoked and the bitterest hate; the hot breath she respired was charged with wishes for her destruction; yet each, and all of these beings, were unconscious of the feelings they inspired; for the honorable Berenza, whose mild philosophy taught him it was only just to conclude that love induced love, and proofs of esteem gratitude, regarded his wife with an unvarying tenderness. The innocent Lilla placed confidence in her smiles, and courteous demeanour; while Henriquez, absorbed in the contemplation of an adored mistress, remarked not the impassioned glances of another directed towards him, nor the pointed attentions by which they were at times accompanied.

---

1 Compare to Bienville's *Nymphomania*: "They dwell only on the fatal object, who is the cause of their disorder; they see but him alone; all the powers of their mind are, as it were, unmoveable." (See Appendix A.)

Eminently indeed calculated to excite an ardent love in youth, was the mind and person of the orphan Lilla. Pure, innocent, free even from the smallest taint of a corrupt thought, was her mind; delicate, symmetrical, and of fairy-like beauty, her person so small, yet of so just proportion; sweet, expressing a seraphic serenity of soul, seemed her angelic countenance, slightly suffused with the palest hue of the virgin rose. Long flaxen hair floated over her shoulders: she might have personified (were the idea allowable) innocence in the days of her childhood. Her very situation had a powerful claim upon the heart of sensibility, for the blooming Lilla was an orphan: no ostensible protector had she under the face of heaven, since an old and feeble relative, whose very existence from day to day appeared precarious, could not justly be deemed so; this very circumstance it was, that drew most powerfully towards her the benevolent soul of Berenza, and ardently he longed for the expiration of the allotted year, that she might obtain, in the arms of his brother, a safe and honorable refuge.

Time rolled on, and the effervescence of Victoria's mind increased almost to madness. Nothing but the consideration of the proposed marriage between Henriquez and Lilla being, in conformance with the religious scruples of the latter, protracted, kept her within the bounds of discretion, necessary even for the accomplishment of her own purpose. But as she beheld time passing away, and that still Henriquez, the idol of her thoughts, remained wholly insensible to the most open insinuations, almost avowals of the feelings he had excited, she became nearly frantic with desperation, and resolved to risk every thing to obtain her point.

The most wild and horrible ideas took possession of her brain; crimes of the deepest dye her imagination could conceive appeared as nothing, opposed to the possibility of obtaining a return of love from Henriquez. To see him, and to see him bestowing upon the envied Lilla marks of the tenderest attachment, made her wild with the furor[1] of conflicting passions: now it was, that she truly felt she had never *loved* the injured Berenza, but that circumstances, the situation of the moment, and a combination of events alone, had first induced her to attend, and ultimately to fly to him, as the only being who would afford her protection. She now viewed him as a philosophic sensualist alone, whose conduct towards her had been solely actuated by selfish motives. Was he not considerably her superior in years? It was plain, then, that his regard for her had been of the most unworthy kind, and his anxiety to ascertain her love for him, ere he took advantage of the situation into which she had thrown herself, a refinement of the grossest artifice. But Henriquez, the lovely Henriquez,

---

1 made her wild with the furor of conflicting passions.: Dacre's use of furor, for *furor uterinus*, or nymphomania, had shocked the reviewer for *Monthly Literary Recreations* (see Appendix B and introduction for a full discussion).

was more upon an equality with her, and it was for him that the selfish Berenza should have reserved her.

Thus it was, that she ungratefully reflected upon the delicate and noble conduct of the Conte towards her! forgotten all his honorable forbearance, despised his refined and disinterested attachment; and thus it is, that in the pursuance of some favorite object, the wicked depreciate the benefits they have received.

Retiring one night to her chamber, more gloomy, more repining than ever, she threw herself upon her bed, secretly wishing that Berenza, that Lilla, nay, even the whole world, (if it stood between her and the attainment of her object,) could become instantly annihilated. Her bosom ached with the exhausting conflict of the most violent passions; death and destruction entered her thoughts, and twice she started up, as impelled to execute some dreadful purpose, she knew not what! Horrible images possessed her brain, and her heart seemed burning with an intense and unquenchable fire. She became even herself astonished, at the violence of the sensations which shook her, and for an instant believed herself under the influence of some superior and unknown power.

Transported nearly beyond the bounds of reason; almost expecting, in the wildness of her distempered fancy, to behold somewhat that should corroborate her idea, perhaps even to soothe the agony of her bosom; she started up again from her thorn-strewed pillow! But no — all was peaceful without — the rage and the confusion was in her breast! A dim light, at the further end of the chamber, emitting a few solitary rays, revealed the surrounding loneliness and gloom; she pressed her hand on her throbbing temples, her heart beat with violence; and, once more overpowered, she laid her head upon her pillow.

At length she fell into a disturbed slumber; dreams of mysterious tendency began to flit in the disordered eye of sleep. First she beheld, in a beautiful and luxurious garden, Lilla and Henriquez; his arm encircled her waist, and her head reclined upon his shoulder, while he contemplated her angelic countenance with looks of ineffable love. As this vision, a deep groan broke in sleep from the miserable Victoria; she endeavoured to turn her eyes from them, but could not, and, while the most horrible and raging pains shot through her heart, they suddenly disappeared from before her, and she found herself alone, in a remote part of the garden. Presently she beheld, approaching towards her, a group of shadowy figures; they appeared to hover in mid air, but at no great distance from the earth, and, as they came nearer, she discerned, that though of a deadly paleness, their features were beautiful and serene. These passed gradually; when, as if from the midst of them, she beheld advancing a Moor, of a noble and majestic form. He was clad in a habit of white and gold; on his head he wore a white turban, which sparkled with emeralds, and was surmounted by a waving feather of green; his arms and legs, which were bare, were encircled with the finest oriental pearl; he wore a collar of gold round his throat, and his ears were decorated with gold rings of an enormous size.

Victoria contemplated this figure with an inexplicable awe, and, as she gazed, he bent his knee, and extended his arms towards her. While in this attitude, her mind filled with terror, she looked upon him with dread, and essaying to fly, she stumbled and awoke.

Reflecting on her dream, she could attribute it only to the disturbed state of her mind; and, desirous if possible to forget for a few moments her pain, she again endeavoured to sleep.

Scarcely had thought become again suspended, ere fancy took the lead; she now saw herself in a church brilliantly illuminated, when, horrible to her eyes, approaching the altar near which she stood, appeared Lilla, led by Henriquez and attired as a bride! In the instant that their hands were about to be joined, the Moor she had beheld in her preceding dream appeared to start between them, and beckoned her towards him; involuntarily she drew near him, and touched his hand, when Berenza stood at her side, and seizing her arm, endeavoured to pull her away. "Wilt thou be mine?" in a hurried voice whispered the Moor in her ear, "and none then shall oppose thee." But Victoria hesitated, and cast her eyes upon Henriquez: the Moor stepped back, and again the hand of Henriquez became joined with Lilla's. "Wilt thou be mine?" exclaimed the Moor in a loud voice, "and the marriage shall *not be*!" — "Oh, yes, yes!" eagerly cried Victoria, overcome by intense horror at the thoughts of their union. — In an instant *she* occupied the place of Lilla; and Lilla, no longer the blooming maid, but a pallid spectre, fled shrieking through the aisles of the church, while Berenza, suddenly wounded by an invisible hand, sunk covered with blood at the foot of the altar! Exultation filled the bosom of Victoria; she attempted to take the hand of Henriquez; but casting her eyes upon him, she beheld him changed to a frightful skeleton, and in terror awoke!

Her mind was now in a chaos of agitation and horror, from which she found it difficult to recover; endeavouring, however, by a violent effort to recall her scattered ideas, and to resume her usual firmness, she became collected enough to review the leading features of her dream.

The image which, upon this review, presented itself most forcibly to her mental vision, was that of the Moor, whose person she had a confused idea of having seen frequently before. After a minute's reflection, she identified him for Zofloya, the servant of Henriquez. Why *he* should be connected with her dreams, who never entered her mind when waking, she could not divine: but certain it was, that his exact resemblance, though as it were of polished and superior appearance, had figured chiefly in her troubled sight. She next reverted to the terrible moment in which she beheld joined the hands of Lilla and Henriquez, but that Zofloya had offered to prevent the marriage. On this incident she pondered with a sensation of pleasure, and Berenza, bleeding and dying at her feet, she contemplated as a blissful omen of her success. The more she considered, the more she inferred, the less reason she perceived for interpreting ill the visions of the night; and the conclusion which at length she drew was this, that every barrier to the gratification of her wishes would ultimately be destroyed, and that she should at length obtain Henriquez: all else she considered as irrelevant to the true purport of her dream, and the fantastic ebulitions of a disturbed mind. The frequent introduction of Zofloya she judged to be merely in consequence of her beholding him daily, sometimes attending behind the chair of his master at meal times, and on other occasions; while Henriquez, changing to a skeleton when she obtained his hand, was emblematic only, she conceived, that he would be hers till death.

The following day, when at a late hour she entered the apartment where they usually dined, the first object that caught her attention was the tall, commanding figure of the Moor, standing near the chair of his master; she almost started as she beheld him, and, the image in her dreams flashing in her mind, she marked how exact was the similitude, in form, in features, and in dress. She seated herself, however, at the table, but involuntarily stole frequent glances towards him: once or twice she imagined that he looked upon her with a peculiar expression of countenance, and strange, incongruous ideas shot through her brain; ideas which, even to herself, were indefinable. She became at length gloomy and abstracted, from mere incapacity to develope her own sensations; but to be gloomy and abstracted, had of late ceased in her to become remarkable; and, while the excellent Berenza in secret deplored this change in his beloved Victoria, he forbore the slightest reproach, endeavouring only, by the kindest and most delicate attentions, to disperse her frequent melancholy: the innocent Lilla too, with gentle sweetness, would sometimes approach, and seek, by endearment or lively converse, to remove what was so evident to all.

But the efforts of the lovely girl appeared rather to injure than to benefit Victoria; they roused her from her dejection indeed, but excited strong irritability, and feelings of the bitterest nature. Solitude in general seemed to delight her most; and, as she had denied to Berenza that she possessed any definable cause of melancholy, in that he permitted her to indulge; hoping, unsuspicious of the evil in her heart, that her mind, by its own efforts, would recover its tone.

As for Henriquez, though he treated her with friendship and respect, as the wife of his brother, he did no more: first, because he was absorbed in Lilla; and, secondly, because being so completely, both in mind and person, the reverse of that pure and delicate being, he not only failed to view them as two creatures of the same class, but almost thought of Victoria with a tincture of dislike, from the very circumstance of her being so opposite to his lovely mistress.

CHAPTER XVIII

The Moor, Zofloya, was beloved by all, save one, in the pallazzo of Berenza; this single exception of the general sentiment was discernible in a man called Latoni, a domestic who had resided for some years in the service of the Conte: envy and hatred filled his heart in contemplating the superior qualities of Zofloya, whose elegant person was his least recommendation. He could dance with inimitable grace, and his skill in music was such, that in excursions on the Laguna he frequently, at the request of his master, occupied one end of the gondola, to charm the company with the exquisiteness of his harmony. These rare distinctions, and the estimation in which the Moor was held by his superiors, so preyed upon the mind of Latoni, that he abhorred to look upon him, and sought every occasion to irritate him, that, in some quarrel or fight, he might do him a mortal injury. The Moor, however, disdaining Latoni, treated him with sovereign contempt, and no bitterness of language could extort from him other reply than a smile of most expressive scorn. This behaviour would enrage Latoni to a pitch of madness, but not daring to wreak his vengeance upon so universal a favorite, he had no alternative but to rush from the spot, and vent in curses the malignant fury of his breast.

It happened that, some few days after the singular dreams of Victoria, while their impression and their tendency still occupied her mind, that the Moor, Zofloya, became suddenly missing! As he was so highly prized by Henriquez, and admired by all, this circumstance caused infinite consternation throughout the pallazzo; and none indeed did it affect more strongly (most inconceivably to herself) than Victoria. Every place that he had ever been in the habit of frequenting, where even there was the remotest probability of his having been, was scrupulously sought, and referred to; people were sent different ways, throughout Venice, to gain, if possible, some intelligence respecting him; but all in vain. — Several days elapsed, and not the smallest tidings could be obtained.

Conjecture at length became weary, and hope began to fail; all further attempts to learn the fate of Zofloya were considered to be vain, and time alone was expected to develope the mysterious circumstances of his sudden disappearance. In the midst of this, the domestic Latoni was seized with sickness, and confined to his bed. Berenza, who regarded him as an old and faithful servant, used every endeavour to promote his recovery; but his disorder rapidly gaining ground, the physicians confessed the inability of medicine to save him from approaching death. This final opinion being conveyed to Latoni, he was seized with the most terrible pangs, from which he only recovered to entreat the presence of a confessor, his master, and Signor Henriquez, ere he resigned his breath.

This request of a dying man, the benevolent Berenza readily complied with; Henriquez likewise consented to accompany him, and Victoria, she knew not why, begged permission to be present. All together, then, entered the chamber of the expiring Latoni, who, soon as he beheld them, raising himself in his bed, spoke as follows:

"My Lord Berenza, and you Signor Henriquez, execrate not a dying penitent, but listen with mercy and forgiveness to his confession. It is I, Latoni, who know all concerning the disappearance of the Moor Zofloya. *I* envied his beauty, his accomplishments, and hated him for the admiration which they obtained him. I sought many opportunities of provoking him to quarrel with me, but he treated me with contempt, and this increasing my rage against him, determined me to take his life!"

"Wretch!" exclaimed Victoria.

"Signora, peace, I beseech you, for I must be brief; and the pangs I now endure, may almost expiate my crime —

"One evening, the evening he was missing — I followed him from the pallazzo; I watched his footsteps, but kept at a distance. I observed him on St. Mark's; my heart panted with uncontrollable fury, and desire of vengeance, for the bitter moments he had given me. — I saw him raise his eyes to heaven, and contemplate the spangled sky — he stood almost close to the brink, over the canal, and I longed to push him in headlong; but the idea that this might not effect completely his destruction, and that he might save himself by expert swimming, stayed my eager hand, and softly I approached him from behind. — He heard me not. — I took, trembling with fear of failure, my dagger from my belt, and plunged it repeatedly into his back, ere he could even attempt to defend himself; I then, satisfied that he must perish, tumbled him into the water, from which he never rose, and hastily fled the spot! — An avenging conscience pursued me however, and prevented me from enjoying the fruits of my crime; death approaches, and the torments of Hell are open to my view."

As Latoni concluded, strong convulsions seized him, and he fell back upon his pillow. His confession had eased his conscience, but could not prolong his life. He lingered a few hours, then praying for mercy, though almost despairing to obtain it, he breathed his last.

Great was the grief of Victoria on hearing, thus circumstantially detailed, the loss and destruction of one who had began so deeply to interest her thoughts. She found it impossible to account for the degree of feeling which affected her; she had never been conscious of the slightest predeliction in favor of the Moor, and, till the circumstance of his impressing her mind from appearing in her dreams, had never even cast a thought more than common upon him. From that period, indeed, she had been most inexplicably interested about him, nor could she for any length of time banish his idea from her mind.

It was vain, therefore, that she essayed to feel indifferent to the reflection of his unhappy fate; she found it impossible, and experienced a weight at her heart, as if under the impression of having sustained a heavy loss.

Zofloya, though a Moor, and by a combination of events, and the chance of war, (in the final victory of the Spaniards over the Moors of Granada,) reduced to a menial situation, was yet of noble birth, of the race of Abdhulrahmans. He had, after severe vicissitudes, when still young, fallen into the hands of a Spanish nobleman, who, pitying his misfortunes, considered him rather as a friend than an inferior, and bestowed high polish upon the education he had received. Henriquez having become acquainted with this nobleman during his travels, to divert the sorrows of his love, he formed with him a strict friendship, founded, in some degree, upon similarity of situation as well as sentiment. Unfortunately, however, in the height of their friendship, the Spaniard became involved in a quarrel, which terminated in bloodshed. He received a wound, which was pronounced to be mortal, and Henriquez had the melancholy office of attending a friend in his dying moments: at this awful period it was, that he, among other charges, recommended to his future protection the Moor Zofloya. Henriquez promised implicit observance to all his wishes, and Zofloya was in consequence taken immediately, after the death of his first master and protector, into the service and guardianship of Henriquez.

These peculiar circumstances, besides his excellent and ingenuous nature, considerably endeared the Moor to him, and he loved him not only for the sake of his departed friend, but for his intrinsic worth as well. His loss, therefore, by Henriquez, was most sensibly and deeply regretted, and the confirmation of his frightful death received with sentiments of acute grief.

Nine days had now elapsed since the death of Latoni; nothing had as yet been heard to contradict his dying account of the end of Zofloya, when, to the surprise of every one, on the evening of the tenth, he entered the apartment where the family of Berenza were assembled! All started from their seats, and Victoria, overcome with mixed emotions, sunk into hers again; an explanation of his astonishing and unlooked for return was hastily demanded by his master, when, gracefully bowing, the Moor gave of himself the following account:

"Of the cause of Latoni's hatred towards me I am wholly unconscious; he frequently sought my life, and on the night that he followed me with murderous intent, and wounded me repeatedly with his stiletto, I discerned whose hand aimed the blows, but was not empowered to make effectual resistance, being, as it happened, wholly unarmed. I struggled with the base assassin, however; but not aware of his intentions, he pushed me, faint as I was with loss of blood, over the edge of the steps on which I was standing when he first attacked me, into the canal below. Here, undoubtedly, I must have perished, but that an honest fisherman, returning to Padua, was the means of my preservation, by extricating me from the water, assisted by the feeble struggles for life that I was yet enabled to make. Fortunately, none of my wounds proved to be serious; and being in possession of a secret transmitted to me by my ancestors, for speedily healing even the most dangerous ones, I remained at the hut of the fisherman till I was perfectly recovered, and enabled once more to present myself before the honorable family to whom I owe my highest gratitude and respect."

Here ended the narration of Zofloya, who, when he had received the congratulations of every one upon his miraculous escape from destruction, appeared to learn with evident surprise the death of Latoni. He demonstrated, however, visible joy at the intelligence, and returning thanks, submissive yet dignified, for the kindness manifested towards him, respectfully withdrew from the apartment, casting, as he went, a look of the most animated gratitude upon Victoria, as though his *heart* thanked her for the interest she had appeared to take in his story, beyond what his respect would permit him to express.

As for Victoria, in proportion as she had been miserable at the disappearance of the Moor, in so much was she rejoiced to behold him again. Her heart dilated with an unaccountable delight, with which the image of Henriquez was deeply connected; for she thought of him with less of jealous agony, and more of confidence and hope, as though, strange as it appeared, the mere presence of Zofloya possessed a secret charm to facilitate her wishes. This idea gave an animation to her countenance, and a flow to her spirits, that for some time had not been perceptible in her. The change delighted the unsuspicious Berenza, who flattered himself that it was the dawning triumph of vigorous reason, over the morbid refinements of a sickly fancy. The innocent Lilla, too, caressed her with heartfelt pleasure, and Victoria returned her caresses with a gloomy eagerness, as the murderer might be tempted to fondle the beauty of the babe, whose life he intended to take. Henriquez, always participating in the pleasures and sorrows of his mistress, paid too a more than usual attention to Victoria; but it was an attention in compliment to Lilla, to a brother whom he loved, and not the spontaneous effusions of his heart to her.

On this night Victoria retired to bed with feelings of delight, that teemed with woe to others. Hers was not that innocent vivacity which springs at once from the *purity* and *sanity* of the heart; it was the wild and frightful mirth of a tyrant, who condemns his subjects to the torture, that he may laugh at their agonies; it was the brilliant glare of the terrible volcano, pregnant even in its beauty with destruction!

Scarcely had her head reclined upon her pillow, than the image of Zofloya swam in her sight, she slumbered, and he haunted her dreams; sometimes she wandered with him over beds of flowers, sometimes over craggy rocks, sometimes in fields of the brightest verdure, sometimes over burning sands, tottering on the ridge of some huge precipice, while the angry waters waved in the abyss below. Often the circumstances were so strong, that the bounds of fancy contained them no longer, and, hastily awaking, scarcely could she assure herself that Zofloya stood not at the side of her bed! At one time the delusion was so strong, that she even fancied, after gazing for a minute at least, that he was a few paces from her bed, and that she saw him turn, and walk slow and majestically towards the door. At this, being no longer able to resist, she started up, and called him by his name; but as she did so, he seemed to vanish through the door, which still remained shut. Surprised, she passed her hand over her eyes, and looked round the chamber; all was lonely, she beheld no further traces of his figure, and, difficult as was the persuasion, she endeavoured to believe the whole a delusive dream.

At length, she laid down, and closed her eyes again; the weariness of sleep oppressed her to such a degree as to deprive her wholly of motion, but, notwithstanding this, her eyes half opened involuntarily. A grey silvery mist filled the chamber, shedding a sort of twilight; the curtains at the foot of her bed opened wide, and in the same spot again stood the figure of Zofloya! With one hand he seemed to hold Berenza, whose countenance, of pallid hue, seemed convulsed in the agonies of death. On his bare bosom appeared large marks of livid blue, and his eyes stretched wide, gazed mournfully upon the oppressed Victoria. In his other hand, the Moor held, by her beautiful and flaxen tresses, the orphan Lilla; her thin and spectral form seemed arrayed in transparent shade, her lovely head drooped, and on one side of it was seen a deep wound, from which the blood had streamed adown her aerial robes. While still incapable of volition, Victoria gazed, Berenza and Lilla vanished back, and she beheld instead, her own likeness and that of Henriquez stand on either side of the Moor. She seemed to stretch forth her arms, into which Henriquez appeared impelled, but hastily retreating, she saw that his bosom was disfigured by a dreadful wound. Suddenly, Berenza and Lilla again drew nigh; resplendent wings, which dazzled her eyes, came from the shoulders of Lilla; with a seraphic smile she extended her hands to Berenza and Henriquez, and rising with them from the ground, Victoria beheld them no longer; her heart beat violently, her brain throbbed, and, essaying to rise, she found herself no longer incapable of motion.

CHAPTER XIX

Victoria having passed a night of restlessness and agitation, fell into a slumber towards morning, from which she did not awaken till late in the afternoon. When she entered the saloon to join the family at dinner, her eyes irresistibly fixed upon the figure of Zofloya, who flew with alacrity to procure her a seat; during dinner she was silent and abstracted, and her regard continued involuntarily to turn towards him. In one of those hasty glances which pride alone would permit her to steal, it occurred to her that the figure of the Moor possessed a grace and majesty which she had never before remarked; his face too seemed animated with charms till now unnoticed, and his very dress to have acquired a more splendid, tasteful, and elegant appearance. — True it was, that great was the beauty of Zofloya, to a form the most attractive and symmetrical, though of superior height, deriving every advantage too from the graceful costume of his dress, was added a countenance, spite of its colour, endowed with the finest possible expression. His eyes, brilliant and large, sparkled with inexpressible fire; his nose and mouth were elegantly formed, and when he smiled, the assemblage of his features displayed a beauty that delighted and surprised. But still, to the present period, all this had been unnoticed by Victoria: the oftener she looked towards him, the more her astonishment increased that it should have been so, and she could not help thinking that Zofloya, before his sudden disappearance, and Zofloya, since his return, were widely different of each other.

Whenever she cast her eyes upon the Moor, she could perceive that he observed her; and not observed her only, but regarded her with a tender, serious interest, that filled her soul with a troubled sort of delight. At times she even thought he looked at her with a peculiar earnestness and animation, yet her pride felt no alarm; but, on the contrary, she took pleasure in knowing that he gazed upon her. His place was near the chair of Henriquez, yet he was assiduous in attending to her: in every motion he displayed some new grace, and in the eyes of the vain Victoria his beauty increased every moment.

For this once, though Henriquez was in her mind and in her soul, another occupied her attention, and in spite of every attempt to divert it to other objects, on that one (as if by the irresistible force of magnetic attraction) it perpetually turned. To relieve herself from an indefinable oppression, she soon rose from table, and wandered into the garden: there, throwing herself on a seat, she began to brood over her criminal passion, and the wildest thoughts rioted for pre-eminence in her brain.

"Detestable Berenza!" she suddenly exclaimed, inspired by the basest hatred and ingratitude towards him. "Detestable Berenza, selfish and unworthy wretch, that played upon my youth, and deluded me into the misfortune of becoming thy wife! had it not been for thee, and thy cursed arts, Henriquez ere now would have been mine. The baby, Lilla, I would have banished from his heart; I would have rooted her thence, or from the earth! but, that my energies are all enslaved, my powers fettered, by the hated name of wife, Henriquez should have yielded to my love; he should not have yielded only, but gloried in it. Who is the minion, Lilla? A friendless upstart! *she* was no obstacle; I think not of her: detestable Berenza! I say again — mean, calculating philosopher, it is thou — thou that I should wish annihilated!" As she concluded, a faint echo seemed to repeat her last words, in a low, hollow tone, as if sounding at a distance, and borne by the wind.

"What was that?" said Victoria, mentally; but the sounds returned not — "Ah, it was some mockery," she pursued, while a deep sigh burst from her guilty bosom! She drew her hand mechanically across her eyes for a moment, and as she removed it, she beheld Zofloya standing, though at a respectful distance, before her. Surprise, accompanied by an emotion of anger, lightened through her mind, that an inferior should thus presume to intrude upon her retirement: this latter sentiment, however, faded in an instant before the majestic presence of the Moor; she looked upon him with an anxious air, but did not speak, and observed that in his hand he carried a bouquet of roses.

"Beautiful Signora!" he said in a gentle voice; and gracefully inclining his body, "pardon me that thus I venture to appear uncalled before you; but these roses I gathered for you; suffer me to strew them at your feet." So saying, he attempted to scatter them before her.

"Zofloya!" cried Victoria, while her eyes wandered with admiration over the beauty of his form, "no — you shall not strew them at my feet; give them to me, and let me place them in my bosom."

"There are too many for your bosom, sweet Signora! but I will select you some, and of the rest I will form you a carpet." He took the choicest rose from the bouquet, and strewed the remained at the feet of Victoria: then, extending his hand, he presented to her the rose which he had selected.

Victoria stretched forth her hand to receive it; when, as she did so, a thorn ran deep into one of her fingers, and the blood issued in a large drop. Zofloya, in apparent consternation, opened his vest, and, tearing some linen from his bosom, cast himself upon his knees, and applied it with trembling eagerness to the wound. Victoria felt too surprised — almost gratified to repulse him, and the Moor continued, unchecked, to press the blood from her finger, and to absorb it with the linen, as it flowed. At length it ceased to do so: Zofloya pressed the crimsoned linen to his heart, and tearing from it every particle that remained unstained, he folded it up as a sacred relic, and placed it in his bosom. Then seeming suddenly to recollect himself, he appeared struck with confusion at his own audacity: he dared not raise his eyes to Victoria; and a dark-red blush animated with lurid colour his expressive countenance.

Victoria, feeling irresistibly impelled, laid her hand upon his shoulder, and in gentle voice said, "Rise, Zofloya, and be not ashamed, for you have not done aught amiss."

"Say *you* so, Signora? I rise then with confidence;" and, rising as he spoke, he humbly retreated a few paces from her.

"But, why, Zofloya," inquired Victoria, with a smile, "have you deemed that piece of linen worthy of preservation?"

"Worthy, lovely Signora!" answered the Moor, raising his fine eyes to her countenance, and crossing his arms upon his bosom; "it is of more worth to me than language can describe; it is of equal value to me with yourself, for it is a part of you — your precious blood! chary[1] will I be of it; and, safely placed upon my bosom, no earthly power shall tempt me to resign it." As he concluded, his countenance glowed with a brilliant fire, and increased animation spread itself over his graceful form.

The vanity of Victoria was flattered: in no guise did she disdain flattery; but was astonished at herself, however, that with such disparity of situation, it should be sweet to her. She desired to banish all hostile reflection; and, gazing upon the attractive Moor, she saw such unconquerable fascination, that her eyes sought the ground, as fearful to express the conscious emotion of her bosom.

"Wherefore, Zofloya," she involuntarily said in a tremulous voice, "do you remain at such a distance?"

"*May* I then approach, Signora?"

"You may."

The Moor drew nigh; but, as Victoria still remained in a recumbent attitude, he seated himself upon the earth, at her feet.

An oppressive gloom now took possession of the mind of Victoria; a weight of misery seemed pressing on her heart, and, covering her face with her hands, she heaved a deep sigh.

"You sigh, sweet Signora!" said the Moor, in a sympathising accent; "may Zofloya venture to demand the cause?"

"The cause, Zofloya — Ah! it is a cause which you cannot remove; it is a wound from which there is no balm."

"Not so, perhaps, Signora."

There was little in the words of Zofloya to excite hope in the bosom of Victoria; yet enlivening hope shot through her bosom, and she half rose from her reclining attitude.

"Zofloya," she said, in a doubting accent, finding that he did not proceed, "what hope could *you* offer me?"

"Some, perhaps, Signora — name your grief."

She started wildly from her seat — "Moor!" she exclaimed, "your words are big with meaning; they contain more than meets the ear! Quick, and tell me, boldly, all you would say."

---

1 chary: meaning treasured or dear.

Zofloya rose from the ground: he presumed to take the hand of Victoria, and led her again to her seat; in a moment she was calm — "Now, Signora, deign to acknowledge to me what secret oppresses, and has for long oppressed your soul; the Moor, Zofloya, may repay you for your confidence."

The secret of Victoria hovered on her lips; hitherto it had remained unknown to mortal soul; in the gloomy solitude of her own perturbed bosom, had she till now preserved it, where, like a poisonous worm, it had continued to corrode. She was now on the point of betraying her inmost thoughts, her dearest wishes, her dark repinings, and hopeless desires; of betraying them, too, to an inferior and an infidel! The idea was scarcely endurable, and she scorned it; but, in the next instant, she cast her eyes upon the noble presence of the Moor: he appeared not only the superior of his race, but of a superior order of beings. Her struggles died away, and, in hurried accents, she involuntarily exclaimed — "Oh, Henriquez! Henriquez!"

The Moor smiled —

"Why dost thou smile, Zofloya?" cried Victoria, with momentary indignation.

"You love Henriquez, Signora."

"Yes, yes — to madness! — to distraction! — how canst thou smile, unfeeling Moor?"

"Are you not a holy catholic, Signora? — yet to love so much an earthly being —"

"Mock me not at this moment, Zofloya; for *that* being I would forfeit my hopes of heaven! You smile again; I perceive I have condescended too far; you dare to make sport of my miseries?"

"No, no, beautiful Signora; I smile only at your innocence."

"*My* innocence!" she repeated with surprise; for conscience whispered *that* long since had fled.

"Yes, Signora, at your innocence; that, in the midst of wishes so consuming, could not instruct you to obtain them."

"Oh say — Can *you* instruct me? can you arrange? can you direct the confused suggestions of my brain?"

"I think I could *assist* you, fair Signora!"

"Oh, Zofloya, you would bind me for ever to you!" eagerly exclaimed Victoria.

"Enough, lovely Signora! To-morrow, at the dusk of the evening, deign to meet me again here. I see approaching towards us Il Conte Berenza and Signor Henriquez."

"Ah! I see them too — the hated Berenza," she said; while stronger loathing against him took possession of her heart.

"Farewell, Signora, till to-morrow," said Zofloya; and precipitately leaving the arbour, he took a contrary path to that in which Berneza and Henriquez were advancing.

Victoria continued, with indescribable sensations, to gaze after his graceful figure, as it disappeared from her view; then reluctantly leaving the arbour, she joined the Conte and Henriquez. With tremulous delight, and with feelings of diminished pain, she stole frequent glances at the unconscious possessor of her soul: he observed her not; for the blooming Lilla was hastening towards them. In an instant he quitted the side of Victoria, and flew towards her: at this sight hate kindled fiercer than ever in the bosom of Victoria; she regarded the lovely orphan with the eyes of a basilisk,[1] and wished that, like them, they possessed the power to destroy. Vain this evening were the mild endearments of Lilla: she repulsed them with haughtiness; for the feelings in her bosom raged too strong to permit the assumption of kindness, and she experienced, that, however her conversation with Zofloya might have imparted hope, and have soothed in a degree the anguish of her mind, still it had increased, to the highest point of irritability, every violent and bitter sensation.

---

1 eyes of a basilisk: The basilisk is a mythical serpent with a poisonous gaze.

CHAPTER XX

Scarcely, on the following evening, had the artificial shades of twilight increased the gigantic outlines of the far-seen mountains, ere Victoria hastened to the spot where the Moor, Zofloya, had said he would await her. On her arrival, she found him already there, and on perceiving her, he hastened forward.

"Be seated, fair Signora," he said, respectfully leading her to a sloping bank, overshadowed by a spreading acacia.

Victoria obeyed; the manner of Zofloya was such as inspired involuntary awe: he took his station beside her. The soul of Victoria was a stranger to fear, yet uncommon sensations filled her bosom, as she observed her proximity to the Moor. The dim twilight increasing to darkness, which now began to spread its sombre shadows around, threw a deeper tint over his figure, and his countenance was more strongly contrasted by the snow white turban which encircled his brows, and by the large bracelets of pearl upon his arms and legs. Yet his form and attitude, as he sat beside her, was majestic, and solemnly beautiful — not the beauty which may be freely admired, but acknowledged with sensations awful and indescribable.

"Signora," he began, in an harmonious voice, while every uneasy feeling of Victoria's bosom vanished as he spoke — "I am not to learn that dreadful oppression of soul weighs you to the earth; but the cause of your unhappiness I desire to hear from your own lips, more explicitly than you have yet acknowledged it. Think not, beautiful Victoria, that in the spirit of idle curiosity merely, I would dive into the recesses of your bosom; no, it is from a hope I entertain, that I possess a power equal, almost to my wishes, of alleviating the sorrows you endure. But even should I not possess that power, even then there is a delight, of which you will speedily become sensible, in confiding them to a sympathising breast."

Victoria hesitated — the Moor proceeded:

"Does the Signora believe, then, that the Moor Zofloya hath a heart dark as his countenance? Ah! Signora, judge ye not by appearances! but, if you desire relief, make me at once the depositary of your soul's conflicts, and trust to the event."

Scarce had Zofloya opened his lips, ere uneasiness, as we have said, vanished from the mind of Victoria. As he proceeded, the most agreeable sensations fluttered through her frame, and in her brain floated fascinating visions of future bliss, that passed too rapidly to be identified. Scarce had his silver tones sunk on her ear in thrilling cadence, than she felt even eager to express to the Moor her inmost thoughts: excessive, yet confused pleasure, filled her heart — she looked upon his still discernible, though darkened figure; upon his countenance, where, like two diamonds, revealed by the force of their own casual rays, his eyes emitted sparks of lambent flame. — Involuntarily softened towards him, she said —

"Whether or not thou canst assist me, Zofloya, is unknown to me; but, feeling strongly impelled to reveal to thee every movement of my soul — the fatal, I almost fear, the remediless cause of my misery, I hasten to acknowledge to thee all. I have already hinted to thee concerning my love; although the wife of Conte Berenza, my inmost soul doats franticly upon the young Henriquez; to complete my hopeless distraction, the orphan Lilla, that presumptuous and dependant intruder, hath for long been in possession of his heart, an heart of which she knows not the value, for her person is not more puerile than her mind. But, it is not the artful insignificant ascendancy this girl has acquired over him that bids me despair; it is — it is that I am wedded to a wretch whom I abhor! — who stands between me and happiness, and who was only sent upon this earth to seal the fiat of my miseries. Were I but once freed — freed from those hated fetters that bind me to Berenza, I would soon drive from the superior mind of Henriquez the silly passion which now occupies it; I would make him feel that he was destined to nobler fate, to confer and to receive the highest happiness; not merely to yield himself a sacrifice to the undiscriminating fancy of his boyish days. Oh, Zofloya! this would I do, were opportunity allowed me — but never, oh, never will such bliss be mine!"

She leaned her head upon her hand, and paused; then quickly resuming: "I have now told thee of the agony which racks my breast; I have even revealed my wishes — my depair. — Say, say quickly — what consolation canst *thou* offer in return?"

"I would bid you, Signora, not despair.

"And is this *all* thou canst say, Zofloya?"

"Are you of a firm and persevering spirit, Signora?"

"This heart knows not to shrink," she answered, forcibly striking her bosom, while her eyes flashed fire; "and in its purpose would persevere, even to destruction!"

"Are such the attributes of your character, Signora? Then what earthly wishes are not to be atchieved by the united force of firmness and perseverance?"

"I see not how firmness and perseverance can avail me here, however valuable in themselves may be those qualities."

"Not so, beautiful Victoria."

"Your words are ambiguous, Zofloya; deign to be explicit," said Victoria hastily.

"Will you consider me so, when I assert, that if you determine to act up to what you have just said, no accidental combinations can prevent you from obtaining your utmost wishes?"

"Hah! say you so, enchanting Moor?" exclaimed Victoria, half frantic with joy at the meaning contained in his words; and, breathless with contending emotions of hope and doubt, seizing his hand, she pressed it to her bosom.

"Signora! be calm, be composed," cried Zofloya, "and honor not thus, unworthily, the lowest of your slaves."

"Speak on then, Zofloya; your words are magic, they soothe my soul, and I feel *hope!*"

"And if I speak on, you will not bid me cease; you will not shrink, Signora."

Victoria's only answer was an expressive smile and gesture.

Zofloya then resumed —

"Before, Signora, by the unhappy defeat of my countrymen, in Granada,[1] by Ferdinand of Arragon, I became the property of the Spaniard, who dying, recommended me to Signor Henriquez, I had, from early youth, been addicted to the study of arts as well as arms; botany, chemistry, and astrology, were my favorite pursuits; and this turn of mind was further encouraged and improved by an ancient Moor of Granada, who took pleasure in cultivating my taste, and eventually increased considerably my information on various points, and to a surprising extent. While in the kingdom of Arragon, resident with the Spaniard, my late master, I continued to have full leisure for the pursuit of my favorite branches of study, for he treated me as a friend and an equal, rather than as a miserable captive and domestic."

"Oh, Zofloya! Zofloya!" impatiently cried Victoria, "this is irrelavent."

"Suffer me to proceed, however, Signora," gravely observed the Moor, with an air that repressed the violence, and commanded the attention of his auditor.

"In consequence of the liberty I enjoyed, I devoted myself, as I have said, to my favorite pursuits; I obtained a perfect knowledge of simples and earths, and how drugs are compounded from them. No one could go beyond the infallibility of my calculations, as to their effect. To chemistry, then, I became particularly attached, without, however, resigning my astrological pursuits. Close application, (favored too, as perseverance usually is, by the deductions of accidental observation,) taught me in time, amidst a vast variety of chemical science, to compound poisons with such infinite art, that, from the most speedy and subtile, I could vary their degrees to the slowest and most imperceptible. I tried them (experimentally as it were) first upon animals, and then upon those who had offended me!"

"Victoria started; but the Moor, appearing not to notice it, proceeded:

---

1 the unhappy defeat of my countrymen, in Granada: The Nasrid kingdom of Granada (1235–1492) was the last Muslim state in Spain. In the fifteenth century, Granada's population was approximately 350,000, including some Jews, who like the Moors, were expelled from Spain in 1492. The Muslims were promised safety, a right to their possessions, safe passage out of Spain, and the right to observe Islamic law in their communities. However, Ferdinand and Isabella broke these promises in 1502, and the Muslims were forced to choose between conversion or exile, as the Jews had been forced earlier.

"Upon these I tried, alternately, my speedy and lingering poisons. I have seen the little greyhound, one moment frisking at my feet, and the next, without a struggle, sink, motionless, beside them. I have seen the man I hated, who had forgotten he had ever offended me, smiling in my face, and lingering under the imperceptible but certain influence of the poison that had been administered to him, and which circulated in his blood, gently leading him to the gates of death! for the female who had dared to prefer *another* to *me*, I have first wreaked my vengeance on her lover, and then on herself. By the power of drugs I have given them, their love for each other has been alternately changed to hate; and they have only recovered from the delirium, to be separately destroyed by the effect! In no instance have I ever failed in my calculations of the event. That which I willed came to pass, and came to pass in the *manner* that I willed it! — Many other surprising secrets of art and nature became revealed to me, but, to expatiate upon them now would be, as you have said, irrelevant to the subject; therefore to the point. — I now demand of you, Signora, whether *you* would choose the slow poison, or the swift?"

Victoria was for a moment staggered at this unexpected question, which again the Moor seeming not to observe, took from his pocket a small gold box, which opening, Victoria perceived to contain several divisions; from one of these he drew a little folded paper, and thus proceeded:

"This paper contains one of the most subtile and delicate poisons that ever, by the hand of art, could be composed. It deals unerring death, but deals it slowly. It may be administered in wine, in food — it may even be completely introduced into the system, by the puncture of the smallest pin! It is this which I should recommend to you, Signora, for a beginning; take it and use it as opportunity shall present: should opportunities but unfrequently occur, you will yourself know how to make them."

Victoria stretched forth her hand, and took the paper — for a moment she was silent, and then said —

"This, then, is for Berenza."

The Moor smiled expressively, and waved his hand, as if to say, "that surely requires no answer;" then, assuming a more serious air, he coolly observed —

"When barriers oppose the attainment of a favorite object, the barriers must either be laid low, or the object remain unattained. To remedy an evil, it is necessary to strike at the root. Nothing is to be gained by lopping the branches which arise therefrom. Thus, should you resolve to overstep common boundaries, and that which is termed female delicacy[1],

---

1 female delicacy: another echo of Bienville: "they throw off the restraining, honorable yoke of delicacy, and, without a blush, openly solicit in the most criminal, and abandoned language, the first-comers to gratify their insatiable desires." (See Appendix A).

by openly declaring your passion to Henriquez, and he (even setting defiance to consequence) should return it, how do you imagine, that while the wife of another, you could enjoy unrestrained delight with the choice of your soul? Do you want resolution then, fair Signora, to effect, by means so trifling, your highest wishes? — and did I err," he added ironically, "in the different estimate I had formed of your character?"

"It is not that I want resolution," returned Victoria, somewhat piqued. "I desire, oh, how ardently desire, the death — the annihilation of Berenza; but, by these means, to take his life! — it is not that I hesitate, however!" and ashamed, confused at what she deemed her cowardice, she stopped —

"It is not that you hesitate," in an accent half serious, half disdainful, returned the Moor; "and why *should* you hesitate? *he* had no hesitation in sacrificing to himself your young and beautiful person, for his gratification; and why should you hesitate, now, at sacrificing him for yours? You hate him; yet you receive with dissembled pleasure those endearments which he lavishes upon you. In depriving him of life, you would do him far less wrong. Surely the conscience of Victoria is not subjugated to a confessor? From whence then arises this unexpected demur? Is not self predominant throughout animal nature? and what is the boasted supremacy of man, if, eternally, he must yield his happiness to the paltry suggestions of scholastic terms, or the pompous definitions of right and wrong? His reasoning mind, then, is given him only for his torment, and to wage war against his happiness; yet what cause can be adduced, why *another* must be permitted to stand between him, and his fair prospects, overshadowing them with hopeless gloom? What argument can be adduced against his removal? — For him, of whom we are speaking, he has enjoyed, already, many years of existent pleasure; he must now yield his place to another; for he has not a right to monopolize to his share the pleasures of others. Besides, were he to live a thousand years longer, each day must be but a tasteless repetition of the past; for, in length of time, even the zest of pleasure wears off; and when we come to reflect, after this long disquisition into which we have been drawn, what is the momentous consideration, whether the breath of a man be hastened a few moments sooner from his body, than sickness, accident, or a thousand chances might have propelled it, and in the common course of things have befriended you; — yet, if none of these happen to arise, a mind of enterprise, endowed with the strength and power of right reason, steps with unshrinking foot a little from the beaten track."

Zofloya paused — the cool deliberateness of his manner, in expressing his sentiments, induced Victoria to believe that they were the result of conviction, deduced from accurate reflection, and the having given to the subject the rational consideration of a towering and superior mind, rather than the cruel or forced constructions of the moment. Under this impression, she could not avoid saying —

"Zofloya, you possess strong powers of reflection, and you are eloquent."

"Charming Signora," in a softened voice, answered the Moor, "I am not naturally eloquent, but the wish of promoting your happiness renders me so."

Pride filled the heart of Victoria, and she smiled.

"Ah!" pursued the Moor, "that beauteous form was never made to pine by hopeless love! — no, it was not made to sink to the earth a victim to ungratified sensations, to yield, to fall a sacrifice to imperious circumstances. Ah! Victoria, beautiful Victoria! *Zofloya must fly you in despair, should you disdain his proffered services.*"

Oh, Flattery, like heavenly dew upon the earth, gratefully dost thou descend upon the ear of woman! Indescribable pleasure dilated the bosom of Victoria, as she listened to the honied accents of the delicate Moor. She put forth her hand towards him, and, when he softly seized and pressed it to his lips, the haughty Venetian was not offended.

"Tell me then, Zofloya," she said, with slight hesitation, "how must I use this bland and dangerous enemy?"

At night, in wine, Signora; in morning beverage; when, and how you can; ere long its effects will become discernible."

"The Conte, at a certain hour of the day, drinks lemonade," observed Victoria, which I was once in the habit of administering to him; he used to say it tasted sweeter from my hand."

"Renew your tender offices," said Zofloya, with a meaning smile, "and increase your opportunities: the powder I have given you is of the minutest particles; the smallest atom is sufficient at a time. Using it at the rate of twice a day, it will not be exhausted for ten days; at the end of that period, the perceptible effect that shall have been produced upon Berenza will direct us to proceed. Now, Signora, allow me to conduct you hence." So saying, Zofloya gently taking Victoria by the arm, led her, with a kind of respectful freedom, from the spot.

CHAPTER XXI

With unshrinking soul, and eye unabashed by the consciousness of guilt, Victoria joined at supper the innocent family circle. The high blush of animation flushed her dark cheek with more than usual fire; her eyes sparkled, but it was with a fiend-like exultation, and her nerves seemed new strung for the execution of her dreadful purpose.

Berenza rejoiced at her appearance, and little surmising the cause, approached, in the fulness of his heart, to embrace her; she returned it impatiently, and pushing him from her, surveyed him, with a kind of half smile, from head to foot.

The unconscious Berenza mistook this for the embrace of eager love, repentant at past coldness, and the accompanying action for sportive gaiety only. But it was not so; Victoria hastily embraced him, from the cruel reflection that he would not long have the power of soliciting these marks of an affection that she felt not, nor she the hated task of granting them: — in pushing him from her, she but yielded to an overpowering impulse of the hatred which possessed her bosom; while gazing on him with a smile, she consoled herself with the thought — how soon he would cease to be!

At supper she could forbear sometimes casting her ardent eyes upon Henriquez, anticipating future delight; while his were fixed as usual upon the blooming fairy, Lilla. But her Victoria now regarded only with contempt, from the suggestion that she was an atom too easily crushed to cause a moment's painful thought. Yet she failed not to pay attention to all; and the vivacity of her manner, the brilliancy of her wit, attracted, as it was wont to do, the pleased admiration of all towards her.

"Come, my life," cried the enraptured Berenza, raising the glass to his lips, "Here's to thy happiness, and the success of *thy every wish*: drink all of you the same," he added, looking round the table.

Every one obeyed, and drank to the happiness of her, who, in that moment, meditated their destruction.

"And now," she cried, playfully, "it is my turn: and taking two goblets off the table, she flew to a recess at the end of the saloon, where wines and ices were set out upon a small marble table; filling them to the brim with Vino Greco, and infusing into the glass that had been hers a small quantity of the poison, (which instantly incorporated itself with the wine, and disappeared,) she returned to the supper table with well-dissembled innocent sportiveness, and exclaimed —

"Fill your glasses all round."

All obeyed again, and held their glasses in their hands.

"Here, Berenza, is *my* glass," she cried; drink from it as I will drink from yours — To the *speedy fulfilment of our wishes*!"

The fatal toast was drunk, and "To the speedy fulfilment of our wishes," echoed round the table, while the devoted Berenza, whose only wish was the gratification of Victoria, drank eagerly to promote it the first draught of death! and looking tenderly upon her, exclaimed, "To the speedy fulfilment of *thy* wishes," thus emphatically calling on his own destruction.

Victoria smiling, fixed her eyes upon him — in a few moments she imagined he turned pale: he passed his hand hastily across his eyes, as if sensible of a slight sudden pain in his head; she became apprehensive she had given him more than was prudent for a first dose, and that she would be betrayed: presently, however, her fears subsided, the colour returned to the cheeks of Berenza, and the pain passed away. Uninterrupted gaiety then reigned to the end of supper, and till the lateness of the hour warned them to separate.

From this eventful period, Victoria omitted no opportunity of administering insidious death to the unsuspicious Berenza. Sometimes, with the point of a small fruit knife, which she retained about her for the purpose, she introduced the baleful poison within the fruit, while offering it to him on the point of her knife; thus remorselessly rendering him to himself the dealer of his own death.

After once or twice, the poison no longer took an immediately perceptible effect upon him; the stomach becoming habituated, no longer evinced resistless loathing as it received the gradual destruction, which, blending its baleful influence with its other juices, was conveyed into the system. At the expiration of eight or ten days, a change, scarcely marked by others, but fully perceived by Victoria, became apparent in the hapless Berenza; the blood of his cheeks, which, on first taking the poison, vanished back for a few moments, seemed, as by repeated checks, to have become more languid in its circulation, and tinged them no longer, as formerly, with the vermilion hue of health. A kind of tremulousness began to possess his nerves, and a dry but faint cough gave frequent symptoms that the mischief had begun to work.

Satisfied with these appearances, on the evening of the tenth day, for the eagerness of Victoria (now that she had commenced her dreadful plan) had not suffered an atom of the poison to remain beyond, she sought, as previously agreed, Zofloya, in the appointed spot: when she arrived, she perceived him not; already her dark mind became suspicious of the delay; — "Zofloya! Zofloya!" she cried, in an under voice, "where art thou?"

"Here," replied a voice, like the sweet murmuring sound of an Æolian harp,[1] swept by the breath of the zephyr; and, turning, she beheld at her side the towering figure of the Moor.

---

1 the Æolian harp: a harp played by the wind (Aeolus). It was a favourite metaphor for nature's inspiration of the poetic imagination for Romantic writers such as

She had not seen, neither had she heard his approach; and, ashamed of the doubts she had felt, and the impatience she had evinced, she could not, as his commanding eyes looked down upon her, for the moment speak.

"Well, beautiful Victoria," he said, "behold me here; and suffer me now to ask, does hope begin to cheer your long-benighted bosom?"

"Yes," answered Victoria, "I entertain hope, the fond hope, Zofloya, that I shall have good cause to mark the day, when, irresistibly impelled by the kind sympathy of thy manner, I confided to thee the cause of my sorrows."

And I too, Signora, shall have proud cause to *mark* that day; for it gave to the unworthy slave, Zofloya, the most beautiful and enterprising of her sex."

"It gave thee my friendship, indeed, Zofloya," said Victoria, slightly surprised; "it gave thee my gratitude, not myself; for I am irrevocably, as thou knowest, devoted to another."

"Be not offended, beautifil Victoria, nor let us waste the precious moments in defining terms; for the Signor Henriquez, to whom I am obedient for your sweet sake alone, requires my presence: were it not for you, Zofloya would no longer appear in a character unfitting his state, the character of a menial."

"And what would you then, generous Zofloya? for sure you were the attendant of Henriquez, ere I became known to you."

"Were *you* otherwise than *you* are, fair Victoria, I should not now be here."

"Is it even so? — then am I indeed indebted to you, most excellent Moor, for the sacrifices which you make to my service, and never, never can I sufficiently repay you."

"You will, you do repay me, kind Signora; but time wastes: let me now give what you require, the second powder, for — " He concluded his meaning with a smile; then taking the box from his pocket, he drew forth a second powder, but from a different division, and presenting it to Victoria, he said —

"This powder is a degree more powerful than the last; you will admin-

---

Percy Bysshe Shelley and Coleridge (in his 1795 poem "The Æolian Harp"). In Mary Wollstonecraft's *A Short Residence in Sweden, Norway, and Denmark* (1796), the dangers of the imagination's origins in physical sensation are made evident and implicitly gendered, as they were in Bienville's *Nymphomania*, and in Dacre's *Zofloya*: "what misery, as well as rapture, is produced by a quick perception of the beautiful and the sublime, when it is exercised in observing animated nature, when every beauteous feeling and emotion excite responsive sympathy, and the harmonized soul sinks into melancholy, or rises to extasy, just as the chords are touched, like the aeolian harp agitated by the changing wind. But how dangerous it is to foster these sentiments in such an imperfect state of existence" (*A Short Residence*, 99).

ister it the same, and the effects will be proportionably increased. This, likewise, will last you ten days, and in that time you will observe in Berenza the flame of life become fainter and fainter. To all around his illness will wear the appearance of languor and gentle decay, no one will suspect death to be at hand; by you, some cold draught, and unnoticed at the time, must be fondly alluded to, and suggested as the cause; by tenderness and unlimited attention, by soothing and consolation, you must shut his eyes on the danger of his situation, and administer with your poison the fallacious hope, that his constitution will triumph over the cureless malady; so that no advice, and, if possible, not any medicines, may be resorted to, lest they should counteract or retard the workings of his delicate enemy. You will thus behold him perishing away, like the rose, which carries the canker-worm hidden in its heart, or the tree, that, blasted by the lightning, can never more recover its verdure."

The Moor paused; but Victoria appearing violently agitated, as if overcome by some sudden thought or recollection, remained silent.

Her uneasiness was not unobserved by Zofloya; but he only gazed upon her, without inquiring the cause, leaving it to herself to reveal the workings of her mind.

At length, fixing her eyes upon his countenance, she said in a hurried voice —

"Zofloya, Venice will never do for the seat of action; it would be folly, it would be madness to make the attempt. Such an undertaking as ours, if crowned by success, would prove ultimate destruction; know you not, know you not, Zofloya, that nothing can remain concealed from Il Consiglio di Dieci?"

"But you commit no crime against the state, Signora; you are no heretic."

"True, but the pretended accusation for these crimes are frequently the vehicles of punishment for other offences; hatred, suspicion, or malice, conveys an anonymous line into the lion's mouth; the familiars of the holy inquisition are every where, and, though summoned before its awful tribunal upon false grounds, the torture soon wrests from you a confession of those offences of which you have been really guilty. No, Zofloya, the attainment of my object avails me nothing, if destruction follows the momentary triumph."

"Well, Signora, though I think that your fears magnify the danger, yet the alternative which occurs is easy; persuade the Conte to quit Venice."

But whither to go?" she said, with an embarrassed air; "all Italy is equally dangerous."

Zofloya made an impatient gesture, as if to reprove the hesitation of Victoria; after a moment, she resumed —

"I have heard Berenza speak of Torre Alto; it is the name of a castle appertaining to him, which is situated among the Appennines."

"A retirement there would at least suit your purpose; the prying steps of curiosity will not follow you, and discovery cannot reach you."

"But should Berenza object, as *I* have hitherto done, to a temporary removal thither?"

"Then can you adduce a thousand reasons; a desire for solitude, a wish to visit a spot you have never yet seen, or lastly, a suggestion that change of air and situation might speedily restore his health."

"It shall be so, Zofloya; pity the distraction of a wretch, whose mind is rendered imbecile by misery, and who of herself is incapable of an effort towards her own happiness; aided and advised by thee, I may command success."

The Moor smiled — "Your fate, your fortune, fair Signora, will be of your own making: I am but the humble tool, the slave of your wishes; your co-operation with me alone can render me powerful; but fly me, disdain my assistance, and despise my friendship I *sink abashed into myself, and am powerless*! Farewel, Signora; I have already staid too long; for the present you need me no more." Abruptly then Zofloya turned away, and quitted the presence of Victoria, who took her steps, musingly, towards the house.

At supper, soon as with wine and conversation the spirits of Berenza became joyous and elevated, she artfully seized an opportunity of introducing the subject nearest her heart; she spoke of Torre Alto, and expressed a desire to visit its sublime solitudes, professing herself to be still further influenced from the flattering presumption, (looking tenderly at Berenza as she made the assertion), that change of atmosphere and a more elevated situation might be a means of bracing his nerves, and restoring him to his pristine health.

Whatever the tender and unsuspicious Berenza believed, it was enough for him that Victoria expressed the wish, for him unhesitatingly to comply with it; while the welcome, but fallacious hope pressed upon his heart, that devoted to love and him, and desirous to prove to him that she was so, she abandoned, without regret, the vain pleasures and amusements of the voluptuous city, for a solitude no longer unpleasing to her. Charmed at this return to reason and rationality, he fondly persuaded himself that the evening of his days would close like the brilliant beauty of a western sky declining into the shadows of night. Fearful even that her purpose might change, he expatiated on the beauty, the situation of his castella; and, desirous to offer every possible allurement to her perseverance, he entreated that Henriquez, his fair mistress, and her ancient protectress, would be of the intended party.

To this, Henriquez, who fondly loved his brother, readily acquiesced, and ventured to promise for Lilla and the Signora, as with a smile he looked towards them, to deprecate the possibility of a refusal.

Victoria, perceiving in the hapless Berenza such unhoped-for eagerness in coincidence with her plan, artfully forbore to press the subject further; but her alarm being awakened, lest the relation of Lilla should object to the journey, and thereby (an idea that was not endurable) detain Henriquez in Venice, she exerted the fascinations of her kindness towards her, and observed with seeming pleasure, as if the point of her acquiescence had been settled, what infinite benefit would, in all probability, result to her own health, in consequence of the salubrious change.

The poor old Signora did not exactly think so, but it was enough that Victoria condescended to say it, and to direct towards her unusual attention, for her not to hesitate. Besides, as self-love is no less inherent in age than youth, she felt no little gratification in being deemed of sufficient consequence for solicitation.

All preliminaries being speedily arranged, it was agreed, ere they rose from table, that the following day should only intervene for the conclusion of some necessary preparations, and that on the subsequent morning they would take their departure from the gay city of Venice, for the Castella di Torre Alto, among the Appennines.

CHAPTER XXII

On a lovely morning, early in spring, the party, descending the steps of St. Mark's, embarked on the Brenta for the Appennines.[1] Victoria, seated by the side of Berenza, administered to him the tenderest, the most deceitful attentions; the fair and beautiful Lilla, with her long flaxen tresses almost veiling her fairy form, seated by the side of Henriquez, caught the soft breathings of his love, and, without looking upon him, *felt* the warm glances of his eyes, which thrilled with voluptuous tenderness her innocent soul. The aged Signora, proud to be among the youthful party, though of little interest to any, save her orphan charge, sat contented in the enjoyment of others; for venerable age but rarely attracts the portion of consideration which is due to it. Zofloya, towering as a demigod, with his plumed and turbaned head, his dark form contrasted, and embellished by his bracelets of pearl, and by the snowy hue of his garments, was stationed near the stern of the vessel, and ravished the surrounding party with his exquisite harmony, to which even the undulating waves, in the rapt ear of enthuastic fancy, appeared to keep respectful music.

Never was fatal journey performed under fairer auspices, never with fonder triumph did the bridegroom conduct his long loved mistress to the altar, than the poor Berenza conducted to his solitude, among mountains, the faithless Victoria. He saw no solitude when she was by; to him she was the peopled world of pleasure, and in the fulness of his exhilarated heart, he blest the moment which, by visiting him with sickness, restored him, as he thought, the affections of a wife he had feared was lost to him.

To be brief — their journey concluded, and arrived at Torre Alto, Victoria observed herself, with a gloomy and secret delight, enclosed within the profoundest solitudes, for no town, no hamlet was even near the Castella of Berenza, which was situated in a deep valley, on the borders of a forest. On either side huge rocks towered above its loftiest spires, and half embosomed it in terrible but majestic sublimity, while no sound disturbed the solemn silence of the scene but the fall of the impetuous cataract, as it tumbled from the stupendous acclivity into the depths below, or the distant sound of the vesper-bell tolling solemn from the nearest convent, with, at times, when the wind blew towards the castle, the murmuring peal of the lofty-sounding organ, caught at intervals in the

---

1 Brenta for the Appennines: The Brenta is a river in northern Italy, flowing southeast into the Adriatic. The Appennines are a mountain chain running the length of Italy.

breeze, seeming more like the mysterious music of the spirits of the air
than sounds from mortal haunts.

"Here, then," said Victoria, as on the morning after her arrival ar
gazed from her chamber window upon the beautifully terrific scenery, and
the immeasurable waste of endless solitude which composed it — "Here,
then, without danger, may I pursue the path leading to the summit of my
wishes; no prying eye can pierce through, here, the secret movements
which, to compass my soul's desire, may be requisite. Hail then to these
blissful solitudes, hail to them, since they perhaps may first witness the
rich harvest of my persevering love; and for such a love, perish, all that
may oppose it!"

While thus she continued, her eyes indeed wandering wildly over the
world of mountains, but her thoughts far, far beyond them, she was
roused by the mild voice of Berenza, who gently seizing her arm, smilingly inquired the subject of her reverie.

A faint blush suffused the guilt-bronzed cheek of Victoria, as in a low
voice she merely replied, "I was contemplating the grandeur of the surrounding scenery, my Lord."

"And do you know, beloved Victoria," replied Berenza, "that I fancy
my health already improved from the effects of our journey, this beautiful
seclusion, and these pure airs."

Victoria felt that this idea of Berenza's was indeed mere fancy, for well
she knew that, on the preceding evening, unrestrained by his fatigue, the
circumstances of the moment, or the pallid cheek of Berenza, she had
administered to him his death-dealing draught. The bare assertion, however, that he did not feel ill, disturbed her for the moment, and she secretly resolved, that in the next draught she would mingle more of the poison. For the present, however, she accompanied him from the window,
and joined the party already assembled at breakfast.

Persevering with relentless barbarity, ere the ten days were concluded,
Victoria had administered to the Conte the last atom of the poison; she
therefore, as evening came on, wandered forth, in hopes of encountering
the Moor, with whom, since her arrival at Torre Alto, she had scarcely
found an opportunity of conversing.

She took her way across the almost pathless forest; for the deeper and
more gloomy the solitude, the more probable she thought it, that Zofloya
would choose it for his haunt.

Accordingly, she had not proceeded far, ere, as if informed by sym-
pathetic influence of her wishes, she beheld the stately Moor issuing
from a break among the trees, directly across her path. She called to him
aloud; when, slightly bowing, he arrested his steps till she came up with
him.

Impatience to begin on subjects more important, prevented her from
remarking the cool and haughty conduct of Zofloya, who, instead of proceeding rapidly to meet her, had contented himself with awaiting her
arrival at the spot where he stood.

"Zofloya," she said, as she took his arm, and walked rapidly onwards, "can you not at once deliver me from the tortures I endure? Having embarked thus far, my soul is sick of the delay; I therefore implore, if you desire to serve me, that you will do it speedily and effectually."

"Signora," answered the Moor gravely, "your movements have already outstepped my directions, and your precipitancy has gone near to defeat your views: the present illness of the Conte is of a nature to induce gradual and ultimate dissolution; there is nothing in its *appearance*, which in the common course of things, could warrant the event of sudden death; such an occurrence, therefore, would give immediate rise to suspicion, with every colour of justice on its side: behold, therefore, and pardon my abruptness," he added, "here is that which will cause considerable change in the Conte. Seven days will exhaust it: but it must not be exhausted in a shorter period. Moreover, Signora, I warn you, that if my directions are in the smallest tittle infringed, you weaken the power by which I act, and destroy the effect which strict adherence to the rules laid down can alone produce." Then giving a small paper into the hands of Victoria, with distant air he bowed his head, and, striking immediately into the deep recesses of the wood, became lost to her view.

"Singular being," thought Victoria, as with slow and meditating steps she retook her path towards the castella, "how happens it, that with a thousand questions to ask him, I find time to ask him nothing? and, with a thousand inquiries to make respecting himself, my tongue refuses in his presence to perform its office, and I remain unsatisfied?" Thus reflecting, she increased her pace, for the darkest shadows of evening were beginning to fall. As she approached the castle, she beheld coming, as if to seek her, the youthful Henriquez, unconscious object of the devouring flame that consumed her. At sight of him, her heart throbbed, and various emotions filled her breast.

"I come, Signora," he cried, as he drew near, "at the desire of my brother; he became impatient at your absence, perhaps apprehensive at this late hour, and entreated that I would seek and accompany you home."

"A task," said Victoria, in a reproachful accent, "which you would rather have been spared."

"No, indeed, Signora," coolly, though politely, answered Henriquez, "to give a moment's ease to the bosom of a beloved brother, to attend to his last request, and gratify even his most insignificant wishes, I could never deem a task."

"To wish for me, was indeed an insignificant wish," gloomily observed Victoria.

"I said not so, Signora."

As he spoke, the foot of Victoria striking against a point of projecting stone, she stumbled; Henriquez instinctively caught her arm. Victoria snatched it away resentfully, and, while tears almost started to her eyes, she said —

"No matter, Signor Henriquez, no matter to you if I fall."

"Good Heaven! Signora, why should you think thus? How have I given rise to so unjust a surmise?"

"You know, you know you hate," in an agitated voice, cried Victoria, thrown entirely off her guard.

Henriquez looked towards her with surprise, and, at a loss what to reply, bowed with an embarrassed air.

Victoria remained silent for a few moments, and then in a calmer voice resumed —

"Had the Conte desired you to seek Lilla, with what alacrity would you have obeyed."

"Ah!" returned Henriquez, with animation, "who could have reminded me to seek Lilla? since my eyes, accustomed to dwell upon her, would so soon have missed their wonted delight."

Victoria scowled, with mingled rage and jealousy, upon Henriquez; but he looked not towards her, and if he had, the hour had been almost too dark for him to distinguish the expression of her countenance, which was so terrible, it might almost have been felt by inspiration. By degrees, however, she quelled the violence of her sensations, and, in a smothered voice, observed —

"Henriquez, you love Lilla."

"Love!" he emphatically replied, "I adore her! I idolize her! She is the light of my eyes, the sunshine of my soul, the spring which actuates my existence! Without her, life to me would be a dreary blank; and, if fate snatched her from me in *this* world, I would die, yes, hasten to die, that my soul might rejoin her in the next, and my body repose by her pure form in the grave."

"Oh! madness, madness!" muttered Victoria, and involuntarily grasped Henriquez by the arm.

"Signora, are you ill?" he cried, instantly stopping.

"No, no, no; but I — I was almost on the point of falling again," she answered, gasping for breath; and in that instant she wavered, whether the powder she retained in her bosom should not be destined to Lilla rather than Berenza.

While this idea crossed her mind, she beheld the innocent girl bounding towards them through the gloom, seeming like an aërial spirit, seen by the dubious light, scarcely appearing in its delicate movements to touch the ground. Instantly the rage of her bosom changed into laughing contempt: she felt her least power could at any time annihilate this, the most fragile of nature's productions, and disdained herself, that she had even cast a thought upon an atom so insignificant.

Henriquez flew instantly to meet her, Victoria slowly followed, and altogether entered the castle, the tender Lilla with her right hand holding one of Victoria's, and passing the left round her waist. Proceeding to the room where Berenza awaited them, they found him stretched at length upon a sopha, which being of crimson colour, added a more deadly tinge to the paleness of his complexion; as soon as he beheld Victoria, he stretched forth his hand to her, and exclaimed —

"Oh, my love, whither have you been? I have been wishing for my tender nurse to make me a glass of lemonade."

"I have been walking in the forest, my love," replied Victoria, and I went further than I intended; but let me hasten to prepare your drink."

So saying, she quitted the room, and in a few moments returned, with a glass of lemonade, into which she had already infused a sufficient quantity of poison. Its additional force discomfited, as at first, the debilitated stomach of the unfortunate Berenza, for he had drunk it all with avidity. Complaining of faintish sickness, he motioned for Victoria to sit beside him; and, leaning his head upon her faithless bosom, seemed presently overcome by a profound sleep. Soon, however, it became disturbed and interrupted by convulsive catchings; that innocent breath, which issued from his lips, and passed over the face of Victoria, spoke no reproach to her remorseless bosom. A feverish glow passed over his cheek, and now was succeeded by a deadly paleness; now his hand involuntarily shook, and now different parts of his body yielded to a tremulous convulsion; his lips quivered, his eye-lids became agitated by a nervous motion, and he half-opened his eyes, over which there appeared a dimness like a thin film. Again the heart of Victoria yielded to selfish terror, lest she had administered too powerful a dose of the poison. Berenza, however, was not awake, though his eyes remained half open; she took his burning hand, and, actuated by her fears, strongly pressed it; the action recalled in a moment the fleeting senses of Berenza; he started and opened his eyes, from which the film vanished; then perceiving the false Victoria bending over him, the complaint he was about to utter died upon his lips, and fearful of giving uneasiness to her, who was deliberately consuming his life, he even repressed the look of anguish, straining it into a tender smile, and smothered the sigh of agony which was bursting from his bosom.

"Dear Berenza, you are ill," cried Victoria, gazing with dissembled fondness in his face.

"Only a little languid, my beloved," answered he, "a few glasses of wine will reanimate me." So saying, he rose, endeavouring to conceal the access of weakness, of which he became sensible, from the eyes of every one, but more particularly from those of Victoria; and requesting they might repair to the supper room, he was that night permitted, not from her compassion, but her base policy, to drink his wine unmingled with the baleful poison. Yet bitterly she regretted what she felt to be so necessary an intermission.

CHAPTER XXIII

The allotted week had not expired, ere change sufficient was visible in the unfortunate Berenza, to satisfy even the soul of Victoria, thirsting as it was for his innocent blood. It was in vain that he gazed on her with eyes of dying fondness; it was in vain that, when oppressed by raging thirst, he called on her for drink, and would receive it from no hand but hers: even this disarmed not her heart of its fell purpose, even this touched it not with an emotion of pity or remorse. Still she infused, with hand restricted only by fear of danger to herself, the consuming poison into the coveted draught, which, so far from allaying the fever of his blood, was as oil to the devouring flame.

Still Berenza dreamed not that his death was nigh; true, he felt within him, an inanity as it were, a languor of the heart, with sometimes a kind of distaste and weariness of former objects; he knew not precisely the nature of his own sensations, for they varied occasionally; often his spirits were animated, but then it was an animation which diffused not its vivifying current through the pulses of his heart: it sprang not thence, neither did it leave cheerfulness behind; it seemed independent of himself, as the artificial vivacity which is raised by the power of wine. Always, after the animal spirits had been thus pressed into action, as it were, he became feebler, and more dejected from the strained exertion. This Victoria observing, and instantly concluding that wine, while it exhilarated him for the moment, must still tend to parch up the vital heat, she induced him to drink plentifully of it, thereby causing it to answer the double purpose, of blinding him to his actual danger, and hastening his death.

His cough had now become more serious, exercise was fatiguing to him, and all society but that of Victoria irksome; thus was he completely in her power, but nevertheless she durst not go beyond the directions of Zofloya. The person of the Conte, however, underwent no considerable alteration; his complexion only had become somewhat pallid, though occasionally it glowed with a transparent red; but though feeble, and slightly emaciated, his appetite was increased even to ravenousness.

From this circumstance he could not believe himself in actual danger, but rather coincided with the pretended hope of Victoria, that time, and a naturally robust constitution, would triumph over a disorder that he firmly attributed (as Victoria had suggested) to some neglected and unnoticed cold. The wilds of the Appennines seldom tempted him to roam: with the inhabitants of a few gloomy castellas, scattered here and there, at immense distances from his own, he never associated; and Victoria affirmed, in order to keep him more secure, and avoid the remotest risk of drawing attention towards them, that quiet and rest were absolutely indispensable to his recovery.

Whatever she willed, right or otherwise, was law to the fond, the dying Berenza, who forgot in her present apparent tenderness towards him, and seeming devotement, all former coolness and discontent at the very moment in which, with treacherous hand but looks of love, she held towards him the life destroying draught, in that moment was she dearer to his soul than ever, and often, ere he put it to his parched lips, did he stay his eagerness, to kiss the false hand that presented it.

In vain did Henriquez entreat of his infatuated brother to receive advice, to explain his sensations, only to hear the opinion of a physician: no, he steadily refused; Victoria was all-sufficient, and on her tender care would he alone depend.

The poison, however, being now exhausted, and the week elapsed, Victoria finding that the miserable Berenza was not only yet in existence, but that for the last two days he had not appeared more evidently reduced than he had for some time past, became absolutely impatient to a degree of savageness, and cursed the feeble life that still struggled to retain possession of its worn-out tenement; deeming it therefore requisite to seek Zofloya, she again repaired to that part of the forest where she had last encountered him. This time the Moor seemed awaiting her, and hastening towards her, as she approached, he said —

"You are impatient, Signora, at the strength of the Conte's constitution; is it not so? — But rest satisfied, your end is answered; he cannot long survive."

"Yet does he not appear worse this evening than he did eight days ago," murmuringly observed Victoria.

"Probably not, Signora; yet are the principles of life irreparably sapped, and though you should now resign all further attempts to utterly destroy them, though every aid of medicine might be essayed, yet never now could nature recover herself, for he must eventually and speedily perish."

"But how soon? or he may linger for years, even till old age shall have chilled the ardent fires which now burn in my bosom, till my passions shall have withered away, and my energies become damped! Oh, Zofloya! if you desire to serve me, let it be at once; hitherto you have but trifled."

The Moor started back, and looked scowlingly upon Victoria; never before had she beheld him look so terrible: in an instant her proud rage subsided, her eyes were cast on the earth, and she trembled at what she had suffered to escape her lips. Yes, Victoria, who never before trembled in the presence of mortal being, who did not tremble to agonise and insult a father, to revile a mother, and consign a husband to the grave, trembled now, in the presence of Zofloya. To herself even, the sensation she experienced was inexplicable; and involuntarily approaching the Moor, who was still distant from her, she took his hand, and said — "Forgive me, Zofloya; pardon my abruptness, and attribute it to the irksome delay I suffer in my hopes, which confuses and distracts my brain."

"'Tis well, Signora," answered the Moor, gracefully, yet haughtily bending and waving his hand.

"You forgive me, Zofloya; deign then to advise me."

"I direct, Signora, not advise, and at the same time must observe, that the fullest confidence is to be placed in me; you have not yet found that I have deceived you; it will be early enough for reproaches, when you discover that I have. Spare them, I beseech you then, till the arrival of that period; your doubts must vanish meantime, and, if you wish my assistance, I must be suffered, without comment, to pursue that line best calculated to render it effectual. I told you, that the drug I gave you would work the destruction of the Conte; did I not add, that it would work it slowly? Would you have desired it should be immediate, to frustrate for ever your own hopes, and end at once my business here?"

"Well, Zofloya, I will in all respects follow your directions; relax then the sternness of your brow, and smile upon me as usual."

"Beautiful Victoria! you are resistless," cried Zofloya, dropping on one knee — "'tis I now who sue for pardon, and promise to devote myself to your service."

"Rise, gentle Moor, and accept my hand," cried the vain and flattered Victoria; "never shall I have power to recompense you."

"*You recompense me, Signora, in accepting my services*; deign now to listen to me: you desire that Berenza should be cut at once from the face of the earth. I deem it more advisable that he should be left to the concluding effects of the poison he has already imbibed; but that I may gratify your wishes, and, above all, guard against the possibility of disappointment, I have here a drug which I have known to be immediate in its operations: lest, however, it should accidentally fail in the present instance, requiring perhaps a small addition of some corroborative quality, or an increase of the dose, I would recommend a previous trial upon some indifferent subject —" He paused.

"I know of no subject," said Victoria, musingly.

"Has not the orphan Lilla an old female relative with her?" observed Zofloya; "she is, as far as I can see, a most useless appendage, and hereafter might even prove troublesome."

"True," replied Victoria, "she would answer excellently for an experiment."

The Moor smiled with malice. "I would have you then, Signora, lead the officious dame into the forest; I will shortly appear, as if by your previous desire, with two glasses of wine or lemonade; you will take the one which I shall put next to you, and present the other to the old Signora. She is feeble, and tottering on the verge of the grave; should not an immediate effect be perceptible on *her* swallowing it, we must add a grain for the benefit of the Conte."

"But should it not take instant effect, we shall be betrayed, Zofloya."

"Leave that to me, Signora, and suffer me to proceed: on my having retired, you shall run hastily towards the castle for assistance, pretending, which will be easily believed, that the Signora hath fallen down in a fit."

"But should any marks of the poison become perceptible after her death," interrupted the selfish Victoria.

"They will be naturally attributed to the *mode* of her death; no suspicion, rest assured, shall be excited — trust to me, beautiful Victoria. I have an interest, a deep interest, in preserving you from exposure."

"Well, give me the powder then; I reply implicitly upon you." The Moor gave into her hand a small paper containing the poison, and the following morning was agreed on for the trial of its efficacy. Separating then, each reached the castle by different ways.

On the following morning Victoria, having watched her opportunity, entered a little apartment where the aged and inoffensive Signora was tranquilly sitting by a window, inhaling, through the bars of a blind, the fresh breeze from the mountains. Solitary, and forsaken by the younger branches of the family, even by the gentle Lilla, who had been drawn away by Henriquez, she smiled with pleasure at the sight of Victoria, who, more rarely than any one, deigned to notice her.

"What, entirely alone, Signora," she exclaimed as she entered; "come then," in a gay and conciliating tone, "come, let me lead you out; you will find the open air do you more service than inhaling it through this confined medium."

The poor Signora, surprised and flattered at such wonderful condescension, rose with trembling limbs, yet with all the alacrity she could assume.

"Lean upon me, good Signora," said Victoria, "and let me assist you."

The gratified and feeble Signora respectfully accepted the offer. Panting with weakness, she gained at length, however, the precincts of the forest. Here Victoria, though she cursed and dreaded the delay, was under the necessity of permitting her for a few moments to rest upon her arm. But her evil genius assisted her evil intent; no one appeared in view, and the fresh air having a little restored the imbecile powers of her unsuspecting companion, she prevailed upon her to proceed, and succeeded at length in luring her, by the unusual honor of her attention, to a more gloomy part of the forest, where a rocky acclivity on one side, offered at its base a rugged and projecting seat. Here Victoria, affecting to have selected this spot for its convenient attributes in shading them at once from the sun and the wind, and likewise affording them a seat, entreated the Signora to rest, while, with treacherous kindness, she assisted her to sit.

Appearing then infinitely grieved at her evident weariness, though the poor Signora, from complaisance and gratitude, forbore complaint, she observed to her, "You are indeed fatigued, Signora; I apprehend the exertion has been too much for you; allow me to return to the castle and procure you some refreshment — though, generally, the Moor Zofloya brings me about this hour sherbet or lemonade."

"The Santa Maria forbid!" replied the Signora, "that you should give yourself any trouble; a little rest will quite restore me — but I am no longer young, Signora."

At that moment Victoria beheld among the trees the emerald-covered turban of Zofloya, glittering to the sun-beam; her heart leaped, and she rose to receive from him the glasses of lemonade, which he carried in a silver salver. Punctual in taking for herself that which the Moor held towards her, she presented the other to the unconscious Signora, who received it with palsied hand, but with a thankful smile and a dim eye that looked on her with gratitude.

Scarcely, however, had she taken off the fatal draught, ere, overcome by dreadful sickness, she fell headlong from her seat: she essayed to speak, her sunken eyes rolled dreadfully, and, with violent convulsions, she uttered, "I am — I am poisoned!"

"She will not die," muttered Victoria, in a low voice, to the Moor.

Zofloya replied not, but, stooping over the struggling unfortunate, he compressed her withered throat with his dark hand, and the sounds, half-formed, rattled within it. Then rising, with unruffled visage, he laid his finger on his lip, and pointing towards the castle, precipitately disappeared.

Victoria understood the movement; neither shocked nor alarmed at the frightful outrage committed, she ran from the recess, and, as she gained the castle, called loudly for help. Servants immediately came running different ways, and, when informed that a terrrible catastrophe had befallen the old Signora, they hastened to the spot. Even Berenza conquered his pain and lassitude, to gaze with awe upon the melancholy fate, a forerunner only of his own. The innocent Lilla, almost frantic, exclaimed in agony, as she leaned over the lifeless body of her only relative, that she had now, indeed, no friend, but was a deserted orphan left destitute in the world.

"Unkind Lilla," cried Henriquez, endeavouring to draw her from the painful scene, "have you not a lover, and can you want a friend?"

Lilla replied not, while tears of anguish coursed down her fair cheeks, and melancholy forebodings filled her breast.

Henriquez passed his arm round her waist, and forced her from the spot, while Victoria gazed upon them as they passed with eyes of malignant rage.

Every one believed that the old Signora had expired suddenly in a fit; some said the air had taken too powerful an effect on her debilitated frame; some, that she had been seized with sudden convulsion; while even the wisest attributed the event to the visitation of Providence, and the infirmity of age, that could no longer support the burden of existence. None surmised the real cause: at the dreadful scene of her death there were no witnesses but its cruel perpetrators; in the gloomy solitariness of mutual guilt, the deed was hatched and done.

CHAPTER XXIV

A short time only had elapsed since the dreadful catastrophe of the poor Signora, during which Victoria had continued, though with pining reluctance, the use of the slow poison (the Moor Zofloya having peremptorily refused to administer as yet the final dose), when, frantic with protracted hope, and increasing passion, she sought again the dark abettor of her crimes. It was on an evening, when no appointment existed between them, at an hour too much earlier than she had yet been accustomed to seek the Moor; but the demons of evil raged with such fury in her bosom, that every consideration was lost in their overpowering influence. The wretched Berenza still lived an obstacle to her wishes, and death, death alone, could satisfy her thirsting soul.

She bent her steps towards the thickest of the forest; where the gloomy cypress, tall pine, and lofty poplar, mingled in solemn umbrage. Beyond, steep rocks, seeming piled on one another, inaccessible mountains, with here and there a blasted oak upon its summit, resembling rather, from the distant point at which it was beheld, a stunted shrub; huge precipices down, which the torrent dashed, and foaming in the viewless abyss with mighty rage, filled the most distant parts of the surrounding solitude with a mysterious murmuring, produced by the multiplied reverberations of sound.

Victoria stopped for a moment, and gazed around; the wild gloom seemed to suit the dark and ferocious passions of her soul. She gave way to the chain of thought that came pressing on her mind, her heart was anarchy and lust of crime, and she regretted that she had suffered till now, the existence of aught between her and her desired happiness. "By the dagger's aid," thought she, "I could have accomplished all ere now. I despise, yes, despise my folly, in having deliberated so long, and the contemptible fears that have restrained my hand." Thus buoying herself up to frenzy, she admitted no reflection of danger that was attendant on the open commission of crime; her reason was blinded by the blandishments of guilt, and the despotic sway of evil that triumphed in her heart.

"Oh! Zofloya, Zofloya," she exclaimed, with wild impatience, "why art thou not here. Thou, perhaps, and thou alone, couldst soothe the burning madness of my brain!"

As she concluded these words, she struck her forehead violently with her hand, and threw herself with her face upon the earth.

Of a sudden the sweetest sounds stole upon her ear; they were like the tremulous vibration of a double-toned flute, sounding as it were from a distance; its lovely melody by turns softened and agitated her; it seemed not the solemn notes of the organ from the neighbouring convent; no, it was unlike mortal harmony; besides, the convent was on the other side of the castle, situated half way down a mighty rock, and she had wandered too far to catch the smallest note of its deep sounding music, even had the wind set towards the castle. Still the soft tones continued, and kept her on the rack between pain and pleasure; at one moment it brought before her view the idolized form of Henriquez, in all the grace of his youthful beauty, disposing her to love, and the most impetuous passion; the next, its melancholy cadence, suggested to her sickening soul, that him so franticly adored might never be hers; and that the barriers existing between them could never be overcome. If the turbulent emotions of her mind abated, they gave place to others no less dangerous — still she listened with resistless attention; at length a slight pause occurred.

"Sweet aërial sounds," she cried, "yet painful are the impressions I receive from you, distracting rather than soothing my troubled soul! sooner, yes sooner, would I hear the footstep of Zofloya, or his sweet voice, sweeter than all this music."

"His voice then, and not his step! most beautiful Signora," said a voice which rivalled indeed the sweetness of the music; and Victoria beheld at her side the stately Moor.

"Astonishing being," she exclaimed, "I heard you not indeed; whence came you?"

"I am here, Victoria; will not that suffice?"

"How knew you that I desired your presence?"

"By sympathy, lovely Victoria; your very *thoughts* have power to attract me. Such as you have just indulged would bring me to you, from the further extremity of this terrestrial globe."

"Explain, Zofloya!"

"They are bold and spirited, they convince me that you partake of myself, and that you are worthy of my present devotion. I am satisfied in this conviction."

"But, how have you the power of divining *my* thoughts?"

Zofloya smiled, and regarded her with a piercing eye — "I can read them now, beautiful Victoria! that high-flushed cheek, that wandering eye, are evidences that cannot be mistaken."

Victoria sighed deeply, and concurring in the justice of the observation, inquired no further.

The wily Moor had turned her attention from his mysterious insinuations to her own conscious feelings; these alone regained full possession of her, and every thing else appeared trivial in her view.

"Oh, Zofloya!" she exclaimed, "truly dost thou divine; my soul is indeed disturbed, and unless thou wilt assist me, I am lost."

"Despair not," said the Moor, casting himself beside her, as her figure, half risen from the earth, was supported by her elbow, and her head reclined upon her hand — "Despair not," he repeated, and unrepulsed took the hand which hung down; "say but how Zofloya can serve his lovely mistress, and let him prove to her his zeal."

"Ah! thou knowest, thou knowest, Zofloya," she cried impatiently, when looking upon the serious, yet expressive countenance of the Moor, she more calmly proceeded: "I have hitherto, Zofloya, yielded to thy counsel; I may say, to thy will, for thou wouldst not grant me that which ere now would have set me free. Berenza still lives, still intervenes between me and happiness! Well thou knowest the feverish suspense which I endure; my blood bubbles in my heated veins, and I feel within me as if the powers of life were withering, scorched and dried up by the raging fires of my long protracted love. Oh, kind and pitying Moor, I ask thee — yes, I ask thee for that, which by ending at once the existence of him whose emaciated semblance of what he once was, reproaches, while it mocks my hopes, shall free him from the lingering torments he endures, and give new life to me!"

She paused, and looking on the Moor, beheld his eyes sparkling with such a scintillating brilliancy as it were, that she was compelled to withdraw her gaze, though impatiently she awaited his reply.

"Victoria," said he, at length, in dulcet accents, while the wild emotions of Victoria's bosom began already to subside, "I would not have thee think that in the waywardness of an unkind spirit, I refused thee thy wish; be assured thy present safety, and the ultimate attainment of thy hopes, alone actuated me. When we essayed the poison on the ancient relative of the orphan Lilla, which speedily extinguished within her the feeble flame of life, I ask thee, would it have been expedient, according to thy ill-judged desire, to have administered on the following day a similar draught to the Conte? What terrible and dangerous surmises would instantly have been excited, marring thereby, and putting perhaps an eternal period to all thy hopes? It was necessary that a short time at least should elapse; meanwhile, we have not lost any, for not a day hath since passed, that has not brought him nearer to his grave; because he still breathes, and faintly lives, thou believest that his breath and life are not nearly exhausted: it is not so, however; and the slightest impellant will tumble him headlong into the arms of death. Had we not first essayed the efficacy of the poison upon the old Signora, but unadvisedly had administered it to him, he would have languished for a time, and his situation would have awakened suspicion. Now will I be sworn that success, immediate success, shall attend our attempt, and that Berenza shall die without power to express a word; depend on me then, lovely Victoria; place implicit confidence in Zofloya."

"Ah, if you are indeed anxious to serve me, Zofloya," cried Victoria, with a smile that evidenced the joy imparted by the last words of the Moor, "why did you not seek me at once, and put the speediest possible end to my protracted misery?"

"I did not seek you, because it increases my triumph and my pleasure that you should will me into your presence; with joy do I promote your wishes, but with redoubled joy when you *yourself* invite me. — Besides," added he, "I am almost convinced, that it would be as well even yet to delay for a time —"

"Oh, talk not to me so," interrupted Victoria, "wherefore, wherefore delay?"

"The better to evade suspicion," rejoined the Moor.

"Oh, you are bent upon destroying me, Zofloya;" when perceiving a gathering frown upon the countenance of the Moor, she hastily added —

"Oh, frown not so terribly, Zofloya, but assist me at once; thereby laying claim to my eternal gratitude, and enhancing the benefit you confer."

It shall be so then," replied the Moor, with a beautiful but peculiar smile; "I will yield to your desire, assist you in your attempt, and shield you from all *immediate consequences*; this night removes from your view, one become so obnoxious to it."

"This night! saidst thou Zofloya?" cried Victoria, in an exulting voice.

"This very night," returned the Moor; "within this hour, you shall see your desire fulfilled, and I will preserve you from every danger and suspicion."

"Oh! Moor, I thank thee," exclaimed Victoria, seizing in her joy his hand, and pressing it to her bosom.

The Moor turned upon her his resplendent eyes — "Is not that heart mine, Victoria?" said he, in an impressive voice.

"It is indeed, gratefully bound to you, Zofloya," she answered, looking upon him with a disconcerted air.

"I say it is *mine*, Victoria," returned he; "But," he added smilingly, "fear not, for I am not jealous of your passion for another."

Victoria felt surprise; she lifted her eyes to the countenance of the Moor, but they fell beneath his fiery glances — she would have spoken; she knew not what conflicting emotions chained her tongue, she desired to reprove his boldness, but needing his assistance, she durst not — she beheld herself in his power, and, in the abjectness of her guilt, she trembled.

Zofloya smiled, his hand had remained on her bosom, its hard pressure seemed heavy on her heart! — He now withdrew it, and her confused senses began to rally; she felt released, as from a grasp of iron; again she ventured to turn her eyes towards him, his features had resumed their usual expression, animated, but serene, resembling the returning brilliant calmness of a summer sky, that had looked lurid with the threatened storm. In an instant his ambiguous words vanished from the mind of Victoria, or ceased to make impression; aught was pardonable in the resistless Zofloya, and she faintly smiled.

"Victoria," he observed, "it is yet light, the evening is mild and beautiful, the breeze from the mountains bears temptation on its wings, it promises delight to those in health, and reanimation to the feeble. Berenza will, I think, be induced to venture forth; leave this spot therefore, walk towards the castle, and you may encounter him; if you do, you will see me likewise; should Berenza be sick, let your eyes seek me; when mine meet yours, put forth your hand, and receive whatever I shall offer you; give it to Berenza, and the result will be manifested! — Farewell."

So saying, in a moment he turned, and walked rapidly away; soon Victoria beheld him no more; his movement had been so precipitate, so sudden, that scarcely could she believe she had but just beheld him. With slow and lingering steps she prepared however to depart. The words of the Moor still sounded in her ears, but their import was not clear to her; his mysterious deportment occupied her thoughts, and, though in his presence hope and pleasant feelings diffused themselves through her bosom, no sooner was he vanished than, for the temporary calm she had experienced, accumulated horrors distracted her — the wildest phrenzy of passion, the most ungovernable hate, and thirst, even for the blood of all who might oppose her. In a mind of such gloomy anarchy, was she now traversing the forest, her pace quick, and irregular; already had she entered the path leading to the castle, when a faint and hollow voice uttered her name.

Raising her eyes, she started on beholding before her the heart-touching semblance of what he once had been; the dying, but unconscious Berenza, supported between Lilla and Henriquez; his faded form was before her indeed, but she beheld him not, for her guilty eyes were directed instantly towards his blooming brother, whose sparkling eye, and health-animated form, presented too sure a striking contrast to the feeble being beside him. Sunk was the once brilliant eye, and robbed of its red rose teint, the pallid cheek of Berenza; despoiled of their healthful firmness, his emaciated nerveless limbs; his once expanded chest, expanded now no longer, but contracted, and oppressed by a difficulty of respiration; his elevated figure, his step bold and erect, now changed and depressed by the hard hand of long protracted suffering; the wretched Berenza retained about him no traces of what he once had been, save in the sweet suavity of his unaltered manners, save in the never dying grace that, even in a state so pitiable, accompanied his every movement. The philosophic dignity of his soul, his native strength of mind, forsook him not, but taught him, as through life it had done, to rise superior to his bodily ills — ills which even yet he vainly flattered himself were not irremediable. In the delusive fondness of Victoria's eyes he still read hope; from her well-feigned solicitude he derived consolation, and felt as though while beloved and attended by her, death could not reach him: — her love, her tenderness, seemed to him a protecting shield, through which its arrows could not pierce. Each pulsation of that faintly throbbing heart beat still with unvarying love for her; and, as he beheld her approaching, he disengaged his arm from Henriquez, and hastening towards her, even at the peril of sinking, he leaned his trembling hand upon her shoulder for support, and in an under voice he cried —

"The hope of meeting thee, my love, hath enabled me to proceed thus far. I now feel nearly overcome; lead me where for a moment I may rest myself.

"Canst thou walk a few paces further?" inquired Victoria, leading him onwards to the very spot where the unfortunate Signora had yielded up her life; they were then at no great distance from it, and Berenza, unable to reply, motioned that he might be supported thither.

Henriquez and Lilla joined to assist him. In a few minutes he gained the shady recess, and reposed himself upon that seat that had already been so fatal to another; passing then his arm around Victoria, he leaned his head upon her bosom.

"You are much fatigued, my love," she observed, in an anxious voice, as she sat beside him.

"Yes, my Victoria; and I would I were at the castle, for I faint with thirst."

"What wouldst thou, Berenza; I will hasten for it," said Victoria.

"Drink, drink! No matter what," answered the miserable Berenza, "something to revive my sinking soul."

"Oh, my brother!" cried Henriquez; you drink more than is prudent; and wine but increases the fever which consumes you."

"What, Henriquez!" hastily, and somewhat reproachfully, cried the agitated Berenza, rendered irritable by long suffering; "I named not wine; but if I had, wouldst thou deprive me of *every* consolation, refuse me every desire?"

Never before had the hapless Berenza expressed himself thus to a brother whom he tenderly loved: no sooner, therefore, did he observe that the feelings of Henriquez were wounded, than, stretching forth his hand, while a tear trembled in his eye, he said —

"Forgive me, Brother, forgive me; you do not feel as I do, nor would I have you; without wine I am a wretch; for, while it quenches the intolerable thirst which seems to parch my vitals, it warms and invigorates my debilitated frame; it gives new life to my sinking spirits, and renovates, when they begin to fail, my hopes of recovery —" Here, overcome by weakness, he could only wave his hand; which motion Henriquez comprehending, and vexed to have uttered aught that could in the smallest degree thwart his unfortunate brother, cried —

"Fly, my Lilla, to the castle, and bring our brother some wine; he may need my assistance, here therefore I will remain."

The beauteous Lilla bounded away to execute her mission. Berenza recovered a little; but his heart beat quick, though feebly, and his frame trembled with an increase of debility.

Lilla presently returned; "I met the Moor Zofloya," she cried, as she approached, "and he hastens now towards us with wine. I told him an overflowing goblet for *you*, my Lord;" she said, with a sweet smile, addressing Berenza —

"Did you, my little love?" said Berenza, faintly smiling, in return for her innocent attention.

Meantime, with quick step, Zofloya drew near; at sight of him violent emotion seized the breast of Victoria. Now his last words began to be explained, and she wondered in silence.

He approached and presented to the Conte the goblet of wine which he carried.

"Give it to me, my Victoria," cried Berenza, "from thy hand would I receive it," and with difficulty he raised his beating head from her bosom.

Victoria stretched forth her hand for the wine: her eyes met those of Zofloya; they were pregnant with terrible intelligence, for they spoke that *death* was in the goblet which she received from his hand.

With all her unshrinking hardihood in deeds of horror, the strange, the dreadful expression of Zofloya's countenance shook her inmost soul: nerving her hand, however, she took, with assumed steadiness, the fatal glass, and presented it to the anxious Berenza. He raised it, fixing his hollow eyes upon her countenance; and then, looking up to Heaven, as if to call down blessings on her head, he raised it to his lips and hastily drank its contents, even to the dregs!

Scarce had he done so, ere, with convulsive motion, his hand was pressed upon his heart, that heart seized with an acute and sudden pang; yet he uttered not a word; for, while the fires of Ætna[1] consumed his vitals, respiration was nearly arrested, and he gasped — his lips and cheeks became deadly pale, his eyes closed, his hands fell nerveless beside him, and, bereft of sense, he sunk back! ... Who more collected than the dark Zofloya? He loosed the vest of the Conte, he rubbed his hands and his temples; and, while horror assailed Henriquez, and even the guilty Victoria felt a selfish terror at the sudden accomplishment of her own wishes, he calmly, though with seeming sorrow, expressed his idea that the Conte had fainted through excessive weakness, and would probably recover if conveyed into the castle, where proper remedies could be administered. To this remark Henriquez, though almost insensible with alarm, sadly assented; the Moor then raising in his brawny arms, him whom he well knew would never more revive, hastened with him into the house.

The lifeless Berenza being laid upon a couch, a favorite servant of the Conte's, by name Antonio, proposed instantly to go in search of a certain Monk belonging to the neighbouring convent, who was reported to be highly skilled in physic and the disorders of the human frame. Henriquez, catching at the idea, hastily dispatched him, with every promise of reward, if he used expedition; and, meantime, approaching his brother, assisted Victoria and her wily coadjutor in their pretended endeavours to restore him.

That every effort was vain, is scarcely necessary to be said: yet great was the trepidation of Victoria, lest the reputed skill of the Monk, if it failed in counteracting the deadly *effects* of the poison, should at least reveal to him that poison had been resorted to. This idea threw her into a

---

1 Ætna: Mount Etna is an active volcano on the coast of Sicily, whose name in Greek means literally "I burn."

state of terror, that not all her dependence on Zofloya, nor even the offended glances of encouragement, which, from time to time, he cast on her, could subdue.

After some time of excruciating anxiety, passed by all, though from different motives, Antonio at length returned. He was accompanied by a Monk indeed, but not by him whom he sought, the Reverend Father being absent from the convent on visits of charity in a distant hamlet. The one now with him was offered as a substitute, and highly recommended by the superior, as second at least to Father Anselmo in physical knowledge, and his equal in piety, charity, and good-will towards men.

The Monk approached Berenza, and, after looking at him a few moments, desired that his arm might be uncovered; then, taking his lancet from his pocket, he made a small puncture in the vein. Victoria bent over him with well-feigned sorrow, while Henriquez held his motionless hand. Suddenly, (though, at the first puncture, a single drop had refused to flow,) the blood started forth, and flew in the face of Victoria!

Terror and surprise nearly overpowered the conscience-stricken wife; the avenging blood of Berenza had fixed upon his murderer, and hung its flaming evidence upon her cheek! She dared not lift her eyes, lest those of others should read in them the self-written characters of guilt; but, with trembling hand, raising a handkerchief to her face, wiped away the crimson stains, and then again ventured to bend over his lifeless form, still in terrible expectation of some further fearful event. All was over, however; the blood had just started and instantly ceased; animation was not suspended merely — it was for ever fled!

No one suspecting her guilt, her agitation was attributed only to the acutely painful feelings natural to be excited by an occurrence so affecting. While the thoughts and observation of all were still engaged upon Berenza, she ventured to raise her eyes; the terrible eyes of Zofloya alone encountered hers: in them she read the desperate and gloomy fierceness of determined crime; she could not gaze upon them, but hastily looked away.

Though despairing of the smallest success, the Monk had opened a vein in the other arm of Berenza: the terrors of Victoria were renewed, but groundlessly; no life-warm current followed the lancet's point; the heart was for ever motionless, and the bosom in which once it had beat high in healthful pride, inanimate and cold; hope could no more be indulged — for no swoon but the eternal sleep of death was discovered to have seized Berenza.

Such a fate, so sudden, so terrible for the best of human beings, excited bitter grief in the minds of all but Victoria. Yet even those who lamented him most, felt no surprise; for though immediate death had not been foreseen, no one had ventured to hope that it was far distant. He had not expired in the plenitude of vigorous health; his decay, on the contrary, had been progressive, though rapid, and his dissolution hastened, as Henriquez believed, by the unhappy determination of his beloved brother to refuse all medical advice, in the strange, delusive persuasion of his ever-reasoning mind, that nature must be all-sufficient to triumph in time over her own complaints. Never, is despite of representations most delicately urged, would Berenza give ear to any suggestions of actual danger; and for this pertinacity, Henriquez, too justly, in his mind arraigned Victoria, so tenderly beloved by the Conte; and often had he felt surprise and indignation that she never joined with others in entreating him to alter his fallacious system, when she well knew that her word, or slightest persuasion, would have changed instantly his most obstinate resolve. On the contrary, she would often argue with him, that physicians were ignorant, dangerous experimentalists, and pretend to be herself a convert to the hazardous plan of trusting all to the operations of nature. In consequence of these reflections, the heart of Henriquez involuntarily turned against the infamous wife; he had never viewed her with sentiments of regard, and she was now more than unpleasing in his sight: from an unaccountable combination of ideas, he connected her so intimately with the cause of Berenza's death, by having upheld him in his mistaken notions, that he shrunk almost instinctively from her, with a sentiment of horror. Unhappy Brother! little didst thou surmise, how well, how justly founded, were the feelings of thy breast, wherein nature so powerfully asserted herself.

CHAPTER XXV

When, at a late hour, the inmates of the mansion that so late had owned Berenza for its lord, retired to their respective apartments, more to indulge in solitude their grief for his loss, than to seek repose: it chanced that Victoria, whom no feeling, however, of regret or remorse for the cruel death inflicted by her on the most excellent of human beings, deprived of the power to sleep, awakened soon after she retired to bed from a disturbed and terrifying dream. Starting up in her bed, she gazed around the chamber, still trembling under its dreadful impression. She thought that entering the apartment where the corpse of the deceased Conte reposed, she had drawn aside the curtains of the bed, and beheld his countenance and various parts of his body discoloured and disfigured by livid marks — evidences of the poison which had been given him; that, in the frenzy of despair and terror, she had called upon and reproached Zofloya, who, without deigning to reply, gazed upon her with a stern and bitter smile. Thus, in a state of mind baffling description, she had awakened, and the impression made by her dream was so strong, that, although she endeavoured to view it only as an insignificant vision, caused by the events of the day, she found it impossible to compose herself; the figure of Berenza, discoloured by the effects of the poison, still swam in her view.

At length, determined to end what she conceived to be her superstitious terrors, she resolved to seek the apartment of the Conte, and to satisfy herself with the conviction that her dream was without foundation, phantoms conjured merely by a diseased imagination.

Accordingly, rising from bed, she wrapped herself in a loose white dress, and took in her hand a lamp, which was burning on a marble table at the other end of the room. As she quitted her chamber, it occurred to her, that Zofloya had said he would shield her from suspicion; he might mean only with respect to having *caused* the death of the Conte; he had not expressly said, that *after* his death it should not be possible to ascertain by what means it had been occasioned. This reflection accelerated her steps, and, with pallid cheek and beating heart, she reached the room, where, in awful solitary stillness, reposed the body of the Conte. Pausing, trembling at every step, dreading to discover she knew not what, slowly she approached the bed whereon he lay. The curtains, which were of gause, were drawn close around; still hesitating without, she endeavoured to look through them: but the outline only of the poor Berenza's form was discernible, as seen through a thin mist. Summoning resolution then, she drew the curtains apart; a slight covering still lightly veiled his countenance; desperate, fierce, she snatched it away, when, horrible confirmation of her fears, she beheld the features disfigured indeed, and frightfully changed, even to the most extravagant portraiture of her distempered fancy! — For a few moments she remained rooted to the spot; then resist-lessly impelled to search for, and know the worst at once, however it might increase her consternation and despair, she opened his peaceful and unconscious bosom, whereon large spots of livid green and blue became revealed, and struck her almost senseless with overpowering dread! not the dread of public justice, so much as the dread, horrible to her, that the discovery, or suspicion of her guilt, would prevent, *before* death, the accomplishment of her criminal wishes, rendering thereby use-less and unavailing the enormities she had atchieved for their sake.

These ideas glanced rapidly through her mind; she still remained by the side of the bed, gazing upon the placid though discoloured features of him she had destroyed, and which, had she been susceptible of com-punctious feeling, spoke in their mournful fixedness a thousand reproach-es on her guilt. But no, her thoughts were employed upon the conse-quences likely to ensue to herself; the hour of morning began to approach, and her heart beat with increased alarm, at the idea of the sur-mises that must soon be excited by the altered appearance of the Conte. The terrible Inquisition![1] — its horrid torments, its lynx-eyed scrutiny, pressed upon her brain — at this juncture she thought of Zofloya; a faint hope that he might assist her in the present confusion of her ideas, deter-mined her to apply to him — yet how to seek him? and at this hour how could she, to the presumptuous Moor, excuse the indecorum of summon-ing him?

These reflections, unworthy however the masculine spirit of a Victo-ria, she speedily overcame, in the stronger sense of her embarrassment, and she decided to seek him instantly. She knew that his apartment was situated near that of Henriquez, and cautiously she left the silent cham-ber of death, and retraced her steps along the darksome gallery, dimly illu-mined only by the lamp she held, and which served to guide her steps. As she was slowly proceeding, a ray from her lamp fell suddenly upon the sparkling vest of Zofloya, and partially betrayed his towering figure to her view.

"I was seeking you; I need your advice; hasten onwards, I pray," in a low voice entreated Victoria, too rejoiced to have encountered him, to feel surprise at his unexpected appearance.

"Lead on then," replied the Moor, "I am obedient."

Victoria laid her finger on her lip, and turned back towards the cham-ber of the Conte; the contrast between them, as they moved along, was

---

1   The terrible Inquisition!: The Inquisition often appears in Gothic texts set in Italy, i.e., in Lewis's *The Monk*, Radcliffe's *The Italian* and Shelley's play *The Cenci*. The Inquisition creates a Gothic atmosphere of secrecy ("It has terrible secrets!" says Schedoni in *The Italian*), paranoia, and terror, with characters facing a constant threat of persecution and torture at the hands of arbitrary and absolute power.

peculiarly forcible; the figure of Victoria, slender and elegantly proportioned, arrayed in flowing white, with her raven hair streaming over her shoulders; that of Zofloya so gigantic, and differently attired, yet seeming at intervals, by the dubious rays of the lamp, and the effect of strong shade, increased to a height scarcely human. Once or twice, the deceptive magnitude of his dark shadow on the wall, struck with momentary alarm even the hardy Victoria, and might have excited remark, but that other objects engrossed too deeply her present thoughts.

They now reached the peaceful gloomy chamber of Berenza. "Enter, Zofloya," whispered Victoria, and approach that bed."

The Moor obeyed.

"Open the curtains, and gaze upon the countenance within."

The Moor opened the curtains, and looked upon the face of Berenza; then turning immediately to Victoria, the expression of his features, (though less malignant and severe,) reminded her forcibly of her dream.

"Tell me, Moor," she exclaimed, rendered desperate by her feelings of terror, and grasping with violence the arm of Zofloya, "tell me, what can be done in this terrible extremity?"

The Moor was silent.

"Didst thou not tell me," pursued Victoria, "thou wouldst preserve me from suspicion? Behold those blacked features, that discoloured bosom; who can fail immediately to ascertain that poison — poison hath caused the death of Berenza?"

"Whoever beholds the Conte will clearly ascertain that fact," coolly replied the Moor.

"Zofloya, Zofloya!" cried Victoria, gasping with terror, "what is that you say?"

"I say, beautiful Victoria, whoever sees the Conte, will instantly pronounce, that his death was caused by poison!"

Victoria clasped her hands, and remained mute with consternation and anguish, fixing her regards upon the Moor.

"Victoria!" he cried at length, "if you would have *my* services, I repeat, what I have often urged, you must place *implicit confidence* in me, and firm reliance; retire now to your chamber, and fear nothing for the morrow!"

"But, Berenza —"

"Leave to me all care for your safety."

"But, those marks!"

The Moor knit his dark brows — "I have *said*," he cried, in a stern authoritative voice, and pointed haughtily to the door.

The frame of Victoria trembled, and she retreated towards the door. Horror and awe, at the inexplicable character of the Moor, so wholly possessed her, that though she longed, she durst not require an explanation of his intentions with respect to the body of Berenza. His dark but brilliant eyes, like two stars in a gloomy cloud, pursued her with their strong imperious rays, even to the threshold of the door; she stopped, hesitated, and attempted to speak, but the effort was vain; and without power to offer resistance, she quitted the apartment.

Great alternately were the terrors, and great the hopes of Victoria. On the word of the Moor she had strong reliance, for she had never yet found that he deceived her; but his ambiguous promises, his explicit acknowledgment, that whoever saw the body of the Conte must discover the occasion of his death, threw her again into fits of doubt and consternation; and the hours that she passed in her chamber, expecting every moment some confirmation of her fears, were the just portion of one immersed like herself in blackest guilt.

The morning was not far advanced, when a mingled commotion, and confusion of voices, pervaded the castle; the terrors of conscious criminality prevented her from rising to inquire the cause. Fainting, almost dying, she awaited the result, while cold drops of agony gemmed her writhing brow. At length a loud knocking at her chamber door caused her to start from her seat: the blood flew into her lately pallid cheeks, and as suddenly rushed back to her heart, leaving them again of a livid paleness. The knocking continued: more dead than alive, she tottered to the door, and opened it; various persons, domestics in the castle, burst into the room; strong dismay painted on their faces, and with loud lamentation exclaimed, that the *body of the Conte was missing*!!

END OF VOLUME II.

VOLUME THREE

ZOFLOYA;

OR,

THE MOOR.

CHAPTER XXVI

This dreadful and singular event spread consternation throughout the castle. Victoria alone could have attempted to explain it, and she carefully treasured in her bosom the ideas that presented themselves.

"Oh! most exquisite Zofloya," exclaimed she, in the solitude of her chamber, "well mightest thou say, that *those* who *beheld* the body of the Conte, would be enabled to ascertain the cause of his death, while already thou had'st resolved that it should never more be seen! No — I will doubt thee no longer, powerful Moor, nor thy care for my safety, for well do I now perceive thy infinite depth, and wisdom."

But after the first emotions of joy at her narrow escape had subsided, she began to marvel and reflect upon the sudden and precipitate disappearance of the body. Whither, in that short space, could he have conveyed it? perhaps into some bottomless abyss, where the foaming torrent had embraced, and hid it ever more! — If not so — how then had he disposed of it? — no matter how, so that never more it revisited the light. "Adieu then for the present, to vain and useless surmises," thought she, "I will rest content with the effect that has been produced.

Events, however terrible and strange at the moment of their occurrence, lose by degrees their impression over the mind, for the ideas failing to identify the point at which they aim, relax their attempts, and revert to the consideration of objects more familiar to them. — Thus, after a certain lapse of time, though surprize and regret continued frequently to obtrude on the minds of all, strong anxiety and horror gradually, tho' slowly diminished. — A gloomy calm was perceptible throughout the house, as though every one bore about him the *memory* of some dreadful calamity, which time had ameliorated into a chastened grief.

On the heart of Henriquez had the melancholy death of his brother, and its accompanying circumstances sunk the deepest; — the castle, where so late he had resided, became a gloomy memento in his sight, and the presence of Victoria daily and unaccountably more displeasing to him. — He meditated therefore, to abandon the former, and to quit Italy altogether for some distant clime, where the memory of his misfortunes should no more, in a thousand eloquent and mournful shapes, continue to haunt him.

The time, however, was now fast approaching, when the innocent Lilla would no longer consider it a point of religion or duty to hesitate at becoming his wife. — Till this period, therefore, he decided to remain stationary, to smother the repugnant feelings of his bosom; for he reflected, that unless he remained under the same roof with Victoria, he should be debarred the society of his Lilla, well knowing that her unaffected virtue and sense of decorum would deem it improper to be elsewhere so perpetually with him.

Mean time, the passion of Victoria having now, as she conceived, no further obstacles to surmount, grew to an unrestrained height. — She sought, by every wily blandishment and seduction, to attract the attention of Henriquez. — But vain were her artifices, for his soul was enslaved by the simplicity and innocence of the youthful Lilla; all other women were detestable in his sight — her trembling delicacy, her gentle sweetness, her sylph-like fragile form, were to him incomparable, and being familiarized to the observance of such soft loveliness, the rest of her sex, when placed beside her, appeared, in his idea, like beings of a different order. But, above all, Victoria he viewed with almost absolute dislike; her strong though noble features, her dignified carriage, her authoritative tone — her boldness, her insensibility, her violence, all struck him with instinctive horror; so utterly opposite to the gentle Lilla, that when, with an assumed softness she deigned to caress her, he almost trembled for her tender life, and compared the picture in his mind, to the snowy dove fondled by the ravenous vulture.

At length, with infinite reluctance, and to the bitter mortification of her pride, Victoria acknowledged to herself, that she was not only indifferent to Henriquez, but despised and hated by him. — At this bitter conviction her brain whirled — "Yes, he detests me," she exclaimed in an agony of rage — "but he shall, he must be mine — his boyish caprice shall nought avail him; — ah!" she continued, relapsing into softness — "I will throw myself, my fortune, into his arms, — I will again sacrifice my liberty, and offer to become his wife."

Amidst these reflections the haughty Victoria had scarce allowed herself to believe, that the attachment of Henriquez to Lilla was the cause of his indifference to her. — She resolved to be at once explicit therefore — to make to Henriquez a proposal which she imagined he would not dream of refusing, and to seize the earliest opportunity of doing so.

As if to coincide with her views, Lilla on the same evening, complaining of indisposition, retired early; and Henriquez who felt no desire to remain alone with a woman whom he viewed with sentiments of disgust, arose a few moments after Lilla had quitted the apartment, and bowing distantly to Victoria, was departing. "Stay, Henriquez," cried the determined Victoria, starting from her seat — "I desire a few words with you."

Henriquez bowed, and arrested his steps.

"Be seated — I implore you."

"Have you any thing material to communicate, Signora?" inquired Henriquez, unable to conceal his reluctance to her society, — "or will not tomorrow answer equally well?"

"No," replied Victoria, in an impressive accent, "I request you, Henriquez, to be seated."

Unwillingly Henriquez resumed his seat, when the frantic woman, incapable of restraining her emotion, cast herself at his feet, and, seizing his hand — "Henriquez!" she cried, "Henriquez, my soul adores you! — behold me at your feet, — I offer you all, — all that I possess — my hand in marriage — grant me but your love!"

"Signora," answered Henriquez, with assumed composure, disengaging himself from her grasp, — "as my brother's wife, I tolerated, but never approved you, — since his *death*, my feelings towards you have acquired a stronger cast, — I now," he cried, forgetting in a moment his attempt at coolness — "I now hate and despise you! — Wretch! worthless and insensible as you are, to forget so soon a husband that adored you, and doubly a wretch to confess to me your unhallowed thoughts, whose soul you know to be irrevocably another's!"

Victoria sprang from her abject posture, the feelings which swayed her heart had been irrepressible; she had not intended to be thus premature in her avowal of love, but the violence of passion threw her off her guard! — now the emotions excited by the reply of Henriquez were equally unconquerable.

"Miserable youth!" she cried — "it is enough — your insulting coolness, your bitter reproaches, I could have borne, — have borne, proud as I am, with patience! — but that you should dare, without trembling, to acknowledge in my presence, your love for another" —

"Love!" interrupted Henriquez with enthusiasm — "Love! — say, adoration, idolatry! — by heaven my Lilla is a gem too bright to shed her pure rays beneath this contaminated roof, — oh! wretched Victoria," he continued, with a bitter smile, "and could *you* attempt to talk of love to the lover of *Lilla?*" —

Can language describe the feelings of Victoria? Her brain worked with wildest rage, producing almost instant madness! — Yet revenge, thirsting revenge, was the predominant sensation of her soul, swallowing up every other! — by an effort, and self-command, scarcely credible, she reined in the tumult of her passion, and forebore to recriminate upon Henriquez. — What! drive him from the castle, and lose thereby the power of sacrificing the abhorred Lilla to her vengeance, the pigmy, the immaterial speck, that she had deemed unworthy of a thought! To lose too, for ever, the possibility of softening, (perhaps even yet subduing) the stern insensibility of Henriquez? — No — the sacrifice to frantic rage would have been too great! — Her decision was prompt, and instantaneous. — Covering her face with her hands, she sunk into a chair, and audibly sobbed!

A reply so different to what he had taught himself to expect, knowing the violence of her nature, at once surprised and affected Henriquez. — In a moment he regretted the asperity with which he had spoken, and the reflection obtruded on his mind, that the female whose only fault towards him was the love which she bore him, merited at least a milder return; he hesitated an instant — the goodness of his heart prevailed, and he approached the wily Victoria.

"I would offer, Signora," in a gentle voice he said, (taking her hand) — "some apology for my warmth — I meant not, — I assure you, I meant not to be severe, — will you then," he added, "pardon me, and accept this acknowledgement of my error?"

"Oh, Henriquez!" replied Victoria, redoubling her tears, "it is I alone who am in fault; at this moment I feel within me the reproaches due to my conduct! — The words which I have suffered to escape my lips, now strike me with shame and horror — scarcely can I account for the impulse that forced me to give them utterance! — Noble and generous as you are, forget, if you possibly can, the phrenzy of the moment, and do not — do not," she pursued, casting herself again at his feet, "despise me to the degree that I feel you ought."

Henriquez, infinitely affected, raised in his arms her whom he believed was indeed the abashed and repentant Victoria: he besought her to be composed, and to forgive him the pain that he had caused her.

"Ah, all that I ask is *your* forgiveness," said Victoria, "and your promise that you will not reflect upon what has passed this night, to my disadvantage. Oh, Henriquez! I will shew you, that if Victoria yields for a moment to an unpardonable weakness, that she knows how to conquer and become herself again."

Henriquez assured her, that he would blot from his mind every impression unfavourable to her, and added, that by the immediate revival of noble sentiments in her bosom, and the candour with which she had arraigned herself, she had more than expiated the imperfect part of her conduct.

Victoria, affecting to be satisfied, and grateful for this assurance, took, with well-feigned diffidence and humility, the hand of Henriquez, and raising it to her lips, turned from him, as if unable to restrain her emotion, and hurried out of the room.

CHAPTER XXVII

Reaching her own apartment, the miserable, because guilty, Victoria threw herself upon her bed, in torture too great to be described. The most infuriate passions, forcibly restrained as they had been in the presence of Henriquez, now agitated her breast, and now found vent in terrible imprecations. She cursed herself, the hour that gave her being, and the mother that had borne her; outraged pride swelled her heart to bursting, and its insatiable fury called aloud for vengeance, for blood, and the blood of the innocent Lilla.

"Oh! let me at once destroy the minion," she wildly exclaimed, starting from the bed, and snatching from her bosom a dagger, which she usually carried there, "Let me at once, I say, destroy the puny wretch, who dares to call destruction on her head by thus becoming of consequence."

"Not yet, Victoria," said a melodious voice; and before her stood the Moor, who gently seized her uplifted arm, and smiled.

"How came you hither, Zofloya?" she cried — "your voice, nor your smile, nor your promises, have power to calm me now."

"Beautiful Victoria," he answered, "I come to counsel and to sooth."

"Thou canst do neither, Moor, for Henriquez hates me; — canst thou change the genuine sentiments of the heart? — Canst thou of hatred make love?"

"I can do much, Victoria, if you will confide in me."

"But thou art not a sorcerer!"

"It is possible to have a knowledge of physic, and yet not be a physician."

"Oh, yes, thou hast infinite knowledge, Zofloya — every day proves it beyond doubt — but thou canst not — no, thou canst not charm love for *me* into the heart that loves another."

"Not readily, while that other intervenes, fair Victoria."

Canst thou assist me? — Say at once, canst thou asist me, Zofloya?"

"Lovely Victoria!"

The silver tones of the Moor penetrated to the very heart of Victoria; his wily accent was piteously tender; tears, spontaneous tears, rushed into her eyes, and involuntarily she threw herself into his arms, which opened to receive her, and wept upon his bosom. Zofloya gently pressed her in his arms.

The delusion of Victoria continued but a few moments: she hastily disengaged herself from his embrace, and hesitatingly said —

" 'Tis strange, Zofloya! — I know not why, but thou soothest me ever, and attractest me irresistibly. I do, indeed, believe," she added, with an earnest smile, "that thou art truly a sorcerer!"

The Moor smiled also, and bent, as in acknowledgment, his graceful form; — fascination dwelt in every movement of this singular being, and in nothing was it more evinced, than in the power he held over the proud heart of Victoria.

"Incomparable and lovely mistress," he cried, falling upon one knee, and laying his hand upon his heart, "Deign to inform the most lowly of your slaves, what you would require of him? and, having said, trust to him for the performance."

"Rise then, Zofloya," cried Victoria, flattered and delighted by a condescension of late somewhat unusual with the Moor — "Rise and tell me — ah! canst thou not divine, Zofloya? — Lilla — Lilla! —

"The orphan Lilla stands between you and your love; — is it not so?"

"Yes, yes."

"And you would have her" —

"Die!" cried Victoria, relapsing into phrenzy.

"Calm, calm," in gentle accents said the Moor. — "The orphan Lilla must not die, Signora."

"No!" —

"No — for it would excite instant suspicion, and then farewell to all your hopes — you forget, fair Victoria, that already" —

"True, true," hastily returned Victoria; "but what then?"

"It must not be."

"Oh, madness! — it shall, it must — without your aid, then."

Zofloya looked stern. — "Be it so then, Signora," he cried, and moved with dignity towards the door.

"Oh stay, inconsistent being!" cried Victoria, "and forgive my despair."

"Despair! — despair when *I* have bid you hope — you must confide."

"Oh, be at once explicit, and tell me" —

"Well, then, Lilla must not die; but she shall be at your disposal, and you may inflict on her such misery, that" —

"Such torments!" interrupted Victoria, with demoniac sparkling eyes — "Yes, such torments, as shall pay for those she has inflicted upon me! — But when, oh when, Zofloya, may this be?"

"At to-morrow's dawn be in the forest; proceed through the narrow break on your left, ascend the steep rock which overlooks the wood, making it appear an inconsiderable dell; and when you have gained the summit, remain, and await my coming."

"I will be punctual — but Lilla."

"She shall be with me — enquire no further, Victoria."

Joy and abominable triumph filled the breast of Victoria; well was she now versed, and well could decypher the ambiguous answers of the Moor.

"Zofloya," she cried, in a voice of exultation, "excellent Zofloya, say how can I repay you?" and eagerly taking a brilliant of immense value from her finger, she added, "accept this, and wear it for my sake, but wear it concealed in your bosom."

With a proud and dignified air, Zofloya put back with his hand the offered gift.

"Keep your diamond, Signora; the riches of the world are valueless to me — my aim is higher."

"And what is it you aim at, then, Zofloya?"

"*Your* friendship — *your* trust — *your* confidence — *yourself,* Signora!"

Victoria smiled at what she thought the gallantry of the Moor; the Moor smiled likewise, but with a different air, and bowing respectfully to Victoria as he advanced towards the door, he said, "Farewell, Signora, for the present; watch for the first streak of the morning."

"Sleep shall not visit my eyes, I will gaze upon the firmament, and at the last fading of the stars, will leave my chamber."

The Moor waved gracefully his hand, and retired.

No sooner was he gone, than Victoria extinguished the lamp, that no artificial light might render unobserved the first approach of dawn. Then opening the window, she seated herself beside it, and gazed with unblushing front upon the serene majesty of the cloudless heavens. Patiently did she endure the loss of sleep, patiently attend, like the blood-thirsty murderer, who rendered invulnerable to external ills by the strong nerved fierceness of his mind, lurks ambushed through the lonely night for the unconscious footstep of his destined victim; so did she wake, so watch, anticipating alternately the gratification of her revenge, and scenes of future bliss with the beloved Henriquez. Compelled at length with bitter reluctance to view the blooming Lilla, as the powerful shield presumptuously opposed to her facinations, she determined, while pride and hatred nerved anew her heart, to inflict upon the innocent girl, all that malice or that vengeance could invent.

Meanwhile, Henriquez, being left to the solitude of his reflections, reviewed the conduct of Victoria. He began to fear he had ultimately treated her with too great lenity and forbearance; disgust rose in his soul against her; he compared to her shameless and dishonorable confession, the blushing sweetness, the retiring modesty of the young orphan, Lilla. Ardently he longed for the hour, in which with propriety he could withdraw her from the tainted roof, under which, still rich in native purity, she continued to breathe. Joy and complacent delight diffused itself through his bosom, when he reflected that a few days only need now elapse, ere the pious scruples of his innocent love would be at an end; he might then call her legally and for ever his. The probationary year was nearly expired; he resolved in the moment of its completion, to claim her for his bride, and depart, not only from the spot where he had lost an only and idolized brother, but from his native land, for ever, the very atmosphere of which had now become obnoxious to him. Now his mind wandered into anticipated scenes of happiness; he beheld himself the father of a blooming progeny, the delighted husband of a beauteous wife, and regret passed through his mind, when he reflected that his lost Berenza would never make one among the blissful group, enjoying a felicity he would have delighted to contemplate.

Ah, miserable Henriquez! little didst thou dream that these thy fairy visions of love and happiness were never, never to be realised, but to end, on the contrary, in reduplicated horror and despair.

Victoria remained sitting at the window, immersed in gloomy meditation, till the opening horizon began to shew faint streaks of light between clouds of darker hue, and the blue mists of the distant waters slowly to dissipate. The stars became fainter, and a fresher breeze was wafted from the east, when intent on evil, she stole with cautious footsteps from her chamber. Now with beating heart she gained the court, and passed into the forest, hastening onwards to the path described by Zofloya; the deep gloom rendered almost impervious the lonely way, and the break on the left, to which he had alluded; she ascertained it however, and as she proceeded, a deeper gloom informed her, that she approached the frowning rock, which cast its shadow around. — Though never before had she wandered in the light of day so far, she trusted implicitly to the directions of Zofloya, and prepared to ascend the rocky acclivity.

Morning gradually advanced, but surrounding objects were still rendered indistinct by a delusive mist: — she proceeded a considerable way up the rock, when the loud solemn roar of the foaming cataract, dashing from a fissure on the opposite side into the precipice beneath, broke upon her ear. — She fearlessly advanced, however, till she gained the summit, while louder and more stunning became the angry sound of the waters. Here, for a while she decided to remain; the dim light even yet afforded no correct view over the lengthened rocks; mountains of mist appeared rising above each other, till the last ridge dimly stretched its gigantic outline upon the distant horizon, shewing no world beyond.

The stars had all retired, as though shrinking abashed from the view of so much guilt, but louring clouds obscured the face of heaven, the wind sighed hollow among the trees of the forest, and though the lonely solemn grandeur o, the scene would have inspired in the breast of virtue deep awe and devotion, directing the soul to inward contemplation, yet was it sad and unwelcome to the evil mind, which, bearing within itself an eternal night, feels troubled and appalled in the gloom of nature.

Such was the state of Victoria — restless and impatient for the encreasing light; — encreasing light came on, she arose from the spot where she had seated herself, and gazed around; on one side, the yet shade-enveloped forest, seeming, as Zofloya had said, an inconsiderable dell, appeared far beneath her feet, while, on the other, a dark blue line of mist gave distant warning of the sky-girt ocean, that in oblique ascent seemed blending with the heavens.

The rock on which she stood being an elevated point, had caught the first light of the morning, and to herself she was fully revealed; objects below were still partially engloomed, and eagerly she strained her anxious eyes, to catch the first glimpse of what alone could interest her attention. Every moment which elapsed, appeared to her sanguinary soul like so much time robbed her of her revenge; but at length, to her infinite joy, the sight so ardently desired greeted her view. Hastening onwards with rapid strides along the winding path she had so lately traversed, she beheld the gigantic figure of the Moor, gigantic even from the diminishing points of heighth and distance. — Hanging lifeless over his shoulder, encircled by his nervous arms, he bore the once blooming Lilla — blooming now no longer, but paler than the white rose teint! — Swiftly he approached, and careless of his burthen, bounded like lightning up the rugged rock. — Victoria contemplated, with joyous exultation, the helpless and devoted orphan: her fragile form lay nerveless, her snow-white arms, bare nearly to the shoulder (for a thin night-dress alone covered her,) hung down over the back of the Moor; her feet and legs resembling sculptored alabaster, were likewise bare, her languid head drooped insensible, while the long flaxen tresses, escaping from the net which had enveloped them, now partly shaded her ashy cheek, and now streamed in dishevelled luxuriance on the breeze.

"Shall we hurl her down the precipice?" cried Victoria, while her fierce and jealous eyes wandered over the betrayed graces of her spotless victim.

"No!" said Zofloya, "follow me." He darted down a rugged path on the opposite side of the rock, and, though not with equal swiftness, Victoria pursued his steps. Now he hovered on the edge of a precipice, now ascended a mountainous steep; at length in a narrow valley, or rather rocky division, between two mountains of gigantic heighth, he paused for a moment; an irregular winding path, forming a steep declivity, seemed leading almost to a bottomless abyss. Zofloya, looking at Victoria, observed that she was nearly exhausted with violent exertion to keep him in view.

"Have courage," he cried, "but a few steps further."

Victoria endeavoured to smile, and followed him with new alacrity; for the base passions of her soul stung her with a desperate firmness.

Suddenly Zofloya stopped; he laid his still inanimate burthen upon the rugged path, and with apparent ease, though it seemed to require superhuman strength, removed what had appeared a projecting point of rock, but which Victoria now perceived to be only a huge and independent fragment of it, — a deep narrow opening presented itself beneath; the Moor, raising Lilla again in his arms, entered the aperture, with an inclination of the body; — Victoria still followed, and soon beheld herself in a spacious cavern, gloomily enlightened alone by the opening at which they had entered.

"Here, Victoria," cried the Moor, your rival may be at least secured from the possibility of further molesting you; — now, if the heart of Henriquez be vincible, there is nothing to impede your happiness."

"But," answered Victoria with a gloomy air, "while Lilla *lives*, is there not a remote possibility that she might escape hence?"

"Behold then," said the Moor, "what shall ever remove that vain fear," lifting from the floor of the cavern, as he spoke, a massy chain, which though fixed to the opposite side of the wall, extended in length to the sloping irregular ascent, leading to the mouth of the aperture.

"With this ring at the extremity," he pursued, "while the girl is still insensible, I will fasten it round her wrist; will you then, Victoria, be satisfied?"

"I will endeavour," hesitatingly replied Victoria, still desiring nothing less than the death of one whose beauty was blasting to her sight.

"It shall be done then," said Zofloya, "though wholly unnecessary; for when she returns to the power of thought, how will she be enabled to divine the true situation of the spot in which she will find herself? she will even be ignorant of the means by which she came hither, — as when she awakened, and found me bearing her from her bed, — (for deep in sleep as she was, and smiling, at her dreams of love no doubt, I seized her in my arms, to fulfil my promise to you) — then, vainly struggling within my grasp, she fainted, and has since remained insensible. — How then, unassisted, incredulous fearful Victoria, could she trace out a path which she had not even power to observe? Further precautions than leaving her here are, be assured, unnecessary."

"Still I would wish the chain," muttered Victoria; — "if unnecessary as a precaution, it may have its advantage as a punishment; — come, hasten good Zofloya," she continued, putting in his hand the fair and lifeless hand of Lilla — "let us depart from hence, before our absence is discovered."

Zofloya, smiling with a scornful archness, retained the hand of Lilla in one hand, and holding the chain in the other, while he looked upon it, said to her in a jeering accent:

"Think you, Victoria, that il Conciglio di Deici hath ever confined any of its victims in a spot so remote as this cavern? this ring, this massy chain, seem almost an evidence that" —

At that terrible name the colour of Victoria forsook her cheek.

"Cruel and ill timed remark," she cried, interrupting the Moor in his malicious insinuation — "why at this moment allude to subjects irrelevant? — I pray you fasten the chain, and let us go."

Still with the smile upon his countenance, he prepared to obey the desire of the terror-struck Victoria. — In a moment, the galling chain was clasped around the delicate wrist of Lilla, and Victoria hastening towards the aperture, exclaimed:

"Let us now leave this place — come Zofloya, and precede me hence."

Suffering the devoted orphan to remain stretched upon the flinty ground, both now prepared to quit the cavern; — already they had gained the ascent, when at that moment the miserable Lilla opened her eyes. Without being fully restored to sense, she perceived with dismay her situation; — she essayed to speak, but could not, and starting up, cast herself despairingly upon her knees, raising her innocent hands in agonized supplication. The motion and noise of the chain caused Victoria to turn her head — she beheld the kneeling defenceless orphan — but she saw only her rival, and pausing while a smile of exulting malice passed over her features, she waved her hand as in derision, and instantly hastened on.

As she gained the mouth of the aperture, and retreated from the sight of the wretched girl, who with horror had recognized Victoria, a shrill and piercing scream assailed her ears, but failed to excite in her breast one emotion of pity, for the state in which she had abandoned her.

"Signora," observed Zofloya, as again they took their path across the mountains, — "it is my intention to return hither in the course of this day with provisions for our prisoner, and a mantle of leopard skin which I possess, to serve her at once for bed and covering — I likewise intend" —

"Methinks you are tender of the upstart," angrily interrupted Victoria.

"It is not my intention," coolly returned the Moor, "that the death of your rival should be caused by famine — she shall have food, therefore; for in the spot where she is doomed to breathe the residue of her days, her dissolution will be accelerated in sufficient time."

"Why, there is certainly a pleasure," with a fierce malignant smile, observed Victoria, "in the infliction of prolonged torment; I therefore approve your arrangement."

"You will sometimes visit the young girl, Signora, will you not?"

"It will be an exquisite delight that I shall occasionally confer on myself," she replied, "but if Henriquez prove unkind, she shall have no reason to thank me for my visit."

"A just and excellent combination, Signora," satyrically remarked the Moor; "if Henriquez prove unkind, she deservedly suffers whose memory is the cause; indeed I admire that inflexible spirit you possess, Signora — that unyielding soul, whose thirsty vengeance is never satiated."

Victoria turned her looks upon the Moor, to read if he spoke earnestly — and she rejoiced to behold, in the lambent fire of his ardent eyes, relentless cruelty and mischievous delight, as he had uttered the last words.

The morning was now far advanced, but no beams of the chearing sun irradiated the heavens — light hovering clouds overspread with gloom the deep recesses of the forest, upon which they almost appeared to descend; — all was awful stillness; not even the carol of a bird broke upon the solemn silence, as though the eye of morning paused in grief, upon the crimes that had ushered in its dawn.

The Moor spoke not, and Victoria, absorbed in calculations of the conduct most eligible to be pursued for the attainment of her wishes, sought not to draw him into converse.

In this manner they proceeded till they gained the open forest, when Zofloya observed, it would be expedient to separate before they came in view of the castle. — Victoria acquiesced in the propriety of the idea. — She hastened towards the castle, and he struck into an opposite direction.

CHAPTER XXVIII

Henriquez awakened, in the fond hope of beholding her whose lovely image had visited him in his dreams; he hastened to a certain part of the wood, the most open and chearful, where, as frequent, he expected to find her; for Lilla sometimes inhaled the pure breeze from the mountains at an early hour of the morning.

For some time he traversed this favorite spot with patience, conceiving it possible, that, yielding longer than usual to sleep, she had not yet arisen. Yet the morning was already so far advanced, that every moment rendered this idea more improbable; he determined therefore to return into the house — still he beheld no sign of her his soul adored — impatiently he summoned a female servant, and ordered her to repair to the chamber of Signora Lilla, to awaken her, and to inform her of the lateness of the hour. What alarm then must have seized him, when the servant, returning, informed him that the bed of the young Signora was vacant, and appeared to have been so for some time, but that her clothes remained upon the chair beside it, where they seemed to have been cast on the preceding night.

Henriquez, naturally impetuous, made no remark, but, springing from his seat, rushed past the servant, and flew wildly into her chamber, where failing indeed to behold her, with frantic impatience he searched every part of the castle that was habitable, it is needless to say, in vain. Regardless at length of every thing but his lost love, the door of Victoria's chamber meeting his view, he burst it, with the strength of madness, open, and rushed into her apartment.

The artful Victoria, fully prepared for the scene she expected to ensue, had retired to her bed, on returning from the dreadful deed of the early morning, and as Henriquez forced himself into her chamber, appeared to start up alarmed, as if suddenly aroused from a peaceful slumber. Henriquez, regardless of her seeming terror or surprise, flew towards the bed, scarce knowing what he did, and seizing her by the arm, exclaimed, in frantic voice,

"My Lilla is missing! — tell me, tell me, I implore thee, where she is."

"Lilla missing!" answered Victoria, with assumed surprise — "impossible, Signor;" but observing the air with which Henriquez regarded her, she added, "yet if it be so, would I could indeed inform you where to seek her."

"Oh, I shall die mad with agony!" cried Henriquez, "if my Lilla be not found."

"Retire a moment then, Signor Henriquez," in sympathising accents said Victoria; "I will arise and dress myself, and together we will seek our beloved little friend." Perceiving the despair and anguish of Henriquez painted in his eyes, she continued, "Be pacified, I entreat you, and rest assured the fair girl cannot be far distant."

Henriquez, striking his hand upon his forehead, darted out of the room, and Victoria hastily rising, and dressing herself, followed him into the apartment where they usually assembled. She proposed to the distracted lover, that they should seek Lilla together. Again every corner of the castle was searched, again the forest was inspected, and resounded to the name of Lilla. In vain, in voice of agony, Henriquez called upon that name. The lovely Innocent, naked, chained, and solitary, was far, far beyond the possibility of replying.

Once more they now entered her chamber; the clothes she had worn on the preceding day remained untouched upon the spot where she appeared, upon taking them off, to have cast them. The bed clothes seemed dragged on one side, and lay partly upon the floor; in one place the curtains were twisted and torn, and the net, which was supposed to have encircled her head at night, lay likewise upon the ground, near the door, as though it had fallen off. Upon this more accurate examination, the despair of Henriquez knew no bounds; it appeared as if his innocent love had been torn defenceless from her bed; the terrible idea wound his mind to a pitch of dreadful anguish, and scarcely knowing what he did, he darted like lightning from the house, determined to explore the inmost recesses of the wood, and even to traverse the very mountains in search of her.

After a lapse of many hours, towards the close of the evening, he returned, unable to give the smallest account of where he had been wandering, and with a raging fever burning in his veins. Scarce had he power, distracted as he was, to ask if tidings of his Lilla had yet arrived; ere confirmed by a dreadful negative, in his despair he fell senseless upon the earth.

He was immediately conveyed to bed by order of Victoria. Wild delirium seized his brain; his ravings, and frantic struggles to escape from those who surrounded him, were dreadful to hear and to behold. For three weeks his life was despaired of, and the phrenzy which possessed him scarcely left hopes, that even if it were spared, his mind could ever recover its former sanity.

Meanwhile the poor Lilla, the guiltless cause of so much havoc, continued to linger in her dreadful confinement. The Moor Zofloya attended her with undeviating punctuality, furnished her with provisions, and a mantle of leopard-skin, to preserve her in some degree from the flinty hardness of the ground, and on which too often she was, in her own despite, compelled to stretch her tender limbs. Yet, in this pitiable situation, she still lived and still cherished faint hope in her spotless bosom, that time would end her miseries, and restore her to the world, and to him she fondly adored. Sometimes she trusted to soften the impenetrable Moor, but hope of that soon faded from her heart when he appeared; for though he brought her food, he never uttered a single sentence, and if by chance his eye met hers, the gloomy fierceness of its expression damped the assumed courage of her innocent soul, and the little resolution she might have acquired in his absence.

Faint dawnings of returning reason, and reanimated life, began at length to reveal themselves in the unhappy Henriquez. During the whole of his illness, Victoria had never quitted his apartment, administering to him with her own hands every medicine that was prescribed, and sleeping by night with one of her attendants in his chamber. When the powers of his mind became sufficiently restored to recognize surrounding objects, her attentions,if possible, redoubled; and could Henriquez have divested himself of the unconquerable disgust with which he viewed her, her singular tenderness and care towards him must have excited in him the utmost gratitude and regard.

But vain was her solicitude, rather painful than pleasing to him, and the moments in which his wretched mind felt most relief from intolerable anguish, were those very few in which she was absent from him. But his coldness and repugnance was either unperceived, or unheeded by Victoria — She became daily more passionately tender, more undisguised in her manner towards him, and this as well involuntarily as by the previous decision of her mind. Gloomy melancholy and perpetual abstraction, still, however, possessed the unfortunate Henriquez, when, conceiving that she advanced too slowly, by simply paying the attentions of friendship (so understood at least) to Henriquez, she resolved once more gently to probe the present situation of his heart respecting her; for presumptuously she flattered herself, that her complete devotion to him, throughout a long and dangerous malady, must in some degree have impressed him in her favor.

One evening when she was sitting in his apartment, with the silent meditative Henriquez, he feeling an anxious wish to indulge in solitude the luxury of his grief, gently, though with perfect coolness, observed to her:

"I do not desire, Signora, thus to be a tax upon your time and your friendship; I pray you, now that I am so far convalescent, be less punctilious in your attentions towards me, and use some recreation to relieve your mind."

Determined to let no opportunity pass for touching upon the subject nearest her heart, Victoria replied in a voice of tender reproach.

"Cruel Henriquez! is it thus you address one, who lives but in your presence? forbear, at least forbear to taunt a heart that loves as —"

"Signora!" with agitation interrupted Henriquez — "is *this* a time? — is *this* a subject — I thought it was never more to be renewed."

"I can forbear no longer," exclaimed Victoria, throwing herself at his feet; "Oh, Henriquez! I love — I adore you to madness! — if you have a spark of feeling, of compassion in your soul, reject me not, but pity a wretch who feels it impossible to overcome her fatal passion!"

Henriquez knew not how to reply, for he felt that local circumstances made gratitude due to Victoria; yet her present base avowal, doubly infamous at such a time, — her abject prostration at his feet, excited anew all the gall of his bosom against her, and, spite of every consideration, he found it impossible to treat her with softness. For a few moments, then, he remained in painful silence, but his determination to crush at once those hopes his anguished heart told him he could never realise — shocked too at the cruel indelicacy that so early could attempt to obliterate from his mind all traces of his first and only love — he attempted with impatient gesture to raise her from the ground. — Finding, however, that with still-existing feebleness he was incapable of doing so, he said —

"Signora, I entreat you to rise from your unworthy situation — till then I cannot say any thing."

Victoria, in violent agitation, arose.

"Signora," then pursued Henriquez, "my heart is still smarting with agony in the never to be forgotten affliction of having lost the only being for whom I ever considered life desirable! — I feel, Signora, that the anguish of that heart will not long endure; for though my body becomes sane, my feelings convince me, that the wound I have received no time can heal, and that I shall expire, God grant it soon, of a broken heart! — This alone, Signora, you might deem a sufficient reply to the confession with which you have just honored me; but that I may not, by an undue warmth of expression, leave the shadow of a doubt upon your mind respecting my cooler feelings, or my unchangeable sentiments, let me at once add, that were circumstances even *different* from what they are — were my soul even unattached to the pure heavenly memory of my lost Lilla — had I never even *known* her to become attached, still, Signora, the present feelings of my heart towards you convince me, that even then, I could never have returned your flattering partiality. — I feel that we are dissimilar in every respect; nay more, — whether from a fault of my nature I know not — but I feel likewise, that I could sooner poignard myself," he added, with an encreased elevation of voice, "than bring myself to entertain for *you* the slightest sentiments of tenderness!"

" 'Tis well!" cried Victoria, in accents scarcely articulate, "ungrateful Henriquez! — you are indeed explicit — farewell! — I will no longer pain you by my presence. Yet, ere I go, call to mind, that your Lilla, still mourned for, is no more!"

"But her *memory* still lives! — still triumphs in my bleeding heart?" — cried the agonized Henriquez, starting from his seat, and wildly clasping his emaciated hands; when, overcome by weakness and the conflicting violence of his emotions, he could no longer support himself, but fell enanguished on the floor.

Victoria, returning, flew towards him, and raising him in her arms, laid her head upon his bosom.

"Ah!" she cried, while the bitter smile of disappointed pride and passion passed over her features — "Ah, stubborn relentless Henriquez! thou shalt yet be mine, though death were the consequence!"

"Death — death *will* be the consequence," cried the half frantic Henriquez, who had caught her last words; and perceiving that his head reclined upon her bosom, started hastily from the floor, as though he felt the sting of a scorpion!

Victoria, fearful of returning delirium, spoke no more; but assisting him, against his will, to rise, led him to the side of his bed, and left him to himself.

With perturbed and gloomy spirits, mechanically she bent her steps towards the forest. It was late in the evening; the sky was overcast with black heavy clouds, but unheeding she pursued her way; the thunder now rattled over her head, and the blue lightning flashed across her path; her mind, however, too engaged in its internal warfare, regarded not the warring of the elements, and external circumstances had rarely power to affect her stubborn mind.

"Ah! what means *can* I pursue?" she cried aloud, certain that no one was nigh, "how satisfy my destroying passion? — Shall all I have done be in vain then, and the sole object of my ardent wishes, the goal of my hopes, elude at last my wild pursuit? — no, no, it must not be! — Yet, that he were mine at last, I would not hesitate to plunge my soul in deepest perdition for his sake! for without him I cannot live — this world would to me be an earthly purgatory — Ah, Zofloya? — why art *thou* not here, to offer thy assistance and advice? — Surely thou wilt not forsake me at the period when *most* I need thy aid — or perhaps even thou art powerless to assist me in this."

As she uttered these words, a soul-enchanting melody rose gradually in swelling notes upon her ear; she paused to listen — her mind became calmed, and wrapt in attention. She wondered at the magical powers of the invisible musician. In a few minutes it sunk in thrilling cadence, and was heard no more.

The gloom of Victoria's mind began to return, and, angry that any external circumstance should have had power for a moment to interrupt the despondency of her thoughts, she prepared, disgusted as she was at not having met with Zofloya, to leave the forest. As she hastily turned, however, suddenly she encountered him.

"I am glad, Zofloya, to behold thee," she cried; "but how cam'st thou here? for till this moment I have not seen thee."

"I have followed you, Signora, for some time past."

"And why would'st not thou overtake me?"

"That I might have the frequent, yet ever new delight, fair Victoria, of hearing myself called upon."

"*Then* why did'st thou not reveal thyself?"

"You were listening, I believe, to the music. Soon as it ceased you turned, and we met, — but say, Victoria, how speed your wishes?"

"Alas! miserable wretch that I am," returned Victoria — "much I fear, success will never be mine — Henriquez loaths me. This evening only, did he formally, finally, and coolly reject me."

"And his excuse for refusing the loveliest of her sex?" —

"Love, and ceaseless devotion to the memory of his Lilla; — yet, has he insultingly added, that had a Lilla never existed, Victoria could have had no power to excite his love."

"Most insensible idiot!" indignantly cried the Moor. "He would have loved you, I presume, had you chanced to have *resembled* Lilla."

"Ah! would," cried the degenerate Victoria, "would that this unwieldy form could be compressed into the fairy delicacy of hers, these bold masculine features assume the likeness of her baby face! — Ah! what would I not submit to, to gain but one look of love from the pitiless Henriquez."

"Beautiful Victoria," cried the Moor in a soft flattering voice — "call not that graceful form unwieldy, nor to those noble and commanding features offer such indignity. — Eminent loveliness is yours, — could the tasteless Henriquez but *believe* you Lilla" — he paused — and Victoria fixed her eager searching eyes upon his countenance; — when finding that Zofloya did not proceed, she exclaimed.

"Speak, speak Zofloya; if you have aught to suggest, withhold it not an instant from me."

At this moment, a vivid flash of lightning dividing the skies, Zofloya said:

"Let us seek, Signora, a more sheltered spot — the storm appears encreasing."

"Oh, heed not the storm! — but speak," cried Victoria, "if aught you can adduce to sooth the despair of my mind."

"You heed not the lightning, Signora, neither do I — deign then to answer me; is it now your firm belief that Henriquez will never grant you his love?"

"Alas! I have said so," replied Victoria in a gloomy accent.

"And, under these circumstances, do you still love *him?* — still feel him necessary to your happiness?"

"Sooner then resign all hopes of obtaining him, I would plunge this instant a stilletto in my bosom!"

Zofloya remained a few moments silent, and then resumed —

"If you could only obtain his love, and every mark of unrestrained passion, in the delusive belief on his side, that you were his betrothed Lilla, would you upon *such* terms accept" —

"Oh! yes, with joy, with delight," interrupted Victoria — "say but *how* such blissful delusion could be conveyed to his mind."

"It grows late Signora — the storm becomes more violent; shall I defer till the morrow what further I might say?"

"If you would have me expire at your feet," cried Victoria wildly — "attempt to leave me thus unsatisfied — in the very midst too of the faint hope you have suffered to beam upon my soul. — What of the hour? — what of the storm?" she pursued, as the blue lightning conjured trees of fire, and seemed to dance upon the summit of the mountains; — "what even of the dissolution of nature in a moment like this, when my soul pants for —"

"Well then," interrupted the Moor, "noble intrepid Victoria! mark me, for truly do I love, and glory in your firm unshrinking spirit — I possess a drug, the peculiar property of which it is — not to stupify the faculties, or induce actual insanity, but to cause a sort of temporary delirium upon any particular point optionable with those who shall administer this drug; — for instance, a partial mania as it were, as many that are termed mad may be perfectly sane upon every subject but the individual one which caused their madness. This drug has a singular power of confusing the mind, and of so far deluding it, that those who take it must inevitably believe that which it is desired to convey to their minds. — Thus, those who go mad for love, imagine that in every female they see her who caused their madness, involuntarily pursuing and indulging the conceit which is uppermost in their diseased fancies. — You begin, Signora, to obtain some insight into the nature of my plan — the only one that suggests itself at this pressure for the atchievement of your love; — Allow me to proceed, however, — this drug which I will give you, being administered to Henriquez, suppose this night, when, with a restrained and tranquil tenderness, such as might befit a sister, you give him ere he sleeps some draught of a refreshing or composing nature. During the night it will have leisure to attain its proposed effect; in the morning, on awakening, he will be furious for Lilla, her image having so possessed him during the night, that he will be almost incapable of considering it as the mere delusion of a dream; — in consequence of his possession (strange and unaccountable to those around) being reported to you, considered by all as a proof of confirmed lunacy, you will instantly hasten to his chamber. — Scarcely will you have entered, ere, flying towards you, he will clasp you with wild fervour in his arms, calling you his adored his long lost Lilla."

Victoria, unable any longer to restrain her emotions, threw herself upon her knees, and clasped her hands eagerly together.

"Oh, rapture! oh inexpressible bliss!" she cried — oh, moment for which my heart so long has panted! — shall I then at length be clasped — voluntarily and ardently clasped to the bosom of Henriquez? — oh, enfeebled soul! help me to support the reality of this happiness, which now thou tremblest but to think of!"

"Reserve your transports, fair Victoria — reserve them for that moment which I swear to you shall arrive; mean time arise, and hear me to an end." —

"Henriquez, being fully persuaded, that you are his idolized Lilla, will call you by the name of wife, and believe you such, for his mind will be in that state of anarchy and confusion, he will have no conception of time that is past, nor that his marriage, fixed to have taken place on a given day long since elapsed, has never yet been performed. — He will merely be enabled to combine your appearance with your supposed return, and feel as though after suffering for your loss, deep affliction for a certain space of time, you were at length restored to his arms. The elation of his spirits will be great in consequence, his mind will be attuned to love and pleasure, and you must beware of doing aught to thwart or offend him. — Indulge him with wine, enliven him with music, let an elegant banquet be prepared — humour his delusion, assume as much as possible the character of Lilla and of his wife — in all you do be collected, be firm, and love shall be propitious to your wishes."

Once more, and for the last time, Zofloya drew forth the box, the fatal repository of so much mischief — then placing in the hands of Victoria, a small folded paper containing the philtre to which he had alluded, he bade her, with a serious smile, use well her advantages, and, without another sentence, turned suddenly away. As he retreated into the thick gloom of the forest, a vivid flash now and then revealed his swift moving figure to her view — now emerging from among the trees — now scaling the pointed rock, and now appearing a figure of fire upon its lofty summit.

Victoria, too inebriated with joy at the prospect she beheld of at length obtaining her dearest wishes, to remark or wonder at the precipitate departure of the Moor, thought only of the exquisite happiness he had promised her, and unmindful of the awe inspiring thunder, — unmindful of the red lightning (which gleaming around at quick repeated intervals, shewed mountains, rocks, and forests of fire,) remained with undefended form, but a heart beating high with the fervor of hope, rooted, as it were, to the spot in idolatrous anticipation of future bliss.

At length forcibly rousing herself, she returned to the castle; on her way she beheld no traces of Zofloya, and concluded (an idea not unfavourable to his character) that he had chosen a night like the present, to wander among the mountains: — She proceeded, however, and entering the castle, gently approached the chamber of Henriquez. — With air humbled and abashed, she presented herself before him, and addressed him in a faltering voice of tender humility.

Again Henriquez became the dupe of her artifice — again he regretted his cruel explicitness, and though he could not help feeling for her a certain portion of involuntary disgust, he received her with gentle politeness. She, with well-assumed melancholy softness, but secret exultation, busied herself in silence, in little offices about his chamber; these completed and arranged, she proposed to retire for the night. — Henriquez with a grateful bow, as if for her attention, acquiesced in the movement, when Victoria, retreating with an air of mortified resignation towards the door, pretended suddenly to remember that she had not administered to him a certain restorative medicine, which with her own hand she insisted on presenting to him, every night since his recovery. Hastily returning at the further end of the room, remote from the pensive Henriquez, she prepared his mixture, and infused the drug given her by Zofloya. Approaching him then, with hand rendered unsteady from ravishing anticipation of the effects it would produce, she tendered it to him. Henriquez felt no inclination for his potion, yet unwilling to dismiss Victoria from him with an aching heart, he took it with a soft thankful smile from her hand, and instantly drank it off. — This accomplished so far, with frame still tremulous, and heart wildly beating with the thoughts of the morning, Victoria received back the glass, and bidding him farewell, retired from the chamber.

Henriquez having laid his head upon his pillow, soon fell into a heavy sleep. His mind became gradually disturbed, and the form of Lilla glided in his view; now, as formerly, he beheld her under the same roof with himself, constituting a part of the family, — now she sat beside him — now rambled with him in the forest, and now bestowed on him her innocent endearments, pure as innocence itself. All night these blissful but deceptive visions haunted his fancy, and when towards morning he awoke, so far was the delusion from vanishing with sleep, that scarce could he restrain himself in his bed, though a confused idea of the earliness of the hour, prevented him from arising.

Every moment, however, his infatuation encreased, — he believed that he had been for a long time in a state of mental derangement, that he had only now recovered his senses, and that the image of Lilla being so deeply impressed upon his mind, was owing to his having actually beheld her the day preceding, of which, he even thought he entertained a faint recollection. Unable longer to contend with the powerful delusions of his disordered fancy, he started wildly from his bed, and flew towards the well-known spot in the forest, where frequently they had been wont to ramble. Loudly he called upon the name of Lilla, till his voice obtaining involuntary latitude, he repeated that dear loved name briefly, and incessantly, till he panted for breath. Finding at length, that his search was vain, he returned to the castle. Victoria, anxiously upon the watch, heard all his movements; the better to deceive him, she wore a veil of Lilla's, and such parts of her dress as might suit indiscriminately either the one or the other. His conduct had already evinced to her, how powerfully the philtre was acting, but she deemed it expedient to increase his impatience, that the delusion practised upon him might be the less liable to detection.

She had left her own apartment, and now occupied that of the poor victim, Lilla; — presently she heard the distracted lover pacing to and fro before the well-known door he firmly believed to enclose his mistress. This was the moment for Victoria — she threw open the door of the chamber, as if by chance, and came forth! — Scarcely was she beheld by Henriquez, ere he darted towards her, and seizing her in his arms, exclaimed —

"Wife of my soul! — my beloved — my darling Lilla! — have I then at length recovered the pride of my life? the darling of my bosom! — her, for whom alone existence is worthy the bearing! — oh, my heart's Lilla, speak to me my love, and tell me whence thou comest, and whither thou hast been!"

Who can describe the delight of Victoria at this proof of the extravagance of Henriquez? she clearly perceived his distraction to be at the heighth, and that without fear she might humour the deception; — looking tenderly upon him, she cried —

"Dearest Henriquez be composed — I have indeed never departed from thee since the day of our marriage; but dost thou not remember, on that eve which should have proved so blissful, thou wert attacked by sudden malady, and conveyed to bed? — for nearly three weeks thou wert insensible — nor could'st thou, oh! my love, recognize even thy faithful wife, although she neither quitted thee by night nor day! But no more of the melancholy past — thou knowest me now; — Ah! little durst I hope, when sad and heart-broken I retired from thee last night, that this morning would bring with it such happiness!"

"And wert thou with me last night, my Lilla? — Oh! yes — I know thou wert, for now I recollect" — and he pressed his hand upon his burning forehead — "now I recollect — surely thou hast never once been from me — yet I thought — I thought — fool I must have been! — that thou wert *not* Lilla — but — ah! I must indeed have been severely ill to mistake that heavenly face!"

"No more, my Henriquez — my husband," cried the artful Victoria, "but let this blisful day be dedicated to love and joy; and although we have never in reality been separated — yet let us celebrate this day, as for our restoration to each other."

At these words the heart of the poor Henriquez bounded in his bosom, — for his brain was high wrought fired to phrenzy, and madly eager for noisy revelry and delight. He seized the hand of Victoria, and pressing it to his lips, cried out aloud in a mirthful voice,

"Let us feast, and dance then, on this glorious day, my Lilla! — Let's have a banquet, let's have music, and cause the mountains to re-echo!"

"Yes, yes, my love," interrupted Victoria, joyfully smiling, we will have a banquet, and music; and in these beautiful solitudes, we will be the world to each other."

"Ah! — spoken like my Lilla!" cried Henriquez, "if we were in Venice, we should be tortured with guests, — yet do we need no company, but that of each other, — thou sayest true, — but we must dance then, my Lilla! — Yes," he added with a loud laugh, "we must dance together, — or by heaven I shall die of pent up bliss."

He threw his arm round the waist of the joy-mad Victoria, and, in wild sport, dragged, rather than led, her from the spot.

On this day, high beat her heart — her bosom's fierce triumph flashed from her eyes, as she gazed on the devoted youth, and secretly she swore to bestow upon Zofloya whatever reward he should desire for thus accomplishing her soul's first wish. At once she gave orders for a sumptuous feast, and determined that the day should be dedicated, in compliance to the whim of Henriquez, to mirth and revelry; the most delicious viands, the choicest and most intoxicating wines, constituted the banquet, and as she pressed them upon Henriquez, his blood circulated with wilder rapidity, and the delirium of his brain encreased.

The graceful Zofloya, highly skilled in the science of harmony, and seated at the further end of the banqueting room (retired from others, who occasionally joined him, but a host in himself) drew from his harp sounds of such overpowering melody, as by turns reduced the soul into the most delicious softness, or excited it with transport even to madness! — Now drowned in tender tears, the inspired Henriquez listened with restrained enthusiasm, — now raised to distracting rapture, he leaped from his seat, and his strong emotion found no vent but on the beating bosom of Victoria; her he pressed eagerly in his arms, and on that treacherous breast shed tears of the wildest transport.

In his phrenzy he had desired to dance, and Victoria, with the grace of a sylph, flitted in varied movements to the soft music of Zofloya. — Henriquez gazed with ravished eyes, but soon starting up, seized her by the hands, and joined with her in the dance, while Zofloya struck a wilder note to the no longer measured footsteps.

Till a late hour of the evening the pleasures of the banquet were protracted, even till the high-wrought spirits of Henriquez becoming less violent, though his delusion still continued in full force, he said —

"I am weary, beloved Lilla, of this excess of happiness — my mind feels jaded and confused, as though it stood in need of rest to restore its energies: let us retire then, my life, and in gentle dreams we may retrace the pleasures of the day."

CHAPTER XXIX

Never had the sun risen on a day of equal horror to that which succeeded the one just described; — scarce had its first beam played into the chamber of Henriquez, ere sleep forsook his eyes, and with that all the traces of the wild delirium that had possessed his brain on the preceding day. — Yes, the delusion was at an end! Scarce could his phrenzied gaze believe the sight which presented itself. — Not the fair Lilla, the betrothed and heart-wedded wife of his bosom, but Victoria! appearing Lilla no longer, blasting his strained eyes with her hated image! — Sleep still overpowered her senses, unconscious of the horror she inspired — those black fringed eyelids, reposing upon a cheek of dark and animated hue — those raven tresses hanging unconfined — oh, sad! oh, damning proofs! — Where was the fair enamelled cheek — the flaxen ringlets of the delicate Lilla? — *Real* madness now seized the brain of the wretched Henriquez — his eye-balls, bursting almost from their sockets, furiously rolled, till he could gaze no longer. — A frantic cry escaped his lips — it was the inarticulate name of Lilla; as springing, a raging maniac, from the bed, he snatched a sword that hung on the opposite wall, and, dashing its hilt on the floor, threw himself, in desperate agony, upon its point! — Exposed, defenceless as he was, it entered instantly his beating breast, and he sunk to the ground bathed in his purple gore! — Victoria had awakened as he sprang from the bed, but not in time to prevent his dreadful and unthought for deed; — she reached him only as he fell, and, casting herself wildly on her knees beside him, raised his head upon her bosom.

At her touch, strong convulsive shudderings seized the frame of the dying Henriquez; he sought to lift his head from her breast and dash it on the ground, when finding himself incapable of doing so, his agonies encreased ten-fold? — For a moment his closing eyes glared upon her, as in desire of vengeance, but the strong emotion expired with his fleeting breath, and a harrowing smile — a smile of despairing triumph, passed over his waning features, as though he would have said, "Thus do I escape thee for ever, persecuting fiend!" — No word passed his lips — no sigh heaved his bosom, and, exulting in his agonies, he died!

Thus vanished at once, Victoria beheld her death-reared visions; — frantic rage fired her soul at the thought, and keen disappointment maddened her brain. — Now she clasped her hands, and twisted her fingers in each other, and now tore, by handfuls, the hair from her head, strewing it in agony over the lifeless body of Henriquez. At length her violence subsided; a sudden portentous calm took possession of her mind, and she started on her feet. Wildly she seized her dagger, and, throwing a few clothes over her, revolved in her mind a confusion of horrible intent. Quitting hastily the chamber of despair and death, yet instinctively securing the door after her, she sped her way into the forest.

Scarce was she herself conscious of the dire purpose that throbbed at her heart — yet her steps were directed towards that fatal spot, where, in hopeless imprisonment, the miserable Lilla still languished. Now nerved with hellish strength, she ascended the sloping rock; now the cataract foamed loud in her ears; the rapidity of her movements encreased, scarcely she felt the rugged ground; the mountainous steep appeared a level path, and yawning precipices inspired no dread. At length she beheld herself where instinctive rage and terrible despair had led her. Till this moment, never had she visited the defenceless object of her hate and vengeance; indifferent to her state, whether of death or long-protracted torment, never had she sought of Zofloya aught concerning her, and unnoticed, even on this fatal morn, had she still remained, but for the horrible purpose that had seized her soul — a purpose fitted as the catastrophe to the scenes which had preceded it. — Without pausing to take breath, she rushed hastily down the rugged descent which led into the gloomy dungeon of the orphan Lilla.

The sight that then presented itself nerved, instead of softening, the fierce rage of her bosom. Extended on the flinty ground lay the emaciated and almost expiring girl; her pale cheek reposing upon her snowy arm, barely preserving it from unworthy contact with its rocky pillow. Beside her were some coarse fragments of scanty food. Victoria approaching, raised her dagger, which she firmly grasped, and, seizing her chained wrist, loudly commanded her to rise. — With trembling limbs, the feeble Lilla endeavoured to obey. Over her alabaster shoulders was thrown a mantle of leopard skin, brought her by Zofloya, and her flaxen tresses hung around her in mournful disorder.

Clasping her thin hands upon her polished bosom, and with some of her long tresses, still in pure unaltered modesty, essaying to veil it, she raised her eyes, of heavenly blue, to the stern and frantic countenance of her gloomy persecutor, appearing, in figure, grace, and attitude, a miniature semblance of the Medicean Venus.

"Minion! — accursed child!" wildly shrieked the maddened Victoria, "prepare for death!" for even in this state of forlornness and woe, the seraph beauty of the orphan Lilla, rising pre-eminent to circumstance and situation, excited her jealousy, and renewed her rage. — "Ah, Victoria!" in mournful accents she cried, "is it you — you then who would kill me? — I thought, I hoped, (only that your angry looks bid me doubt) that you came to give me liberty."

"I do, wretch! — puny babbler," she answered, — "Behold!" — unloosing with frantic violence the chain from her wrist, "I come to give thee liberty! — the liberty of death!"

"Alas! Victoria, in what then have I offended you, that you should hate me thus? — Ah, consider I am but a poor and friendless orphan, who can never do you ill."

"Peace, I say, puppet!" shrieked Victoria; "thou hast already done me more ill than the sacrifice of thy worthless life can repay — follow me!"

"I cannot walk: — I cannot follow you indeed," sobbed the innocent Lilla, while the tears rolled fast down her snow-white cheeks.

"Then I will teach thee!" cried Victoria; and seizing her by the arm, dragged her over the rugged ground, and up the irregular ascent, while her delicate feet, naked and defenceless to the pointed rock, left their blood red traces at every step! — still to the uttermost heighth she forced, relentless, her panting victim: —

"Now, look down," she cried. — A bottomless abyss yawned at the mountains base; and from the opposite side the tumbling torrent rushed furious over immense projections, till finding the receptacle of the abyss, it dashed down its rugged sides into the cavity below.

"See'st thou?" cried Victoria again. — "Now then, stand firm, beautiful, unconquerable Lilla! thou whom no art could root from the breast of Henriquez, stand firm, I say! — for now I push thee headlong!"

"Oh, mercy! mercy! shrieked, in accents of agony, the terrified Lilla, clinging, with the strength of horror, round the body of Victoria. — "Oh! sweet Victoria, remember we have been friends. — I loved thee! nay, even now I love thee, and believe that thou art mad! — Oh, think! think we have been companions, bedfellows! — Sweet and gentle Victoria, murder not, then, the friendless Lilla, who for worlds would not injure thee!"

"I tell thee, thou shalt die, wretch. — Wert thou not the beloved of Henriquez?"

"Henriquez! — ah me! I was indeed! — but where, where is Henriquez now, Victoria?"

"Dead! dead!" with a fiend-like laugh, cried Victoria — "Let me send thee to him."

"Dead! — Ah, cruel Victoria! murdered by thee?"

"Murdered by *thee*, viper!" fiercely returned Victoria. — " 'Twas thee who plunged the sword into his breast, — thy accursed image revelling there, impelled him to the frantic deed! — leave thy hold I say, or by heaven I will dash thee at once down the rock!"

Oh, Henriquez! — Art thou indeed gone? — yes, yes, or the wretched Lilla would not be thus! — no one would dare," she sobbed, "while thou wert near, thus to treat the miserable Lilla; — no hope, no happiness for her now, in lengthened life!"

"Die then at once, presumptuous babbler!" exclaimed Victoria, endeavouring to shake off the firmly clinging form of the defenceless Lilla.

"Ah! dearest Victoria — I am afraid of so terrible a death! — If I must die — be it then the same death as my Henriquez suffered, — plunge thy stilletto in my heart."

"That will I do," cried the enraged Victoria, "and dash thee head-long beside. Raising her dagger high, she sought then to plunge it in the fair bosom of the beauteous orphan, but she, suddenly relinquishing her hold, the point of the dagger, wounded only her uplifted hand, and glancing across her alabaster shoulder, the blood that issued thence, slightly tinged her flaxen tresses with a brilliant red.

The courage of the wretched Lilla forsook her — the death she had preferred, her innocent soul shrunk from enduring; but perceiving that Victoria was desperate, and determined, she resolved to make a last effort for her life. — Again the fell poignard was uplifted for surer aim — when springing from her knees, on which she had cast herself, to implore mercy, she forgot at once her wounds and her weakness, and endeavoured by speed to escape her barbarous enemy; seeming, as she wildly flew, the beauteous and timid spirit of the solitude.

Nerved anew by this feeble attempt to escape her vengeance, Victoria pursued her flying victim. At the uttermost edge of the mountain she gained upon her, when Lilla perceiving that hope of escape was vain, caught frantic, for safety, at the scathed branches of a blasted oak, that, bowed by repeated storms, hung almost perpendicularly over the yawning depth beneath. — Round these, she twisted her slender arms, while, waving to and fro with her gentle weight over the immeasurable abyss, they seemed to promise but precarious support.

Victoria advanced with furious looks — she shook the branches of the tree, that Lilla might fall headlong. Enhorrored at this terrible menace, the miserable girl quitted suddenly her hold, and on the brink of the mountain sought despairingly to grapple with the superior force of her adversary! — Her powers were soon exhausted, when clasping together her hands, and looking piteously upon that which had received the wound, from whence the blood now streamed up to her elbow; she exclaimed "Barbarous Victoria! — look down upon me, behold what thou hast done, and let the blood that thou hast shed appease thee. Ah! little did I think, when a deserted orphan, invited by thee to remain beneath thy roof, that such would be my miserable fate! Remember *that*, Victoria — have pity on me — and I will pray of heaven to forgive thee the past!"

The only answer of Victoria was a wild laugh, and again she raised the poignard to strike.

"Is it even so, then?" cried the despairing Lilla. — "Take then my life Victoria — take it at once, — but kill me I implore, with that same dagger with which you murdered Henriquez, because he loved me more than he did you!"

Fired to madness by this accusation, and the concluding remark, Victoria, no longer mistress of her actions, nor desiring to be so, seized by her streaming tresses the fragile Lilla, and held her back. — With her poignard she stabbed her in the bosom, in the shoulder, and other parts:—the expiring Lilla sank upon her knees. — Victoria pursued her blows — she covered her fair body with innumerable wounds, then dashed her headlong over the edge of the steep. — Her fairy form bounded as it fell against the projecting crags of the mountain, diminishing to the sight of her cruel enemy, who followed it far as her eye could reach. Soon as a hollow momentary sound struck on the rapt ear of Victoria, informing her that Lilla was sunk into her grave, no more to rise, she hastened from the dreadful spot in a state of mind, which, if exulting, was far from being at ease — possessed rather with the madness and confusion of hell. A certain trepidation of spirits that she had never before experienced, caused her to rush along with even greater rapidity, if possible, than she had used in her way thither. — Though sinking with fatigue, she durst not abide in these gloomy solitudes to rest — she feared even to turn her head, lest the mangled form of Lilla, risen from the stream, should be pursuing her. — Now precipices yawned at her feet, and now that lovely form, bounding from crag to crag, seemed at every turn to meet her view; — those fair tresses dyed in crimson gore, that bleeding bosom was before her; and now the agonised shriek for mercy rang in her distracted ears! —

At length she passed the rocks, and issued into the forest from the narrow break that led to them; — at this moment the Moor, Zofloya, appeared before her, as if he had there awaited her coming.

"Victoria!" he cried, in a voice less sweet than usual, and with a brow more gloomy, — "thou art too precipitate — and thereby hastenest thy fate! — why hast thou destroyed the orphan Lilla? — the deed was premature, and thou wilt repent it; — mean time enter not the castle, for evil awaits thee there!"

"Who told thee I had murdered the orphan, Lilla?" haughtily returned Victoria — "but if I have, the deed is mine, and I will answer it. — Stand aside Moor — the *castle* is mine and I will enter it."

"Do so," said the Moor, with a bitter smile, "and thereby court the fate thou might'st yet a little have protracted."

"The consequences be on my own head," answered Victoria, — "I will pass." —

"Thou shalt — but remember, poor Victoria, that independently of *me*, thou canst not even breathe!"

With a look of scorn and disgust at the changed manner of the Moor, Victoria turned from him, and pursued her way. — Her mind already in a ferment, could brook no additional irritation; — just as she reached the castle, she beheld Zofloya entering before her, yet she had not seen him pass her, and he had even remained some moments upon the spot where she had encountered him. — This circumstance excited some slight surprise, but objects of higher consequence engaged her mind, and she followed him into the castle.

Her first step was to repair to the chamber of Henriquez. — It immediately appeared to her, that no one had found entrance to it during her absence, the lifeless body bathed in its blood still remained extended on the floor, and all was in the state she had left it. — She decided, therefore, despising in her mind the false prophecies of Zofloya, to secure the door, without as yet making known the death of Henriquez. His non-appearance she readily conceived would excite no immediate remark, he having frequently of late passed the whole of the day in his chamber. Thus, she determined, (for her mind was a chaos, and could suggest no better conduct for the moment) — to make fast the door; repairing then to the solitude of her own apartment, she secured it likewise, and throwing herself upon her bed, desired to take a retrospect of the past, and consider, if possible, respecting the future. — She endeavoured to collect her wandering thoughts, but instead of this, an unconquerable lassitude crept over her, accompanied by a disposition to sleep. — In vain she tried to shake it off, the influence became resistless — her eyelids involuntarily closed, and she was compelled to yield to a power superior to her will.

Total forgetfulness, however, did not ensue; — she experienced a sensation similar to that of persons who have taken too large a quantity of opium to allow of calm undisturbed repose. — To herself her eyes appeared as if strained to their fullest extent — strange visions swam in her sight; yet unable to trust the delusion, she believed herself under the unconquerable horrors of a waking dream. — Now the ringing of bells sounded in her ears, and now she beheld herself transported into an apartment, distant from the habitable part of the castle, and which, ever since the death of Berenza, had not even been opened. — In this room formerly there had stood a huge iron chest, this she had once seen; now likewise it was present to her view, and she recognised it. — Suddenly the door of the apartment was thrown open, and a number of persons appeared rushing in, consisting chiefly of the domestics of the castle. One, however, preceded the rest, and him her mind identified for the old and favourite servant of Berenza, named Antonio.

With horror and perturbation in his looks, Antonio seemed rapidly advancing towards the chest, and calling aloud for some of his companions to assist him, by their joint efforts they raised the lid. — This was no sooner accomplished than a shout of universal horror prevailed, accompanied by the strongest marks of terror and perturbation. The cause was presently explained. — Forth from the chest they drew the disclosed, half mouldered skeleton, that once had been Berenza!

At this sight of horror, it seemed to her, that with animated gestures of indignation and revenge, they unanimously rushed towards her, to drag her from her bed. — In the midst of this terrible scene, Zofloya entered; at once the crowd vanished, the confusion ceased, and in indescribable agony she awoke, while the cold drops of terror bedewed her forehead.

On opening her eyes, the first object she beheld was the Moor, standing in fixed attitude at the foot of her bed. — His aspect was frigid and severe, yet his eyes shone with lambent fire, as a dark thunder-cloud emits the vivid flame. — Conceiving the whole to be still delusion, she cast her eyes anxiously around the chamber — it was gloomy and dim — and the evening seemed far advanced. Surprised that she should have slumbered so long, she sought, in confusion of mind, to throw herself from the bed, when the sweetly solemn voice of Zofloya arrested her movement.

"Victoria," he said, "attend. This morning you unwarily disregarded my words; but, nevertheless, for the love I bear towards you, I desire to preserve you from immediate destruction! — Already have the unrestrained passions of your soul precipitated your fate, and hastened the shame that waits to overcome you; — from that shame, even yet, I offer to rescue you. — Listen to what I shall reveal. — You have dreamt, but it was no fable; you have slept some hours; the sun had not long passed the horizon when you entered your chamber, and now the evening is drawing to a close. — At an early hour of the night the servant of the deceased Berenza, Antonio, will retire to repose; a fearful dream will awaken him, concerning the disappearance of the body of his late master. Actuated by its resistless influence, he will arise, and alarm his fellow domestics — he will relate to them his dream. Naturally weak and superstitious, they will all be induced to accompany him to the solitary chamber, remote from the habitable part of the castle. There — contained in the iron chest within — they will discover the mouldering skeleton of Berenza!" —

"Oh, Zofloya! Zofloya — is this thy truth and thy friendship?" exclaimed Victoria. "Did'st thou not promise thou would'st preserve me from suspicion and from ill?"

"I said not that I could do so for *ever*. Over the body of the Conte I have not eternal power — yet thy own folly and impatience hath hastened" —

"Ah, little could I dream of this reserve," interrupted Victoria, "yet surely, surely, it is in *thy* power to preserve me for ever from suspicion; for, Zofloya, thou possessest superior power — the future is exposed to thy view — thou anticipatest events, and canst therefore guard against them. Save me then — save me, I implore thee, from the shame thou sayest awaits me — or wretch shall I consider myself ever to have confided in thy power, or thy promises!"

The terrible eyes of Zofloya shot fire, as they turned their burning glances on Victoria.

"This is no time," he fiercely exclaimed, "for retrospect or idle observation. — If you repent your confidence, do, in the present instance, without my assistance — writhe between the pillars of St. Mark! — I may *visit* you there perhaps — farewell! — but remember," he added, shaking his finger with a menacing air, "remember there is now no escape for you."

"Oh, strange, mysterious, and, to me, indefinable being!" cried Victoria — "your words, your looks, terrify and confound me; yet go not," she continued, as with angry, though majestic pace, Zofloya moved towards the door; "abandon me not at this crisis, cruel Zofloya."

The Moor turned from the door; fire gleamed no longer from his eyes, but a beautiful and haughty smile diffused itself over his countenance, which appeared like the sun beaming from a gloomy cloud.[1]

"Well then — once more thou entreatest," he cried, "once more I befriend thee; but beware, Victoria, how again I am reproached; — to irritate me now would be vain and impolitic, and sharpen against thyself that sentiment of hate which I bear — but this is irrelevant," he hastily added — "suspicion will, as I said, attach to thee — by what means induced I scarcely need now explain; the terrible Inquisition will drag thee before its tribunal; infinite confusion will reign in this castle; the chamber of Henriquez will be forced open, (for strange surmises begin already to prevail concerning thee) and instantly they will discover that which, of itself, would damn thee. — The body of Henriquez remains bathed in its blood upon the floor of his chamber — beside it lies thy veil, and divers articles of dress in which thou wert seen yesterday. Thy guilt, in the estimation of all, will be made clearly evident; but, forbearing to alarm thee with the knowledge of their discovery, they will secure thee, merely a prisoner in thine own apartment, and dispatch messengers to Venice, for the purpose of making it known and bringing condign punishment on thy head. Need I expatiate upon the events that will follow? — public infamy and public" —

"Oh! spare me," cried Victoria — "horrible is my fate! — yet I swear to thee, Zofloya, that I would meet it with indifference, if Henriquez still lived, and lived for me. Ah, tell me, Moor, didst thou not promise that" —

"Beware, Victoria! — to the very extent of my promise I have performed; — I swore to thee that Henriquez should call thee his, and clasp thee voluntarily to his bosom; — I swore to thee that thou should'st have his love — did I promise thee that his delusion should last for ever? or profess to be amenable for those consequences which should follow the completion of my promise?"

Victoria longed to reply — but awe and terror checked the words that rose to her lips; yet the idea glanced for an instant through her mind, (and bitter was the suggestion) how fleeting, and how short-lived had been the moments of precarious pleasure procured for her by Zofloya, yet how terrible and how lasting the evils they had produced; they were, as the passing shadows, the mere mockery only of what they promised, while real horrors waiting to overwhelm and destroy, attended close upon them.

The Moor, with a piercing glance, seemed to penetrate her inmost thoughts; a shade of severity passed over his features, and he said:

"If you hesitate respecting the path you should pursue at present, I leave you free to chuse."

---

1 like the sun beaming from a gloomy cloud.: Zofloya grows decidedly more Satanic throughout this volume; here Dacre alludes to Milton's description of Satan in *Paradise Lost* 1 (594–96): "as when the sun ris'n/Looks through the horizontal misty air/Shorn of his beams."

Victoria clasped her hands — too well she beheld the desolate prospect before her — too keenly felt the words of the Moor; — there appeared indeed no escape for her.

"Decide, Victoria!" cried Zofloya, with encreased sternness.

"I do! I do!" replied Victoria.— "I confide in you. — I rely on you to save me from the horrors that now encompass me, or to bear me safely through them; — to save me from them, Zofloya," she added emphatically, "for ever."

"To that I pledge myself; — you shall be saved for ever from the disgrace and horrors that here await you; but you must fly."

"Fly!"

"Yes, — for I cannot turn the tide of events, in which I have no concern. — I cannot, Victoria, influence the course of justice, nor prevent that from arising, which arises independently of me. — Whatever you may deem my power, be assured, that although I may induce the occurrence of many events that otherwise might not have been, yet I cannot prevent from occurring aught which is already written in the book of fate."

"And whither then must I fly?" with an abstracted air demanded Victoria.

"Entrust that to me. — A few words more, and I go. — Take heed that you rest where you are — resign yourself unresistingly to repose. — It will be calm, and undisturbed, but deep! — On the morrow, when this abode shall be the seat of confusion — when the city of Venice shall be alarmed, and your person be even vociferated for by the populace who will surround your pallazzo there, then shall you be far from danger, from pursuit, and from Venice!"

As Zofloya concluded, slightly waving his hand, he suddenly turned, and retreated from the apartment with the rapidity of a passing shade.

It was now quite dark; Victoria, was sensible neither of hunger nor thirst, yet felt a desire to retrace the terrible events that had been crowded into her life. — The attempt was vain, a numbing torpor began to creep over her as before; she essayed to conquer it, though contrary to the direction of Zofloya; and her incapacity to do so conveyed a bitter pang to her heart, while she felt that she was no longer mistress over herself or her faculties. — Chill horror took possession of her, and in an agony of mind that words cannot describe, seeming subject as it were to an unknown power, and unable to resist, she hopelessly resigned herself to the arbitrary spell that appeared to be cast over her.

CHAPTER XXX

Darkness and gloomy solitude reigned around, when the eyes of Victoria again opened to the sense of life and perception. She found herself reclining on the bare earth; the thunder rolled aloud over her head, and flashes of vivid flame now and then displayed the terrific sublimity of surrounding objects. — Immense mountains, piled upon one another, appeared to encompass her, and to include within their inaccessible bosoms the whole of the universe. Beyond their towering walls, (capped only by the misty clouds,) the imagination, suddenly thrown back and staggered at its own conceptions, could not presume to penetrate. — Mighty rocks, and dizzying precipices at their base, in which the water, falling from an immeasurable height, franticly battled gloomy caverns, which seemed the entrance to Pandæmonium;[1] Alpine cliffs, that in their fierce projection menaced ruin to the wretch beneath: — Such was the scene that, as the blue lightning flashed, in terrible and stupendous confusion, struck upon her view. — Amidst these awful horrors, with folded arms and majestic air, stationed nearly opposite to her stood the towering Zofloya. To him the scene appeared congenial, and Victoria acknowledged to herself, that never before had she beheld him in his proper sphere. — Common objects seemed to shrink in his presence, the earth to tremble at the firmness of his step; now alone his native grandeur shone in its full glory, not eclipsed by, but adding to the terrible magnificence of the scene.

On him the eyes of Victoria involuntarily fixed; dignity and ineffable grace, were diffused over his whole figure; — for the first time she felt towards him an emotion of tenderness, blended with her admiration, and, strange inconsistency, amidst the gloomy terrors that pressed upon her heart, amidst the sensible misery that oppressed her, she experienced something like pride, in reflecting, that a Being so wonderful, so superior, and so beautiful, should thus appear to be interested in her fate.

As if he penetrated her thoughts, the Moor approached, with a sweet though awful smile, and extended his hand for her to rise. Trembling, as much from consciousness at the confused sentiments she felt arising in her bosom, as from alarm, occasioned by external circumstances, she took his proffered hand.

"Tell me, Zofloya," she said, in a tremulous accent, "Tell me where we now are, and how we came hither."

"Know you not, beautiful Victoria, that we are among the Alps, the

---

1 Pandæmonium: In *Paradise Lost*, Pandemonium is Satan's palace in hell, which the fallen angels build through song.

boundaries of your native kingdom? — how we came hither is surely not material for you to know, — but we are safe."

"But I have no remembrance of our journey. — If I recollect aright, it was evening when last we parted; — it appears evening still, though late, — in what time then." —

"It appears, as it is, late in the evening; — it was, as you justly observe, evening when we parted, — this then infers the probability, that a night and a day have nearly elapsed."

"But how! — Have my faculties been so long suspended?" cried Victoria, with uneasiness, "and it is to you alone that I am now indebted for their restoration? — Oh, Zofloya! I perceive too clearly, how much, how compleatly, I am in your power!"

She sighed deeply as she uttered these words, and the conviction of her subjection pressed heavily upon her mind: — her self-confidence vanished, and uneasy sensations filled her bosom.

Zofloya smiled, and tenderly took her hand. — "Why these reflections, Victoria, and why these inferences? — are you not now secure from the shame and horror that awaited you? — no *common* means could have extricated you in such an exigence, — the case pressed, and required prompt exertion, why then regret, if superior power *was* employed to save and to deliver you?"

Zofloya paused — a loud peal of thunder rattled madly above them, and reverberated in stern and hollow sounds among the echoing rocks; — the pointed lightning fearfully gleamed in long and tremulous flashes, — Victoria's firm bosom felt appalled, for never before had she witnessed the terrible phenomena of nature, in a storm among the Alps. — She drew closer to the proud unshrinking figure of the Moor — he passed his arms round her waist, and gently pressed her to his breast.

Victoria felt reassured — she seemed to herself as an isolated being, possessing no earthly friend or protector, but him on whose bosom she now tremblingly reposed. — Never, till this moment, had she been so near the person of the Moor — such powerful fascination dwelt around him, that she felt incapable of withdrawing from his arms; yet ashamed, (for Victoria was still proud) and blushing at her feelings, when she remembered that Zofloya, however he appeared, was but a menial slave, and as such alone had originally become known to her — she sought, but sought vainly, to repress them; for no sooner (enveloped in the lightning's flash as he seemed, when it gleamed around him without touching his person), — did she behold that beautiful and majestic visage, that towering and graceful form, than all thought of his inferiority vanished, and the ravished sense, spurning at the calumnious idea, confessed him a being of superior order.

While thus they remained in the midst of these terrible and sublime solitudes, as there was a solemn pause in the fury of the storm, (which, exhausted by its own violence, seemed suspended only to collect force for renovated explosion,) the sound of human voices broke on their ears:

lights gleamed suddenly from the rocky heights, which appearing rapidly to move (like flaming meteors athwart a gloomy sky,) were discovered at length to be torches, carried by the hands of men. As they continued to approach, their dress, their arms, and fierce demeanour, revealed them for Condottieri[1] or banditti.

Zofloya. inclining his body, said in a low voice to Victoria,

"Be not alarmed, we shall be presently surrounded by these bands, hordes of whom infest these mountains, particularly mount Cenis, where we now are; but regret not the circumstance, no immediate ill will arise; on the contrary, we may, if we will, procure shelter and accommodation."

Victoria made no reply, for by this time a ring began to be formed round them of armed men, the red flame of whose torches betrayed forms and features of such desperate and horrid cast, that scarcely bore they the semblance of human beings. — One stepping from among them, brandished his dagger, and thus spoke:

"What do ye here, in the midst of this storm? — Whence came ye? — whither are ye going? and what riches do ye carry that ye will resign at once without bloodshed?"

"Whence we come, and whither we designed to go, is now immaterial," answered Zofloya, "the riches we possess are not worthy your notice, but we desire to be led to your chief.

There was a pause among the band; Zofloya resumed —

"You behold that we are unarmed — you have nothing therefore to fear, in permitting us to see your chief — we are neither spies nor enemies with bad intent." — So saying, with an authoritative air, he waved his hand, as if to say, "Lead on without further question."

Thus, at least, the action appeared to be understood; respectfully the ring opened on either side, and him who had first spoken, inclining his head with submissive air to the Moor, motioned to lead the way.

With one arm round the waist of Victoria, and holding a torch that had been tendered to him in the other hand, Zofloya walked stately in the midst of the band, his plumed head towering above all, as the lofty poplar of the forest proudly towers above surrounding shrubs.

"Astonishing being that he is," thought Victoria — "even these ferocious bandit are tamed into submission by the magic power of that fascinating voice." —

They ascended the side of the mountain; then, by narrow and dangerous defiles, gradually declined. — Now they touched on the brink of a precipice, now glided with the ease of habit along the slippery ridges of stupendous rocks. — At length a deep hollow presented itself — they descended its almost perpendicular sides, and reached the rocky valley

---

1 Condottieri:The condotierri were groups of mercenary soldiers used to fight in the wars of the Italian States, particularly from the 13th to the 15th centuries.

below; — a rude projecting mass of rock, (seeming to sustain itself in mid air, as it were) became, by the winding of the path, presently visible; it extended nearly to the opposite side of the mountain, forming thereby a kind of huge irregular arch. — Entering beneath it, a narrow aperture presented itself, through which one by one the band began to pass. Victoria beheld herself in her turn at the darksome mouth of this cavern, (to which the o'erhanging brow of the rock formed a natural and tremendous portico) and again her spirits failed, and her heart began to sink.

Compelled to proceed, however, for the bandit from behind pressed onwards, she consoled herself with the reflection, that Zofloya was nigh, and resumed her courage. — By degrees the opening became more spacious, but turning and winding in an endless labyrinth, while other openings perpetually crossed their path, sometimes divided from each other by an arch, whose heavy summit was indivisible from the roof of the cavern, sometimes by rude pillars of stone forming an irregular colonade. At length they found themselves in an extensive space, whose slimy walls, as the red glare of the torches passed along, reflected the various and blended colours of the rainbow. Victoria looked around; the gloomy cave reminded her of that in which the unfortunate Lilla had been pitilessly immured, and involuntarily she trembled.

One of the banditti approaching a certain part of the cavern, with the butt end of his tromboni knocked loud and distinctly three successive times against it; after a pause of about a minute, the knocks were repeated on the inside; he then drew from his girdle a small instrument, in shape resembling a horn, and applying it to his mouth, he blew a shrill peculiar sound. Immediately that part, which bore no remarkable appearance, but seemed only a plain indissoluble portion of the rocky wall, flew suddenly open, in form of a rude door, as if actuated by a secret spring, and discovered, seated round a blazing fire, with wine and various provisions spread in rude confusion before them, a crowd of bandit, in savage attire, resembling those who now rapidly poured in, as if inspired by an anxious desire to partake of the good cheer they beheld.

In the midst of this horde, the bandit ranged respectfully on either side, elevated by a rude bench of stone from the rest (who merely squatted on the floor) appeared a graceful figure, distinguished by his high and single-plumed helmet and by the fierce eccentric costume of his dress. He looked, and was the chief of the Condottieri, elected unanimously as their leader, on the death of a famed chief who had preceded him. His face was concealed by a mask, which circumstance excited the surprize of Victoria. Beside him sat, (fancifully but splendidly attired) a female, whose countenance, though neither remarkable for extreme youth or beauty, struck instantly peculiar emotion to her breast, in the confused but uneasy recollection of having some where before beheld it; in this idea she was confirmed by the look with which her slight glance was returned; it bespoke instant recognition, and with it fury and unfaded hate.

Zofloya boldly advanced, leading his companion by the hand; the chief instinctively arose, with a dignified and commanding air. As the strangers drew nigh their chief, the tenacious and suspicious bandit sprang on their feet, to a man, and drew, as with one accord, the shining stiletto from their belts, to guard against the bare possibility of treachery or evil intent. Zofloya, observing this movement, haughtily smiled, and waved his hand, as if to imply that their suspicions were erroneous; the chief, by a turn of the head, commanded them to put up their weapons, and Zofloya thus addressed him —

"Signor, we are strangers, but would willingly become friends: we fly from danger and persecution, and request for a while the safety of your protection."

Victoria felt surprize to hear the Moor speak thus; but surprize at *his* conduct had ceased to be a new sensation: she remained silent therefore, and the chief thus replied:

"It is enough — we injure not the defenceless, nor those who throw themselves upon our mercy. Honour is our law, and the lives of those who would place themselves under our protection are sacred. I pray you, then, be seated, and partake, without compliment, of our supper. — Friends, be seated all, and let your daggers remain sheathed." In a moment every one resumed his seat.

"Drink," said the masked chief, and offered to Zofloya a flask of wine, who, receiving it, presented it immediately to Victoria.

This movement appeared to draw towards her the regards of the chief; for a moment they were fixed steadfastly upon her; he became agitated, and laid his hand upon the hilt of the stiletto in his belt, then half rose from his seat, and again reseated himself! — Victoria trembled, she knew not why; the company seemed surprised; Zofloya alone remained collected and unmoved; he pressed Victoria to eat with respectful entreaty. By degrees the chief resumed his composure, he looked no longer towards Victoria with pointed regard, and her uneasiness abating, she accepted the attentions of Zofloya. Reserve wore off, cheerfulness, and at length conviviality, began to prevail; the band drank success to each other, and health to their brave commander; they joked, they laughed, they sang; the female joined in their merriment with indecorous glee, but the chief, though no longer disturbed, remained still silent and absorbed. At length, either displeased at their mirth, or rousing himself by an effort, he said —

"Our brave comrades are all here."

"All," replied several voices at once.

"They go forth no more tonight; let every one retire to repose, save those whose turn it is to guard. For you, Signor, looking towards Zofloya, you must fare as we do. — Victoria! — the Signora I mean — (she is neither your wife or mistress I presume) will find matting to repose on in a separate nook of our cavern."

The words of the masked chief electrified Victoria — surprize possessed her soul, for it was evident she was known to him. She looked towards the Moor, but in his strong marked countenance saw no unusual expression.

"The Signora is not my wife," he replied, addressing the chief, "neither is she my mistress — she will be mine, however, for we are linked by indissoluble bands."

"What, I suppose, the bands of love," cried the female with a loud laugh, as she sat beside the chief, and now resembled a Bacchante.[1]

Again the chief became visibly agitated. "*Your's!*" he muttered — but suddenly checking himself, added — "The accommodations here are scanty — you must arrange for the best therefore;" — then, haughtily inclining his head, he retired beneath an arch at the extremity of the cavern, which appeared to lead into an interior recess. The female, who seemed either his wife or companion, retired likewise.

With skins and matting the Moor Zofloya composed for Victoria a tolerable bed; he spread it in a rugged nook, remote from the band, and, leading her towards it, was retiring, when Victoria's proud, but now almost subjugated heart, touched with the respectful attentions of the only companion her vices and her crimes had left her, extended to him, with softened looks, her hand. — He took it with tenderness, yet delicate reserve, and raised it to his lips — his manner but increased to ardour the feelings of Victoria. The dying embers at the further side of the cavern cast round a dusky light — the form, the features, and, above all, the luminous eyes of Zofloya appeared more than human — they shone with a brilliant fire — resistless fascination dwelt about him. Victoria, as he held her hand to his lips, gazed upon him with admiration and gratitude, and her high wrought emotion vented itself in a flood of tears! — yes, the proud, the inhuman Victoria, conquered and affected by the shew of kindness, wept from feeling, from an emotion of the heart! — but who could withstand the enchanting influence of Zofloya?

"Sweet and gentle Victoria," he cried, in a voice that seemed the music of the spheres, "compose yourself, and retire to rest — why should my trifling attentions call forth this excess of feeling? — believe me, I feel that you will yet repay me all."

"Repay thee, Zofloya! — I am thine ever."

---

1 Bacchante: The Bacchantes, or Maenads, were female followers of Bacchus/ Dionysus, god of wine, fertility, excess, and are best known for tearing to pieces the poet Orpheus. Bacchantes are associated with women's violence and acts of bloodlust and with celebratory defiance of their domestic duties. After women's participation in the storming of the Bastille in 1789 and the march on Versailles, images of women as bloodthirsty Bacchantes were popularly used both in Britain and France to warn of the dangers of women's unrestrained participation in the public sphere, and as an embodiment of the excesses of the French revolution as a whole.

"I know that thou art, in a degree, lovely Victoria — but not sufficiently so."

"Ah, tell me then Zofloya! — can I be more so? — teach me — for I feel — I think that it is impossible — the gratitude of my heart, the sentiments of my soul are thine!"

An indefinable, yet bewitching smile, passed over the features of Zofloya.

"Ah, Victoria!" he softly said, "the time is not yet come — I will not claim thee yet — but when I do, then thou wilt be wholly and compleatly mine — wilt thou not?"

"Ah! Zofloya, Zofloya."

"Thou wilt, thou shalt, fair Victoria, I have sworn it — by myself I have sworn it — but now, — now I leave thee to repose — delay will but encrease the value of my prize."

"Oh inscrutable Moor! — thy language is ever indefinable!"

"Time will explain it — fairest Victoria, good night."

The Moor withdrew, and Victoria sunk oppressed upon her couch, — a couch harder far than any on which hitherto she had reposed; — "Yet the poor departed Lilla!" — whispered conscience, which in the gloomy hour of adversity ever wakes, "the poor Lilla! — she had not even such as this" — Yet for the hardness of the couch, for the pang of conscience, what repaid? — strange to say, the conviction of Zofloya's proximity, who now shed enchantment around, and ravished her deluded mind.

She fell, at length, into a slumber, from which she did not awake till the noise of the bandit, moving to and fro in the cavern, caused her to start and gaze eagerly round for Zofloya, the only being on whom she now considered herself to possess the smallest claim; — he observed her eager looks, and hastening towards her, said —

"I have obtained permission of the chief, sweet Victoria, that you shall quit the cavern, and enjoy the keen air of the mountains; he relies upon the word of Zofloya, that we return to this spot, which has afforded us shelter in an hour of necessity, and that whenever we quit it, we shall consent to be escorted by some of his troop, to the other side of the mountain, or some miles forward, in whatever direction we may desire to go: this to avoid the possibility of evil design on our parts, and to satisfy his mind with respect to us: — mean time, he permits us to go unaccompanied."

"Has he yet unmasked?" whispered Victoria, "and can I see him?"

"He has not — nor does he ever, I understand, in the presence of strangers. Come, I have a basket of provisions on my arm, — let us quit for a few hours this subterraneous abode. — I last night noted the labyrinthian windings of the path leading to and from the mountain, — we shall need no guide."

Victoria gave her hand to the Moor, secretly surprised he should have been able so readily to mark the devious way, — but nothing was impossible to Zofloya; his noble presence seemed to diffuse around respect and admiration, — submissively the fierce bandit fell back as he passed, when, as they reached the rugged ascent leading to the mouth of the cavern, and were on the point of issuing thence, the graceful chief (still masked) appeared before them, with his female companion leaning on his arm. For a moment he stopped with a proud uneasy air, when seeming to remark the respect manifested by the Moor towards Victoria, he slightly bowed, and retreated a few steps, leaving room for them to pass beneath the frowning portico that concealed and overhung the aperture of the cavern. His companion, however, fixed her eyes upon Victoria, with a look at once of hate and malicious scorn; — Victoria felt agitated, and again the features of this woman impressed forcibly her mind; — well she remembered that bold and phrenzied countenance, though appearing far less beautiful than when she saw it first, being now from irregular living, or some other cause, bloated and coarse. But yet the never-fading expression of features, so familiar to her fancy, remained, though the power of memory was vain to identify them.

As they emerged from subterrene gloom to the light of day, Victoria expressed to the Moor the sensations which oppressed her —

"I know not whence it is," she said, "but the stately and solemn deportment of that chief affects me strangely, — his regards, not of an approving kind, are pointed particularly at me. — The sight of the female too, agitates and discomfits me. — Sure I am, Zofloya, that I have somewhere beheld that face."

"It is far from improbable," observed Zofloya.

"But why should she regard me," pursued Victoria, "with looks so hostile and malignant? — why should the chief direct his looks towards me?"

"*Time* will explain all," laconically, though with emphasis, observed Zofloya again.

"But you are not surprized Zofloya; these incidents draw from you no remark."

"I am *never* surprised."

"But tell me at least thy thoughts, I entreat thee."

"*My* thoughts!" said the Moor with a serious air, and looking gloomily upon Victoria.

"Yes — thou takest, methinks, Zofloya, no part in the common occurrences of life — what are thy thoughts?"

"Destruction!" — he returned, in a terrible voice.

Victoria involuntarily shuddered —

"True," — he pursued — "I take no part in the common occurrences of life — *common* occurrences do not interest me. — The dreadful, the terrific, the surprising alone of nature, have power to call me forth, — nor even in them do I mix, unless invited or allured!"

"Oh, Zofloya!" cried Victoria, "wretched and friendless as I am, yet ever to lament that thy converse to me is unintelligible."

"It will not *always* be so, Victoria — but seat thyself here beside me, and let us discourse on other subjects."

Victoria obeyed — for it was impossible for her to resist the smallest proposition of the Moor; — he placed himself near her, and entreated her to partake of the provisions he had brought, but she felt an oppression at her heart, and could not eat. — Perceiving her uneasiness, he passed his arm round her waist, and said —

"Fair Victoria, why this discontent? wherefore this gloom; canst thou not place thy entire confidence in me? — or canst thou not be happy with Zofloya? — say at once, for thou knowest, lovely creature, that we are affianced." —

Victoria started involuntarily. — "Zofloya, what mean you?"

"A truce, fair Victoria, to folly! — am I not thy equal? — Ay thy superior! — proud girl, to suppose that the Moor, Zofloya, is a slave in mind!"

Victoria repented her ill-timed check — she felt herself in the power of the Moor, while his manner, at once proud and imperious, carried with it an irresistible charm, a somewhat that penetrated her heart, and took from her the wish, as well as the power, to offer further reproof.

"Victoria," resumed the Moor, "remember, that I have been thy willing instrument, and that literally I have performed to thee the promises I made."

The heart of Victoria did not assent; she felt that his promises had been fallacious, or indefinitely performed; but still she forbore remark, and he proceeded as though he understood her thoughts.

"Am I to blame, if circumstances operated to make my services unpropitious; have I not sacrificed all future prospects to save thee from disgrace, and accompany thee in thy flight? — Thou canst not be displeased, Victoria, — am I to blame for the unkindness of fortune?"

The speciousness and futility of his arguments were sufficiently evident to Victoria, yet her soul involuntarily became softened. Graceful beauty shone conspicuous in the form of the Moor, and a fascinating sweetness dwelt on his features; — his resplendent, yet tender beaming eyes, sent their powerful softness through her bosom, and her heart dissolved in willing pleasing delusion, delighting to cherish, while it felt its weakness. — A triumphant smile now lighted up the expressive countenance of the Moor; he took her hand, and presssed it to his lips with haughty tenderness.

"Yes, too sure I feel," cried Victoria, unable to contend with the emotions of her heart, — "that for thee, Zofloya, I could at this moment resign the world, — nay life itself! — Yet my soul sickens at the prospect before me, — say, how long must we reside amid this savage Condottieri?"

"Yet awhile, lovely Victoria; — and when thou quittest these solitudes" — he pursued, while his eyes sparkled with more than mortal fire — "Then art thou mine — *for ever!*"

Victoria ventured to look upon him, but did not speak.

"Say, — wilt thou not be mine?" resumed Zofloya — "yet why do I ask — since there is no appeal for thee," he added, with a terrible smile — "thou, in reality, being mine already." — As he concluded, he grasped the hand which he held in his with violence.

A faint exclamation of pain escaped the lips of Victoria, but looking in his countenance, illumined as it was with wild and singular expression, she attributed his violence to uncontrollable ardour, and only smiled. — The Moor seized her in his arms — then pushing her from him, surveyed her from head to foot.

"Yes, yes, — thou wilt be *mine!*" he exclaimed, "to all eternity!"

CHAPTER XXXI

Some time had now elapsed, since Victoria had been the associate of Banditti — the vile and lawless outcasts of society — her constant companion and presumed lover a vile Moor, introduced originally to her notice in a menial capacity. Banished from the world by her crimes, and her vices, and seeking, in the depth of an almost unfathomable obscurity, safety from the punishment their due.

Such was now the situation of one, whose early character and propensities (naturally evil) required in youth the strong curb of virtuous example to reprove, and ultimately reform them. Maternal imprudence, and maternal indiscretion, by destroying the bonds of respect, rendered abortive all future attempt to preserve from baleful example the hopeless victim of premature corruption. — Thus, too, noble emulation was perished, and with the character became identified as cureless habits, errors which time and strict education would have withered in the germ.

In moments of solitude, which occurred but seldom, the wretched Victoria, reflecting upon her early youth, what she *might* have been, and what she *was*, cursed, (terrible to say) the mother that first had weakly indulged, and then, by her own example, tempted and destroyed her.

During the whole of the time that she had resided among the Condottieri, never once had she beheld the countenance of their chief. Yet in her absence Zofloya had said, that he unmasked. "He hath a reason," added he, for concealing his features from you; but time will develope all, and then you will know it."

In manners however, the haughty chief was considerably changed — he seemed to have remarked, and approved the terms on which Victoria and the Moor continued to live; ever delicately respectful in his presence, though incomparably tender at other times, was the manner of Zofloya towards her — the more distant indeed, the more reserved and punctilious he appeared, the more did the chief unbend, and the more appear pleased; but if by a word, or even a look, he expressed aught of tenderness or warmth, then did he become agitated, lay his hand upon his dagger, or start uneasily from his chair. In his voice there was a something that powerfully awakened the attention of Victoria — his manner affected her less for its solemnity, than for other reasons, which she could not define, and she would at times have given the universe for a glance at his features.

As for the mistress of the chief, her manners underwent a considerable change; she behaved to Victoria with civility, sometimes even with attention, but at others, particularly in the absence of the chief, she would regard her with a look that wanted only the *power* of destroying.

The Moor Zofloya occasionally accompanied a chosen troop of the bandit in their adventurous excursions among the Alps; and Victoria could not avoid observing that when he did so, they were such generally as were esteemed most desperate, and were most in repute for their ferocity and contempt of life; such too, as were considered by the rest capable of any enormity, and troubled neither with the weakness of compassion, qualms of conscience, or a distaste to bloodshed; they were, in fact, ruffians rather than robbers, and the blood hounds of the band. — These Zofloya chose to select, when he went forth with any, and unanimously they swore, that when he was among them, they felt impelled to deeds which otherwise would have remained unattempted.

One gloomy evening, seated on the declivity of a mountain, Victoria reflected involuntarily upon this circumstance; — she loved, yet trembled at the inscrutable Zofloya — but lost and abandoned — seeking an object to fix on, she yielded without struggle to his fascinations. — That he loved her, she believed; yet such was the dignity, sometimes haughty repulsiveness of his manners, that even in his softest moods, she watched the turning of his eye with secret dread, fearing and dubious of what the next moment might produce. Never, even had she been compleatly at ease with him; there was always a proud reserve about him, in the midst of his tenderness; — his softness resembled more the condescension of a superior than the devotion of a lover.

"Strange mysterious being," she mentally exclaimed, "thy looks, thy words, thine actions, have ever to me been indefinable. — Better, ah! better perhaps it were" she added with a sigh, "that I had never known thee." — She paused, her ideas reverted to her past life, she retraced its black and disastrous career, — "Ah, mother, mother!" she cried, "all is attributable to thee; why did'st thou, when in early youth, — when my passions were strong, and my judgment weak, why did'st thou imprudently bring before my eyes scenes to inflame my soul, and set my senses madding? — It was thou first taughtest me, to put nor check, nor restraint, upon the incitements of unholy love. — 'Twas thy example too, which caused me to deem lightly of the marriage vow. — Thy heart wandered from its allegiance to thy husband, my heart wandered from mine. — Thy husband died through means of thee, — mine died by poison, which I administered — yet wherefore do I thus retrace?" she added, casting herself upon the mountain, — "do I repent me of that which I have done? No, — I regret only the state to which circumstances have reduced me. — Wretch! that I am, Zofloya, — oh, Zofloya! thou hast helped on my destruction — yet am I now so bound, so trammelled to thee (by what magic arts I know not,) that though at this moment I feel strong wish to fly thee, yet it is counteracted by conviction that the attempt is impossible." She sighed deeply, then in a mournful voice resumed — "Here must I wait thy coming, for into the cavern I will not descend — the gloomy silence of the chief oppressed my soul, while the now cool, now ferocious looks of his mistress, throw my senses into confusion!"

She remained still prostrate on the side of the mountain, till, wearied with grievous and unavailing reflection, she closed her eyes. By degrees sleep stole over her faculties, and she dreamed, that gliding lightly over the highest rocks, she beheld a beautiful and seraphic form approach. — When it came near, it seemed to her that her eyes could not sustain the exceeding brilliancy which shot from the countenance, the hair, and the garments of this celestial vision.

"Victoria!" it pronounced in a sweet and awful voice, "I am thy good genius; I come to warn thee at this moment, because it is the first, for many years, in which a spark of repentance hath visited thy guilt-benighted soul. — The Almighty, who wishes to save his creatures from destruction, permits that I appear before thee. — If thou wilt forsake, even yet, the dark and thorny path of sin, if thou wilt endeavour, by thy future life, to make amends for the terrible list of the past, even yet shalt thou be saved! — But above all, thou must fly the Moor Zofloya, who is not what he seems."

At that instant, Victoria saw beneath the feet of the resplendent vision, the Moor Zofloya — he lay prostrate — stripped of his gaudy habiliments, and appearing monstrous and deformed! — Still she recognized him for Zofloya.

"Attend," pursued the Angel: — "Fly immediately the false pretended Moor, and heaven will direct thy steps. Retire for a while from the world, look into thine heart — *Repent* — and thy sins shall be forgiven thee! — Yet mark!" and loud thunder seemed to rattle from above, — "If thou pursuest thy present path, speedy death and eternal destruction will be thine!"

As the splendid form pronounced these words, the earth opening at its feet, shewed an immeasurable abyss — down headlong it spurned the Moor, who uttering terrific yells, which echoed through the mountains, sunk struggling from view. The celestial vision ascended, pointing, as it rose, its fair finger to heaven. — The awful voice of the thunder solemnly sounded — the dazzled eyes of Victoria beheld the heavens open as the spirit drew towards them; the music of the spheres in loud choral harmony struck for an instant on her ravished ears; her high-wrought fancy could bear no more, and she awoke.

Opening her eyes, she beheld that all around was still and gloomy; yet so far was she still possessed by her dream, that even yet she beheld a stream of radiance in the air, and fancied she could identify that spot in the sky at which the Angel entered its bright abode. Celestial shapes and sparkling corruscations still swam in her view; and when she closed her eyes she saw them with encreased brilliancy in imagination's eye.

By degrees the vividness of these impressions subsided. She felt ashamed to yield observance to a dream, yet still her soul was touched.

"But whither and how can I fly?" she cried; — "yet destruction awaits me if I stay. — Oh, no, it cannot be — I will not yield thus to a vision — a frolic of the fancy, let loose when the senses slumber — and for that to quit Zofloya; — ungrateful Victoria! no, I feel, I feel that to be impossible!"

Scarce had the unhappy Victoria pronounced these words when, darting from a cleft in the mountain, the Moor appeared before her! — even through the dusky gloom Victoria beheld the fire which sparkled in his eyes; his whole figure seemed more proudly dignified, more lofty than ever. — If she hesitated before to adopt the conduct she was warned to pursue, that hesitation now vanished. — She remembered her dream no longer; the presence of Zofloya put reflection and consideration to flight — he took her hand, and in a gentle voice said —

"You would not forsake me, Victoria!"

Victoria started, for this remark implied a knowledge of her thoughts.

"How is this Zofloya?" she said, and faintly smiled: "You seem to read" —

"Your thoughts! fair creature," added the Moor — "and have I not always read them?"

"True, true," aid the embarrassed Victoria — "but how?"

"No matter!" cried the Moor. — "You are mine, I have gained you, and lose you now I neither can nor will. — You do not hate me, Victoria."

Victoria replied not; her thoughts were confused respecting the Moor, and again a sentiment of fear predominated over every other sensation.

"Come," he resumed, nothing checked by her silence, "come, let us remain here no longer, but return to our home; it is more chearful than this gloom, my Victoria, and will disperse thy melancholy."

He passed his arm gently round her waist, and led her on: — though her scruples ceased to occupy her, her heart was oppressed, and she could not speak.

In softest language the Moor addressed her as they walked; by degrees the sweet tones of his harmonious voice, his honied flattery, and soft attentions, produced their wonted effect: — again the changing Victoria began to feel irresistibly rivetted to him, and the more, from the temporary gloom that had affected her in his absence.

"Wert thou always with me, Zofloya," she at length said, in a low voice, as they approached the cavern, "black melancholy and gloomy visions would never agitate my soul."

Zofloya pressed her hand. "While thou livest," said he, "I will remain with thee — and death shall have no power to tear thee from me."

They now entered the cave; in the midst of a few straggling bandit sat the chief, still masked, with his bold companion by his side, showily habited, and looking the wild genius of the terrible abode. The chief sat solemn and reserved, listening, rather than partaking in the conversation of his band. Some of them sat cross-legged, some reclined, talking over deeds of bloody outrage, while the red fire-light cast upon their marked features an additional tinge of ferocity.

Victoria seated herself among them, and the Moor took his station beside her, though at a respectful distance. The chief looked towards them, (not unkindly) but did not speak; his fierce companion scowled upon Victoria, to whose features exercise and agitation had given an unusual brilliancy: — the look, as usual, caused a thousand dim remembrances to rush into the mind of Victoria; — for an instant she almost identified the countenance before her, but, at all events, returned the malignant glance with visible contempt and indignation. Fire flashed from the eyes of the female; she half rose, but the chief, who silently observed both, caught her arm, and restrained her on her seat. At this instant three loud distinct knocks were heard outside the door; one of the robbers started up, and returned them on the inside with the hilt of his stiletto; then sounded, without, the loud shrill noise of the horn, and the robber instantly touching a spring, the door flew open.

Several of the bandit entered; in the midst of them was a female, supported by and leaning on the arm of one of them; her figure, though faded, was still beautiful; her features were haggard and pale; tears streamed down her cheeks, and on her temple appeared a wound, from whence the blood flowed over her bosom, which was bare, and cruelly bruised; her long dark hair hung wild and dishevelled, her clothes were torn to tatters, and one fair arm, gashed at the wrist, hung useless by her side.

This miserable object was led, or rather brought into the midst of the assembly. The chief drew near, and regarded her for a few moments with agitated but stedfast air; then staggering back several paces, he laid his hand upon his heart with convulsive emotion.

"Is it possible?" in a voice of smothered agony, he cried. Hardly had he spoken, when more of the band rushed in, with daggers drawn in their right hands, and securing with their left a man of tall majestic figure, in whose countenance was discernible traces of the deepest rage and the most gloomy ferocity. — In an instant the attention of the chief was attracted towards him; he gazed no longer on the pitiable object before him, but approached, with uneven pace, the stranger thus forcibly secured. — Scarce had he seemed to fix his eyes upon his countenance, ere he recoiled, horror struck! — then hastily returned, and looked again, as doubting the testimony of his senses; now he appeared dreadfully convinced, his whole frame trembled with violent emotion: — madly impelled, as it were, he snatched the stiletto from his belt; he rushed towards the unarmed stranger, and tearing him from the grasp of the banditti with the strength of a raging lion, he buried it to the hilt in his panting bosom!

At this the wounded female, uttering a cry of horror, sunk upon the floor, but, as if new strung by this very circumstance, the chief, with tenfold fury, tore the reeking dagger from the breast of the stranger, and plunged it unnumbered times in different parts of his body! — The band perceiving this unusual and sanguinary violence on the part of their chief, and that he no longer required of them to secure the object of his rage, resigned entirely the hold they had resumed, and retired to a distance.

Exhausted, then, by horrible and repeated wounds, the stranger sunk down, bathed in his blood. The chief bent over him, still gasping with unsated vengeance; he knelt on his mangled form, and with his left hand pinioned him to the earth, then raising his dagger high, transfixed it in the centre of his panting heart!

"Die, infamous and thrice damned villain!" he cried, in a tremendous voice. "Thus die! — for this moment I importuned incessantly just Heaven — and Heaven, in its justice, has at length granted my prayer." — As he uttered these words, he tore off his mask, and throwing back his plumed helm, Victoria recognised — her brother! —

"Now, wretched Victoria," he cried, gazing full upon her, with stern and piercing eyes, "Dost thou know me? — and dost thou know the wretch who lies there weltering in his blood? — Him, who within this instant," he exultingly cried, "has met by *my* hand the punishment his due — dost thou not *know* him? — methinks, unhappy girl, *thou* should'st remember — Ardolph! — the vile Ardolph — the betrayer of thy miserable mother — of that mother, who now lies extended on the ground, in the wretched person of that dying female!" —

Victoria was on the point of speaking, when Leonardo, rushing wildly towards the bleeding body of Ardolph, exclaimed, with a convulsive laugh,

"What! — did the wretch hope to escape for *ever* the vengeance of my soul! — Villain and coward!" he pursued, spurning the body with his foot, "that put thy trust for safety in the weakness of my youthful arm! — did'st thou believe it would remain for ever weak? — and that thy infamy would pass unpunished? — to rob us of our mother — to destroy our father — and to blast for ever the fair honor and the happiness of their children! — Ah, villain and coward! — did'st thou dare to hope that the young and boyish Leonardo would forget thee? — No, no — he, whose soul could feel disgrace and injury sufficiently to fly the spot where it had overwhelmed his miserable family, could never, never forget the wretch who had caused it! — could never forget those accursed features, stamped in indelible characters upon his burning brain! — No, no, I tell thee — nor age, nor time, nor circumstances, could hide thee with a veil so thick that outraged honor could not pierce it! — a Venetian's outraged honor! — For this blessed hour my young heart panted — for this my maturer feelings, encreasing as I grew in bitter sense of the wrong done us, and in desire of revenge, longed with wilder enthusiasm! — For this I implored Heaven, and Heaven," he cried, falling on his knees, while a fierce but noble enthusiasm burnt in his eyes, "Heaven has listened to me. — Father! — my injured father! — *thy* wrongs are avenged!" — He smiled exultingly on the disfigured corpse of the once gay, but now justly punished Ardolph, and arose from his knees.

At this moment the wretched Laurina uttered a faint sigh. Leonardo started, and appeared recalled to himself; he clasped his hands, and tears started to his eyes; he approached his wretched mother, and Victoria followed; between them they raised her in their arms. Leonardo turned fiercely towards the silent, though surprised banditti, who stood around, and in an angry voice exclaimed —

"Which among ye have dared thus to maltreat a female?"

"Not any of us," in one voice, answered the banditti.

"How came she thus wounded?"

One of the band stepped forward, and replied, "We had wandered far, and were returning homewards, when loud shrieks from a distance first called our attention, — we turned again, and hastened to the spot from whence they appeared to proceed; there we discovered him who lies bleeding yonder, cruelly beating this Signora. — On perceiving us, he attempted to drag her forward, — she fell, and cut her temple against the point of the rock; — on this, he redoubled his blows and barbarously kicked her; the Signora must have upon her head wounds more dangerous than that which is apparent: we secured the inhuman Signor, however, while some of our bravos seized the mules and baggage, which were following at a distance — they could not retain possession, however, without encountering the servants and muleteers, whom they soon routed, some one way some another — we then" —

"No more," cried the chief, haughtily — "I have heard enough."

The offended bravo bit his lips, and muttered somewhat between his teeth to Zofloya, who stood beside him, and regarded him with an approving air.

"What! — how sayest thou, villain!" — exclaimed Leonardo, passionately.

"I say we did our duty — and"

"Peace, — base born ruffian!" cried the chief, "I'll hear no more."

The vindictive bravo laid his hand upon his dagger — the action was not un-noted by Leonardo; — he left the feeble Laurina in the arms of Victoria, and rushing towards him, with one blow levelled him to the earth.

"Insolent ruffian!" he cried, "darest thou to rebel against thy chief? lend me a dagger," he called aloud, "it shall drink his heart's blood!"

Seventy hands at once tendered their daggers; Leonardo seizing one, brandished it for a moment over the prostrate robber; — then seeming to consider the object unworthy, checked his rage, and bade him rise.

The wily robber rose upon his knees, and crossing his arms upon his bosom, declined his head in token of submission.

The chief threw the weapon from him with a smile of contempt.

"Thou art unworthy of death from *my* hand," he cried "arise reptile!"

The robber rose on his feet, and joined his comrades with a sullen air.

Leonardo returned to his mother; — he regarded her with an air of pity, and supporting her in his arms, brought her forward, and offered wine to her lips. The wretched Laurina swallowed a little, and it appeared to revive her. — Leonardo then commanded that a bed should be prepared, the very best that the cavern could afford; when ready, with his own hands he endeavoured to render it more commodious, but still it was a sorry couch for one who had till now reposed on beds of down, and made the grievous transition at a period like the present. On this, however, her languid limbs were stretched, — the wounds on her head were bathed, and her gashed wrist bound up. — All these tender offices were performed by Leonardo, while Victoria stood silently by, regarding her wretched mother with a stern unpitying air, or, wholly indifferent to what was passing, conversed with Zofloya in another part of the cavern.

At length the miserable Laurina sunk into a slumber, and Leonardo, quitting then her lowly couch, rejoined his companions. Supper was prepared, and, while partaking of it, those of the bandit that had been out detailed more at large the particulars of the evening's adventure. Little more of moment was, however, related, than what the bravo had already specified; — still Leonardo listened with the deepest attention, making, however, no comment, while Victoria (terrible to say) seemed to exult in the awful fate that had overtaken her deeply punished mother.

The wine passed briskly about — the banditti resigned themselves by degrees to the arms of sleep, reclining round the expiring embers of the fire. — Victoria retired to her usual place of rest, while Leonardo, motioning his female companion to retire, approached the uneasy pillow of his mother with intent to watch beside her during the night.

Thus, by the wonderful and inscrutable ways of Providence, were gathered together under the same roof, those whose fates were so intimately connected with each other. The one suffering under the dreadful visitation of her crime, — her children under its fatal consequences; while the infamous author of all had met, unprepared, the fate due to his guilt, as to his barbarity towards the woman he had betrayed.

Not long had the hapless Laurina retained that unworthy love for which she had made such sacrifices; — the injured Loredani no more, — her son Leonardo fled, no one knew whither, — Victoria eloped from the confinement in which she had been placed; — no further obstacles, no further alarms to encounter, the passion of the ungenerous Ardolph cooled apace, nought existing, nought occurring to give it the required zest. He began to regret that he had resigned his liberty for a woman, whose almost constant melancholy damped his spirits, or whose strained attempts at gaiety but reproached him for expecting the effort. He became first indifferent to, and at length even hated the wretched victim of his artifices; — he retained no longer traces of the fascinating elegant Ardolph, but degenerated gradually into the harsh and savage tyrant. — Grief had stolen the roses from the cheeks of Laurina, remorse had faded her graceful form — she was no longer an object of triumph or of envy, to exhibit to the worthless ephemera of the day, and she was reproached with her broken charms. The gay, the infamous seducer became weary of his acquisition; by degrees he absented himself from her for lengthened periods, — mirthful and joyous when away, he returned to her gloomy and severe. — Next, frequent infidelities struck the barbed arrow of despised love into her soul. — Bitter reproaches, and at length personal ill treatment, even to a degree of barbarity, closed the list of her outrages, and filled up the measure of her punishment and misery!

It was in these dreadful moments — or in those of cheerless solitude — smarting to agony beneath the pangs and indignities of brutal tyranny, that the wretched Laurina reflected upon her past conduct, — upon the husband and the children she had abandoned — upon the husband, the fond husband, that for her had died, —upon her children, hating her and flying from her presence. — Ah, terrible and severe must be the compunctious visitings of the mother, who stepping aside from the path of honor and of virtue, becomes amenable for the distraction and death of a doting husband, for the crimes and miseries of her offspring! Awhile, faintly may you triumph, sad daughter of infamy! — glitter awhile the vain and despised pageant of the hour, but short-lived is your ignoble glory — bitter and premanent your punishment and regret!

Among other vices resorted to by the vile ungrateful Ardolph, was that of deep play. In this he engaged with a spirit of enterprize, so hazardous and wild, that his fortune became rapidly impoverished: — It was the conviction of this that determined him to quit Venice, and retire to Switzerland. — In haughty terms he expressed his intention to Laurina, and brutally added that his exile from the gay world would be pleasing, if unaccompanied by her; but the lost and broken hearted mourner replied not to the insinuation; — to accompany him she felt unavoidable, for spite of his baseness, spite of his inhumanity, she loved him still.

On their journey, notwithstanding, he continued to treat her with the utmost harshness and severity. Not till the period of their encounter on the Alps, however, with Leonardo's band, had he resorted to personal ill usage. Thus did it happen, that his aggravated crimes and cruelty caused him to rush upon his fate, — for, terror for her life, excited by the violence of his blows, extorted loud shrieks from the terrified Laurina; these shrieks attracted and guided the robbers to the spot; the barbarian was immediately secured by ruffians less ferocious than himself, and deservedly met his death by the hands of one, on whom he had entailed misery and destruction! Such are the retributions of a just Providence, which, though sometimes tardy, are generally sure, even in this world.

CHAPTER XXXII

About noon the following day, the wretched Laurina, (who had not, during the night, nor till the present period uttered aught but incoherent exclamations, appearing wholly unconscious, and insensible to surrounding objects) — opened her dim eyes; — they fell first upon the countenance of Victoria, who happened to be standing near her, — she gazed for a few moments — by degrees, weakened memory resumed its power; she identified her daughter, and faintly shrieked! — she passed her feeble hand over her eyes, then raised it trembling to heaven, and extended it towards Victoria.

"Daughter! — beloved daughter," in broken accents she said — "by what chance do I behold thee? — but no matter — I have not time to ask, — forgive — forgive me!"

Victoria answered not, neither did she extend her hand — but the soul of Leonardo was more noble; — he likewise stood beside the death-bed of his mother, though she knew him not; — he bent over her, and took her feeble hand, which had sunk again upon her miserable couch.

"Mother," he cried, glancing angrily towards the cruel Victoria, "Mother, dost thou forget thy son Leonardo?"

The wretched parent turned upon him her heavy eyes; Nature spoke resistless in her bosom, and in the strong marked features, the muscular figure of the chief of a banditti, she recognized the once delicate and blooming boy, that she had nurtured in her bosom! and an anguished sigh convulsed her heart.

"Oh, God!" she murmured, "can this be; — and dost *thou* pardon me — say, dost thou, whom I deserted and abandoned?"

"Mother, as I love and pardon thee, may Heaven look down and speak peace to thy soul."

"Oh, my Leonardo! — thy nature was ever noble, — raise me in thine arms, — beloved — injured son — raise me in thine arms — if — if — thou dreadest not pollution," she added, shuddering violently.

The cavern at this time contained only Victoria and Leonardo; — at the further end blazed a bright wood fire, but still it served not wholly to reveal its gloomy expanse to the dim sight of the expiring Laurina. Near her abject couch, upon a fragment of stone, serving for a table, burned a lamp, which shed its red rays full upon the objects near her, and partially revealed the rude horrors by which her last moments were encompassed. Here plumed hats, here stillettos, swords, and other instruments of murder, hung around; and there the spoils of the slain were scattered in lawless profusion; — the body of the murdered Ardolph had been removed, and cast perhaps — (meriting no other burial) down some measureless abyss, but his unwashed blood still dyed in a dark red stream the flinty ground, while his garments, crimsoned over, and pierced in unnumbered holes by the fierce dagger of the avenging Leonardo, remained awful mementos scattered near.

Upon such a scene of massacre and confusion, Leonardo, in her last moments raised his mother in his arms! she gazed wildly round — but at this fearful moment thoughts of higher import appeared to possess her soul. — Her eyes reverted again towards her daughter, who remained still standing beside her, with folded arms and the stern countenance of a relentless fiend.

"Daughter," — in a hollow voice cried the dying mother, clasping the weak hand, which she could just move, over that which was wounded, and incapable of motion, "daughter, — thy dying mother prays to thee for pardon! — ah, — look not so unkindly upon her, — unbend those stern features — let me not enter the presence of offended God — unpitied! — unforgiven by thee! — Daughter I say — oh, Victoria! —"

A deep and shuddering sigh interrupted further utterance, and she remained gasping in the arms of Leonardo.

"Speak! — speak to thy poor mother, Victoria," cried the superior soul'd Leonardo — hast thou been in thine *own* conduct so faultless, and so pure, that thou should'st deny to thy mother the assurance of love and pardon in an hour like this?"

"Hah! — that is the very point," exclaimed Victoria, with a wild frightful laugh, — "that which I have been, my mother made me! — Mother," she pursued, addressing the anguished Laurina — "why did'st thou *desert* thy children, to follow the seducer, who hath justly rewarded thee? — 'Tis thou who hast caused *my* ruin; on thy head, therefore, will all my sins be numbered. — Can I — oh can I reflect upon my deeds of horror, without arraigning thee as the primary cause? — thou taughtest me to give the reins to lawless passion, — for that I dishonoured my husband; — caused the death of his brother, and murdered a defenceless orphan! — For these crimes — all, all, I say, rising out of *thy example*, I am now a despised exile in the midst of robbers — of robbers, of whom the noble son who supports thee in his arms is *Chief!* — for this" —

"Infamous, abandoned girl!" exclaimed Leonardo, "palsied be thy tongue! — can'st thou, wretch! without one compunctious pang, strew with sharp thorns the dying pillow of thy mother? — kneel, monster of barbarity! kneel and solicit heaven and her for pardon."

The fierce countenance of Victoria relaxed into a smile of contempt, and she remained immoveable.

Laurina still gasped in the arms of her son; convulsive shudderings seized her shattered frame; — her eyes, fixed on Leonardo, beheld his noble features, irradiated with filial love and tenderness. — In the agony of approaching death, she could only grasp his hand, but the grasp spoke eloquent to his heart the anguished gratitude which filled her own! —

once more she turned her piteous looks upon Victoria, who unfeelingly regarded her pallid countenance (rendered doubly pallid by the blood stained bandage which bound her wounded forehead,) but spoke not.

Excess of agony pressed upon the burning brain of the wretched mother; the pulsation of her breaking heart encreased to violence — then it nearly ceased — the film of death crept over her eyes, cold damps bedewed her brows, and in accents scarcely articulate she murmured —

"Terrible — yet just God! — oh, pardon — pardon — *mercy!*"

The last word quivered on her lips — violent and universal convulsion seized for a moment her frame — it was the last struggle of life with death — the struggle ended, life became extinct for ever!

When Leonardo could no longer doubt that his mother had expired, he reclined her gently upon the rugged pillow, now no longer uneasy to the departed sufferer, and kneeling beside her corpse, pressed her cold hand to his lips, and bedewed it with the heart-wrung tears of bitterest anguish.

"Fool!" exclaimed Victoria from the opposite side of the couch — "how can'st thou weakly lament over the death of one who hath made thee what thou now art — the vile chief of a band of robbers? — Let the noble chief weep then — well he may, when he remembers, that instead of being thus distinguished — he should have figured the highest nobleman in Venice!"

"Base obdurate hearted wretch!" replied Leonardo, with dignity, "the vile chief of a band of robbers can lament at once over the *errors*, and over the miserable *fate* of a misguided mother — deeply, too deeply, by the death bed *thou* hast given her, independently of the punishment her errors have received, hath she expiated the wretched delusion of the moment. — Nor wholly on her, abandoned girl, dare to affix thy guilt and crimes — far, far beyond what her example ever taught thee. No, Victoria, thy base mind was naturally evil; — a mother's example might have checked thy depravity, but could never have rendered thee virtuous!"

"But for her," gloomily returned Victoria, "the accursed pleasures of illicit love would never have tempted me to sin — she *first* corrupted and allured my mind — her example opened wide the flood gates of passion in my soul — from its resistless turbulence, bearing down all before it, *first* came my crimes, if crimes they are; and — But who art thou that presumest to reproach me? — Why do I reply to thee? — Did'st thou not attempt to *murder*, in his sleep, the man who never injured thee? — did'st thou not spill the blood of thy sister — did'st thou not forsake thy brokenhearted father? — and art thou not now an outcast of society? — a lawless captain of banditti? lurking amid dreary mountains, to seize as he passes the unwary traveller! — to despoil him of his all — perhaps to kill! — No doubt, many a precipice among these solitudes (safe but for thee and thy horde) hath received the frequent corse of the defenceless, butchered victim! — no doubt —"

"Babbling and aggravating fiend! provoke me no further," cried the enraged Leonardo, starting on his feet.

The horrible Victoria burst into a loud laugh, and flew to the extremity of the cavern. Leonardo's blood boiled in his veins, but he cast his eyes upon his mother's corpse; her livid features, which still wore the cast of anguish, appealed to his heart; they seemed to say — "At such a moment, forbear!" A sacred sentiment pervaded his bosom; by a powerful effort, conquering his indignation, he wreaked not merited vengeance upon a wretch that he remembered was his sister, but turning hastily away, he cast himself across the couch of his mother, and covered his face with his hands.

At this juncture the figure of Zofloya presented itself to Victoria, at the entrance of the cavern; he was unperceived by Leonardo, and beckoned to her with his finger; she flew joyfully towards him: — the Moor received her with a smile, but strange meaning appeared on his features, and he pressed his finger on his lip, to enjoin her silence. Victoria spoke not, for to Zofloya she was all yielding and obedience.

He gently took her arm, and led her from the cavern; they proceeded in silence till they gained the mountain, when Zofloya, desiring her to be seated on a rugged projection, and taking his station beside her, spoke thus: —

"Victoria, thy brother hath offended thee, but ere long thy revenge will be complete! — Dost thou remember the bravo that he struck last night, Ginotti by name? — I stood beside him."

"I remember him well," answered Victoria.

"*I* stood beside him — did'st thou mark?"

"I did."

"Bitter hate, and thirst of vengeance, instantly filled his bosom against thy brother. At the first streak of dawn, he stole from the cavern; sleep had not closed his eyes during the night: he went forth with the resolution of hurling destruction upon the head of his chief, and, rather than not sacrifice him to his vengeance, implicate the whole of his associates. Ere now, he hath given information to the government of Turin, and betrayed the caverned recess, deemed, without clue, impenetrable. At an early hour on the morrow, Savoy's duke will have dispatched a considerable force to Mount Cenis; the avenue from the cavern will be surrounded, and for those within there will be no escape! — Thy brother will fall, perhaps, the first, and" —

"And what will be my fate?" eagerly enquired Victoria, with her usual regard for self, "must I fall likewise, Zofloya?"

"Have I forsaken thee yet?" sternly enquired the Moor. "Return without fear to the cavern; even were the troops already within its walls, I would rescue thee!"

"But wherefore return, Zofloya?"

"I will it so!" replied the Moor, in a loud voice. "Learn to rely upon me even in the heart of danger. — Now let us converse no more," he added, in a softened voice, "upon this subject."

Victoria durst not reply. They continued wandering for a short time among the mountains. Zofloya then caused her to return to the cavern, but, to her infinite dismay, did not himself follow. At the usual hour, still without having seen him, she was compelled to retire to repose, indifferent respecting the fate of others, but tormented with selfish terrors for her own.

CHAPTER XXXIII

It was the hour of noon, on the following day, when Leonardo, who had never quitted the cavern since the death of his unfortunate mother, heard the usual signals for entrance given without.

The band were not often in the habits of returning at this hour; he therefore conceived that somewhat extraordinary must have occurred, and hastened to give them entrance. Several of the robbers rushed tumultuously in, with looks of horror and alarm.

"We are lost!" they exclaimed, in terrified accents, "we are betrayed! — our retreat is discovered: — an armed force now hastens to surround the entrance to the cavern; every avenue of escape will be blocked up; such of our comrades as are out will stand no chance, for they will be secured by innumerable soldiers, awaiting them in ambush; for ourselves, our temporary security will be presently penetrated; we shall all be sacrificed, unless our captain can discover to us any secret paths, by which we may find a passage under the mountains, and evade our foes."

"My brave comrades," returned Leonardo, with a cool and dignified air, "if the case be such as you represent, all is over with us. — I know of no secret paths leading from this cave, nor do I believe there are any, its own concealed and secret situation, its o'er-hanging portico, and labyrinthian avenues, having ever been deemed sufficient protection: — malice or treachery could alone have revealed us; all I can recommend, therefore, is, that we sell dearly our liberty and our lives, and yield not an inch that is not purchased by blood!"

While thus he spoke, the signals from without were rapidly repeated.

"Some of our brave fellows have found means to elude the vigilance of the guards," cried Leonardo. — "Our signal is unknown to any but ourselves — haste and give them entrance — perhaps they bring further intelligence."

At this time the cavern contained only an inconsiderable number of banditti, their chief Leonardo, his mistress, and Victoria, who sat beside her, trembling with apprehension of danger, and dismayed at the non-appearance of Zofloya, whom she began to fear intended to abandon *her* in the common ruin.

The order of Leonardo was obeyed; the signals were exchanged, the door thrown open, when in rushed, to the horror of all, a numerous band of armed soldiers, headed and conducted by Ginotti! the dastard whom Leonardo in momentary passion had struck.

Surprized and shocked, even the brave soul of the chief was daunted! — The soldiers hastened to surround him. — With the pride of genuine nobility, he waved his hand, and instinctively they fell back! —

"But a few moments, Signors," he cried, "and I am yours:" — for in an instant he beheld that resistance against an host would be vain. — "I would but speak," he continued, "a few words to this female, the companion of my fortunes, then will I no longer claim your courtesy."

He approached his mistress, who, more surprized than intimidated, remained sitting beside Victoria.

"Megalena Strozzi!" he exclaimed.

The name in a moment electrified Victoria — she beheld herself seated next a dire foe, surrounded by death and danger! — she looked for Zofloya; he was no where to be seen, and her soul shook within her — she sat in fearful silence, listening to the words of Leonardo.

"Megalena Strozzi!" he cried again; then, lowering his voice, he proceeded, "I will not reproach thee now. — I will not tell thee that thy delusions misled my youthful mind, or have ultimately caused my ruin. — No, I will not tell thee so — for the original cause lies deeper, and more remote! — but look around. — At this moment, oh! Megalena, I consider only the love that I have borne thee, — the years that we have been united, — that thou hast uniformly shared my perils and my miseries,- and at the remembrance, my soul freely pardons whatever evil thou hast caused me! — Yet less lightly wilt thou be judged of by others, and suffer common ignominy with the lowest of our band — a disgraceful death!"

"I have security against *that*," in an agitated but low voice, interrupted Megalena, snatching a stiletto from her bosom. — "I, — but first, thou infamous Victoria! who, in the splendour of youth, crossed my path and robbed me of a lover, thus do I thank the fate which has thrown thee in my power!" — Then springing on the defenceless Victoria, she would have plunged the weapon in her bosom, when suddenly between them stood the Moor Zofloya!

"Victoria is *mine*," he cried in a voice of thunder.

Fired to phrenzy, Megalena, without further hesitation, buried the dagger in her own breast! — "Thus, Leonardo," she exclaimed, "*I* escape an ignominious death!"

"And thus," cried Leonardo, rushing upon Ginotti, and (ere his intention could be surmised) plunging a poignard in his heart, — "thus do *I* reward a traitor, and disappoint him of his expected triumph!"

Ginotti fell, bathed in blood, and uttering hideous imprecations. — The guards hastened to seize the frantic Leonardo, but breaking with the strength of madness from their grasp, he fled to the extremity of the cavern, and before he could be again secured, had given himself repeated wounds with the poignard, still reeking from the heart of the treacherous Ginotti! — Fainting, bleeding profusely, he staggered, and would have fallen; the soldiers supported him in their arms, and some attempted to staunch his wounds, but even in the agonies of death he struggled furiously to prevent them, crying out repeatedly, in broken accents of frantic joy —

" 'Tis too late! — 'tis too late! — Heaven be praised." — He endeavoured to dash himself upon the earth, when finding he was forcibly restrained, and that his strength failed him, he rolled his wild eyes around, as in contempt of their further power, and resigning himself calmly into their arms, expired, with a smile of triumph on his features!

Finding that the chief of the robbers had thus escaped them, the soldiers hastened to secure, with all possible diligence, the remainder of the band. Some approached, and offered to seize Zofloya, supposing him to be at least second in command.

"Oh! we are lost," whispered Victoria to him in accents of alarm.

"Fear not," softly returned the Moor, "but accustom thyself to rely upon me wholly. Signors," he cried, addressing himself to the guards, "retire immediately from the cavern — if you persist in remaining, evil must betide you! — you impede my movements, and will yourselves suffer, — here is my dagger, take it, and be now convinced, *I* meditate not to escape your hands by means of self-destruction."

Selfish terror, or awe, perhaps both, acted involuntarily upon the minds of the soldiers, and they retreated to a distance. Zofloya, then passing his arm round the waist of Victoria, stepped back a few paces. — Suddenly a frightful noise like the rumbling of thunder was heard, — the cavern, and even the mountain itself, seemed to shake to the foundation! huge pieces from the walls, and from the roof, became as it were forcibly disjointed! — the soldiers, frantic from terror, no longer retained their hold of the banditti, but rushed in one common croud towards the entrance of the cavern, pressing tumultuously forward to escape, as expecting to meet death at every footstep! — Even Victoria, though supported by the arm of Zofloya, yielded to the terrible impressions excited by this scene of dismay, — the reiterated shouts of the soldiery, of "An explosion! an explosion!" and the feeling she had of her own inevitable danger; — her senses became over-powered, confused horrors danced in her sight, her eyes closed, and, unable to preserve her fleeting faculties, she swooned. — On recovering, she beheld herself in the midst of a spacious plain, reclining in the arms of Zofloya, and encompassed by myriads of guards — she gazed wildly around — scarcely could she believe that still she existed!

"Oh, Zofloya, Zofloya!" she cried, in a voice of horror, — "where are we? — no longer in the cavern, but in a situation equally perilous; — oh! dost thou not mean at last to preserve me from impending fate? — behold how we are surrounded, — no hope of escape. — Would that, like Leonardo, I had preserved myself from the ignominious death that too well I see awaits me!"

"Wilt thou not trust to me then?" in a terrible voice cried the Moor. — "I tell thee I can save thee from the fate thou dreadest — though surrounded by numbers, we are beheld of none! — Swear then thou wilt confide in me, — trust me wholly, and, in an instant, I bear thee from the midst of them!"

"Oh I swear, I swear!" cried the agonised Victoria.

More swift than a point of time was the transition: — she beheld herself no longer in the midst of armed soldiers, but on the summit of a mighty rock! — Zofloya led her to its uttermost brink; extreme terror filled the soul of Victoria, but she could not speak. — Involuntarily she cast downwards her eyes, — a dizzying precipice, that made the senses stagger, yawned at her feet; far, far in its bottomless abyss, battled the deafening cataract, which, from the summit of the adjacent rock, tumbled a broad tremendous stream, till broken mid-way in its course by some rude projection, it divided into numberless dancing sprays, and branches of foam, uniting again at a considerable distance beneath, and thundering as it fell with resistless fury down the rugged sides of the precipice, whose hollow bosom sternly re-echoed to the mighty sounds.

Victoria trembled, for the spirit of the beauteous Lilla seemed to rise to her view from the depth of the frightful abyss! — mournful it appeared, and mangled with many a wound. — Victoria remembered, that for her she had felt no pity. The images of the dying Berenza, of the destroyed Henriquez, glided before her on the rocky steep — *remorse* filled her guilty soul, but filled it too late, for it came accompanied by *despair!* — In utterable anguish she gazed around, and wildly clasped her hands. —

"Now then, Victoria!" cried the Moor, but not in the gentle voice in which he had been wont to address her — "Now then, thou art emancipated from falling ruins, from hostile guards, from fear of shame, and an ignominious death, — already hast thou witnessed my power, therefore thou knowest what I am capable of. — I have watched thee, followed thee, and served thee until now: — If, then, I save thee for ever from all future accidents — all future worldly misery — all future disgrace; say — wilt thou, for that future, resign thyself entirely to me?"

"Alas, Zofloya!" answered the terrified Victoria, "am I not already in thy power — can I chuse then but be thine?"

"No evasion, woman!" sternly cried the Moor, — "no forced concessions, — hast thou not always promised to be mine? Have I ever," he added, in a softened voice, "have I ever availed myself till now, of that promise which thou madest? — but yet I cannot, Victoria, compel thee, nor, so dearly do I covet thee, will thy forced compliance satisfy me; — say then at once — wilt thou unequivocally give thyself to me, heart, and body, and soul?"

"Oh, yes! yes, for ever!" answered Victoria, rejoiced at even the semblance of returning softness in the Moor, in whose power she so completely beheld herself. — "Oh, yes for ever! but rescue me, I implore thee, at once from this frightful situation, and hereafter thou shalt dispose of me as thou wilt. — Taunt me no more, oh Zofloya! with hopes of safety and of peace, for my soul grows sick within me at the view of surrounding horrors!"

"Yet awhile, fair Victoria! — thou must first swear to abide by what thou hast now said."

"I swear, then!" answered the trembling Victoria.

"And thou hast said it often, rash girl!" replied the Moor, bursting into a loud laugh, and fixing on her his terrible eyes, from whose fiery glances Victoria turned enhorrored! — "Nay, turn not away," he tauntingly pursued, — but look again, and — see to *whom* thou hast sworn!"

Victoria raised her eyes — horrible was the sight which met them! — no traces of the beautiful Zofloya remained, — but in his place, stripped, as in her dream, of his gaudy habiliments, stood a figure, fierce, gigantic, and hideous to behold! — Terror and despair seized the soul of Victoria; she shrieked, and would have fallen from the dizzying height, had not his hand, who appeared Zofloya no longer, seized her with a grasp of iron by the neck!

"Dost thou mark, vain fool!" he cried in a terrific voice, which drowned the thundering echo of the waters — "Behold me as I am! — no longer that which I appeared to be, but the sworn enemy of all created nature, by men called — SATAN! — 'Tis I that lay in wait for frail humanity — but rare, too rarely it is, that by allurement or temptation, I seduce them to my toils! — Few venture far as thou hast ventured in the alarming paths of sin — thy loose and evil thoughts first pointed thee out to my keen, my searching view, and attracted me towards thee, in the eager hope of prey! — yes, *I* it was, that under semblance of the Moorish slave (supposed the recovered favorite of Henriquez) — appeared to thee first in thy dreams, luring thee to attempt the completion of thy wildest wishes! — I found thee, oh! of most exquisite willingness, and yielding readily to all my temptations! — But what hast thou gained? for I have deceived thee throughout; — yet hast thou permitted thyself to be led along! — thou hast damned thy soul with unnumbered crimes, rendering thyself, by each, more fully mine. — Thou hast enjoyed no moment of peace, nor even the smallest of those fruits for which thou wast reduced so deeply to sin! — Thus hath my triumph been richly compleated, thou art at once *betrayed* and *cursed!* and the glory of thy utter destruction is *mine!* — *Thus* then," with a terrible laugh, he pursued — "*thus* do I now perform my promise to thee of saving from future *worldly* ill!" — As he spoke, he grasped more firmly the neck of the wretched Victoria — with one push he whirled her headlong down the dreadful abyss! — as she fell, his loud demoniac laugh, his yells of triumph, echoed in her ears, and a mangled corse, she was received into the foaming waters below!

———

Reader — consider not this as a romance merely. — Over their passions and their weaknesses, mortals cannot keep a curb too strong. The progress of vice is gradual and imperceptible, and the arch enemy ever waits to take advantage of the failings of mankind, whose destruction is his glory! That his seductions may prevail, we dare not doubt; for can we otherwise account for those crimes, dreadful and repugnant to nature, which human beings are sometimes tempted to commit? Either we must suppose that the love of evil is born with us (which would be an insult to the Deity), or we must attribute them (as appears more consonant with reason) to the suggestions of infernal influence.

FINIS.

Appendix A

From Chap. II. *A general description of the Nymphomania, or Furor Uterinus*

By the *Nymphomania* is understood an irregular, and disturbed motion of the fibres, in the organical parts of woman. This disorder is different from most others which are sudden in their attack, and declare, nearly at once, by evident symptoms, all their malignity; the *Nymphomania* on the contrary, lurks, almost without exception, under the imposing outside of an apparent calm, and frequently hath acquired a dangerous nature, when not only its progress, but its beginnings elude our perception. Sometimes the fair one, who is attacked by it, stands with one foot upon the precipice, without suspecting that she is in peril. It is a serpent which hath insensibly glided into her heart; and fortunate must she be, if before it can have mortally wounded her, she should exert a powerful resolution, and flee with speed, from this cruel and destructive foe.

This disorder frequently surprizes the younger part of the sex, at a marriageable age, when their hearts, premature in love, have warmly pleaded in favor of some youth, for whom they feel a desperate passion, the gratification of which is opposed by insurmountable obstacles.

Debauched girls who, during a long time, have lived amidst the disorders of a voluptuous life, are on a sudden, attacked by this malady. This is frequently the case, when an involuntary retreat drives them far off from the opportunities of indulging their fatal inclinations. Married women are not exempted from this distemper, particularly, when they are united either to an husband of so feeble a temperament, as to exact continence in his pleasures, or to a cold mate, but little sensible of the delights of enjoyment.

To this disorder, young widows are frequently liable, especially if death hath deprived them of a strong, and vigorous man, during a commerce with whom, by acts briskly repeated, they had acquired an habitude in pleasures, the delicious remembrance of which too often affects them with that bitter regret, which produces uneasinesses, agitations, and motions at the first involuntary, but which, in the end, soon throw the mind into the most alarming situation.

In a word, all, when once they yield themselves a prey to this disorder, are uninterruptedly busied with equal perseverance and eagerness in the search of such objects as may kindle their passions at the infernal firebrand of lubricity; and if they engage with particular ardor in the pursuit, it is because they are impelled to it, by the natural vehemence of their constitution.

This natural vehemence must be simulated, and increased, when they read such luxurious novels as begin by preparing the heart for the impression of every tender sentiment, and end by leading it to the knowledge of all the grosser passions, and causing it to glow with each lascivious sensation. They also add fuel to the flames which devour them, by learning the most amorous songs: their impassioned voices incessantly accompany the tunes, and words of these which breathe into their souls the poison destined to destroy them.

In their particular conversations with their companions, they are so far from using any efforts to banish the most seducing subjects from their imaginations, that they are assiduous in making them the leading topics. If, in spite of all their art, they cannot prevent the discourse from taking a turn quite opposite to their passions, they sink into languor, and pine under an incurable disquiet, which they have not the power to conceal.

They perpetually dishonor themselves in secret by habitual pollutions, of which they are themselves the unfortunate agents, until they have openly passed the bounds of modesty; but when impudence enlists itself on their side, they are no longer fearful of procuring this dreadful, and detestable pleasure from the assisting hand of a stranger.

Always disposed to listen to the flattering, and seducing compliments of the men who surround them, they shudder at the most trifling employments whensoever they prove capable of turning them, for one moment aside from those lascivious subjects, which are the favorite pleasures of their imagination.

From the walks, where the most innocent sports of nature are, in their pre-occupied minds, the lively attractions of voluptuousness, they proceed to luxurious tables, at which the sharp, stimulating, and poisoned meats give the finishing stroke to that horrible disorder, into which the blood had previously been thrown.

Strong wines with which they are incessantly drenched, spirituous liquors which they swallow, as if they were water, the abused, and excessive use of chocolate;[1] all these articles, (a single one of which is capable of corrupting the animal harmony) when united, impart additional fury to the flames which burn for their destruction; all these throw such sparks amongst the passions, as set fire to the most shameful and unbridled lust.

I grant that all these alarming accidents, of which it is impossible to draw a picture sufficiently hideous, are, at the first, supportable; but the dismal events which they produce, soon become of the highest concern,

---

1 [Note by Wimot, Bienville's translator.] The coloring in one part of this picture is, probably, a little heightened. Wine drank to a certain excess, by a person of strong and lascivious passions, and not accustomed to intoxicating draughts, *may* add fuel to this flame of lust; but in a confirmed habit of *swallowing spirituous liquors like water*, the amorous desires are gradually dying away, and must shortly, be entirely extinguished. This is a truth which I know some husbands do not, and, let me add with inexpressible concern, I fear, some ladies cannot call in question. The immoderate use of chocolate was, in the last century, considered as so violent an inflamer of the passions, that *Joan, Franc. Rauch* (in his *Disputatio*

unless the most prudent means to repress their course, be instantly and earnestly embraced. On the contrary, the women who have neither the resolution, nor the power to turn back, after having taken their first step in this labyrinth of horrors, fall insensibly, and almost without any perception of their conduct, into those excesses which, having wounded their reputation, conclude by depriving them of life.

These sufferers are continually absorbed in the same thought, and their greatest apprehensions are lest they should be withdrawn from it, for a single moment. They dwell only on the fatal object, who is the cause of their disorder; they see but him alone; all the powers of their mind are, as it were, immoveable; they neither perceive, nor understand any thing which passes near them; one principal and sole business engages their attention; they absolutely neglect every other, and even that on which depends the proper management of their family, and, of course, their fortune. Sad, and melancholy, they become fond of repose, and silence; if they interrupt this silence, it is only to talk to themselves. But woe be either to him, or to her, who shall dare to trouble this delightful, still retirement. The violence which they do themselves, by endeavoring to conceal that dreadful flame which consumes them, is the completion of their miseries. But this violence doth not last long.

A beautiful youth presents himself to their view; yet, what do I say? a man, such as they chuse to imagine him to be; for in the whirlwind of flames which compose their atmosphere, the sparks of fire which dart from their eyes may well cast such light and brilliancy over any object, howsoever deformed, as would change *a Vulcan* into an *Adonis*. This man, then, let him be what he will, becomes, in an instant, the object of their desires. They listen with the most eager attention to the slightest flatteries, and even the customary compliments which he pays them are, in their opinion, a train of well-designed seductions. They answer him in a tone of voice, and by gestures expressive of a lively passion; and they consider as serious the usual pleasantries which arise in their mutual conversation. They not only surrender themselves up in the most unresisting manner to those desires, which they imagine that they have inspired; but it more frequently happens, that they outstrip the inclinations of their supposed lover, by an immodestly which disgraces their sex.

---

medicodioetetica, de aëre, et esculentis, nec-non de potú. Viennæ, Austrian, Schilgen, 1622, & 1624. in 4to). Warmly enforces the necessity of forbidding the *monks* to drink it; and adds, that if such an interdiction had existed, the scandal with which that *sacred* order hath been branded, might have proved more groundless. This work is a *rara avis* which is but seldom caught, even by the most indefatigable of the *Virtuosi* in uncommon libraries. It is indebted for its scarcity to an equally singular and ridiculous circumstance. The *monks*, fearful of losing their characters, or, what, perhaps, was dearer to them, their chocolate, were so diligent in suppressing almost every copy, that the *connoisseurs* reckon but five in Europe. W.

This distemper, already too violent, is not yet arrived at its last stage. In each access, it rages with redoubled malignity, and every symptom becomes daily more alarming. The real sensation of pleasures, added to those the different ideas of which are incessantly filling their imaginations, in a short time renders these wretched sufferers furious, and ungovernable; it is then, that breaking down, without the least remorse, the barriers of modesty, they betray each shocking secret of their lascivious minds by proposals, to the expressions of which even ears not uncommonly chaste cannot listen without horror, and astonishment; and soon the excess of their lust having exhausted all their power of contending against it, they throw off the restraining, honorable yoke of delicacy, and, without a blush, openly solicit in the most criminal, and abandoned language, the first-comers to gratify their insatiable desires. Although they meet with a repulse, yet they flatter themselves that they shall conquer, by employing all the arts of seduction. In order to accomplish this point, how wily are the snares in which, by conversation, and by gestures, they endeavor to trepan[1] the objects of their passion? when such advances meet with their deserved contempt, these monsters in human shape abandon themselves to an excess of fury, during which they asperse their despisers with the most unjust reproaches. They pursue them with scandalous accusations, intended to destroy their same; they persecute them with unremitted obstinacy and clamour; and after having by a thousand fruitless stratagems conspired against their peace, and reputation, they violently, and sometimes even without precaution, indulge their vengeance in the perpetration of the most cruel and tragical crimes.

Hitherto, this malady, in how horrible a point of view soever I may have represented it, hath not passed the bounds of a melancholy *delirium*; but we shall soon perceive it raging in all the excesses of a confirmed madness.

It is then, that, as if afflicted with continual symptoms of insanity, they hiss, applaud, deny, affirm, assume ridiculous gestures, throw their bodies into strange contortions, attempt to stimulate the passion of the men by the loosest language, and, to ensure success, affect a disregard for attire, approaching to nakedness, weakly imagining that it will be attributed to their piercing distractions, which, however, are not so artfully feigned as to impose on the simplicity of even the least experienced youth. If, notwithstanding all this, the men should reject their advances with disdain, they will fall on them with the most implacable fury; and so sudden will be the violence of their frenzy, that to find time for an escape from their assaults may scarcely be in the power of those against whose persons they are directed.

---

1 trepan: to snare with a deceptive device

[Source: M.D.T. Bienville, *Nymphomania, or A Dissertation Concerning the Furor Uterinus*. Trans. Edward Sloane Wilmot. London, 1775. Published with *Onanism* by S.A. Tissot in *Onanism / Nymphomania*. New York: Garland, 1985.]

Appendix B: Select Contemporary Reviews of *Zofloya*

1. *Monthly Literary Recreations* 1 (July 1806) 80.

Induced by the puffs so liberally bestowed by some of the daily prints upon this work, we took it up, but without being extremely sanguine of being repaid for our trouble; as the extracts which were laid before us were by no means calculated to impress us with a very high opinion of Rosa Matilda's performance. And, alas! we found that we were by no means mistaken in our anticipations of the little pleasure we should receive in its perusal. Indeed we may safely affirm, that there has seldom appeared a romance so void of merit, so destitute of delicacy, displaying such disgusting depravity of morals, as the present. It is a humble, very humble, imitation of the Monk, possessing in an eminent degree all the defects of that wild performance, but entirely destitute of all its beauties. The Monk, at least, has language to recommend it. The supernatural agent introduced is not unnecessary to the story; in order to tempt Ambrosio, he has great difficulties to encounter. As a contract to the wicked, some virtuous, interesting characters are brought upon the scene—and, though we may reprobate the tendency of the work, we cannot help being attracted by its perusal. Here the language in general is bombastical; new words are introduced, such, for example as *enhorred* and *furor*, the latter of which is certainly used in the language of medicine, but in a sense which delicacy will not permit us to explain. Here the sentences are often constructed in an affected, artificial manner, as to render the sense obscure. Here the greatest number of the characters are so depraved, as to excite no other sentiment but disgust; and there are, in the great number of characters introduced, but three that can be called good, and they are brought forward only for a short time, and then fall victims to the machinations of the guilty. The three good we allude to, are Loredani, Henriquez, and Lilla. For Berenza, the husband of Victoria, before marrying her, makes her his mistress; and that the delicate and feminine mind of the author calls honourable love. The supernatural agent is totally useless, as the mind of Victoria, whom Satan, under the form of Zofloya, comes to tempt, is sufficiently black and depraved naturally, to need no temptation to commit the horrid crimes she perpetrates; and thus Rosa Matilda has sinned against one of the long-established laws of composition.

Nec deus intersit, nisi nodus vindice dignus
Interdit . . . .   HORACE.[1]

---

1 Horace, *Ars Poetica* 1.191 ("Let not a god interfere, unless the difficulty demands his aid").

In short, we never read a more odious and indecent performance than the present; and would advise Rosa Matilda to keep to the humble walk of versifying for the newspapers, and to leave the profession of romance writing to females who possess more delicacy of mind, more facility of style and purity of sentiments, than she, in the present work, has exhibited.

2. *The Annual Review* 5 (1806) 542.

THE principal personages in these wild passages are courtezans [sic] of the lewdest class, and murderers of the deepest dye: shielded by the broad title of a *Romance*, which is ignorantly considered as granting indulgence to every species of improbability, no extravagance of character is too extravagant, to be pourtrayed [sic]; no absurdity of action too absurd to be narrated.

If we are not deceived in our judgment, both the style and the story of Zofloya, are formed on the *chaste* model of Mr. Lewis's "Monk:" at any rate, there is sufficient similitude to warrant the suspicion. Ambrosio falls a victim to the supernatural fascinations of an evil spirit, who to accomplish its purposes, assumes the form and character of such a lovely woman, that not to have been seduced, would almost have been as great a sin, as the yielding to her seduction; and Victoria is urged to the perpetration of every dreadful crime by Satan himself, in the graceful semblance of Zofloya.

We are sorry to remark, that the "Monk" seems to have been made the model, as well of the style, as of the story. There is a voluptuousness of language and allusion, pervading these volumes, which we should have hoped, that the delicacy of the female pen would have refused to trace; and there is an exhibition of wantonness of harlotry, which we should have hoped, that the delicacy of a female mind, would have been shocked to imagine.

3. *The New Annual Register* 27 (1806) 372–73.

This lady, who used to write stimulating love verses in the newspapers under the name of Rosa Matilda, has here composed a stimulating novel after the manner of The Monk — the same lust — the same infernal agents — the same voluptuous language. What need we say more?

4. From *The General Review of British and Foreign Literature*, vol. 1 (London: DN Shury, 1806) 590–93.

This novel abounds with characters of mischief and vice, drawn with little preparation, and employed in adventures which constitute a plot not remarkable for its art nor striking in its management, but so closely imitated from Lewis's Monk, as to force the reader upon a comparison between the two works incomparably to the prejudice of the one before us;—this novel is, notwithstanding, sufficiently striking for its occasional strength of description and exhibition of persons to entitle it to our notice somewhat more fully than those articles which are concisely enumerated in our catalogue.

The author acquaints us that an historian who would wish his lessons sink deep into the heart, in order to render mankind virtuous and more happy, must not simply detail a series of events, but must ascertain causes, follow effects, draw deductions from incidents, and ever revert to the actuating principle of his narrative. Though this introductory declaration is not remarkable for its perspicuity, we think we understand it sufficiently to apply it to the work so prefaced; and from this work we gather that ladies, who marry very young, ought to take care not to fall in love with accomplished seducers; that in case such ladies should run away with their seducers, it will be particularly incumbent on their daughters not to turn out as bad as their mamas; and more especially, if the devil should appear to them in the shape of a very handsome black man, they must not listen to him — for he will lead them from one crime to another, telling them the most horrible lies, and at length, when the crimes and the consequences have arrived at the utmost pitch, he will push them headlong from a rock, or finish their sublunary existence by some equally dreadful catastrophe.

We are well aware that the sublimest efforts of the imagination may be travestied and made ludicrous by a mere verbal effort, denoting very little ingenuity in the writer who may descend to such a performance. Far be it from us to court the smile which might be thus excited. By our present remark we mean to assert that Zofloya has no pretension to rank as a moral work. As a work of imagination or entertainment it will be read with some interest from the immediate incidents and the manner in which they are treated. Its merits as a whole or entire composition are very slender.

[lengthy plot summary omitted]

Thus ends this mass of unqualified vice and unqualified mischief, begun without plan, continued without preparation, and terminated by death in all its several parts, with little of contrast and still less of judicious arrangement. It must be confessed, however, that the author tells her tales of indiscriminate horror in many instances with great force, and if the plot had been more original, we doubt not that this Novel would have obtained an higher rank in the public estimation than it is now likely to acquire.

5. From *Literary Journal*, n.s. 1 (June 1806) 631–635.

AFTER all, it must be confessed that the devil is on many occasions a very ill used gentleman. Notwithstanding the liberal old saying, "give the devil his due," many people act as if they thought that the devil had no right to expect justice in any form or mode. They have, perhaps, been led to think so from the selfish notion that Satan was a very convenient scape goat, and that they might safely lighten the burden of their sins by placing the better part of them on his shoulders. The devil likewise has, no doubt, been a great sufferer from his never having appeared openly in a court of law either as plaintiff or defendant, a circumstance which seems to warrant the idea that he may be libelled with impunity. The fair Rosa Matilda must be of this opinion as she has laid a variety of crimes to the charge of the devil which, it is more than probable, never entered into his infernal brain, or into any other brain but her own. The reader, in order to be convinced of this, has only to attend to the nature of these charges and the evidence by which they are substantiated.

The scene is laid in Venice which, undoubtedly, the devil has often visited in the way of business, and witnessed transactions that astonished even him. Victoria de Loredani was the daughter of a noble Venetian, and was but very young, when her mother thought proper to elope with Count Ardolph, whom it appears she thought a more agreeable companion than her husband. The consequence was that Victoria's father was killed in an accidental encounter with Ardolph in the streets, the latter having plunged his stiletto in the bosom of the former in self defence. Upon this Laurina, like a dutiful mother, took her daughter Victoria to the home of her paramour. In a short time Victoria proved that the example of her mother had not been lost upon her, for she found means to become the mistress of a Count Berenza who was afterwards induced to marry her. Now this Berenza had a brother named Henriquez, whom after mature consideration Victoria thought preferable to her husband. But then she was married, and Henriquez was in love with another woman. The latter obstacle, however, she thought she could easily overcome, if she could only get rid of the former. It so happened that Henriquez had a Moor for his servant who having been missing for some time, was thought to be dead, but who returned again to the great joy of all, but more particularly of Victoria, for she had dreamed that by his means she had attained to the summit of her wishes. Nor were her dreams without some meaning, for this Moor, according to our fair authoress, happened to be no other than Satan himself, who had come to the assistance of Victoria, and had the decorum to lodge himself in a black body, so as to be something in character. Now the first thing to be accomplished was the death of the husband, and for this purpose the devil very civilly furnished a slow poison, which Victoria administered until Berenza died. But her purpose was not yet answered. She found it not so easy to gain the love of Henriquez as she had imagined, and in this dilemma applied to her sable counsellor.

He, ever ready to gratify her wishes, presented her with a drug which was to have the admirable effect of turning the love of Henriquez from his former flame to herself. The expedient succeeded for a short time, but when Henriquez recovered from the effects of the philtre, he stabbed himself with his own sword most tragically. The enraged Victoria upon this sought her rival and murdered her, and to avoid detection fled to the mountains with her close friend the devil. He conducted her to a den of thieves. There they remained till surprized by the troops of the government. The devil, however, contrived to carry her away, and in some retired situation declared to her that he was no Moor, but Satan himself, after which he very rudely seized her by the throat and dashed her in pieces against a rock. This was the more uncivil because Victoria had fallen in love with his infernal majesty, who in his disguise of a Moor appeared to her a very fine fellow. During these transactions the devil had presented her with some roses, and one of the thorns, having accidentally pierced her finger, he with great eagerness applied his handkerchief to the wound in order to collect the blood. He then put the handkerchief in his bosom, which she thought a very gallant proceeding, while he regarded this as a sort of contract by which he should be his both "soul and body," this it seems being his infernal manner of adjusting matters of this sort.

Now like a trusty jury, resolved to presume the very devil innocent of the particular crimes of which he is here accused, till he is proved to be guilty, we must examine the evidence which the fair accuser adduces in order to substantiate her charges against the foul accused. The principal, and indeed the only direct evidence, is her own assertion; but we cannot take assertion without considering what were her means of information, and whether she might not by probability or possibility have been deceived. One is naturally led to ask how the lady came to be so well acquainted with the devil as to be thus let into the secret of his transactions. But be that as it may, we have no doubt she herself, supposing her testimony false, has been imposed upon. Now it so happens, that in such cases, ladies of her description may be, and very often are, imposed upon. The reason is that unfortunately they have the seeds of nonsense, bad taste, and ridiculous fancies early sown in their minds. These having come to maturity, render the brain putrid and corrupt, and the consequence is the formation of millions of the strangest maggots that one can conceive. The truth of this is now so notorious that it would be idle to enter upon any proof of it, however much it may appear to favour the exploded doctrine of equivocal generation. Now the effects of this disease of maggots in the brain are somewhat similar to those of brain fever. The patient raves incessantly, sees things that never were seen before, and says things that were never before said. In short he creates a world of his own, which he fills with everything but what is rational and human. Some of those afflicted with this malady shew [sic] a particular partiality for the agency of the devil, whom they cause to think, speak, and act, in a manner that astonishes the very devil himself. Indeed even Satan must have pitied them if the devil were capable of pity. This, perhaps, may explain the reason why the devil bears so patiently the ill-usage which he meets with from these unfortunate creatures, for he must be worse than a devil that could derive any pleasure from tormenting poor people in their situation. That our fair authoress is afflicted with the dismal malady of maggots in the brain is, alas, but too apparent, from the whole of her production, and therefore there seem to be good grounds for the conclusion that the devil has been libelled, as he has been on many other occasions; that he is guiltless of the crimes laid to his charge, and that the whole originated in the above-mentioned disease. Besides this, it is to be considered that it is quite out of the devil's ordinary course of proceeding to become a retailer of arsenic or any other poison. He is too cunning to do any thing more than is necessary. If he can tempt sinners to deal in poison he knows that this is sufficient, and that the poison is to be had at any apothecary's shop; though he is certainly often charged with the temptation when he has had no hand in it. In addition to this, it seems pretty clear that the devil has too much business on his hands to be able to attend closely for a long time in *propria persona* on one person. This would be supposing the devil to be a fool as well as a knave, which is certainly doing him injustice, for though he is undoubtedly a knave, yet he generally leaves the folly with maggotty-brained ladies. The influence of this fatal malady therefore appears in all its force when we find that the devil is represented as "swimming in the sight of Victoria, as haunting her dreams, sometimes wandering with her over beds of flowers, sometimes over craggy rocks, sometimes in fields of the brightest verdure, sometimes over burning sands, tottering on the ridge of some huge precipice while the angry waters *waved* in the abyss below; as spreading a grey silvery mist around her chamber when she *laid* down and closed her eyes; as holding the thin and spectral form of the orphan Lilla, which seemed arrayed in transparent shade." Instead of crediting this extravagant account of the devil's occupations, one is apt to think of Humphrey Gubbins's cousin Bridget in her romantic fits, and to say with him, "poor creature, how long have you been in this situation."

But the influence of the disease appears not only in libelling the devil, but also in murdering the English language, for how, alas, could the afflicted patient be expected to talk or write rationally? When we hear of "enslaved energies," or mirth being "like the brilliant glare of the terrible volcano pregnant even in its beauty with destruction," of "dreams of mysterious tendency flitting in the distorted eye of sleep," of "images presenting themselves to mental vision," of "boldly organized minds," of persons "capable of deeds which in conception dilated and seduced the soul, but which they could neither comprehend nor identify;" that is, of deeds which could be conceived but not comprehended; when we hear of these and many other things of the same sort, we must wonder at the power of the maggoty disease in applying extravagant language to common things, and in overwhelming all meaning in a multitude of words.

Sometimes, however, we may form a pretty probable conjecture respecting the sense of certain expressions; for instance, when it is said that Victoria "*laid down*," we may suppose that our fair authoress means to say that she *lay* down, or that she laid *herself* down. It is not often however, that in cases of this kind we are so fortunate. But this malady of maggots in the brain is rendered still more dreadful by its being infectious. The ravings of persons under its influence, whenever they are heard or read, have a sensible effect upon brains of a weak construction, which themselves either putrify and breed maggots, or suffer a derangement of some kind. It might be a charitable thing to have an hospital for the reception of these unfortunate people while under the influence of the disease, where they might be confined in such a manner as not to infect others; the incurables beings of course kept separate from the rest. Now it evidently appears that our fair authoress must have been strongly attacked by the disease when she wrote these volumes and treated the devil, English, and common sense so scurvily. But whether she is among the incurables or not time must shew [sic].

Appendix C: Poems from Dacre's *Hours of Solitude (1805)*

1. "The Mistress to the Spirit of her Lover"

THE MISTRESS

To the Spirit of her Lover,

Which, in the phrensy occasioned by his loss, she imagined to pursue continually her footsteps.

Attempted after the manner of Ossian.

The spirit of my lover pursues me in the wild; I fancy to see his wan figure at my side; he follows me, and speaks in a low murmuring voice, His form is habited in robes of mist, and his silvery hair undulates upon the gale.

Oh! my love, let me hear thy voice when I seek repose; let me not, when I close my eyes, lose sight of thy heavenly form. Be present still to my fond view, and let me never miss thee from my side.

Ah! thou dost not breathe; yet sometimes methinks upon my glowing cheek I feel thy breath, but it is cold and damp, not ardent as in the days of our love.

Can I not press thee to my bosom? Oh! miserable mockery! thou would'st evaporate in my embrace.

Yet do not quit me. Thy features are sunk and wan; they diminish to my troubled sight; yet they are a faint resemblance unto the charms of my beloved; and thy hair, which seems luminous, falls over thy shadowy form.

Sometimes thy features seem to waver — it must be in the twilight, when all has a dubious shade; but I cannot always catch those loved features — it appears to me as though they were fading wholly away; but suddenly, by an effort of the imagination, I again identify them, and secretly determine never more to look off of them.

How celestial dost thou appear, skimming over the tops of the hills. A faint moonbeam catches thy robes of silver mist. I respire eagerly the bleak breeze that passes over thy dubious form; I inhale it with ardent, melancholy delight, for it is impregnated with thy spirit.

Soon will this heart of clay cease to beat; then will *my* soul too be free. My body, which is of concentrated atoms, shall lie by thine in the narrow grave, which it will not deny me to share with it; and then together shall our spirits wander over the mountains, and re-visit the scenes of our youth.

2. THE MISTRESS

To the Spirit of her Lover

VERSIFIED

Wilt thou follow me into the wild?
    Wilt thou follow me over the plain?
Art thou from earth or from heaven exil'd?
    Or how comes thy spirit at large to remain?

Vision of beauty, vision of love,
    Follow me, follow me over the earth;
Ne'er leave me, bright shadow, wherever I rove,
    For dead is my soul to the accents of mirth.

Thou formest my pleasure, thou formest my pain;
    I see thee, but wo is my eye-sight to me;
Thy heavenly *phantom* doth near me remain,
    But ah! thy *reality* where shall I see?

In the darkness of night, as I sit on the rock,
    I see a thin form on the precipice brink;
Oh! Lover illusive, my senses to mock —
    'Tis madness presents if I venture to think.

Unreal that form which now hovers around,
    Unreal those garments which float on the wind,
Unreal those footsteps that touch not the ground,
    Unreal those features, wan vision, I find.

Oh! vain combination! — oh! embodied mist!
    I dare not to lean on thy transparent form;
I dare not to clasp thee, tho' sadly I list —
    Thou would'st vanish, wild spirit, and leave me forlorn.

Ah! wilt thou not *fall* from that edge of the steep?
    The pale moon obliquely shines over the lake;
The shades are deceptive, below is the deep,
    And I see thy fair form in its clear waters shake.

Yet ah! I forget, *thou* art light as a breath;
That aerial form, which no atoms combine,
Might dizzily sport down the abyss of death,
Or tremble secure on the hazardous line.

That hand unsubstantial, oh! might it but press
These temples, which beat with the madness of love;
Oh! let, if thou seest my frantic distress,
Some sign of emotion thy *consciousness* prove.

Lo! see thy dim arms are extending for me;
Thy soul then exists, comprehends, and is mine;
The life now is ebbing which mine shall set free;
Ah! I feel it beginning to mingle with thine.

3. THE SKELETON PRIEST;
OR,
THE MARRIAGE OF DEATH

The winds whistled loud the bleak caverns among,
The nightingale fearfully lower'd her song,
The moon in dark vapors retir'd;
When forth from her chamber, as midnight was told,
Irene descended, so fearless and bold —
For love had her bosom inspir'd.

Her white veil it flutter'd as onward she flew,
Not regarding the tempest, tho' harsher it blew,
Nor chill'd by the deep-piercing cold;
The fire of passion that burn'd in her breast
All other emotions disdain'd and repress'd —
For the power of love is untold.

Now sudden a flash that divided the skies,
And struck the lone maiden with awe and surprise,
Illumin'd the desert around;
She saw herself close to a precipice brink,
And as in mute horror she from it did shrink,
"Beware!" cried a terrible sound.

"*Who* bids me beware?" she trembling exclaim'd;
"Say, art thou a guardian who may not be nam'd,
Or was it my fancy alone?"
Again she proceeded, determin'd to dare,
When slowly again cried the voice, "Oh, beware!"
And sunk in a shudd'ring groan.

"What horror this night does Irene betide?
Orlando, my love, I shall ne'er be thy bride;
    This night is the night of my doom.
Oh, spirit of darkness! wherever you be,
I ask but *this* night for my happiness free;
    Let the *rest* be o'ershadow'd with gloom."

Once more she attempted the spot to depart;
She heard not the voice, and light grew her heart,
    No longer by terror subdu'd;
But scare had she taken three steps of the way
When a lady, whose dress was more fair than the day,
    Of a sudden her footsteps pursu'd.

"O be not afraid, lovely maiden," she cried,
"But grant me the favor to walk by your side;
    My road is the same as your own:
The bride of Orlando you hasten to be,
But that is an hour you never may see,
    And 'tis gloomy to wander alone."

"Oh, prophet of woe!" said Irene, "forbear!"
And turn'd to the stranger with looks of despair,
    But enhorror'd withdrew from the sight:
A mouldering skull in her hand was display'd,
With a lamp the red blood on her bosom betray'd,
    And chequer'd the earth with its light.

"You start, lovely maiden! What folly is fear!
And what in this skull can so hideous appear,
    Since you may resemble it soon;
Unless you consent to be guided by me,
Return to your home, live contented and free,
    Or you journey *may end in the tomb*."

"No, never, while life in this bosom shall reign,
Will I treat my fond love with such cruel disdain,
    Or deny him my husband to be:
This night will I *wed* him, in despite of fate,
And fly with him, too, wheresoe'er he dictate,
    Whatever the sorrow to me."

The stranger sigh'd deep as in autumn the wind;
She turn'd her pale visage, so sad and resign'd,
    On Irene, and shuddering said,

"*Orlando is wedded.* This night, to be thine,
He committed on heaven and nature a crime
     Which in vengeance his soul must be paid.

"Still art thou resolv'd thy fond vice to pursue
In vain, for Orlando is hid from thy view,
     And wanders despairing alone:
His crime is his torment; by demons possess'd,
He gloomily wanders, depriv'd of his rest,
     In a desert by mountains o'ergrown.

"Then court not perdition; take homeward thy way,
Alone let *me* wander, alone let *me* stray,
     Or dread the reward of thy crime:
Forbear thou the union *cemented by blood*,
A *bond* of destruction to lure thee from good;
     The murderous compact resign.

"*Return*, and the past but a vision shall seem,
Appear on the morrow no more than a dream,
     Forgot in the glories of day:
Proceed, and before a short hour is told
Again, to your horror, you shall me behold,
     Your *blood as the forfeit to pay.*"

"Your name!" had Irene but faintly exclaim'd —
The stranger had vanish'd; no traces remain'd;
     The silence of *death* was around;
The wind had subsided, the moon now appear'd,
Its beauteous refulgence the nightingale chear'd,
     And again did her harmony sound.

"Who dwells in this forest of gloom and despair?"
Cried Irene — "What horror impregnates the air?
     Do demons assemble to sport?
They envy those raptures they cannot divide,
The rapture to be of Orlando the bride,
     And this is their infamous court.

"They mock at my feelings, they laugh at my pain,
But all their delusions they essay in vain —
     Orlando, *I still will be thine!*"
Then onward she sprang. At the foot of the hill
Orlando impatiently waited her still,
     And their arms in fond rapture entwine.

But the arms of Orlando than ice were more cold,
As in them Irene he seem'd to enfold;
    His features were hid from her view;
His voice seemed hollow, he mournfully sigh'd;
A chilling despondence crept over the bride,
    A mistrust that she dar'd not pursue.

"Orlando, what demons have lurk'd in my way
Thine Irene from all that she lov'd to delay,
    And say thou wert wedded from me?"
"No more, fair Irene! The hour is right;
"I little expected thy presence to-night:
Our wedding shall speedily be.

"Behind this green hill, just close to the beach,
Is a vessel in which our castle we reach,
    Now gloomy, and anxious for *you*.
Come, quickly depart — time onward does fly;
Since here you have ventur'd you must not deny."
    And forward Irene he drew.

Now approaching the beach, lo! a vessel was there;
Of mist seem'd the cables, the sails vapors fair,
    No creature to guide it was nigh;
Orlando took charge of his terrified bride,
It seem'd like an arrow the waves to divide,
    And swifter than fancy to fly.

Now reaching the opposite shore, he convey'd
From the vessel of shadows the heart-frozen maid,
    When instant it faded from view:
He forc'd her still on through a rocky descent,
Her feet and her bosom were cruelly rent,
    And blood did each footstep pursue.

They enter'd a cavern: an altar was there;
A priest to unite them does slowly prepare;
    Their hands are together entwin'd;
When *casting* his robe, lo! what horrors beneath!
The *skeleton priest* was no other than *Death*,
    Whom the maiden in marriage had join'd.

"Thou art wedded, but *not to Orlando* — behold!
For, maiden, thy love was imprudent and bold —
    Thou art wedded, and must to *my* home.
Orlando no longer — dissolv'd is the spell;

Thy nuptial rejoicing must be a death knell,
    For thou art the *wife of the tomb.*

Irene, despairing, remember'd the wood —
Before her the spectre now menacing stood —
    "The wife of Orlando was *I*;
He sent my soul wand'ring, thy beauties to gain;
I warn'd thee, alas! but I warn'd thee in vain,
    For *thou* wert determin'd to die."

Alas! sad Irene no more can depart;
The numbness of death slowly crept round her heart,
    And, palsied, her nerves seem'd to shrink:
The *skeleton priest* now approach'd them again;
He seiz'd on the victim — her struggles were vain —
From the world, lo, together they sink!

4. "To the Shade of Mary Robinson"[1]

How sadly, sweet seraph, I mourn that I never,
    I ne'er was so happy thee living to know!
How sadly I mourn that the time is gone ever!
    And the wish of my bosom must end in vain woe.

How sadly I mourn, lovely seraph, while thinking
    That now, in the cold gloomy night of the tomb,
Thou know'st not one heart for thy sorrows is sinking,
    One heart that bemoans, with regret, thy sad doom.

How oft, too, I mourn that an heart form'd to love thee —
    An heart which responsive had beat to thine own,
Can from thy cell narrow now never remove thee,
    Where tranquil thou liest, unconscious and lone.

---

1 "Mary Robinson": Mary Robinson (1758-1800) was a prominent poet, novelist
   and republican feminist writer who was associated with Mary Wollstonecraft's
   political circle as well as the Della Cruscan poetic circle, and a regular contribu-
   tor to *The Morning Post* (as was Coleridge) in the days when it was a pro-reform
   paper (before Nicholas Byrne took over. Robinson had led a sexually scandalous
   life, having been the mistress of the Prince Regent, which, in combination with
   her radical feminism and republicanism, made her the object of much public
   conservative scorn, including pornographic satire.

Oh, world, cruel world! how I shrink, how I tremble
    An angel so gracious should be so forlorn!
Oh, world, cruel world! there is none that resemble,
    Among you, an angel like her that is gone.

Like a cedar amid the rude desart high soaring,
    And looking contempt on the shrubs that surround,
Enduring for years the tempest loud roaring,
    And scorning to yield until *broke to the ground.*

Ah! then, with what joy, ye shrubs so presuming,
    Ye rustle and wave o'er the cedar's *proud* grave!
But degrading your safety, and mean your assuming,
    Adversity's storm only buffets the brave!

Oh, thou! whose high virtues, angelic, yet glorious,
    At once move my wonder, my pride, and my tears,
Still, still in the grave dost thou triumph victorious,
    Thy fame sounding loud in thine *enemies'* ears!

The wretches, who envied, who fear'd thy perfection,
    O'er the threshold of life drove thee trembling away,
Shall yet shudder and sicken, when harass'd reflexion [sic]
    O'erwhelms with remorse the retributive day.

Oh! say, from thy cold, narrow, bed, lovely Mary,
    Say, couldst thou not wander, to smile upon me?
Oh! why not, sometimes, in thy form light and airy,
    Deign in the deep wild my companion to be?

Oh! why not, sometimes, when I wander in sadness,
    Glide distant before me — seen dim thro' the trees?
Or how would my heart bound with mystical gladness
    If thy *voice* were heard, sounding sweet in the breeze!

Or why not, o'ershadow'd by yon drooping willow,
    At eve let me mark thee reclining beneath?
Or by moonlight upborne, on the edge of the billow,
    Fantastic, and light as of zephyr the breath?

Ah! around thy sad tomb not a weed gaily flaunting
    Could Matilda's devotion permit there should be;
But vile weeds thy path were *once* cruelly haunting,
    To blight the fair rose that they sicken'd to see.

Yet the thorns of contempt, with mild dignity arming,
    Kept aloof the base upstarts that sought to molest:
Contempt is to cowards the power disarming,
    Turns each shaft to a feather, each sting to a *jest*.

Then grant, O great God! since to Mary 'twas given
    Most perfect among erring mortals to be,
That chief of thy slaves she may serve thee in heaven,
    And bear, when I die, my frail spirit to thee.

The
DÆMON OF VENICE,
An Original
ROMANCE.

Tegg's Edition

The Dæmon precipitating Arabella from the Rock

LONDON:
Pub. by Tho.ˢTegg, 111, Cheapside.

1810.

Courtesy of the Special Collections Department, Temple University Libraries, Philadelphia. Note that the first page of the chapbook spells the title "The Demon of Venice."

Appendix D

THE

DEMON OF VENICE

A ROMANCE

BY A LADY

The Marchese di Lenardi having been married sixteen years to Lucretia de Ponari, had two children within two years after their union. These youthful parents little comprehended the extent of the mischief they were doing; they would not suffer the fair faces of their dear children to be disfigured by tears or vexation; the consequence was that Arabella, at the age of sixteen, though beautiful and accomplished, was proud, vindictive, and cruel, always bent upon gaining the ascendancy in whatever company she was. Orlando, who was a year older than his sister, was equally the victim of an injurious fondness; like her, he was violent and haughty, but at times capable of sacrificing himself to a sentiment of gratitude.

On the birth-night of Arabella most of the nobility of Venice were assembled at the pallazzo of her parents; among them was a young gentleman of rank and fortune, who was a German by birth. Count Jaques, for that was the name of this nobleman, had been banished by the Marchese di Lenardo to stay a month. After a few days Lucretia perceived that his guest was more inclined to be melancholy and serious. One evening as she was pensively walking down the garden she suddenly beheld Jaques before her pale and dejected. Looking tenderly at him she asked in a soothing voice if he were ill? He immediately threw himself at her feet, and declared his ardent passion for her.

For some time Lucretia stood amazed, at last exclaimed, "My husband!" and made an attempt to disengage herself from the Count, who was pressing her hand with all the ardour of affection.

"Oh, my dear Lucretia," said he, "you must be mine! I adore you, and if you will not consent, I shall kill myself."

"Hush!" replied Lucretia, in a faltering voice, and looking wildly at him, hastily snatched away her hand from the deluding Jaques. She flew from his presence, and in the solitude of her chamber gave vent to her emotions.

Jaques availed himself of every opportunity to see Lucretia by herself, and at length succeeded in winning the heart of the once affectionate and faithful wife of Lenardi. Resolving to have her wholly to himself he assured her that it would be adding to her guilt in a most abominable degree to remain under the roof of him who could no longer call her his.

"Oh no, no!" answered the wretched wife; "leave me for ever, cruel Jaques! Here will I die, the victim of the most infamous of crimes!" The artful Count now took her hand, and vowed that as long as he lived he would adore the woman who had suffered so much for his sake.

"My children! oh, my children!" cried the agitated Lucretia.

"May those children," exclaimed Jaques, looking up to Heaven, "perpetrate my destruction, should my heart ever become cold towards their mother. Dear Lucretia, I will take care that every thing shall be ready this night for our departure." He partly acted as he had promised, for preparations were made, and he bore away his victim from the arms of her husband and the embraces of her children.

Who can describe the vexation of Lenardo when he discovered the villainy of his friend and the infidelity of his wife. He now beheld himself the only guardian of the forsaken children; but scarcely had he recovered from his alarm when he heard that Orlando, his son, the pride and heir of his house, had, as soon as he was told of the flight of his mother, rushed from home and never could be found. Every friend was questioned, and day after day elapsed, but still he came not.

Arabella was now the idol, the only hope of the Marchese. A year had elapsed since the departure of Lucretia, as, when Arabella was silently sitting by the side of her sorrowful parent, "Why," he affectionately said, "why do you debar yourself of pleasure to sit with me? Why do you not invite your friends, and visit them in return?"

"Because," Arabella returned, "they will not come."

"Why?" enquired the Marchese. "My mother has disgraced us," replied the unfeeling daughter.

The wretched father sprang from his seat and rushed out of the room. He had wandered about till the cool breezes of night came on. He beheld a man wrapped in a cloak before him; the Marchese looked at him with dread; he thought that in the stranger he beheld the villain Jaques, who had blasted all his happiness. Not knowing what he did, he pursued the person, and tearing off his cloak discovered the wretch whose very name filled him with horror.

"Draw monster and defend yourself!" exclaimed the husband, snatching his stilletto from his bosom.

"I have no sword," said the Count; "but I have a stilletto." The Marchese struck at him with great fury. The indignant Count plunged his dagger into the breast of the unfortunate Lenardo.

As soon as the Marchese fell Jaques concealed his stilletto and hastened to the spot. There, weltering in his blood, the injured Marchese might have remained to die, had it not been for the arrival of some passengers, who, knowing his rank and residence, took him to the pallazzo.

The surgeon who had been called in dressed his wound, and at the earnest enquiries of the Marchese felt compelled to pronounce it mortal.

"Let my daughter be sent for," said the Marchese. Arabella was called; she entered the chamber with slow and trembling steps, then gazed upon her ghastly father with horror and regret — horror at the situation in which she saw him, and regret at the thought of having given him a few hours before a pang so deep. "Oh, my child, my Arabella," he cried, "I am snatched from thee at a time and season when least thou canst afford to lose me." He stretched out his feeble hand; she took it, and, pressing it to her bosom, fell upon her knees.

"Ah, my dear girl," he continued, "correct, if possible, the errors of your disposition."

Overcome with pain and weakness the Marchese suddenly stopped. It was now past midnight; a pale lamp emitted its faint rays over the spacious chamber, and shewed Arabella the pallid features of her father; the gloomy silence was only interrupted by her sobs. "Oh, my Arabella!" he faintly said, "you will be left unprotected!" and a deep sigh rose from his heavy heart.

The door of the apartment suddenly flew open and in rushed the unfortunate Lucretia. "Oh heavens! do I behold her again — no, no, it cannot be! Oh, can death be so near!" cried the agitated Lenardi.

"Oh my husband! my injured husband! I implore your forgiveness! Curse me not with your last breath." So saying the frantic Lucretia threw herself prostrate on the ground by the side of the bed, where her dying husband lay.

Lenardi raised his head upon his hand, he looked upon the prostrate wretch beside him with the look of a pitying angel, then waving his hand to Arabella, he said, "Retire, my child, for a moment."

When the daughter withdrew, "Lucretia," said he, in a low solemn voice, "arise." She raised herself on her knees, but covered her face with her hands. "Lucretia, look upon me," continued he; the eyes of his guilty wife met his; then taking her hand he proceeded — "It is yet in your power to repair, in some measure, the evil you have done. When I am hurried search for your son, who left his home as soon as the discovery of your flight was known. If you should prove successful retire with your children far from Venice."

"Oh!" cried the wretched Lucretia, "I will."

"Let my Arabella now enter," said the Marchese, almost breathless; "I have not long to live."

Lucretia rose and told Arabella to come in. As she approached, "be quick my child," cried Lenardi, "and embrace your mother. Lucretia, now swear to protect your daughter, and in future to set her a good example."

"I swear!" exclaimed Lucretia, and pressed her daughter to her bosom.

"Arabella, do you promise to forget the errors and imitate the future virtues of your mother."

"I promise father," answered Arabella. "Oh heavens! I thank thee!" gasped the dying Marchese. "I forgive you, my dear wife, and die content." Lucretia wept bitterly over the dead body of her husband.

Jaques, it seems, had been obliged to return to Venice upon business; he took a lodging under a feigned name, hoping in this manner to remain undiscovered. When he left the wounded Marchese and hastened home, Lucretia was astonished at the sternness of his countenance, and his unusual seriousness of manners. She approached, and tenderly taking his hand, enquired if any thing had happened. "Yes, Lucretia; but before I tell you, only say you will not hate me."

"Hate you!" passionately echoed this deluded woman. "Oh, my dear Jaques, though you had committed murder, I could not hate you."

"Murder!" returned he gloomily, "I hope not; but I certainly have wounded your husband."

Lucretia screamed aloud; she flew from the presence of Jaques, and hastened to her injured husband, as has been already related. Jaques was determined to try every method of recovering Lucretia. He immediately disguised himself, and walked towards the pallazzo. It was the second day after the death of Lenardi. He knocked at the door, and as soon as it was opened, put a letter into the servant's hand, desiring him to give it to his mistress directly. Lucretia was lamenting the loss of her son, when Orlando, at the very time that the domestic entered with the letter. She opened it and read as follows:

"Dear Lucretia,

"It will not be fit for you to remain here and act as the wife of the deceased Lenardi. The proud relatives of the Marchese will never look on you more. You will be thought the most infamous of women; therefore I would recommend it to you to depart from the hateful place as expeditiously as possible with him, who still remains,
"Your faithful admirer,

"JAQUES."

As soon as she read the letter she put it on the table, and, flinging herself into a chair, said, "What, what am I to do?" She covered her face with her handkerchief, and sobbed out, "Oh my daughter! my Arabella!" She was disturbed by a servant, who told her that the messenger had been waiting ever since for an answer. She then hastily wrote as follows:

"Jaques, or cruel Jaques!

"Dare I acknowledge that I still love you, a seducer and a murderer! Oh horrible! But my determination is fixed — I will never see you again. With Arabella, the innocent sufferer for her mother's crimes, it is my intention to quit immediately the roof under which I am, and shall retire for some time into a remote province; and when the remembrance of my infamy has ceased, I may again endeavour to mix with society, not for my own sake, but for the sake of her, my dear daughter, whom I have so cruelly wronged.
"So farewell ever,

"LUCRETIA."

Having dispatched these few1 lines, the weeping matron began to p.. pare for her journey. Scarcely had an hour elapsed before the same messenger returned with another letter to the following purport:

"You would retire from Venice with your daughter! Mark me, Lucretia, do not trifle with me; I shall expect that you will this night leave your present above, and bring with you Arabella. On the canal opposite your window I shall wait your coming. You must go with me to Montebello, the villa which I hired on my arrival here. The situation is retired and distant from the city. There we may remain free from suspicion; for it is still the general opinion, that the Marchese met his death by the hands of bravoes. Lucretia, never think to escape from one who loves and watches you.

"JAQUES."

The almost heart-broken Lucretia now hastened with her daughter to meet her seducer. They soon arrived at the villa, and day after day the frail Lucretia still loved more and more the murderer of her husband! Jaques no longer liking his retired situation was resolved to keep company. Montebello was only a few miles distant from Venice. Among the gay Venetians who frequented their society was one called Count Amiens, an extraordinary character. He remembered the once virtuous wife of Lenardi, but now looked upon the false Lucretia and her paramour with contempt. Yet he regarded with eyes of no common interest the young Arabella. Pride alone forbade his soliciting her hand, for never yet had Amiens beheld a female, whose character was, in his opinion, formed to constitute his happiness. So ardent in his admiration was the misguided philosopher, that the more he saw Arabella the more he was alarmed. He was determined to try every method to induce her to become his mistress, and therefore resolved to seek the earliest opportunity of obtaining a private interview with her. An opportunity soon presented itself, and having declared his passion for her, he delicately but frankly prepared to her the plan on which they should live together as man and wife.

This being the first lover that Arabella ever had she thought within herself, "My other lives happy with Count Jaques, and so may I with Count Amiens."

Impressed with this idea she gave him her hand, he ardently seized it as the earnest of consent, and seating himself by the side of his intended mistress, who smiled with unusual joy, began to arrange the means by which they should quit Montebello unexpected. Arabella listened with pleasure, and even hinted that they should lose no time. He rose and tenderly embraced her.

At this critical moment in rushed the half frantic Lucretia. "You insolent girl!" she exclaimed, seizing with violence the arm of Arabella, "is it thus you recompence my indulgence! is it thus you reward the fond, the foolish confidence which your mother has ever placed in you? And you,

Signor Amiens, are not you a monster, a villain, thus to blast my only happiness by seeking the ruin of the innocent Arabella?"

"Indeed, madam," replied Amiens, with a scornful smile, "you are well qualified to arraign those who trample on the rights of hospitality."

Arabella gently withdrew her hand from Amiens, and walking up haughtily to her mother, said, "I am resolved to leave this house immediately."

"Oh, my child! my child!" cried the distracted Lucretia, almost sinking to the ground, "would you then abandon me?"

"You abandon me, my brother and my father," sternly replied the unfeeling Arabella. "Oh my child! my daughter! this from you —."

"Yes, you have eternally disgraced me;" and, she added, "no one thought me worthy of their esteem but Count Amiens; therefore I will accept his kind offer and be happy. Why should a mother's permission, who, while a married woman, loved Count Jaques, and fled with him, regardless of the misery you brought upon my father —."

"Cease, ungrateful girl, cease, for heaven's sake!" cried Lucretia in agony. "Let me then depart with Count Amiens; recollect it is your fault," continued the undutiful girl, "that ever I saw him. Had you kept the promise which you made to my father when on his death-bed ——."

These reproaches from a child were too much for the guilty Lucretia to endure; she interrupted her daughter by a scream and sunk upon the floor in strong convulsions. Amiens, who at first listened with pleasure, was now surprised at Arabella's cruelty. He now approached and raised the wretched Lucretia from the ground. On her recovery he respectfully assisted her to her chamber, and whispering Arabella in a serious tone of voice to be more tender hearted to her mother, left them together.

The gloomy countenance of Amiens and his altered air, as he waved his hand to Arabella when departing, had not failed to make a strong impression on her mind; her vivid imagination easily led her to trace the occasion of this sudden change in his behaviour. She saw that her unkind language to her mother had excited his disgust. Alarmed at the idea of becoming indifferent to him, she instantly determined on regaining his esteem. Approaching her distressed parent the artful girl thus addressed her, "My dear mother, be comforted." The weeping Lucretia then took her daughter's hand, and bathed it with tears. "Ah, my dear child," she cried, "retire and promise me never to see that man again."

As soon as Arabella left her she flew instantly to Jaques, and with many tears related to him the disagreeable circumstances which had taken place. She declared she would quit him the next day, and retire at once with Arabella to some seclusion, which, experience now convinced her, she ought long since to have courted.

Jaques listened without interruption, and when she had finished her story, with tender seriousness remarked, "It is hard that we should be made unhappy through an imprudent forward girl. My dear Lucretia, listen to what I have to propose, and let Arabella, as she ought, reap the fruits of her audacity. It would indeed be easy for me to forbid Count Amiens the house, to imprison your daughter in her chamber, and thus prevent them ever seeing each other. But I shall act more prudently and less violently. It is most probable that Count Amiens has never had occasion to correspond with Arabella; he is therefore ignorant of her handwriting — do you then draw up a few lines to the following effect:

"Dear Amiens,

"Owing to the unhappiness of my mother I have agreed to deny myself for a little time the pleasure of seeing you. I beg of you to return to Venice for awhile, when the effect produced by present circumstances shall in some degree have abated. I will instantly write to you to return."

"Let these lines," continued Jaques, "be immediately conveyed to Amiens. The instant he departs for Venice Arabella shall quit this abode."

"Oh heavens! interrupted Lucretia, "without me do you mean?"

"I have thought of an excellent scheme, my dear Lucretia; we will both accompany her to your cousin, the Signora di Tabetha. In our excursions last year we made a short stay there you know, and were very well received; no place can be more retired."

Lucretia now wrote the letter which Jaques had dictated, and it was given to a female servant to be given to Count Amiens; she was desired not to wait for any answer.

The next morning Lucretia entered the bed-room of her daughter, and informed her in a tone of affected surprise of the departure of Amiens.

The haughty Arabella was mortified at this intelligence; rage flew into her face, and looking fiercely at her mother, she said, "I am sure he did not willingly leave me; I dare say he has been driven from the place, but I shall soon know; if he went of his own accord, he will take no measures to see me; but if he has been banished from hence he will write to me, and inform me of the truth."

"Certainly," said Lucretia, who, as she had been advised by Jaques, gave way to her daughter; "I dare say you will receive a letter; in the mean time to amuse ourselves we will take an excursion somewhere. Arabella almost believed that her mother was serious from the innocent manner which she so well assumed. "When are we to go then?" she enquired.

"We shall depart immediately, if you have no objection," returned her mother; and taking her by the hand, she continued, "it is the wish of Count Jaques that we should pay first a visit to the Signora di Tabitha at her delightful retreat near Treviso."

"What to that formal disagreeable old woman," muttered Arabella.

"Hush, my love, recollect that she is a relation; we shall only stay there a few days. I am now going to make preparations for the journey; do you also get ready, my dear girl."

On her mother's departure Arabella mused — she then said to herself,

"Surely Amiens has never left me of his own accord; no, he would have told me the reason. It must be some wild scheme of my mother; but time will reveal the truth.

She had just prepared her things when Jaques and Lucretia entered the room. "Are you ready?" said the Count.

"Yes," answered Arabella.

"And so are we," rejoined Jaques, taking her by the hand, which she hastily withdrew, and followed them in sullen silence.

The coach was waiting for them; their journey was so long and tedious, that they were not sorry when they reached the spot. Jaques was received very friendly by the old dame, but Lucretia and her daughter met with a very indifferent welcome, as Signora di Tabitha had heard of Lucretia's elopement from her husband.

As soon as Arabella had left the room to go to rest Jaques informed the old lady of the cause of their visit, and advised her if Arabella, on their departure, behaved unruly to confine her to her chamber.

"Oh, but madam," interrupted Lucretia, "use her not unkindly; she is not used to harsh treatment."

"I shall act towards your daughter," replied the old lady, "as a good christian, for I shall endeavour to save her soul."

The next morning at sun-rise[1] Lucretia and Jaques departed for their home, while Arabella remained wholly unconscious of what was passing. At ten she rose with more spirits, imagining she should soon leave the hated place; but how was she surprised and disappointed at not seeing her mother.

"What! has not my mother yet risen?" she enquired in a polite manner.

"Oh yes," said the Signora, "some hours." "And where is she?" eagerly enquired Arabella.

"Gone!" said Signora, with a malicious smile. "Gone!" echoed the affrighted girl. "Good heaven! and has she left me here?" "Well! is there any thing disagreeable or horrid in keeping me company for a few months?" said the Signora harshly.

"Cruel, cruel mother!" exclaimed Arabella, "I shall remember this." She now rushed out of the room and sought her chamber, where she gave full vent to her grief.

When the clock struck one she was resolved to go to dinner, as she felt rather sick, not having had any breakfast; but to her greater vexation, she found the door locked on the outside. She could scarcely contain herself. In about a quarter of an hour it was unlocked, and a short girl made her appearance with some bread and water.

---

1 sun-rise: The text reads "sun-set," but an unknown hand has corrected the chap-book to read "sun-rise."

"For whom is this?" enquired Arabella. "For you, miss," answered the girl. "What have I done to merit such treatment?"

"I don't know, miss, but I heard the Signora say that pride must be brought down."

"You may tell your mistress," said Arabella, burning with rage, "that she need not trouble herself in sending up such scanty fare, for I would sooner starve than eat it."

The girl immediately delivered her message to the Signora, and likewise told her that the young lady looked exceedingly ill. This alarmed the Signora, who for the future sent her usual meals. In this manner passed three months, during all which time Arabella heard neither from her mother nor Count Jaques.

"Now," said she to herself, "it is plain Count Amiens has by some foul device been sent from our dwelling; but no matter, I will be revenged, and will leave this detested house. I shall be able to find an opportunity, since the Signora has said I may walk in the garden."

When the girl brought up her dinner, Arabella for the first time spoke kindly to her. "Come her, my good girl, do you like this diamond ring?"

"Yes, miss," said she, curtseying. "It shall be yours then," rejoined Arabella, "if you will consent to a proposal I have to make." "Certainly, miss, if it lie in my power. What is it pray?" "I will tell you," said Arabella. "You must change clothes with me." "Oh, miss," interrupted the girl, "I shall soon be found out not to be you." "But," continued Arabella, "I do not mean that you should pass for me; it is merely to disguise yourself when I am out; I shall stand a better chance in not being insulted when in mean apparel."

The girl complied, and Arabella gave her the ring, the value of which amounted to ten guineas. The girl let her go through a door in the garden that led to a wood.

"And now," cried Arabella to herself, "Mother, I wish you farewell for ever! Never more do I wish to see you." Then pausing for a few minutes, "I think," added she, "there can be no harm in my seeking Amiens; I am determined to see him if possible."

She now undertook a journey to Venice on foot; but, unfortunate girl! her route was soon stopped by a river, and she had no money to go in a gondola. She sat herself down by the side of a river, and eat a few biscuits which she had preserved for that purpose.

Just as she had finished her repast she saw a gondola approach. She called to the rower, told him she was an unfortunate girl, whose friends were all at Venice, and that she had no money to take her there.

"Well," said the rough gondolier, "I don't mind doing a pretty girl a service. Aye, aye, I can see your face for all that slouched hat."

Arabella now slipped into the gondola, and to her infinite joy soon reached Venice. She thanked the man for his kindness, who assured her she was very welcome.

Arabella was quite faint on her arrival; she had only eaten three small biscuits since her departure from the Signora's house, and the cold earth had been more than once her bed. She walked up and down the streets of the city till at last she was so exhausted that she was obliged to sit down on the steps of a house to keep herself from fainting.

She now had a full view of the people returning from a masquerade, and to her great joy she perceived Count Amiens amongst them. She hastened towards him, and standing before him, said, "Do you not recollect me?"

"Oh yes," replied Amiens, "that beauty can never be concealed; by any kind of dress."

How Arabella's heart beat at this unexpected meeting! She suffered Amiens to lead her into his house, where, to her infinite surprise, she found every thing in the most elegant style. She told Amiens all that befallen her since his departure.

"Alas!" he cried, "you must be very much fatigued and hungry; do not exert yourself till you have supped."

A most sumptuous entertainment was then produced. Arabella ate very hearty. As soon as she had finished Count Amiens shewed her the letter which was sent to him in her name.

"Cruel mother!" exclaimed Arabella with rage. The night was now far advanced, and they departed for their separate beds. Arabella soon fell asleep, but Amiens remained along while awake doubting whether Arabella loved him as he did her. "I fear," said he to himself, "that it is a home she seeks at present; but I will treat her as a sister till I am sure of her affection, and even then I cannot, must not think of marrying a girl, whose mother bears so bad a character."

The next morning Arabella was agreeably surprised to see in the place of her former dress a very elegant one. When she entered the breakfast parlour she found Amiens waiting for her; he told her to be seated and make breakfast. "My dear girl," continued he, "you must now be mistress over this house, and make what arrangements you think proper. I have business which calls me out to-day." Soon after breakfast he wished her good morning.

During his absence strange thoughts entered the mind of Arabella; she sometimes feared that she was not loved by Amiens. At dinner they met, and the Count requested her to prepare herself to go with him to St. Marks Place. She attended with pleasure, and happy was the vain Arabella to find herself again the admiration of the gay world.

As they were returning home, a lady appeared to look at her with indignation. When she had reached her lover's palazzo, she asked Amiens if he had noticed her. "I did," he replied, "and I must candidly tell you that woman was in love with me, and was much chagrined because I did not return it. But I must assure you Arabella, that my mistress must be wholly mine; if ever I perceive her encourage another, or listen to the voice of a flatterer, I cast her off for ever! Nay, if she once deceive me, nothing but her blood can wash away the stain! And now, my dear Arabella," continued he grasping her, "have you, after this declaration, the courage to become my mistress and my friend?"

"Yes, my dear Amiens, I have sufficient courage I assure you." Count Amiens advised her to think of it better, and to beware of rash promises.

One night when the Count returned from a walk he found Arabella stretched on a sofa; a thought struck him as he entered the room to sham sleep. He accordingly seated himself by the side of her, when his attention was attracted by Arabella's pronouncing his name. "You do not love me, Amiens." The Count could scarcely breathe. "I swear I love you," she again said.

This was enough for Amiens; but all of a sudden Arabella started up, as if in a fright. "Do you say I don't love you?" and opening her arms, as if to embrace him, she pretended to awake; then affecting shame held her hands to her face.

The Count now took her hand. "My dear," said he, "I hope I don't interrupt your sleep." Arabella had now become more dear to him than ever.

Arabella, when she went to bed that night, could not help thinking of the scornful look which she had received from the unknown female on their return from St. Mark's Place.

Amiens had been asleep about half an hour when Arabella thought she heard a rustling behind the window curtains. She felt much alarmed, the noise still encreased. Just as she was dosing, a footstep, as if walking across the room, made her start. Presently she saw (the chamber being faintly enlightened by a lamp) a man advance towards the bed, and drawing the curtain aside he earnestly examined the face of the Count, then drew out a dagger preparing to strike Amiens; but heaving a deep sigh retreated a few steps. He did not see Arabella, for her arm was thrown over her head. The intruder kept his face under his cloak, and after a few minutes he rose his head up, and with sudden resolution prepared again to strike. Arabella suddenly seized his wrist, and the dagger accidentally fell on her shoulder. The noise awoke the Count, who endeavoured to seize the assassin, who, during the struggle, dropped his mask.

By this time the fainting Arabella opened her eyes, and fixed them on the assassin, when, "Oh heavens!" she exclaimed, and once more fell senseless on the bed. The villain who was going to murder Amiens was her brother, Orlando, who had suddenly quitted his home on the elopement of his mother.

Amiens finding his struggles were of no use went to assist Arabella, who by her groans he knew was wounded. In the interim Orlando made his escape through the window.

"My dear Arabella," said Amiens, "you are dreadfully hurt;" for he now perceived the sheets were covered with blood.

"Only slightly, my Lord," replied she; "I would suffer ten times more to prove the sincerity of my love."

Count Amiens now alarmed the servants and dispatched them for medical assistance; for a whole week he did not once leave Arabella's chamber, and as soon as she was well, so persuaded was he now of her love for him, that he made her his wife.

We shall for awhile leave the new-married couple to relate all that befell Arabella's brother, the unfortunate Orlando.

When first Orlando left his father's home he wandered about the streets, till worn out by fatigue he leaned against a tree to support his trembling frame.

A lovely Florentine lady approached him, and in a soothing voice said, "You appear a stranger here, but your dress and air bespeak a noble birth." She then proposed to him to accompany her home, and as there was no other house near he cheerfully complied with her offer, which he imagined proceeded from pure kindness.

Wilhelmina (for that was the lady's name) had come to her villa to spend a few days, thinking thereby to punish Amiens, who had slighted her love. She was highly pleased with the elegant form of Orlando, and thought he would become a fit instrument of revenge. Three months having elapsed, during all which time Orlando was under her protection. Wilhelmina made proposals to return to Venice. Orlando had made known his secret to Welhelmina, who solemnly swore never to divulge it. They arrived at Venice, and Orlando passed for a near relation. But how disappointed she was when she saw Arabella with Count Amiens at St. Marks Place. This was the lady who cast on Arabella the scornful look which she could never forget.

Welhelmina on her return had a private interview with Orlando. "I want you," said she, "to prove your love to me this very night. When I went out I met the man who was my first seducer, he used the grossest language as I passed him, and the woman, whom he has picked up, gave me such a violent push in my side that it is with difficulty I breathe. You must this very night stab him in his bed!"

"Stab him!" echoed Orlando; "murder is a horrid crime, it makes me shrink to think of it; but you have been my preserver," he continued, "and shall not be insulted."

"Oh, my kind Orlando," interrupted the malicious Wilhelmina, "this infamous man seeks my life!"

"Indeed," cried Orlando; "then give me a stilletto —." Saying this he put on a mask and cloak. She pointed out the way and hour, and told him the window was easy of access. How he succeeded is already related. When he returned with his mask in his hand, and his cloak torn, Wilhelmina enquired if the deed was done.

"Yes," he replied, in a frenzied manner; "one of your enemies has suffered —."

"Count Amiens I hope," said she.

"No!" replied Orlando, "but my sister; she was your unfortunate rival." Orlando concluded that Arabella must be dead before he reached home.

"Thy sister!" said Wilhelmina in a fiend-like[1] voice, "I had rather it had been the Count!"

"Good Heaven!" exclaimed Orlando, "what a horrid deed!"

"But where is the stilletto?"

"I left it in the arm of my unfortunate sister!"

"We are undone!" rejoined Wilhelmina, "it had my name engraved on it. Let us lose no time, we must hasten back to our villa."

They departed from Venice that very night, and as Orlando got into the coach, he said to himself, "Oh mother! mother! I may thank thee for all this."

A few weeks after the marriage of Arabella and Amiens, they heard a loud ringing at the bell, when, to the Count's great surprise and joy he beheld an affectionate brother enter the room. Amiens, introduced his wife to him, who, as soon as she saw Franciso, repented of her marriage with his brother. Francisco related to the Count the cause of his coming to town. A young lady had long possessed his heart, but as she was recently left an orphan, "decency," continued he, "will not suffer us to be married for some months; her father died only a fortnight ago. With your leave, brother, she shall become an inmate in your house."

The Count immediately consented, thinking that Agnes would be company for his wife.

Francisco brought the young lady next day, but as soon as the Countess saw her, her simplicity, her beauty, and her gentleness of manners, gave her great uneasiness. Indeed Arabella's love for Francisco almost approached to madness. Horrid ideas rose in her mind, and she despised both her husband and Agnes.

Francisco had brought with him a Moor servant, whose form was interesting, and whose manners were engaging. He very much attracted the attention of the Countess Amiens, who thought she might make him the tool of her diabolical purposes.

One evening as the Countess was walking in the garden, she saw this Moor advancing towards her.

"Your spirits seem very much dejected lady," said he; "perhaps if I play a tune it may enliven you."

"Ah, Abdallah," returned the Countess, "your appearance differs very much from the situation to which you have been used."

Abdallah smiled, then artfully replied, "It may be in my power to assist you in whatever you wish, notwithstanding my situation; therefore confide in me, let me know the cause of your sorrow."

She now frankly told him of her love for Francisco and hatred for her husband and Agnes. "Well," said Abdallah, "then you wish them out of the way?" "I do, I do!" eagerly exclaimed the Countess.

"I have some poison," said the Moor, "which you may put into his

---

1 fiend-like: The chapbook reads "friend-like" but fiend-like seems more likely.

wine; it is of so slow a nature, that no one will think he was murdered." "I thank you from my heart," said this infamous woman.

They now separated, and at night the poison was given to Count Amiens, who, when he took it, said, "Here's to the speedy fulfilment of all our wishes."

Two months elapsed, and at the end of the third month Agnes was to be married to Francisco. The poison had worked so slowly that the Countess began to doubt its efficacy. She hinted her fears to Abdallah, who told her that he must have more. "But who will give it to him?" "You shall; I will bring it in a goblet of wine; he will be thirsty — he will call for drink."

The Count soon became feverish, he incessantly called for wine. His brother wished him to refrain from taking more but Count Amiens declared that wine alone could assuage his pains. "Ring the bell, dear Arabella." She rung the bell, and Abdallah appeared with a goblet in his hand. He gave it to the Countess, who trembled as she presented it to her husband. "Thanks, my dear Arabella," he cried, then hastily drank the contents, dropped the glass, and expired. His wife screamed, and the Count died innocent of her perfidy.

The distracted brother immediately sent for a surgeon. The deceitful Arabella appeared anxious for his coming. The surgeon opened a vein, and suddenly the blood spouted on Arabella's face. She tumbled. It seemed to point out the murderer. Another vein was opened, but no more blood issued. The surgeon then declared he was dead.

Francisco and Agnes were exceedingly affected. Arabella appeared to be so. In a few hours after she again visited the body of her husband, and was exceedingly alarmed at finding it black and discoloured. She called Abdallah — he attended. "Look there," cried she, "what do you think?"

"Every one that sees the body now," returned the Moor very coolly, "will know he was poisoned."

"Then I shall be ruined," cried she.

"Trust to me," said Abdallah with a smile; "return to the company, and say no more."

The next morning the servants all appeared alarmed and confused. Arabella heard them talking of the body. She dreaded that they had noticed its discoloured state, but to her great surprise and joy she was told the body of her husband was stolen. "Ah," thought she within herself, "the Moor has taken care the body should not be seen." She pretended to be much concerned, and joined Francisco in his lamentations.

This night the innocent Agnes, overcome with grief, complained of a head-ache. "Go to bed my dear," said Arabella, "and I will follow you very soon;" for ever since the death of the Count she and Agnes slept together.

As soon as Agnes was out of hearing the Countess said to Francisco, "Then you really like Agnes?" "Like her," answered Francisco, "I love her to my soul!" "Oh say not so," interrupted the Countess, throwing herself at his feet; "excuse my weakness, I love you, and without you cannot live!" "Infamous woman!" returned Francisco; "I abhor you! Was this the affection you bore for my brother? Tomorrow I shall leave the house; my dear Agnes shall no longer stay here."

Arabella gave vent to her rage by tears. Francisco thinking they were tears of repentance, and judging it better to part in friendship on account of Agnes, shook hands with her, but determined in his own mind to remove his intended wife as soon as possible.

When Arabella entered her chamber she looked at Agnes, who was asleep, and seizing a dagger exclaimed, "Am I then to be disappointed? It shall not be! This night she dies!" "Not so soon," answered a voice, and in a moment the Moor stood before her. "Astonishing being," cried the Countess, "how came you here, I did not see you enter? Ah, Abdallah, I know not how it is; but your presence always soothes my sorrow. Say, why should she not die so soon?" "Have you so soon forgot that you have committed murder? Avoid then a repetition of the fault, leave it to me, I will remove Agnes. You must go to the forest, and turn to your left. I will follow with her in my arms while she is asleep." "Oh, my dear friend," said the Countess, "accept this diamond ring as a small token of gratitude." "Keep your ring," returned Abdallah; "it is not wealth I look for, it is your friendship, your confidence, yourself." "I am solely yours," cried Arabella; "I would forfeit Heaven's bliss to serve you." " 'Tis well you will find me obedient to your will; Francisco shall be in your power."

Saying this he left the room, and she thought as he quitted it that he looked a head taller than before.

"Surely," said she to herself, "he cannot be a natural being." This idea made her tremble; but she soon forgot it when she thought of the happiness she would have in forcing Francisco to her embraces.

She instantly repaired to the forest, where she had not been long before she saw Abdallah advancing towards her with the lovely Agnes hanging almost lifeless over his shoulder; he soon reached Arabella; "Follow me," cried he to the wondering Countess.

They descended steep rocks, when Abdallah with great ease moved what appeared to be a stupendous stone. Arabella's surprise was very great to see how he raised it with such facility. They then entered a cavern, where a lamp was burning.

"Here," said the subtle Moor, "your rival is secure from mortal eyes." "But is there no fear of her escaping?" cried Arabella. "I would rather she was dead!" "Hold!" said the Moor, "I will put this chain round her wrists, she shall not be able to move her hands. Are you now satisfied?" "It is my duty to be so," replied Arabella sullenly. "I admire your spirit," said Abdallah ironically. "Your thirst for vengeance is never satisfied. Now let us return to the house, but not together, as we may be suspected."

Early next morning Francisco went to meet Agnes, but alas! no Agnes appeared. He then in a voice of madness called aloud, "Where is my dear Agnes?" Arabella pretended to awake, and be surprised at seeing Francisco in her bedchamber. "What is the matter?" said she. "Alas! too well you know," said he. "You have hid my dear Agnes!" "Hold!" said she, "I assure you I would do Agnes no injury whatever. Retire for a few minutes while I dress myself, and I will assist you in searching for her." Many hours being spent in a fruitless search, a delirium seized the brian of Francisco, and by Arabella's orders he was conveyed to bed, where she attended him.

Agnes, all this time, continued to linger in her solitary confinement. Abdallah had brought her a leopard's skin to keep her warm, and plenty of food. The Countess never thought of her. She was taken up in attending Francisco, who one evening said to her, "It is not my wish Signora that you should confine yourself in attending me." The Countess thought this a fit opportunity to address him on the subject nearest her heart. "Oh, Francisco," said she, "I take delight in convincing you how dear you are to me." "And is this a time to talk upon a subject which you know I hate? Let me tell you, Signora, that even if I had never seen the amiable Agnes I would sooner plunge a poignard in my breast than become the husband to so vile a woman!" "You speak plain," said the mortified Countess; "but you shall repent of your unkindness to me." She now added, "Remember that Agnes is no more!" "No more!" He then started out of bed, and said, "Death be my portion"! "Yes, yes," cried the Countess, "death shall be the consequence if you do not consent to be mine."

Then assisting him against his will to the bed she left the room, and in her way met Abdallah. "Well," said she, "I have not succeeded." "Patience!" cried Abdallah, "suppose you were to take the form of Agnes." "Ah," said the Countess, "what would I not give to be able, but my masculine face is against me." "Cease," said the Moor, "do not abuse your exquisite beauty. Mix this powder with the medicine that Francisco takes; it will put him in a kind of stupor; he will then take you for Agnes, and you may receive his affectionate embraces." The Countess seized the box, and thanked the Moor, then hastened to Francisco, and gave him the powder. He soon fell asleep, and Arabella repaired to her chamber.

Early in the morning he awoke and got up; all that had passed concerning Agnes seemed to him as a dream. He went to the garden, where soon after Arabella made her appearance. "My dear Agnes," said Francisco, "how happy I feel myself." "Ah, Francisco," said Arabella, "I rejoice that you are recovered." She then told him that he had been delirious for three weeks.

"Well," said Francisco, "with your consent we will this day be married." "I shall feel myself happy, my dear Francisco," said this perfidious woman, "in making the day of your recovery our wedding day." Thus it was agreed, and Arabella danced to the soft music of Abdallah.

At dawn Francisco awoke. Arabella had no longer the resemblance of Agnes. He gazed on the sleeping cheat, darted out of bed, snatched a sword, and threw himself on the point of it. Arabella awoke, but too late to prevent the desperate deed. She flew out of bed, and exclaimed, "Oh,

Francisco!" He opened his eyes, and faintly uttering, "Dear Agnes, I shall soon be with you!" expired.

A mad fit immediately seized Arabella, she tore her hair, she wept, she groaned. In a few moments the madness ceased; she then started up, and seizing the sword that was in the body of Francisco, put on a large cloak and repaired to the forest. She soon reached the spot where Agnes lay. She entered her dungeon, and bade her to arise. Agnes endeavoured to obey, but her feeble frame could to support her. "Did you not hear me?" said the Countess. "Prepare to die! for I might have been happy but for you." "Oh!" she exclaimed, "I was in hopes you were come to restore me to liberty. But those fierce looks bespeak your purpose."

"Liberty!" exclaimed Arabella, "yes, you shall have it," and unchaining her wrists, she dragged her towards a precipice. "Do you see this?" said she, pulling out the sword that was stained with the blood of Francisco, "I will plunge this into your heart, then throw you down this precipice."

"Oh, my dear lady, in what have I offended you? Alas! take pity on my youth!" "Peace!" cried Arabella, "you have done me much injury. So follow me." "I cannot," said Agnes; "my feeble frame will not permit me to walk." "Then I will make you," vociferated the Countess, at the same time dragging her by the hair of her head up a higher part of the precipice, and holding the sword ready to strike.

"Oh for Heaven's sake mercy!" shrieked the affrighted girl. "Remember, my dear lady," continued the innocent Agnes, "we have been friends. Pray then do not murder me! I would not for the worth of worlds injure you!" "Not injure me! Were you not the beloved of Francisco?" "I know I was. Ah where is he now?" "See you not the blood on this sword that you are to die with?" "Oh heavens! what do I hear?" said Agnes, "tell me true, my dear lady, where? where is he?" "Dead!" cried Arabella, "and you shall follow." "Dead!" echoed Agnes, "and murdered by his cruel sister-in-law!" "Cease viper!" exclaimed Arabella, "he was murdered by you. Let go thy hold, or I will dash thee down the rock."

"Oh, Francisco! thou art then dead," said the weeping Agnes. "Yes, I believe it now. Ah me! there's no hope of happiness." "Die then at once vile wretch!" cried Arabella, trying at the same time to pull the defenceless girl from her hold.

"Oh, my dear lady!" exclaimed Agnes, "if I must die remember my tender years. Pray let me not suffer so terrible a death! Give me the same that my dear Francisco had." "That you shall have," replied Arabella. Saying this the unfeeling woman raised her hand to strike. Agnes lifted hers, thinking to escape the fatal blow; but the sword ran through the side of her hand, and the blood flowed down her flaxen hair. Once more she threw herself on her knees to sue for mercy. The Countess quitted her hold in order to take breath; a sudden thought now glided across the mind of Agnes, and not heeding her wound she suddenly got up and ran as swift as lightning down the rock.

Arabella pursued her victim with such rapidity that she soon reached her. Agnes in despair caught hold of a bending oak; she twisted herself round it, while the oak threatened every moment to sink beneath her weight. The wicked Countess attempted to shake it, intending to throw her down the abyss.

Agnes exclaimed, "Barbarous woman! See the blood you have shed, will not that content you? Oh! little did I think that this would be my fate! Alas! I may well regret being left an orphan! Oh pray have pity on me! I will invoke heaven to forgive you your crimes."

The only answer she received from Arabella was a loud laugh; again she raised the sword to strike. "Well, be it so," cried Agnes. "Yes, take my life, and let it be with the same sword you murdered Francisco." Incensed by this cutting remark she seized the trembling girl by the hair, and stabbed her in the bosom. Agnes sunk upon her knees, and uttered, "Francisco, I am coming."[1] Arabella then took up her body, and threw it down the rocks. She followed it with her eyes as far as she could. The Countess was now repairing to the house, while the voice of Agnes suing for mercy still sounded in her ear. Presently the Moor stood before her. "So you have murdered the orphan Agnes." "Who told you I had murdered her?" Abdallah said, "Your guilty countenance." "Well," resumed Arabella, "the crime is my own." She now hastened to her dwelling, where the body of Francisco lay. She threw herself on the bed, and a frightful dream awoke her, when she saw the Moor Abdallah standing before her. "Signora," said he, "it is fear for your safety that brings me here. Will you consent to be mine, and save you from the shame that awaits you." "I swear," replied Arabella, "to do whatever you will on this condition." "Then rise and follow me."

She hastily dressed herself and went with Abdallah. Having proceeded a long way they were stopped by robbers; but as soon as they saw the Moor the chief invited them to his cave. They entered the cave, and the captain of the robbers presented Abdallah with a glass of wine. When they had retired to rest Abdallah told the Countess that she must stay in this cave several days. "But," enquired Arabella, "will the captain and his lady unmask?" "No," replied the Moor with a smile.

Two or three days having thus passed some of the robbers rushed in one evening dragging in a man with them and a female fainting in their arms. The captain started up, and seizing his dagger stabbed him to the heart. "Die, infamous villain!" at the same time pulling off his mask, when she beheld in the captain of the banditti her brother. "Wretched Arabella!" continued Orlando, "is it possible that you know me and not know that villain. It is Jaques and that unfortunate woman is your mother!"

---

1 "Francisco I am coming.": An echo of Antonia's dying words in *The Monk*, "Mother, I come!"

Arabella was answering when Orlando rushed forward to the body of Jaques, "Ha! did you think to escape me? No, heaven has heard my prayers, and I have revenged my father's wrongs."

As he said this a sigh from his mother called him to his senses. Then turning round, he said, "Which of you has used a female thus?" "None of us," they all replied. "We were returning home, when loud shrieks assailed our ears. We then perceived that man, who there lies bleeding, beating his lady in a barbarous manner. We rushed forward. "Peace," interrupted Orlando. "We did our duty, Sir." "Did you not hear me speak?" said Orlando. At this instant the bravo took out his dagger, and levelled him with the earth. "Insolent ruffian! give me a dagger, and I will instantly punish him for raising his arm against his chief." A dagger was presented to him — "I will not be your murderer," he said; "Rise, reptile!" He then returned to his mother, whom he found in a gentle slumber. Orlando perceived that his sister seemed to take delight in the punishment that had met her mother's distress. She retired as usual to her rest, while Orlando sat up to watch over the emaciated frame of his parent.

This unfortunate woman had been kept so long in confinement by Jaques that all the colour forsook her cheeks. He then began to despise her, and after a deal of ill usage, told her to prepare for a journey to Venice. As soon as he had got her into a wood, he thought, unmolested, he could wreak his vengeance on the defenceless woman. It was at this critical moment that he was seized by the robbers, and met his due punishment from the son of her whom he used so ill.

The next morning Arabella went to visit her mother, and found her brother sitting by the side of her bed. She had not been long in the room before she caught the attention of her bewildered mother, who said, in a low voice, "Ah, my dear child, by what miracle do I see you here? Alas! I have not long to live, so forgive your guilty mother." The cruel daughter answered not; but the more noble hearted son extended his hand to his dying parent, "My dear mother," said he, "do you forget Orlando?"

She turned her eyes towards him, "Oh, God!" she cried, "and do you pardon me?"

"Mother!" he cried, "may heaven pardon thee as freely as I do."

"Oh, my son! thy heart was ever noble." He raised her up. "Daughter," she said, "look not so angrily at me, but oh pardon your dying mother."

Here a deep sigh broke forth, and she fainted away in the arms of Orlando.

"Why do you not speak to your mother at such a time as this?" cried Orlando sternly. "Pray have you been so pure and faultless yourself?"

"Ah, that's the reason," replied Arabella with a wild laugh. "I may thank her for all my crimes. Oh, mother! why did you desert your children to follow a base seducer? Can I reflect on my crimes without horror? I have murdered a fond husband — I have been the cause of the death of his brother — I have destroyed a defenceless orphan! for this, I may thank the example of a worthless mother!"

"Infamous wretch!" exclaimed her brother, "fall on your knees and — —." Here he was interrupted by the groans of his mother, who faintly uttered, "Terrible, but just." This last word quivered on her lips, and she expired in the arms of her son. High words now ensued between Orlando and his sister, when suddenly the Moor entered and pacified them.

The next day a band of soldiers attacked the cave. The ruffian with whom Orlando had quarrelled had made known the retreat. They hastened towards the captain.

"Give me leave," said Orlando, "just to speak to my wife."

"Wilhelmina," said he, "I will not accuse you of corrupting my youth, but I must regret the shameful death that awaits you."

"I will avoid that," said she, drawing a dagger from her bosom; "but first your sister Arabella dies, for robbing me of my true love."

She was just going to lodge the dagger in Arabella's bosom when again the Moor stood before them. "She is mine!" said he.

Wilhelmina then put a dagger into her own breast, and fell immediately. Orlando then addressed the ruffian, "You shall not have the pleasure which you expected of seeing me die a public death." He then plunged the dagger, which was warm with the blood of Wilhelmina, into his own heart, and expired without a groan.

The Moor took Arabella from this scene of horror; their departure was invisible to the soldiers. When they had reached a rock, which was immensely high, "Now, rash lady," said he with a loud laugh, "look to whom you have given yourself, to whom you have devoted your body and soul." Good Heaven! what a sight now met her eyes; no longer the beautiful form of a Moor, but that of a hideous devil appeared to view. He seized her by the neck, "Yes, it was I who resembled the Moor, vain fool! Behold, I am the Demon of Venice! Now I will show you what danger I have saved you from." So saying he held her tighter by the neck, and threw her headlong down the rock, accompanying her screams with loud and hideous roars of triumph. Thus the precipice was the grave of two, the innocent Agnes and the wicked Arabella.

FINIS

Bibliography

Works by Charlotte Dacre

Dacre's four known novels have been reprinted in Arno Press's Gothic Novels series, and her volume of poetry by Garland; these should be available in most university and research libraries, and each contains an introduction, not always biographically accurate. *Trifles of Helicon*, written with her sister Sophia King, is available through *The Eighteenth Century* microfilm series. Frederick S. Frank's *The First Gothics* (1987) contains brief plot synopses of each of Dacre's novels. *The Libertine* went into three editions in 1807, and *Confessions* into three editions by 1807. The advertisement for the third edition of the *Confessions* promised a "Portrait and Memoirs of the Fair Author," but I have been unable to locate a copy of the third edition in order to confirm this.

Confessions of the Nun of St. Omer. London: D.N. Shury for J.F. Hughes, 1805. 3 vols. New York: Arno Press, 1972.
George the Fourth. London: Hatchard, 1822.
Hours of Solitude. A Collection of Original Poems, now first published. 1805. 2 vols. in 1. New York and London: Garland Publishing, Inc., 1978.
The Libertine. London: Cadell & Davies, 1807. 4 vols. New York: Arno Press, 1974.
The Passions. London: Cadell & Davies, 1811. 4 vols. New York: Arno Press, 1974.
[Charlotte King and Sophia King]. *Trifles of Helicon.* London: James Ridgway, 1798.
Zofloya; or, the Moor: A Romance of the Fifteenth Century. London: Longman, Hurst, Rees and Orme, 1806. 3 vols. New York: Arno Press, 1974.

Works in Translation

[*The Libertine*] *Angelo, comte d'Albini, ou les Dangers du vice, par Charlotte Dacre Byrne connue sous le nom de Rosa Matilda, traduit de l'anglais par Mme. Élisabeth de B***.* 3 vols. Paris: A. Bertrand, 1816.
Zofloya, ou le Maure, historie du XVeme siècle, traduite de l'anglais par Mme. de Viterne. 4 vols. Paris: Barba, 1812.

Authorship in Question

The Dæmon of Venice. An Original Romance. Tegg's Edition. London: Thomas Tegg, 1810. [The title on the first page reads: "The Demon of Venice, A Romance. By a Lady."]

The School for Friends: A Domestic Tale. By Miss Dacre. London: Thomas Tegg [n.d.]. [This chapbook contains a frontispiece and title page illustration by Thomas Rowlandson.]

Secondary Material on Charlotte Dacre

Craciun, Adriana. "'I hasten to be disembodied': Charlotte Dacre, the Demon Lover, and Representations of the Body." *European Romantic Review* 6 (1995): 75-97.

Erdman, David. "Byron's Mock Review of Rosa Matilda's Epic on the Prince Regent—A New Attribution." *Keats-Shelley Journal* 19 (1970): 101-17.

Frank, Frederick S. *The First Gothics: A Critical Guide to the English Gothic Novel.* New York : Garland, 1987.

Jones, Ann H. "Chapter Eight: Charlotte Dacre." *Ideas and Innovations: Best Sellers of Jane Austen's Age.* New York: AMS Press, 1986. 224-49.

Knight-Roth, Sandra. *Charlotte Dacre and the Gothic Tradition.* (Diss. Dalhousie University) 1972.

McGann, Jerome J. "'My Brain is Feminine': Byron and the Poetry of Deception." *Byron: Augustan and Romantic.* Ed. Andrew Rutherford. Houndsmills, Basingstoke, Hampshire: Macmillan, 1990. 26-51.

Miles, Robert. "Avatars of Matthew Lewis' *The Monk*: Ann Radcliffe's *The Italian* and Charlotte Dacre's *Zofloya, or The Moor.*" *Gothic Writing 1750-1820: A Genealogy.* London and New York: Routledge, 1993.

Peck, Walter Edwin. Appendix A: "Shelley's Indebtedness in *Zastrozzi* to Previous Romances." *Shelley: His Life and Work.* Vol. 2. Boston and New York: Houghton Mifflin, 1927. 305-309.

Pollin, Burton. "Byron, Poe, and Miss Matilda," *Names XVI* (1968): 390-414.

Reiman, Donald. Introduction. *Hours of Solitude.* By Charlotte Dacre. New York and London: Garland Publishing Inc., 1978.

Summers, Montague. "Byron's Lovely Rosa." *Essays in Petto.* 1928; Freeport, NY: Books for Libraries Press, Inc., 1967.

—. Introduction. *Zofloya.* By Charlotte Dacre. London: Fortune Press, 1928.

Varma, Devendra. Introduction, *Zofloya, or The Moor.* By Charlotte Dacre. New York: Arno Press, 1974.

(See also each introduction to the Arno reprints of Dacre's novels.)

Select Bibliography

Adorno, Theodor, and Max Horkheimer. *Dialectic of Enlightenment.* Trans. John Cumming. New York: Continuum, 1993.

Barker-Benfield, G.C. *The Culture of Sensibility: Sex and Society in Eighteenth-Century Britain.* Chicago: Chicago UP, 1992.

Behrendt, Stephen. Introduction. *Zastrozzi and St. Irvyne*. By Percy Bysshe Shelley. Oxford and New York: Oxford UP, 1986.

Bienville, M.D.T. *Nymphomania, or, A Dissertation Concerning the Furor Uterinus*. Trans. Edward Sloane Wilmot. London, 1775. Published with *Onanism* by S.A. Tissot in *Onanism/ Nymphomania*. New York: Garland, 1985.

Blain, Virginia, Isobel Grundy, and Patricia Clemens, eds. *The Feminist Companion to Literature in English*. New Haven: Yale UP, 1990.

Brissenden, R.F. *Virtue in Distress: Studies in the Novel of Sentiment from Richardson to Sade*. New York: Barnes & Noble, 1974.

Butler, Judith. *Bodies That Matter: On the Discursive Limits of Sex*. New York and London: Routledge, 1993.

—. *Gender Trouble: Feminism and the Subversion of Identity*. London and New York: Routledge, 1990.

Carter, Angela. *The Sadeian Woman and the Ideology of Pornography*. New York: Pantheon Books, 1978.

Castle, Terry. *Masquerade and Civilization: The Carnivalesque in Eighteenth-Century English Culture and Fiction*. Stanford: Stanford UP, 1986.

Craciun, Adriana. "Charlotte Dacre." *Encyclopedia of British Women Writers*, 2nd ed. Eds. Paul Schlueter and Jane Schlueter. New York: Garland, 1997.

Day, William Patrick. *In the Circles of Fear and Desire: A Study of Gothic Fantasy*. Chicago: U of Chicago P, 1985.

Deleuze, Gilles. *Masochism: Coldness and Cruelty*. New York: Zone Books, 1991. (Published with Sacher-Masoch's *Venus in Furs*.)

Doane, Mary Ann. *Femmes Fatales: Feminism, Film Theory, Psychoanalysis*. London: Routledge: 1991.

Donoghue, Emma. *Passions Between Women: British Lesbian Culture 1668-1801*. London: Scarlet Press, 1993.

Ellis, Kate Ferguson. *The Contested Castle—Gothic Novels and the Subversion of Domestic Ideology*. Urbana: U of Illinois P, 1990.

Foucault, Michel. *Madness and Civilization: A History of Insanity in the Age of Reason*. Trans. Richard Howard. New York: Vintage, 1988.

—. *The History of Sexuality: Volume I: An Introduction* Trans. Robert Hurley. New York: Vintage Books, 1990.

Groneman, Carol. "Nymphomania—The Historical Construction of Female Sexuality." *Signs* 19 (1994): 337-67.

Grudin, Peter. *The Demon-Lover: The Theme of Demoniality in English and Continental Fiction of the Late Eighteenth and Early Nineteenth Centuries*. New York and London: Garland Publishing Co., 1987.

Haywood, Eliza. *Love in Excess; or, the Fatal Enquiry*. Ed. David Oakleaf. Peterborough, ON: Broadview Press, 1994.

Hughes, A.M.D. "Shelley's *Zastrozzi* and *St. Irvyne*." *Modern Language Review* 7 (1912): 54-63.

Hunt, Lynn, ed. *The Invention of Pornography*. New York: Zone Books, 1993.

Kelly, Gary. *English Fiction of the Romantic Period*. London and New York: Longman, 1989.

Laborde, Alice M. "The Problem of Sexual Equality in Sadean Prose." *French Women and the Age of Enlightenment*, Ed. Sonia Spencer. Bloomington: Indiana UP, 1984.

Laqueur, Thomas. *Making Sex: Body and Gender from the Greeks to Freud.* Cambridge: Harvard UP, 1990.

Lewis, Mathew G. *The Monk.* 1796. New York: Grove Press, 1952.

Lonsdale, Roger. Introduction. *Eighteenth-Century Women Poets.* Ed. Roger Lonsdale. Oxford: Oxford UP, 1990.

Malchow, H.L. *Gothic Images of Race in Nineteenth-Century Britain.* Stanford: Stanford UP, 1996.

Matus, Jill L. *Unstable Bodies: Victorian Representations of Sexuality and Maternity.* Manchester: Manchester UP, 1995.

McCalman, Iain. *Radical Underworld: Prophets, Revolutionaries, and Pornographers in London, 1795 1840.* 1988; Oxford: Clarendon Press, 1993.

McGann, Jerome. "'My Brain is Feminine': Byron and the Poetry of Deception." *Byron: Augustan and Romantic.* Ed. Andrew Rutherford. Houndsmills, Basingstoke, Hampshire: Macmillan, 1990. 26-51.

—. *The Romantic Ideology—A Critical Investigation.* Chicago: Chicago UP, 1983.

Mellor, Anne. *Romanticism and Gender.* New York: Routledge, 1993.

Michie, Helena. *The Flesh Made Word: Female Figures and Women's Bodies.* New York & Oxford: Oxford UP, 1987.

Milner, Max. *Le Diable dans la littérature française: de Cazotte à Baudelaire, 1772-1861.* Paris: Librairie José Corti, 1960. Vol. 1.

Piguenard [sic], J.B. *Zoflora, or, The Generous Negro Girl. A Colonial Story.* 2 vols. London: Lackington, Allen & Co., 1804.

Polwhele, Richard. *The Unsex'd Females: A Poem.* London: Cadell & Davis, 1978. Published with Mary Ann Radcliffe's *The Female Advocate*, New York and London: Garland, 1974.

Poovey, Mary. *The Proper Lady and the Woman Writer: Ideology as Style in the Works of Mary Wollstonecraft, Mary Shelley, and Jane Austen.* Chicago: U of Chicago P, 1984.

Radcliffe, Ann. *The Italian, or The Confessional of the Black Penitents. A Romance.* Ed. Frederick Garber. 1968; Oxford: Oxford UP, 1981.

Rogers, Pat. "Fat is a fictional issue: the novel and the rise of weight watching." *Literature and Medicine During the Eighteenth Century.* Eds. W. F. Bynum and Roy Porter. London: Routledge, 1993. 169-87.

Ross, Marlon. *The Contours of Masculine Desire: Romanticism and the Rise of Women's Poetry.* New York: Oxford UP, 1989.

Rousseau, G.S. "Nymphomania, Bienville, and the rise of erotic sensibility." *Sexuality in eighteenth-century Britain.* Ed. Paul-Gabriel Boucé. Totowa, N.J.: Barnes & Noble, 1982. 95-113.

Sade, Donatien Alphonse François, Marquis de. "Reflections on the Novel." *The 120 Days of Sodom and Other Writings.* Trans. Austryn Wainhouse and Richard Seaver. New York: Grove Press, 1966.

Swinburne, Algernon Charles. *The Swinburne Letters*. Ed. Cecil Y. Lang. New Haven: Yale UP, 1963. vol. 5.

Williams, Anne. *Art of Darkness: A Poetics of Gothic*. Chicago: Chicago UP, 1995.

Williams, Raymond."Violence." *Keywords: A Vocabulary of Culture and Society*. Glasgow: Fontana/Croom Helm, 1981.

Wolf, Edward. *Rowlandson and His Illustrations of Eighteenth Century English Literature*. Copenhagen: Einar Munksgaard, 1945.

Wollstonecraft, Mary. *A Short Residence in Sweden, Norway and Denmark*. Ed. Richard Holmes. Harmondsworth: Penguin, 1987.

Yaeger, Patricia. "Toward the Female Sublime." *Gender and Theory: Dialogues on Feminist Criticism*. Ed. Linda Kauffman. Oxford & New York: Basil Blackwell, 1989.